Idle Tuesday

At first, Rae Ann thought her imagination was in overdrive. She blinked several times to clear her vision, but the image remained. Kyle was ahead of her about a hundred feet down the trail, lying on the ground and not moving. Rae Ann was suddenly immobilized. A sob caught in her throat and tears blurred what little vision she had. She directed her skis toward the motionless form and dug her feet in towards each other to stop beside him.

"Kyle," she cried above the raging wind, "oh God, Kyle, I'm so sorry." She ripped off her gloves and felt around his body for any indication of his injury. "Kyle talk to me," she grumbled low in her throat. The wet snow was melting through her thin jeans and she could feel her core begin to freeze. She had told him it would be okay and it wasn't. None of it was. She should never have brought him back here and involved him in her problems.

Rae Ann wanted to lay her head down beside him and just cry, but what good would she be to either of them if she gave in to her tears. She struggled back to her feet, when behind her a snapping twig rung out in the night. Something hard came down on her shoulders and an envelope of darkness slowly sealed around her.

Janine ~

I hope you enjoy it!

Courtney E Michel

What They Are Saying About

Idle Tuesday

Ms. Michel has written a very intriguing mystery, weaving in and out with many twists and turns that holds you on the edge of your seat. This book is jam-paced with fast pace action. It deserves five stars. Ms. Michel's creativity, when she puts pen to paper, draws the reader into the story until the last page. A terrific suspense that creates different twists and turns that blend well into the story line. A plot with so many turns that will keep you guessing until the end.

—Linda Lattimer
Skeletons Too Close To Home

Idle Tuesday is an exciting who-done-it that will keep you on the edge of your seat from start to finish. It is a Cinderella story about *Rae Ann Lewis*, who all of her life is raised without a loving family to support her... *Courtney E. Michel's* book portrays the struggle of her heroine who, after years of loveless relationships, finally allows someone into her heart... Rae Ann sets out to reestablish her life and regain her professional reputation. The question remains, will Rae Ann ever be able to establish real love in her life?

—JoEllen Conger
Return Of The Goddess

Wings

Idle Tuesday

by

Courtney E. Michel

A Wings ePress, Inc.

Romantic Suspense Novel

Wings ePress, Inc.

Edited by: Leslie Hodges
Copy Edited by: Lorraine Stephens
Senior Editor: Lorraine Stephens
Executive Editor: Lorraine Stephens
Cover Artist: Nathan Tumulty

Wings ePress Books
http://www.wings-press.com

Copyright © 2005 by Courtney E. Michel
ISBN 1-59088-594-5

Published In the United States Of America

September 2005

Wings ePress Inc.
403 Wallace Court
Richmond, KY 40475

One

"Wisconsin's own Senator Francis Showalter is in the news again tonight with the recent allegations of misusing campaign monies."

Rae Ann Lewis stood in the dark wings of the television sound stage and marveled at the on camera chemistry between the two news anchors. She soundlessly mouthed the words of the news story as they moved across the teleprompter and pretended that she was sitting behind the news desk with Rob Daniels instead of the pretentious Marley Cavanaugh. Being a highly recognized television anchor had been Rae Ann's dream and here she was so close to realizing it. Growing up in New Jersey, Rae Ann had never imagined she would make it this far and was determined to not let anything get in her way. It wasn't unusual to find Rae Ann meandering onto the sound stage and even settling into one of the comfy chairs used on the morning show set to study the anchors at their craft. This particular day the set was alive with people moving back and forth behind the cameramen setting up toys for the annual Christmas drive that was just around the corner. The weatherman stood, bored, in front of his blue wall until the camera was pointed in his direction. He gave a brief thirty-second forecast before the news broke for commercial.

To Rae Ann's left a woman from the local zoo had brought in an armadillo for the news' Talk of the Town segment and the small animal was running in between the stuffed bears and remote control cars of the toy drive. Rae Ann watched Marley Cavanaugh through

1

narrow eyes. She didn't trust the woman's beautiful face and flawless appearance. Through the grapevine, Rae Ann had been told that Marley had been offered a network position and Rae Ann wondered what the back stabbing anchor had done this time to get a job like that.

In fact, Rae Ann was so self-absorbed in loathing the current anchorwoman that she didn't hear Eduardo Torres sneak up behind her. "Hey, Scoop." Eddie leaned in close to Rae Ann's small frame and sniffed. "Is that a new fragrance you're wearing? It's Jealousy, right? Not very becoming of you, Scoop."

"It's better than cigarette smoke, right?" Rae Ann gave him a small shove and smiled in spite of herself.

"Yeah, when are you going to quit that nasty habit anyway?"

"Not now, Eddie. I'm so nervous I could smoke a whole pack." Eddie was Rae Ann's favorite cameraman and only friend at the WZZY station where she worked, as well as the entire city of Madison. He had called her Scoop ever since the day she had made her first on air appearance as a field reporter.

When Bob Ashcroft, the news director, had finally given Rae Ann the break she had been waiting for, she had wanted desperately to impress him. Rae Ann had researched the news piece thoroughly and confided in Eddie that she was willing to do anything to scoop the other reporters in the station, no matter what the story. Rae Ann had gone so far as to buy a new suit and the tallest heels she could find to compensate for her lack of height. What she hadn't realized was that this particular news story took place on the side of a mountain. Rae Ann had stood teetering on the unstable rocks and reported the story with a smile. Despite her inappropriate footwear, Eddie liked Rae Ann's energy and dubbed her 'Scoop'. Rae Ann liked the fact that Eddie could be ready at a moment's notice, even at one in the morning. The two had become an instant team. Unbelievably, almost four years had now gone by and Rae Ann couldn't imagine having to adapt to another cameraman's style.

"Looks like Showy's got himself into some deep shit now," Eddie said referring to the news story on Senator Showalter. After the controversial Senator was elected to a second term, he seemed to be showing up in the news more and more. It was evident that he was a media hound and so someone at the station affectionately nicknamed him "Showy". Every time something major in Madison happened you could bet that Showy was there just dying to get his face on camera.

An unheard voice from the director in the control room gave the cue and the story went to a tape of last year's library fundraiser. It showed a very tan Showy walking amongst "his people" looking more concerned about his appearance than the cause. Mrs. Showalter walked stiffly beside him with rigid posture and a plastic smile.

Unfortunately for Showy, most of the press the Senator got these days was negative. Rae Ann didn't hide the fact that she didn't trust the Senator and just knew he was involved in something corrupt. If only she could figure out what he was involved in, Rae Ann knew the anchor position, up for grabs, would be hers.

During the tape, the two anchors whispered like a secret club of schoolgirls telling secrets and continued to ignore Rae Ann and Eddie. "That guy has got to be pilfering money from somewhere, "Eddie whispered, "It looks like he vacations on the sun. You just can't get a tan like that in Wisconsin. Hell, I'm *from* Mexico and I'm not even that dark." Rae Ann smiled wider and waved a hand to shush him.

The floor director glanced in their direction and Rae Ann mouthed the word sorry. "Hey, are you still going to ask Big Bob about the wench's job?" Eddie whispered moving up beside her.

"Yeah," Rae Ann shrugged, indifferently, the smile leaving her face, "What can it hurt?" "That's the spirit. Way to have confidence in yourself," Eddie said sarcastically as he rolled his eyes. Rae Ann turned in Eddie's direction to defend her honor, but was instead struck speechless when she saw his outfit.

Eddie was not a tall man, only five foot ten. His Mexican roots had given him skin the color of caramel and hair as black as night. Rae Ann stood six inches shorter than her male friend and had to tilt her neck skyward to take in his entire exterior. And what Eddie didn't have in height, he made up for in appearance. "Jesus, Eddie, was it half price day at the Goodwill?"

"What?" Eddie acted shocked as he gave himself the once over. He straightened the old green fishing vest he wore over his Hard Rock

Café T-shirt, then dusted at the thighs of his khaki shorts that were worn over red thermal knit underwear. Rae Ann started giggling and couldn't stop. She motioned for Eddie to follow her into the hall before they got kicked off the sound stage.

Finally able to talk in a normal voice, Rae Ann glanced at her watch, "Oh God, Eddie, it is almost time for the meeting."

"Hey, what happened to that confident, I-don't-need-anyone attitude that you usually have?" Eddie asked, running a hand through his jet-black hair.

"My future is in Bob's hands, Eddie. You know, with him, there is no gray area. He can either make your life wonderful or miserable."

"Well, he made your life wonderful by giving you this field position didn't he?"

"Yes, well now its time for a promotion. I deserve this job." Rae Ann glanced again at her watch and declared, "Time for the meeting. How do I look?" Rae Ann smoothed a hand over her shoulder length blonde hair and brushed lint from her clothes.

Eddie glanced quickly at the crisp, white button down shirt Rae Ann wore under a blue suit jacket and matching skirt. She was beautiful as usual, of course. The suit was tailor made for Rae Ann's petite body and the blue of her suit matched her expressive eyes perfectly. Of course, Eddie would never say any of that out loud. Instead, he joked, "You look like a stewardess."

"Eddie," Rae Ann groaned and gave him a light punch in the shoulder.

"Hey, you asked," Eddie shrugged, "I'll be in the dungeon when you're finished. We'll grab some lunch at Mama Torres'." Eddie's family owned a small authentic Mexican restaurant in downtown Madison. The festive, brightly colored atmosphere seemed out of place in the mostly frozen surroundings of Wisconsin but it had the best margaritas in the whole United States. "Oh, and Mama wants you to come over for Thanksgiving again this year."

Rae Ann nodded and took a deep breath. She had appeased him for now, but Rae Ann knew she wouldn't be accepting the invitation to the Torres Thanksgiving dinner, no matter how many times Eddie

4

asked her. Last year, Rae Ann had finally relented, to Eddie's continuous badgering, to come to his parent's house for the holiday.

Until then, Rae Ann had spent Thanksgiving working or home alone. It was depressing and relieving all at the same time. For many years she had tried not to focus on not having any family. Having someone to finally share in the celebration, Rae Ann thought, might just make her feel like she belonged. But all during the day, Eddie's family's jubilation and closeness had left Rae Ann feeling more isolated and alone than ever before. She left the Torres house feeling small and unimportant. Rae Ann vowed never to put herself in that situation again. She would spend this Thanksgiving at the office working herself to the bone, in hopes of getting the soon-to-be-available weekend anchor position.

Rae Ann watched Eddie take the stairs to the basement, where the technical staff worked endlessly on their computers, to piece together footage and pulled news stories from around the world via satellite uplink. Everyone referred to the basement as the dungeon, since the lighting was always dim to cut down the glare on the computer screens in the editing bays. The dungeon was also where they stored all of the tape segments for the past five years.

Almost like the coach of a professional sports team, Rae Ann would often pull the tapes of her segments and study them at length in hopes of improving her already flawless performance on camera. Now was her chance to show Bob that she could really shine. Rae Ann turned on her heel and headed in the other direction. It was time for the staff meeting that the news director and assignment editor held every week. Rae Ann had sat in the meetings, all but silent, since becoming a field reporter almost four years ago. Today she would be heard.

Rae Ann grabbed a pen and paper from her desk in the newsroom, then headed into the conference area. She immediately felt self-conscious, even though the other reporters sitting around the table continued to ignore her. The world of television could be a very cut-throat, competitive environment and making friends was not an easy task when you jumped up the ladder without any concern for seniority or experience. Even after four years, Rae Ann was not one of the most well liked reporters at the station. This suited Rae Ann just fine, since it gave her an excuse not to get close to anyone there. Relationships shrouded with emotion were not Rae Ann's specialty. She wasn't even sure she would know how to love, given the opportunity.

Rae Ann settled into the uncomfortable, thread worn chair three away from where she knew Bob would sit. Her anxiousness was evident in her continual fidgeting. At that moment, she would have given her life for one cancerous filled drag of a cigarette. Instead, Rae Ann studied her pen at length and then bent over the pad of paper hoping to appear busy when Bob finally entered the room. She remained still for as long as she could, but when it became evident that Bob was running late she nervously shifted positions. Rae Ann glanced at her watch, then crossed and uncrossed her legs just for something to do.

Rae Ann wished Eddie were there so she would have someone to chat with. The need to remain silent was building steadily inside her. She was uncomfortable and, even though the room was all glass, Rae Ann felt suffocated. She was beginning to regret wearing a button down shirt as the collar was slowly creeping down her back and she had to continually readjust the button flap so her bra wouldn't show between the gaps. Rae Ann wiggled her toes inside her shoes and became obsessively focused on the feel of the toe seam of her pantyhose. Rae Ann took a moment to scan the glass walls in search of Bob Ashcroft. When she didn't see him anywhere in sight, Rae Ann ducked her head down under the table to reposition her hose.

"Look alive people, look alive."

Damn!

Rae Ann jerked her head up from under the table. She certainly hadn't wanted Bob to catch her in that unprofessional position. She quickly replaced her smart navy pump and sat up at full attention as her boss came storming into the room. Bob Ashcroft slammed a sheaf of papers onto the conference room table and leaned over them, balancing precariously on all ten fingertips. As always, Bob looked positively stressed and just this side of a stroke.

At nine o'clock in the morning, his tie had already been loosened and the top button of his white shirt was undone. "Okay, we've got a homicide up in Sheridan and I need coverage." There were four other reporters in the room besides Eric, the assignment editor, Bob and Rae Ann. No one seemed remotely interested in Bob or reporting on the homicide. One of the woman field reporters to Rae Ann's right spent the better part of a minute eyeing the cuticles on her left hand and two of the anchors spoke in hushed whispers about the outcome of last night's football game.

"Bob?" Rae Ann spoke tentatively. She cleared her throat nervously and then continued, "I would—"

"No" Bob cut in quickly, "Laura, cover the story."

The woman with the cuticles dropped both hands heavily in her lap and threw a look in Rae Ann's direction. Everyone else appeared relieved to have not been selected. The sports buffs went back to their conversation. Flabbergasted at both being shot down and at everyone else's attitudes, Rae Ann sat momentarily stunned.

"What have we got on Showy this week?" Bob asked the room. All eyes turned to the political reporter, Tom Levin, who looked like a deer caught in the headlights. Rae Ann remembered a couple of months ago when he'd asked her out. She had politely turned him down, even though he seemed nice enough. The next day at the station she had heard two people whispering about the rumor that she was a lesbian. It just wasn't in Rae Ann's nature to get involved with someone she worked with, or anyone for that matter. Long ago, she had sworn off relationships as just something else to deal with. In her life, Rae Ann had seen how relationships could ruin people's lives and it had left her emotionally crippled. In hot pursuit of her career goals, Rae Ann just did not have the time or energy to date.

"Showy has been laying low since the embezzlement claim," Tom explained, "But I hear he's going to be the guest of honor at the grand opening of Pine Trails."

Rae Ann rolled her eyes at the mention of the new ski resort just outside of the Dells in Rockingham. It had dominated the news non-stop for a month and Rae Ann was appalled that so many newsworthy stories were being put on the back burner to make coverage for what Rae Ann considered to be nothing more than daycare for rich people.

Now, here it was the grand opening and undoubtedly it would be top headline for the next week.

"Does anyone else have anything?"

Rae Ann wanted desperately to say something, but she didn't want to blurt it out in front of the other reporters. She took a hand from her lap and raised it slightly before dropping it back down, hoping no one had witnessed her moment of hesitation.

"Fine," Bob said, giving a nod of his head to dismiss the room. When no one made an attempt toward the door, Bob shouted "Move people. I am paying you to be here." His booming voice reverberated off the walls like thunder. Without further delay, the station staff scurried to scoop up their paperwork and head out the door. Everyone except Rae Ann.

"Don't look at me like that, Lewis" Bob said shaking his head and attempting to find some order with his own stack of papers. One of the middle papers kept tucking under itself and the lack of cooperation was showing in Bob's red face.

"I just don't get it, Bob. I mean, clearly no one else wanted the story." Rae Ann rose from the chair and circled the table toward her boss. "Bob, I heard..."

"You heard what?" Bob asked, breathlessly, giving up on the papers.

"I heard that Marley Cavanaugh is leaving and—"

"Oh, Rae Ann, don't start."

"Bob, you're the one that said I could do this. You knew there were more qualified reporters with more rank, but you gave me the field assignment position. I never had a day of on camera experience, but you knew I could do it. You know that you made the right decision. I give everything to this station."

"Rae Ann, listen. You are a good reporter. You only started here six years ago. You jumped from intern to research to field reporter in just two and a half years. That's more advancement than half of these people will ever do in their whole career. It's the reason why they look at you like they do. But this is a small market. You need to branch out."

Rae Ann inhaled deeply and stared at her boss intently, "you know as well as I do that coverage is the most important thing. I don't want another market or another station, Bob. I love it here at WZZY. I just need a hot story if I am even going to be considered for weekend anchor." She tried to keep her voice in check, but it was getting difficult. Rae Ann didn't understand why Bob was suddenly trying to hold back the career that he had molded with his very hands.

"You will have your chance. Just not this time," Bob ended dramatically by tucking the disorderly papers under his arm and turning to go. "Hey," he called back over his shoulder, "why don't you put together something for Sunday's Talk of the Town segment?"

"Bob, you don't understand. I need something high profile. I need to get my face on that television." Rae Ann followed Bob to the door and almost ran into him when he stopped abruptly.

"Fine. You want something big?" Rae Ann nodded eagerly and grinned like a child on Christmas morning. "Take Eddie up to Pine Trails on Saturday night. Remember what Tom said, it's the official grand opening."

Rae Ann crinkled her nose and said, "That's a fluff piece."

"You want exposure or not?" Bob eyed her, daring her to give him another reason to shout. "Besides, Showy's going to be there. It might just be quite the party."

"Fine," Rae Ann conceded, crossing her arms over her chest, "I'll take it, but it's going to be the best fluff reporting you've ever seen," Rae Ann shouted even as Bob shut the door firmly between them.

Two

Saturday, November 18th

Rae Ann threw her overnight bag into the back area of the van and slammed the door shut. She had been less than thrilled when Bob assigned the Pine Trails story to her, but her up-and-comer attitude had won out again. The last thing she was going to do was give the resort some fluff coverage on how luxurious the carpet was.

Rae Ann, along with the rest of Madison, had heard about the ruthless competition for the property between Grant Spencer and Elliot Logan. When they finally realized that working against each other would ensure the loss of the property, the duo formed a partnership and purchased the property together. Although, savvy businessman Grant Spencer had finagled the deal to where he would be buying out Elliot Logan's half within one year of ownership. To boot, Grant Spencer was old friends with Wisconsin's own man of the hour, Senator Francis Showalter.

Rae Ann was determined to cover the story from every possible angle. After doing all her research into the trio, Rae Ann had been chomping at the bit to cover the story. She had learned that the resort had actually opened its doors in October for staff training and last minute details, but the official grand opening happened a week before Thanksgiving, just in time for the tourists to book their ski vacations for the coming winter months. Rae Ann pulled a cigarette from her pack and lit it. The weather was miserable. A steady November drizzle had dampened her hair and her mood. She pulled the wool overcoat tighter around the thin velvet dress she wore and took a long drag off the cigarette. Before the end of the year, Rae Ann vowed to quit.

"You'd better finish that thing now 'cause you ain't smoking it in the van." Eddie was leaning against the door of the van hidden mostly by the hood of his heavy coat.

"Yeah, we'd better get on the road. I think this rain is only going to get worse." Rae Ann dropped the butt of the half smoked cigarette and crushed it under her heel. It would take slightly less than two hours to reach Pine Trails Resort and Rae Ann wanted to rehearse the questions she had prepared for her interview with Showy and the resort's owners.

About an hour into the drive, Rae Ann heard Eddie groan. "I think we have a problem here." Rae Ann raised her head from the notes she had jotted on her pad of paper and looked out the windshield. Sometime during the drive, the temperature had dropped considerably and the rain had turned to a slushy ice. Ahead of them, Rae Ann could see miles and miles of red tail lights. Eddie slowed the van to a stop behind the traffic and rolled his driver's window down. "Looks like an accident."

"Oh, this is just great," Rae Ann slammed her pen onto the note paper, "We're going to be late. I'm going to miss the story and Bob is going to freak out."

Eddie continued to inch the van along the stretch of highway, when they weren't stopped completely, but the going was slow. Rae Ann was so furious with the gridlock that she got out of the news van twice to smoke. She paced the length of the vehicle, in her strapped velvet dress and heels, cussing hotly under her breath.

It took nearly forty minutes, when it should have taken ten, for them to creep down the highway to their exit. When at last they were able to maneuver around the traffic and make it onto the right road that would lead to the Pine Trails Ski Resort, Rae Ann could feel her blood pressure rising to the limit. Here was her chance to prove to Bob that she could be anchor and it was going to be ruined by a traffic jam.

Now out of the congestion of the highway, Eddie pushed the gas pedal to the floor and slid recklessly around a corner. They made their way up the mountain with white knuckles and fast beating hearts. Rae Ann barely had a chance to take in the three other buildings that housed a gift shop, a ski equipment rental store and a bar and grill before Eddie cruised through the slush in the parking lot and slammed the van into park. Rae Ann jumped out of the passenger seat and took a moment to straighten her dress and coat before making her way towards the entrance. Eddie was behind her with the camera and microphone. The frozen ground threatened to trip her up as her heel clad feet tromped through the ice. Her face and ankles were frozen and stiff as Rae Ann slid through the revolving door and was ejected into the lobby of the plush resort.

The ribbon cutting ceremony had come and gone and people were moving into the banquet area to begin a night of drinking and dancing at the owner's expense. Neither Showy nor the never seen before Grant Spencer were anywhere in sight. Rae Ann groaned and threw her hands into the air.

"Great! We've missed everything. We've got no story, no visual." Rae Ann smoothed a few loose strands of hair back into the slowly falling French twist.

"Hey, calm down, pretty lady. And look at it this way," Eddie glanced around, "there is still great food to be eaten." He scooped a handful of hors d'oeuvres off a passing tray and into his mouth, grinning all the while. Rae Ann rolled her eyes and shook her head at the sight of Eddie's cheeks puffed out with crab cakes, like a squirrel storing up for the winter. Rae Ann motioned for Eddie to get footage of the foyer and grand staircase.

Even Rae Ann had to admit, the resort's interior was beautiful. Rich hunter green carpet flowed throughout the entrance, feeling under foot like chocolate melting in your mouth. Dark mahogany wainscoting crept halfway up the walls, to meet creamy eggshell paint that continued up to the vaulted ceiling. Various paintings of mammoth size were illuminated by tiny, well placed light fixtures. The only other light in the foyer came from low hanging chandeliers that were at least four feet in width.

By far, the most extraordinary part of the room had to be the grand staircase. It was located directly across from the revolving entrance door where Rae Ann stood. It was so large and winding that Rae Ann felt sure she wouldn't be able to conquer it all in one day. Just thinking about climbing the mammoth staircase made her tired. The intricately carved mahogany rails began at both the right and left corridors of the upper floor. Swooping down to meet in the middle and then continuing to the lobby floor, its base widening at the decent. To Rae Ann it looked like a waterfall, cascading over the rich and famous.

Rae Ann descended the two stairs onto the sunken lobby floor. The check in terminals and coat check were to the left of the stair case and the reception area was to the right. Four chairs and a love seat had been positioned around a large fireplace set into an island in the middle of the room. The logs crackled and shifted, sending a spray of embers up through the chimney as Rae Ann passed on her way to the ballroom. She gasped at the sight of the darkened inner sanctum of the large room, her hand fluttered to her neck.

People were packed into the room by the hundreds and more were elbowing past Rae Ann. Thousands of sequins on the women's fancy dresses caught the twinkling of the disco ball causing the illusion of tiny camera bulbs flashing continuously. A live band filled up the stage and music spilled endlessly from well hidden speakers. The tuxedoed men migrated to the south end of the well stocked bar to talk politics and sports while the women cut up the parquet dance floor and criticized each others taste in outfits. The pretentious air had become too thick for Rae Ann to breath; she pulled back into the lobby to search for Eddie. He was flirting with a young girl at the coat check counter and Rae Ann dragged him towards the entrance door so he could hear her talk.

"I think we should just go. We can tell Bob what happened with the traffic and pretend like we never even got here."

"Yeah, all right. Let me just get my coat," Eddie, said straightening his tuxedo printed T-shirt and eyed the girl at the coat counter.

"Make it quick, lover boy," Rae Ann mused. As she waited for Eddie's return, Rae Ann wandered to the wall by the check-in desk. On it was an enlarged map of the resort and the surrounding ski trails. There were seven trails in all. Two bunny trails, three intermediate trails and two difficult runs. The most difficult dubbed The Menace.

"Thinking about a ski run?" A voice rang out behind Rae Ann and at first she didn't realize the man had been addressing her.

"I'm sorry?" she questioned as she turned toward the voice. It belonged to a handsome gentleman with an award winning smile. His chestnut hair was combed back straight from his face and his warm brown eyes were searching Rae Ann's. She suddenly felt like a bug under a microscope.

"Skiing? Do you like to ski?" the man rephrased his question.

"Oh no, I'm not here on vacation," Rae Ann explained, "I rather think this overpriced ski school is a waste of money and good land." Rae Ann gave a fleeting look around the lobby, but Eddie had seemed to disappear into the mass of people. She turned her attention back to the man. "I am a reporter for Channel Eight news out of Madison. Rae Ann Lewis," Rae Ann stuck her hand out for the man to shake. His touch was firm but soft. He opened his mouth to speak, but Rae Ann muttered a quick 'excuse me' as she spotted Eddie coming towards her.

"Ready?" Rae Ann started. But even as she spoke, she was already walking slowly in the opposite direction of the entrance, toward the couple that had crossed the threshold into the main lobby from the bank of garish gold elevators. Eddie followed her lead and swung the camera onto his shoulder. "Senator? Mrs. Showalter? Rae Ann Lewis, Channel Eight news. Do you have a comment on the opening of the lodge? Do you approve of them tearing out the trees to make room for this expensive, unnecessary resort?" Rae Ann shoved the microphone toward the senator's mouth for a response and fought the urge to step backwards as the couple continued to walk towards her.

Seeing that she wouldn't be swayed, the Senator gripped his wife's elbow and she stopped on command. Francis Showalter smiled coyly and tightened his grip on the missus elbow as a signal for her to smile as well. "Miss Lewis, I believe you should be directing these questions to the man of the hour. May I introduce, Grant Spencer? Grant owns and operates Pine Trails."

Rae Ann turned her attention and microphone in the direction of where the Senator was holding out his hand. The handsome man from the check in desk was standing stealthily behind her. Rae Ann's breath caught in her throat at the sight of the attractive man that she had virtually insulted only minutes ago. She suddenly felt extremely underdressed and very underprivileged. Grant bowed his head slightly to her and smiled generously, his big brown eyes twinkling all the while. "Miss Lewis and I have met, but I didn't get a chance to say how pleased I am to have you in my resort. I am so delighted that we can accommodate your request for an interview, but don't be mistaken. We only cleared a few trees for the lodge itself. The land where the trails are marked were not stripped of their vegetation." He ended the speech with his award winning smile, that no doubt caused many a woman to faint. It was a nice touch.

"Oh," Rae Ann said, the woman inside her silently fought the journalist exterior she was trying hard to uphold. "I mean," Rae Ann stammered, regaining her composure, "how do you explain the four semi trucks that hauled out trees for three days straight?"

"Well, I see someone has been doing their homework." Grant quipped and the Showalter's obliged with a forced laugh. Grant Spencer shook his head and sighed as if he were about to explain something very complicated to a small child. "Miss Lewis, the ground floor of the resort is nearly sixteen thousand square feet. How many trees do you think that is?"

Before Rae Ann could respond, Grant straightened his bow tie and ushered the Senator and his wife into the party. "Nice guy," Eddie muttered lowering the camera off his jean-jacketed shoulder.

"Listen, Eddie, just get a shot of the guests and let's get the hell out of here." Eddie shuffled back into the ballroom, leaving Rae Ann to her thoughts. She wandered toward the front doors, silently scolding herself for letting Grant Spencer control the interview. She was a professional and professionals weren't swayed by beauty or charm, which is exactly what she just let happen. She hadn't even got to ask about the obviously absent Elliot Logan.

Rae Ann wrestled a cigarette from her purse and began picturing Grant's million dollar smile. She turned back towards the lobby to wait for Eddie when the million dollar smile beamed full force in front of her. "Miss Lewis, I am glad I caught you before you left." Grant Spencer was five feet away and closing the distance fast. "I hope this little interview won't cause any problems with your superior. I just felt the need to justify myself, especially in front of the Senator."

Rae Ann cocked her head to the side and narrowed her eyes to slits. "Why in front of the Senator, Mr. Spencer?" Her journalist instincts kicked back in full force.

"Well, he is an upstanding man and probably wouldn't want anything to do with an establishment that tears down the very wilderness he fights for with his campaign."

Rae Ann gave a half smile and turned toward the door. "That's great, Mr. Spencer. Enjoy your party."

"Well, I would enjoy it a lot more if you stayed for a dance... with me, of course." Eddie, who had walked up in time to hear the proposition, raised his eyebrows to the ceiling.

"Mr. Spencer," Rae Ann started, intending to tell the man just what she thought of his Senator pleasing, tree killing resort when Eddie interrupted. "It would be good for the station, Scoop," he muttered out the side of his mouth as he pretended to fiddle with the lens on the camera.

"I'd love to," Rae Ann finished through clenched teeth. She took Grant's hand and let herself be guided into the adjoining room. Rae Ann shot a look back over her shoulder at Eddie, but he was too busy mock kissing the camera lens. The stunning couple continued onto the dance floor as the guests parted like the Red Sea around them. A slow waltz filled Rae Ann's ears and they began twirling around in time to the music. She hadn't danced all that often, but Grant was a wonderful lead and rather impressive dancer. He was pulling her close one minute and then sending her flying the next. The dance seemed to last forever and in between nine o'clock and eternity they became just Grant and Rae Ann. Two people brought together by a million tiny twists of fate.

Eventually, Rae Ann sent Eddie onto the motel without her. She stayed on Grant's arm feeling like a queen as he paraded her around the room. First introducing her to important people and then shuffling her onto the dance floor for another moment cheek to cheek. For the first time in Rae Ann's life, she wondered if this was how love was supposed to be. Being the focus of a man's attention that wouldn't take *no* for an answer. Rae Ann decided that maybe relationships weren't so bad after all.

At the evening's end, Grant, the gentleman, walked her out into the parking lot. "I had a wonderful time tonight," she said as a sleek black limousine belonging to the resort pulled up to the curb, white smoke billowing from its tail pipe. Grant kissed her lightly on the side of the mouth, "So did I."

Without another word, Rae Ann stepped into the darkness of the limo and was off into the night. Never in all of her life could Rae Ann remember feeling the way she did. Grant was so handsome, so intelligent and so fun. Growing up, Rae Ann would have never imagined her life as she lived it now. She thought back to her past existence. One she had tried so hard to out run. Rae Ann closed her eyes and relived her childhood as if it were a movie playing silently behind her eyelids.

~ * ~

Rae Ann's mother, Ronette, had been a career waitress in a small diner called the Hot Stop in the seaside town of Brights, New Jersey. In her youth, Ronette had set off New York bound to pursue an acting career. It was the same story as old as time and Ronette was a classic case. The girl told herself day after day that it was only a matter of time before her persistence would pay off and she would get the acting gig that would take her far, far away from New Jersey. Of course, she never got that big break and ended up waiting tables on tourists and truckers for the better part of twenty years.

Rae Ann had been conceived in the women's bathroom of the diner one terribly snowy night when everyone else had had the good sense to stay home. Her father was a long haul, over the road truck driver who knew nothing of Rae Ann's existence until a nearly a decade later.

Rae Ann, herself, had been a quiet child. She grew up silently in the back booth of the non-smoking section at the Hot Stop. She reported there every day after school and spent her summers filling the sugar jars for pocket change. Randy, the owner of the diner, never minded Rae Ann's mild mannered appearance and even let her hang out with the fry cooks during the slow hours of the afternoon. Rae Ann knew no other existence and was content with what life had given her. Rae Ann and her mother had no real family to speak of and got along just fine on their own until shortly before Rae Ann's tenth birthday.

Even now, shivering from the cold and excitement of the night, Rae Ann could remember the pleasant spring day when the man that would be her step-father stumbled into the Hot Stop. He was lost and hungry, a traveling salesman named Paul from upstate New York. Rae Ann literally watched her mother fall into immediate love with the sandy haired man and his brand new Buick. Paul was not an unattractive man, but to Rae Ann he was an acquired taste. His forehead seemed a bit large, but he artfully covered it by letting his hair grow long on top. It flopped over into his eyes and Rae Ann often caught her mother brushing it out of Paul's vision. He had a sharp nose and a cleft chin set beneath small dark eyes. Rae Ann could tell that something in his eyes wasn't to be trusted. Suddenly Paul's chance encounter in the diner became a recurring event until even Rae Ann noticed that there was more going on between her mother and the salesman than just the Sunday specials.

On one of his weekend trips to New Jersey, Paul decided that he no longer wanted to be a self-proclaimed bachelor. He resolved to take Ronette away from all of the heartache of the diner and give her the wonderful life that she had always dreamed about in New York. Up until that point, Paul had tolerated Rae Ann's existence. He had even gone so far as to take Rae Ann to the zoo to celebrate her "A" in Grammar at the end of the school year. Unfortunately, now that he was engaged to her mother, Paul did not see any room in his life for Ronette's illegitimate child—or any children for that matter.

At first, Ronette was troubled to learn that her future husband did not want to include her daughter in their new life. But after a lot of artificial promises, Ronette, who wanted more than the swollen ankles and smell of grease she took home every night, decided it was time that Rae Ann went to live with her father. Paul helped Ronette track down Rae Ann's father through the trucking company he had worked for all those years ago.

Needless to say that Joe Danner, the man who had given her life, was less than thrilled to learn that he had a young daughter. He argued mercilessly that he knew nothing of children and was not equipped to deal with her. He insisted she be placed in foster care and threatened to do just that once she was in his custody. In the end, he only agreed to bring her to his home because he realized she would be cheaper than hiring a nurse to care for his ailing mother.

As Rae Ann had pulled out of the Hot Spot parking lot, for the last time, in her father's semi truck, Rae Ann turned away from her mother's waving hand and forced tears, vowing to never need anyone again for the rest of her life. Two weeks after her eleventh birthday and having never been asked her opinion on the situation, Rae Ann moved into her father's tiny clapboard house in Pennsylvania. The very next day, her father went to his boss and asked to be assigned to a longer route that would take him farther from home for longer periods of time. After that Rae Ann rarely saw him, but it did not hurt her feelings. She had become callused to the entire situation and instead turned her energy to helping Sally, the elderly woman that was her grandmother, recover slowly from a stroke. Sally soon became Rae Ann's only solace. Sally encouraged Rae Ann to do well with her school work, taught her to knit and filled her in on the sketchy Danner family history. Rae Ann made a point not to become close with any of the girls she went to school with, knowing that she wouldn't be staying in Pennsylvania forever. When it came time for Rae Ann to leave, she did not want any emotional ties to prevent her from moving on with her life.

Around the time of Rae Ann's thirteenth Christmas, Sally took her to the basement and directed her to dig way back into the small storage closet. The elderly woman held the ladder steady while Rae Ann searched through the years of dust and found the square, blue velvet box that Sally was looking for in the closet. Rae Ann scampered down while her grandmother dusted off the box and then opened it to reveal the hidden contents. Inside laid a single strand of cultured pearls with an elegant golden clasp. It was the most beautiful necklace Rae Ann had ever seen. Even in the dim light of the storage closet as the dust settled back into its undisturbed slumber around her, the pearls radiated a sense of beauty and peace. Rae Ann reached out a hand to touch the smooth orbs and after two years finally felt a connection to the family that never knew her.

"Your grandfather gave those to me as a wedding present," Sally explained to her, "He bought them in Europe where he was stationed during the war. I never showed them to Joe. He would have sold them, in a heart beat."

Sally waited another breath and then spoke again, "I want you to have them, Rae Ann. You should wear them on your wedding day and I pray that you will be as happy as your grandpa and I were. They have been a special part of my life and thankfully, so have you. Your father may not have wanted a daughter, but I have always wanted you, even before I knew you existed. Your coming to this house has made me young again. I want you to promise me that you will finish your education and then give yourself to the world. The world will be a better place for it."

Rae Ann took the box firmly in her hands and looked at her grandmother. The overhead light cast a shadow around the woman and for the first time, Rae Ann could see the frailty of Sally's bones. A second stroke nine months ago had all but taken her life and Rae Ann didn't have a clue as to what would become of her when the woman finally succumbed to her sickly body. "I won't let you down, Grandma."

Three years later, the old woman died silently in her sleep. Rae Ann's father did not even come home for the funeral. He did, however, show up three weeks later when the lawyer was scheduled to read the will. As Joe had expected, Sally had left everything to her only son, but he had not anticipated that she would set aside a rather substantial sum of money for Rae Ann. Joe waited only two days before heading back out to work. Living in the house with a virtual stranger made for an endless string of awkward conversations.

Therefore, he had not anticipated seeing Rae Ann standing with packed suitcases by his rig.

"I want to go with you," Rae Ann stated simply.

Joe stared at the young woman before him. She was still petite and girlish around the edges, but he could see the makings of a real beauty showing through. *My daughter,* Joe thought. He did not think about or even care that being on the road meant she would no longer go to school. At sixteen, he assumed she was old enough to make her own decisions. He gave a quick nod of his head and Rae Ann scampered into the cab before he could change his mind.

Rae Ann sat stoic for most of the journey looking only out the passenger window at the passing landscape. She didn't care where they were headed, hadn't even bothered to ask. The few stops they made were carried out with no grandeur. Rae Ann paid for her own meals and motel rooms with the money her grandmother had left her. There was no late night, sob filled father-daughter relationship reunion. Rae Ann had not expected one.

One morning while she drank coffee from a chipped cup in the restaurant across from their motel, Rae Ann felt Joe approach her small table. "Loads delivered. I'll be heading back to Pennsylvania now."

She raised her chin to look at him and in the steadiest voice she could muster said, "I won't be going with you." Rae Ann concluded that by the slight nod of Joe's head, he had seen this coming and was more than happy to leave her. He tucked his thick fingers into the pockets of his jeans and sighed. Rae Ann thought he might feel obligated to say something so she turned her head back to the coffee cup.

From under her eyelashes, Rae Ann watched his rig roll out of the parking lot, belching black smoke as it gathered speed. Signaling down a passing waitress, Rae Ann asked exactly where she was. The woman was not much older than Rae Ann with a large pregnant belly and a red slash of a mouth. "Madison, Wisconsin," she muttered before setting off behind the counter. The journey had not taken her as far as she had wished, but when she took a deep breath and peered out of the diner's large picture window she caught sight of the endless rolling hills. The white, snowy mounds wore haloes of wispy, thin clouds all set against the clearest, blue sky. Although just hills, they looked massive and intimidating, but full of immense strength and promise. Rae Ann smiled at the mental comparison she made between the hilly landscape and her new life. It was at that point that she concluded that only good things were to come for her here in the capital city of Wisconsin. And for so long they had been good. Almost too good to be true, really.

And now there was the possibility of Grant.

~ * ~

The limo slowed to a stop outside of the motel where Rae Ann and Eddie were staying. She floated up the stairs to her room and didn't even mind that Bob had put them up in less than acceptable accommodations. As soon as she had shut the door to her room, a soft knock sounded. "Go to bed, Eddie."

"But, Scoop..." Eddie's barely audible voice came at her from under the door jam, "I waited up all night for this."

"Eddie we have a two hour drive back to Madison tomorrow. I will tell you all about it then." Rae Ann finished slithering out of the black dress and snuggled in between the sheets. "If you stay up any longer, you'll be too tired to drive and I guess I'll just have to take control of the van."

"Ah, hell no, woman, you ain't driving that van," Eddie joked, "sleep tight lover girl." Rae Ann smiled as she slowly drifted off, dreaming of Grant Spencer.

Three

Tuesday, November 28th

Grant Spencer awoke with a start and sat straight up in bed. At once he knew he was not alone. *Christ, have I done it again?* Grant thought to himself as he glanced over at the figure lying beneath his expensive sheets.

The dark headed woman was sleeping soundlessly with her head turned away from Grant. He ran his hands over his face to wipe away the rest of the sleep and then as quietly as possible removed himself from the bed. This was not the first time Grant had tied one on a little too tightly and awoke beside a strange woman. Didn't he realize it was time for him to grow up and stop acting like such a careless playboy?

Grant gathered his boxer shorts and a robe from off the floor and moved swiftly through the room trying to escape before the girl woke up. He desperately tried to recall the events of the previous evening and couldn't put together exactly what happened shortly after he'd left the bar at Spencer's Grill. It was amazing that he had even found his way back to the main lodge but, of course, that is probably where the girl entered the picture.

Grant started to step over a pile of clothes that belonged to the woman when his foot stopped in mid-air. A housekeeper's uniform peeked out from beneath a sweater and pair of white socks.

Dammit, Grant, he scolded, *not the staff.*

This was really the last straw. It was time he restructured his life and took hold of his priorities. This sort of thing could interfere with the resort and he knew he would lay his life down before he let that happen. Grant took a glass of juice from the refrigerator in the small kitchenette and used it to down four aspirin. Maybe he would give that reporter a call. She seemed like a pretty levelheaded woman. And beautiful to boot. Just the type of woman that could tame his wild side and get him to settle down into the business-like façade he presented. Grant belted the robe loosely around his waist and took the glass of juice with him to the office just across the hall from the suite. He would call Rae Ann Lewis and invite her up to the resort. With any luck, the nameless woman in his bed would be gone before he got back.

Four

Friday, December 1ˢᵗ

Rae Ann slammed the drawer shut on her desk and shuffled through the papers on her desktop. The receptionist had said there was a message from Grant Spencer waiting for her on her desk, but she'd be damned if she could find it. Rae Ann sat back from the desk and took a moment to collect herself, before rifling through the paperwork for the ninth time in search of the tiny pink message. She was acting like a lovesick school girl for Christ's sake.

It had been nearly two weeks since the grand opening of the resort and Rae Ann hadn't heard a word from Grant Spencer. She knew he must be an extremely busy man with the resort and surely Grant had family to spend the Thanksgiving holiday with, but still thought he would have called by now. And now he had, but she couldn't find the number to call him back.

Rae Ann slammed the sheaf of papers back onto her desk and the rush of air sent several contents from her desktop floating down onto the floor. One of those items was Grant's message. Rae Ann snatched it from under her rolling chair, abandoning everything else, and gathered up the phone. She cradled it between her ear and shoulder as her trembling fingers dialed the number to the Pine Trails Resort. It rang only twice before the line picked up and a female voice said, "Pine Trails, how may I direct your call?" Rae Ann was caught off guard momentarily. She had expected Grant's voice on the line, not an operator.

"Oh, yes, Grant Spencer, please," Rae Ann stammered.

"One moment." The line appeared to have been cut off as Rae Ann heard not so much as a buzz on the other end. She was about to hang up when Grant's voice sprang from the receiver. "Grant Spencer."

"Grant, its Rae Ann Lewis," Rae Ann smiled into the phone. When Grant didn't respond, she continued hurriedly, "I got the message that you called."

"Rae Ann, of course. How are you today?" Grant's voice was deep and smooth. Rae Ann remembered the soft kiss he had placed on her cheek that night.

"I'm fine. Thank you."

"I got to thinking about your story and thought maybe you would benefit from a private tour of the resort. Unless, I'm mistaken, you didn't really get what you came for at the grand opening," Grant mused.

This was not what Rae Ann had hoped he was going to say. It was true that Bob had been less than thrilled with the coverage she and Eddie had brought to him about Pine Trails. Rae Ann was sure that Bob would love this exclusive tour plus it would give Rae Ann a chance to see Grant again. "Grant, that would be great. When could I impose?" Rae Ann recovered from her momentary disappointment and regained her composure as a professional.

"I was hoping tomorrow."

"Tomorrow is Saturday," Rae Ann flipped through her date calendar nonchalantly, "It appears that I'm free. I will see you then."

"Oh, Rae Ann?" Grant's voice reached out over the distance, "that isn't the only reason why I called." Rae Ann felt her heart skip a beat and she held her breath until he continued. "I want to see you. On a personal level. I mean a date," Grant sputtered, "wait this is coming out all wrong. I would like for you to stay at the resort for the weekend. I know this is short notice but I happen to be free this weekend and I would like to spend it with you. We could ski, have dinner and, of course, you would get your interview."

Rae Ann giggled like a child and put a hand over her mouth to suppress the laughter. She was certain that Grant Spencer had probably never been this tongue-tied in his life. Especially over a woman. He had appeared so confident and pulled together. "I would love to, Grant. I can be there by noon tomorrow."

"Fantastic."

Rae Ann set the phone down just as Eddie walked up and perched on the edge of her desk. He was eating a yogurt and took in a huge spoonful before noticing her giddy expression. "What?"

Rae Ann leaned far back in her desk chair and swiveled from side to side. "You will never guess who just called."

Five

Saturday, December 2ⁿᵈ

Rae Ann stood in the middle of her bedroom with nothing on but her bra and panties. She couldn't seem to find anything suitable to wear on her date with Grant Spencer. Rae Ann scolded herself for calling it just a date when she was going up there to work. A business suit seemed too professional and jeans were entirely too informal. She put her fists on her hip and glanced over to the bedside clock. The large red numbers silently told her that she was going to be late if she waited any longer. Rae Ann looked at it one of two ways. She could either sit in the middle of her closet and sulk or she could get off her ass and find something suitable to wear. In the end, she grabbed a pair of black corduroy pants and a gray cable knit sweater. On her way out of the apartment, she grabbed her voice-activated tape recorder and her car keys.

An early December snow had blanketed the ground with beautiful white powder. Rae Ann craned her neck to see the resort perched precariously on the hillside as she approached the turn off. She slowed cautiously as she wound up the road that would take her to the resort's parking lot. An elderly man was in front of the building shoveling snow and happily whistling a tune.

"Good day," he said, cheerfully and raised a hand from the shovel to wave at Rae Ann. Rae Ann smiled and waved back.

She hadn't seen him, but Grant had been waiting for her. He came out of the smoked glass doors, his breath pluming in front of him. His twinkling eyes made her breath catch and his smile was as beautiful as the freshly fallen snow. Her corduroy pants and turtleneck sweater made her feel seriously underdressed next to his expertly tailored business suit, but if Grant noticed it never showed.

"I'm so glad you could come," Grant said, taking both of her hands and kissing her cheek.

"Thank you for the invitation. Your resort is even more beautiful in the daylight."

Grant chuckled as he remembered Rae Ann's first impression of his grand resort and then squeezed her hands simultaneously. "Well, I did promise you a private tour. I know you didn't exactly get the story you came after at the grand opening," Grant blushed at his own words and Rae Ann felt her face flush when he referred to the evening they had spent together. "Well, anyway, we should get inside."

Rae Ann followed his lead as a bell hop took her keys and retrieved her suitcase from the trunk. Grant led her away from the check in terminals, but not before Rae Ann noticed that they were gathering quite a few looks. As they walked onward toward the elevator, Grant tried to distract her with conversation, but she couldn't help but notice how everyone seemed to stop what they were doing when Grant walked by them. It was as if at the sight of him, they completely forgot the task at hand and had to stop a moment and regroup after he was gone. Rae Ann was trying to take it all in as they stepped onto the elevator. She looked out again at the lobby as the doors began to close. All the people seemed to have broken free of Grant's trance and gone back to their business.

All but one.

Rae Ann couldn't make out the face of the person standing just to the side of the fireplace. She couldn't be sure of who they were in the dim light of the rapidly closing elevator, but the look of the person made her extremely uncomfortable. Of course, she was just being silly and reading too much into the situation. The person probably wasn't even looking at them. Although, why wouldn't people stare, Rae Ann and Grant did make a rather handsome couple.

Rae Ann opened her mouth to point the person out, but the elevator doors snapped shut and they were gone. Rae Ann watched

Grant insert a special key into a lock on the elevator panel and push the button for the third floor. For fear of appearing paranoid, Rae Ann decided not to say anything and the two continued to ride the elevator in silence until he doors opened on the third and top floor.

"This floor only consists of four rooms and a housekeeper's closet. My office is at the very end on the right hand side. My suite is across the hall. Down here," Grant continued, pointing to the opposite end of the hallway, "is the guest suite that I reserve only for very special people."

Rae Ann flushed again when he smiled in her direction. He began walking when Rae Ann laid a hand on his arm, stopping him and mid-stride. "And the room across from the guest suite?" she asked in a soft voice.

"Oh. For now I'm just using it as storage," he explained and then continued on to the room where Rae Ann would be staying. Grant took hold of another key from his ring and opened the door in the sitting area of the suite. He held the door open while Rae Ann walked slowly into the fairy tale of a room.

It was the most breathtaking sight she had ever laid eyes on. She didn't voice this anecdote, but was certain that her apartment in Madison, her father's house in Pennsylvania and the trailer in New Jersey would all fit into the suite. The whole room was done in the softest shade of lavender. Lilacs were stuck in vases and on paintings all around the room. Two floral patterned chairs were posed in front of the burning fireplace and a silver tea set sat between them on a small oak table. The double doors that led into the bedroom area were open and beckoned Rae Ann to enter them. The monstrous four-poster bed stood directly across the room. It was so loaded down with purple pillows Rae Ann thought the legs might give out.

Delicate lavender fabric was draped from post to post and shimmered in the light from the huge windows along the back wall. Somehow her suitcase had beaten her into the room and had made itself at home on the chaise lounge at the end of the bed. Matching oak furniture pieces were placed around the room creating an old fashioned feel. A large armoire stood to the left of the bed, its handles tied neatly with a purple bow. A vanity table was on the right with a fabulous full-length mirror that reflected Rae Ann's look of amazement. Grant had placidly followed her into the bedroom and was obviously pleased that she admired the room so much. "When you are here you may use this room at your leisure." Rae Ann tried to speak, but was unable to form the words. Instead she wrapped her arms around him and hugged him. To her surprise and his, Grant hugged her back.

"I thought, today, we could go skiing and then have a nice dinner," Grant said, "You do like to ski, don't you?" He reluctantly pulled from her embrace.

"I love to ski," Rae Ann exclaimed, perhaps a little too breathless with the memory of his touch, "but I don't have any equipment."

Grant smiled down at her pixie face and felt twenty-five years old again. Just being with her made him realize what life was all about. Maybe, just maybe, this woman could straighten out his life. "Well, then, I hope you don't mind, but I took the liberty of having some things sent up for you." He directed her attention to the armoire. "In there you should find everything you need for skiing and something for dinner later."

"Grant, I don't know what to say."

"Don't say anything. Just meet me in my office in half an hour." Rae Ann waited until Grant shut the door to the outer sitting room before approaching the armoire. She ran her hand lightly down the smooth textured surface and then let it settle on the bow. With one tug, it untied easily and floated soundlessly to the floor. Rae Ann held her breath as the wide doors swung open and revealed the treasures that lay inside. Tucked neatly against the back of the armoire was a pair of skis, ski poles and boots. Hanging in front was a pair of ski pants, a wool sweater and a nylon parka. The ensemble was all the purest shade of white Rae Ann had ever seen.

In a bag at the bottom of the closet, Rae Ann found gloves, earmuffs and goggles to complete her skiing needs. It had seemed as though Grant had thought of everything. Rae Ann took the clothes and ski equipment out of the armoire and placed it on the bed. She could tell that everything was brand new and no doubt the best on the market. During her time living in Madison, Rae Ann had ventured up

31

to the mountains a time or two and had found quite a love for skiing. Her first skiing encounter came when she and Eddie went to cover a news story. At that time it was all Rae Ann could do to stand on the skis. She quickly realized how to adjust to the extra length on her feet and had become quite proficient on the slopes.

Even now, she knew to check the release bindings on the skis to make sure they were in proper working order and then stood one of the skis up beside her to check its length. When she raised her arm above her head, the tip of the ski fell just between her wrist and her elbow. The skies were a little short for Rae Ann but, after all, Grant did not know that she could ski. He had undoubtedly asked for the shorter skis because they were easier to maneuver. She quickly dressed in the sweater and pants and then turned to shut the wooden doors.

That is when she noticed the garment bag. It was hanging far back in behind the shelves, but was still visible from where Rae Ann stood. She wondered what beautiful outfit Grant had picked out for their date. She reached for the zipper on the bag, but decided to leave it be a surprise for later. Sighing with a smile, Rae Ann shut the doors. She continued to dress, pulling on the obviously expensive ski boots and picked up the parka. She tucked the gloves in one pocket and the earmuffs in the other. As an afterthought, she slipped the jacket on despite the warmth of the room and she secured the goggles on top of her head like a headband.

Rae Ann also retrieved the voice-activated recorder and slipped it into her coat pocket just in case she wanted to document something for her story that she saw while they were skiing. Taking the skis in hand, holding them together base to base, Rae Ann swung them up on her right shoulder. She grabbed the poles in her left hand and started out of the suite. She emerged from her room just as Grant and another man stepped out from Grant's office. Rae Ann noticed that Grant had changed out of his business suit into all black skiing attire. The other man was, however, dressed professionally, his face flushed with anger.

"I assure you, Elliot, this will be taken care of immediately."

"I should hope so, Grant. I really do. A deal is a deal and I don't want to think about what could happen if..." The man's voice trailed off, but the two men continued to exchange stares.

They had yet to notice Rae Ann and she was unsure of what to do with herself. She didn't want to eavesdrop on the conversation but there was nowhere for her to go. With the skis on her shoulder, she would have to come completely into the hall and swing around before going back into the suite. But if she did this they would surely see her. She couldn't back up for fear of knocking into the silver tea set on the table, sending it crashing to the floor. So there Rae Ann stood half in and half out of the room.

The heat inside the parka was steadily rising and she felt a small bead of perspiration begin a trail from her shoulder blades to the waist of her ski pants. Finally Rae Ann decided she had no other choice than to remain where she was and hope the conversation ended soon. Besides, the dialogue exchange was beginning to pique her interest.

"Elliot, we shouldn't make a big deal out of this. I told you I would take care of it. I said that didn't I?" The entire time Grant talked, Rae Ann could see his fists clenched tightly at his sides and could hear his voice start to take on a high-pitched tone.

"Yeah, you said it. But I haven't seen anything happen yet, Grant," the man quickly retorted, "You'd better make good on this deal. I would hate to have to send my boys."

The skis on Rae Ann's shoulder started to feel like they weighed a thousand pounds. The men just kept talking and if Rae Ann stood there any longer, she was sure she would collapse. The entire situation was making her extremely uncomfortable and the sudden need for nicotine was unmistakable. Rae Ann concluded that it was time to make her presence known even though the reporter inside her was trying to figure out what the hell these two were talking about. She walked all the way into the hall and pulled the door shut behind her. At this, both men turned in her direction.

"Rae Ann, you're early."

"Grant, I'm sorry if I've interrupted something. I can come back." Rae Ann put her hand back on the doorknob.

"Don't be silly. Let me take your skis." Grant came quickly to her side and relieved her of the skis and poles. He propped them against the nearest wall then turned back to the awkward situation with his unexpected company. "Rae Ann, this is a business associate of mine, Elliot Logan. Elliot, may I introduce Rae Ann Lewis of Channel Eight news in Madison."

"I'm pleased to meet you, Mr. Logan." Rae Ann stuck her hand out for the man to shake. His smile was phony and forced. "Yes, hello."

With that she was dismissed. The man turned back to Grant as if Rae Ann had never interrupted their conversation. "Grant, remember what I said and enjoy your day skiing." Elliot Logan shouldered past Rae Ann and continued down the hall to the elevator. The doors clanged open as if on cue and the man quickly disappeared inside.

Rae Ann raised her eyebrows in Grant's direction and crossed her arms across her chest. Grant waved his hand as if to clear the air of Elliot Logan's presence and smiled brightly. "Don't you worry about that. Let's hit the slopes." Rae Ann nodded at Grant and began walking toward the elevator in the same path that Elliot Logan had used to storm off.

"Oh no. This way," Grant said, pointing to his private quarters, "I have a deck built off the back of my office. We can take the steps down to my private slope."

"Your private slope?" Rae Ann asked incredulously, "I am impressed."

"Yes, well," Grant blushed, "I was hoping the main slopes would be so busy that there would be no room for my bumbling and stumbling."

Grant's office was exactly as Rae Ann anticipated it to be. It was beautiful and dark except for an unshaded set of French doors directly across from where Rae Ann stood. The wooden flanked walls and floor were the color of night. A set of filing cabinets and the large desk were the same shade. A silver box was open on the desk and it seemed to glow as it caught the light from the doors. It contained cigars and a book of matches from Spencer's Grill.

Grant rounded Rae Ann and opened a door that Rae Ann had at first not noticed was there. It was a built in closet that held his skis and skiing equipment. They manipulated all of their gear around behind his mammoth desk and out of the glass doors. The view was stunning and the crisp, cool air burned Rae Ann's throat when she gasped at the sight. She laid her equipment down on the deck and just peered over the railing for a full minute before regarding Grant.

"It's amazing," she said enthusiastically.

"Thanks. I had it designed so I could just take a break whenever I wanted. Instead of parading down through the resort, I just step out here for a quick run and then go back to work. It rounds out down by the kitchen of the restaurant. I just take the rear steps back up and go on with my day."

As Grant spoke, he moved ever closer to Rae Ann. Despite the cold, his stare was making her sweat even more under the parka. "Unfortunately, it's good for only one run down since the ski lift does not come around to this part of the mountain. To make it enjoyable you just have to take it slow and not rush things."

Rae Ann broke away from his intense gaze and felt her face redden. She had never been so giddy and foolish in front of a man before. It actually felt good. "Well, I think it is wonderful—not just the trail, the entire property is remarkable. Just how did you come to acquire the most desirable piece of real estate in Wisconsin?"

Grant shrugged as if to say it was no big deal. "Just business, you know? My associate that you met earlier wanted the ground and so did I. It was only natural that we enter the venture together. Actually, the hardest part of the negotiations was getting the previous owner's to sell at all."

Rae Ann stared intently, absorbed in the story. "Harold and Lou Spellman owned the entire property. When Lou got sick, Harold thought it would be a good idea for them to get a smaller place and sell off all this unused acreage. In the middle of the deal, Lou died and Harold suddenly couldn't bear to sell what he had shared with his wife of fifty-seven years."

Rae Ann leaned in close and whispered, "How did you convince him?" Grant glanced out over the deck and laughed quietly to himself.

"Well, I did and I didn't. The old man wouldn't budge until I offered him a job. We built him a small log cabin at the base and asked him to be the groundskeeper." Rae Ann smiled remembering the adorable old man that waved at her when she happened upon the resort. "He is an extremely loyal employee and a hard working individual. Sometimes I catch him working late into the night. Says he has nothing better to do with his time. I guess it gave him a greater purpose in life and he has been able to get over the death of his wife."

"That was wonderfully thoughtful of you, Grant."

Again, Grant shrugged and looked back in her direction. She reached down to grab her gear and then hustled down the steps to the top of the mountain ready to begin her run. It was then that she noticed the huge house nestled in amongst the trees further into the woods.

"My goodness," Rae Ann whispered, her hand fluttering to the base of her throat, "Is that your house?"

Grant skipped down the steps to stand beside her. "Yes. It is still in the process of being built. The outside is almost finished, but I'm afraid the interior is suffering due to my lack of fashion sense."

Rae Ann stared, open-mouthed. The wall facing the resort was entirely made of glass, but the rest was covered in cedar siding that all but blended it in beautifully with the surrounding trees. It was a two-story wonder and for a second Rae Ann let herself imagine that she could live there. She shook her head to dismiss the thought and silently scolded herself for being so presumptuous.

"If you have such a beautiful home, why are you still living at the resort?" Rae Ann asked. Then wished she could take the words back even as they were coming out of her mouth, "I'm sorry. That was extremely rude of me."

"No, no," Grant shook his head to stop her apology, "that is a very good question." He leaned over to begin pulling on his skis. "Actually, right now, the resort still needs my full attention and it is just easier to be living there right now." He now stood on both skis and then started in on his gloves and goggles.

"Also," he continued, "I was hoping to be able to find someone to share the house with before I got completely settled. You know...

someone like Harold's Lou." His voice trailed off into a whisper as he looked at Rae Ann in earnest. "Would you mind terribly if I kissed you?"

Rae Ann smiled into his handsome face. "No, I certainly would not mind." Grant leaned in swiftly and pressed his surprisingly hot lips to Rae Ann's. He put his arms around her waist and drew her as close to him as two nylon parkas would allow. It lasted only a few brief seconds, but even after he pulled away, Rae Ann could still feel the urgency in his kiss. Her own lips were on fire and for the moment she was speechless.

Grant looked down as if embarrassed and dropped his hands quickly from her waist. "We should ski now."

"Yes." Rae Ann nodded in agreement still dwelling on afterthoughts of their kiss. For once in a long time, she felt young and alive.

The snow was soft underfoot and splayed in an arc behind her as she swished from side to side down the trail. Grant was somewhere behind her making his own path. His black ski ensemble made it easy for her to keep him in view. As she came to the end of the trail, she pulled her feet together and slid to a stop. Rae Ann plunged the ski poles deep into the earth and slipped her goggles up onto her head. She watched Grant glide gracefully down the trail towards her and stop effortlessly at her side.

"You're a good skier," Grant commented, slightly winded.

"You expected less?" Rae Ann bent to unlock her boots from her skies.

"From what I know of you so far, no." His smile was as fresh as the snow and just as white.

"Shall we go again?"

"I've got a better idea—The Menace," she replied. Grant raised his eyebrows at her daring attitude.

"One run and you think you're ready for the most difficult trail?"

"Race you to the chair lift," she taunted. Without another word she began sloshing through the snow as she heard Grant call out behind her. He jumped out of his skies and followed.

Grant and Rae Ann spent the next few hours riding to the top of the ski lifts and swooshing down the trails at full speed. Rae Ann was exhilarated and despite every effort felt the carefully built walls around her heart begin to crumble. What she didn't know was that Grant was also entranced. He was falling in love for perhaps the first time in his entire life. He wanted to tell her what he was feeling, but knew it was too soon. Grant sensed that Rae Ann was not an open person and kept herself guarded. In time, Grant knew he would be able to get past her protective outer layer.

Around three o'clock, Grant skied to her side and pushed up his goggles, "I have some work that needs my attention. You are welcome to use any of the services in the spa while getting ready for dinner. Just call down to the kitchen and they will deliver you some tea or coffee or hot chocolate or whatever you like."

Rae Ann smiled at the thought of a warm bath and a hot cup of tea. "That sounds wonderful, Grant. Thank you again for such a wonderful time."

"But the day isn't over yet," Grant said, tilting his head towards her.

"I know, but trust me," Rae Ann smiled, "I'm going to have a wonderful time."

Grant moved in close and kissed her mouth again. This time it was long and deep and Rae Ann's head was spinning by the time he pulled away. She watched him gather his equipment and start to lead her back into the resort through the kitchen. Several of the staff called out hello to Grant and he returned the courtesy, calling each one by their name. The girls giggled behind their hands and the men looked smugly satisfied with themselves. They took the rear stairs up from the kitchen and if they hadn't been carrying the cumbersome ski equipment, Rae Ann might have challenged Grant to a race to the third floor. Grant deposited her in front of the guest suite and glanced down towards his office.

"Meet me at six o'clock?"

Rae Ann nodded eagerly and let herself into the room. She couldn't quite bring herself to close the door until she watched him retreat down the hallway. The black ski attire showed off his lithe, masculine form and Rae Ann felt a stirring inside her that had been dormant for a very long time. The office door opened and welcomed him inside. Once he was out of sight, Rae Ann shut the door to her suite and leaned against the wood. A heavy sigh escaped her and she wondered how this amazing relationship would end.

"Dammit, Rae Ann," she scolded herself out loud. She was so pessimistic about love. Her life had never been filled with loving relationships and she honestly didn't know how to handle them. She'd had very few boyfriends in her life and tried not to depend on anyone for anything.

After her father had left her in Wisconsin, it had been up to Rae Ann to make a life for herself. She'd rented an apartment with the money her grandmother had left her and began looking for a job. It took Rae Ann almost five years to realize that she was doomed to relive her mother's miserable existence if she didn't pull herself together. It had happened in a moment's time, one that she was thankful for to this day.

Rae Ann had been a waitress in a small restaurant in downtown Madison pouring coffee for two gentlemen in suits. One of the men was thin, the other heavyset. The collar of the thin man's shirt was too big and he constantly ran a hand up to his neck to adjust it. It was obvious to Rae Ann that the two men were on their lunch hour from some important office job as they talked endlessly about politics and the weather.

Rae Ann had finished topping off the thin man's coffee when the conversation switched to the heavyset man's daughter. The girl had just finished high school and was debating on which college to attend. Over the summer, the man explained, she had wanted to volunteer at the homeless shelter but even the volunteers were required to have a college degree. The thin man guffawed at the absurdity and said, "Nowadays you have to have a college degree for everything."

Rae Ann walked away from the table feeling sorry for herself. She didn't even have a high school diploma, let alone a college degree. She didn't want to be a waitress for the rest of her life but her inheritance was dwindling and she had to make ends meet. At twenty-one years old, Rae Ann decided to take hold of her future. She had made a promise to Sally and she intended to keep it.

~ * ~

Rae Ann moved serenely through the vast suite into the bathroom and ran the water from the tap into the tub until it was hot. It was a mammoth tub that would accommodate several people and Rae Ann was looking forward to soaking in it. The bathroom itself was all white with gold fixtures; pristine and clean everywhere she looked. She absently wondered if she was the first person to ever stay in the room. She stuck her hand out and tested the temperature of the water; it was hot and seared her flesh deliciously.

Just yesterday she would not have recognized the woman she was now. A woman that was allowing herself to get wrapped up in the enigma of Grant Spencer. To be spoiled by his generosity and submissive of his take charge attitude. She undressed slowly and hung the expensive skiing gear on a hook on the back of the bathroom door. Rae Ann let herself be swallowed by the open mouth of the tub. Perhaps it was time to start a new lease on life. To want and need someone was normal and she knew she wanted Grant Spencer. It felt foreign to Rae Ann but she allowed the last of her resolve melt off into the depths of the steamy bath.

Suddenly Rae Ann's eyes jerked open and she thrashed about momentarily, unaware of her surroundings. The water in the tub splashed out around her and sloshed over the side of the tub, hitting the floor wetly. Rae Ann gulped in deep breaths of air and grabbed the tub to steady herself. She had been dreaming but of what she couldn't remember.

Rae Ann scrambled out of the tub and glanced at the clock ticking silently above the bathroom door. She had been in the tub for almost forty minutes and had fallen asleep. *My God, I could have drowned,* Rae Ann thought. She wrapped up in the warm terry cloth bath robe and walked into the bedroom portion of the suite. What had awoken her? A noise of some sort?

Rae Ann stopped to listen for a reoccurrence of the sound but heard nothing. She moved to the wardrobe and threw open the heavy wooden doors. It was now empty of everything except the long garment bag. Like a child on Christmas morning, Rae Ann clawed at the zipper and ripped into the valise. Inside was an exquisite champagne colored gown of the smoothest satin, a small matching handbag and simple heels that would just fit Rae Ann's tiny feet. She smiled into the wardrobe, the awful memory of the dream she had had in the bathtub no longer on her mind. Rae Ann rushed back into the bathroom to continue getting ready. She didn't want to miss a moment of what Grant had in store for this evening.

~ * ~

Rae Ann stood before the full-length mirror of the vanity admiring her reflection. The sleeveless gown fit her perfectly as if it had been tailor made for her frame alone. The satin fabric of the neckline fell just below her collarbone in a gentle slope and then cinched in tight around her small waist. The skirt was bias-cut and hung straight to the floor, ending in a small train behind her. She turned to gaze at the back of the dress, which was by far the most spectacular part. Her bare skin was visible from neck to waist interrupted only by the shoulder straps and a single strand of the satin that snaked its way down the middle of Rae Ann's back. She had stacked her hair high on her head, securing it with a gold clip she had found in the vanity. A lone piece escaped the fastener and she tucked it astutely behind her ear. Rae Ann filled the tiny champagne colored handbag with lipstick, a mirror, her money and driver's license. A final glance told her she was ready to face Grant. How she would ever thank him for the day, she didn't know.

Rae Ann made her way to the door of Grant's suite and fidgeted nervously. *Should she knock? Should she wait?*

Without further contemplation, Rae Ann quickly rapped twice on the door and then busied her hands on the clasp of the tiny purse. Butterflies slammed vehemently into the sides of her stomach. She didn't think she had ever been so jumpy around a man before—but then again, she had never been with someone so wealthy or handsome or kind.

When it was evident that no one would be coming to the door, Rae Ann turned toward Grant's office. Just then a noise behind her stopped her from taking another step. She turned expecting to see

Grant but instead saw a young woman dressed in a housekeeper's uniform pushing a cleaning cart into the small closet. Rae Ann had no idea where she had come from or how long she had been on the floor but perhaps she knew where Grant was.

"Excuse me," Rae Ann said, timidly. The housekeeper did not turn in her direction as she shut the closet door and locked it with a key. Rae Ann thought maybe the clatter of the cart had drowned out the sound of her voice, so she took a step forward and spoke up, "Excuse me, do you know where Grant Spencer is?"

The housekeeper, still with her back to Rae Ann, walked to the elevator and pushed the button.

"Ma'am?" Rae Ann asked, aware that she was being ignored. The elevator doors clanged open and took in the housekeeper. Rae Ann took another step towards the elevator in attempt to get the woman's attention. She was being rude and Rae Ann intended to call her on it. Wearing the tall heels made for slow going and by the time Rae Ann reached the elevator, the doors had closed and it had begun its descent.

"How strange," Rae Ann muttered.

"Rae Ann?"

Rae Ann whirled around and saw Grant Spencer standing half in and half out of his office door. She quickly composed her self and replaced the frown she was wearing with a dazzling smile. "Grant, I was just looking for you."

He was dressed handsomely in a black tuxedo with a matching black vest and business style tie. His shirt was blindingly white and when he reached his arms toward her, Rae Ann caught a glimpse of his tiny gold cuff links.

"Here I am and you, you look beautiful." Grant approached her, taking her elbows in his hands. He quickly kissed her cheek and then stood back to admire her some more.

"All thanks to you. The gown is lovely," Rae Ann replied breathlessly.

"No, my dear, you make the gown. You give it life." Grant's smile was entrancing and Rae Ann blushed at the comment. "Shall we have dinner?"

During the trip to the main floor, Grant explained that there were two restaurants located on the vacation resort's premises. Spencer's Bar and Grill was located in its own building just down the road from the main structure and Antiquities was the formal restaurant situated just off the main lobby.

To Rae Ann it didn't look like a restaurant at all. It looked like a room right out of a fairy tale. It was plush and luxurious from the brocade covered chairs to the sterling silver stemware.

"Your table is waiting, sir." A waiter in a white tuxedo jacket and black trousers appeared out of nowhere and directed Grant and Rae Ann into the dining area. Rae Ann had doubts that Grant's table was ever not ready.

It was situated in the far corner of the restaurant overlooking the main dining area. Since it was elevated above the floor by two steps, Grant nimbly held Rae Ann's hand as she made her way up to stand beside him. He pulled out the chair for her, then settled himself opposite her at the round table. From his vantage point, Grant could observe all of the other diners. Rae Ann could see nothing but Grant and the wall behind him. She moved to pick up her menu when a familiar voice rang out behind her.

"Grant, old buddy, how are you this fine evening?"

Grant Spencer stood from the table with a smile and moved towards the voice. Rae Ann did not hesitate in turning around to look at the senator.

"Francis. Millicent. You both are looking fine tonight," Grant said, reaching out a hand for the senator to shake. He also bent to kiss the surgically enhanced cheek of Mrs. Showalter. "You've both met Rae Ann Lewis."

"Yes, of course, Miss Lewis. We've been seeing a lot of you these days," Francis Showalter said curtly.

"How are you senator? Mrs. Showalter? I hear the embezzlement claim against you has been shelved for the moment. That's nice to know." Rae Ann watched the Senator's dark leather like skin become pasty and a hardness crept into his voice.

"Yes, thank you. I was sorry we were unable to accommodate your request for an interview."

The comment stung deep and Rae Ann narrowed her eyes reflexively. Just after Thanksgiving, Rae Ann had received an anonymous tip that the Senator was seen traveling out of the country on more than one occasion. Rae Ann took the story to Bob and asked to do an expose on the private life of the senator. Bob had granted his approval and Rae Ann set out to secure an appointment with the senator and his family.

Showalter had been less than pleased with her plea and called Bob to complain. The senator asked that Tom Levin, the political correspondent, do the story. Of course, Tom had cast the story in such a positive light that the senator came out smelling like a rose. Rae Ann had been furious.

"Some other time." Rae Ann gave a forced smile and turned back to the menu.

"Well, anyway, we should get going. Millie has her eye set on the Veal Oscar."

Seated again, Grant leaned across the table and took one of Rae Ann's hands, "I see that you and Francis have no great love for each other." Rae Ann couldn't help but smile despite the topic and nodded her head.

"He is my professional cross to bear, I'm afraid. There is just something about the man that strikes me as odd and I have every intention of getting to the bottom of whatever it is he is hiding."

Grant pulled back suddenly and his tone became unnaturally harsh. "What makes you think he is hiding anything?"

Rae Ann was flabbergasted and speechless at Grant's sudden turn of character. "I don't know," she stammered, "I have been following his career since I started working at the station. In that time he has been investigated for bribery, embezzlement and now he is mysteriously traveling outside the country."

"Some people just don't get a break do they?" Grant retorted. Rae Ann stopped to collect her thoughts. She did not want to ruin a perfectly good day with this man by arguing about Senator Showalter.

"Listen, Grant, I'm sorry if I offended you. I don't know why I am discussing work anyway." Rae Ann sipped out of the glass of ice water that had been waiting on the table and waited for Grant to reply.

She was thankful when he too resolved to let the discussion go. Grant smiled again and reached back across the table.

"I apologize, too. I shouldn't get so defensive about the Senator. It's just that I relate a lot of what he goes through to my own life. As somewhat of a local celebrity, there is a lot of hassle that you have to put up with. Especially from the media." He said the last sentence from beneath his brow to show Rae Ann that it wasn't a personal attack.

"I was actually surprised to see Showy here. Just how is it that you know each other?" Rae Ann said, trying to steer the conversation back to Grant.

"Showy?" he asked, with an arched brow.

"Private joke, sorry."

"No, I like it and very appropriate. Francis and I go way back. Our families are old friends and we attended Columbia together."

"But the senator is..." Rae Ann wasn't sure how to finish the sentence.

"Old?" Grant laughed out loud and Rae Ann smiled in agreement. "Francis was actually doing his graduate studies when we met and I was just a lowly freshman." Still, Rae Ann thought that would make Grant Spencer almost ten years older than her thirty-five years.

As if reading her mind Grant asked, "does it bother you?"

"Does what bother me?"

"The age difference."

"Not at all," Rae Ann sipped again at the water.

Did the age difference bother her? She had never really thought about it.

Grant and Rae Ann finished their dinner with little need for further conversation. The food was exquisite and Rae Ann was disappointed when she had consumed the last of her Lobster Bisque and Steak Marsala. The couple lingered over dessert and coffee and, for awhile, Rae Ann believed she was the only other person in the room. Not once did Grant take his eyes from her face or scurry off to correct some problem in the kitchen. He did not get up to mingle with the other patrons of the restaurant or acknowledge each passerby.

Grant took a spoonful of the velvety cheesecake and slid it into Rae Ann's mouth. She mulled over it and closed her eyes to the taste. She wondered if this is what it felt like to fall in love.

~ * ~

"I told you I would have a wonderful evening," Rae Ann said, as they stepped off of the elevator onto the third floor. Grant held her hand lightly in his own. "I still don't know how you pulled all of this off. The dress, shoes, all in my size."

Grant blushed and stopped in front of her suite door. "I admit I had help."

"But who would have..." she started to say before realizing the culprit. "Eddie."

Grant smiled again but did not reveal his source. He looked deep into her eyes and brushed a strand of loose hair behind her ear, "I had a wonderful time, too. More wonderful than I could have imagined. Sleep well. I will be right down the hall if you need anything." Grant gestured toward his suite and Rae Ann had to wonder if he meant more than just needing a glass of water. "Tomorrow we will do the interview for your story."

As he turned to go, Rae Ann felt herself drawn to him.

"Grant?" she whispered, stopping him with just that one word, "thank you."

The sentiment was not intended for the dress or shoes or skiing that they had enjoyed earlier but for the freedom. Grant Spencer had opened up a part of Rae Ann that she had closed down a long time ago. He had shown her that it was okay to want and to be wanted. For so long she had not known what it was like to feel so liberated. She had been rejected so many times that she was determined not to let anyone in the protective cocoon in which she had shrouded herself. But here was Grant Spencer, inching his way through the emotional wreckage and to Rae Ann's surprise, she was helping to clear the path.

Grant placed a hand on the back of her neck and slid his arm around her back. He pulled her close against his taut body and let her linger there before melding his mouth to hers. Rae Ann gave herself over to him, heart and soul. Perhaps this is why she had been guarded

46

for so long. Desperate for love, she knew she was falling for this man and falling fast. She did not want to think about what would happen tomorrow or the next day. For tonight, she was his if he wanted her and by the kiss she could tell that Grant wanted her. He pushed her up against the door to her suite and moved his mouth down over her neck and shoulders. Their breath was in unison coming fast and labored. He moved both of his hands up the bare flesh of her back and she shifted her arms to encircle his neck. Their kiss became demanding and Rae Ann wondered if she could wait to get the door open to start taking off his clothes.

Without warning, the elevator bell rang out loudly and the doors slid open to reveal its contents. Rae Ann gasped and pulled back from the kiss, dropping her arms and purse in the process. The purse's tiny clasp broke free sending her lipstick and money scattering about. Grant whirled to see the intruder, cursing hotly under his breath. Rae Ann bent to retrieve her belongings as Grant approached the elevator.

The housekeeper that had ignored Rae Ann earlier stepped into the hallway and took in the scene. Her face was red and she dropped her eyes, turning at once back towards the elevator. The doors had not completely closed yet and she hopped back into the elevator.

"I didn't realize." Rae Ann heard the woman say before the doors shut completely.

Grant, who had been walking towards his employee, stopped when the doors had closed. Rae Ann collected the last bit of change and stood up, embarrassed.

"I'm so sorry," Grant started to apologize but Rae Ann held up her hand.

"It wasn't your fault. I should get some sleep." Grant nodded in defeat and bid her good night.

Rae Ann entered the suite and went right to the bathroom. She opened up the window above the toilet and lit a cigarette. Rae Ann blew the smoke out from her mouth and it mixed with the cool December air.

Had her only chance at love just been disrupted by a rude housekeeper's untimely entrance? Rae Ann thought silently. And was she just going to sit back and let it pass her by? Rae Ann finished the cigarette and dropped the butt into the toilet to be flushed. She went to her overnight bag and pulled out the long peach nightgown and dressing gown that she had packed for her stay. "I guess these will just have to do."

Rae Ann quickly changed out of her evening gown into the nightwear and brushed her hair out of the up-do. As an afterthought, she also brushed the cigarette taste from out of her mouth and vowed again to quit. Rae Ann peered out of her suite into the desolate hallway and listened. She could hear nothing. In bare feet, she stole down the hallway to Grant's door and pressed her ear to the wood exterior. No sound emerged from inside and for a moment she reconsidered her reckless behavior. Then, recalling the kiss she had shared with Grant only moments ago, Rae Ann knocked lightly. She was an adult and perhaps it was time that she lived outside the controlled world to which she had become accustomed.

Almost instantly, the door swung open and Grant stood before her, naked from the waist up wearing only dark blue silk pajama pants. Without a word, Grant took Rae Ann's hand leading her into his immense living quarters. Only when the door was shut securely behind her did Grant kiss her gently, then swept her tiny body into his arms. Her own arms circled his neck and she ran a hand through his thick, chocolate colored hair. For as long as she lived, Rae Ann was certain that this day would be etched in her memory forever.

~ * ~

They made love all through the night and well into the next day until business summoned Grant from the bed. Rae Ann watched him go before she crashed back into the pillows on the large bed, her body still tingling from his touch. She was absently amazed that she hadn't smoked a cigarette in nearly seventeen hours. Maybe Grant could be her new addiction, Rae Ann mused silently. She knew then that this one would not let her get away. Grant would not allow her to make up some excuse as to why she couldn't share her heart. Rae Ann prayed for this to be true.

Six

*Saturday, February 14th*

Two months later, on Valentine's Day, Grant and Rae Ann were to be married in a lavish ceremony at Pine Trails. Their engagement had been nothing more than a breathless acceptance of the large solitaire diamond Grant placed on Rae Ann's finger during one of her weekend stays at the resort. For the first two weeks, Rae Ann couldn't move her hand without taking a moment to admire the beautiful stone. She just knew that it would sparkle brilliantly under the lights in the television studio when she finally made anchor.

Grant had made most of the wedding arrangements and sent an open invitation for everyone who was staying at the resort for the weekend. Although Grant told Rae Ann that it was simply a gesture for everyone to share in their special day, Rae Ann secretly knew it was because she had very few people that she wanted there on her behalf. Bob Ashcroft and his wife along with two other curious reporters from WZZY sat in a row of chairs. Her old boss from the tiny restaurant where she used to work brought his girlfriend and three girls that Rae Ann barely knew from college made up the rest of Rae Ann's guest list. She had invited Eddie's family but they were unable to come due to the restaurant. And, of course, Rae Ann's one true friend, Eduardo Torres, would be walking her down the aisle. She had not bothered to try and contact her mother or father.

Rae Ann stood again before the vanity mirror in the guest suite where her romance with Grant had begun and admired the white wedding gown that she wore. It was simple and elegant with delicate beading on the bodice. Rae Ann had chosen it specifically to compliment the pearl necklace that her grandmother had given her. She wore it now with pride, wishing the old woman could be there to see the wedding.

"Scoop?" Eddie's muffled voice came from the hallway as Rae Ann secured the veil over her face. They would take the elevator down to the second floor where Rae Ann would make her grand entrance down the magnificent staircase. She nervously opened the door and stared openly at Eddie. Had she not known who it was in the smart attire, Rae Ann would have never recognized him. Eddie was dressed attractively in a sleek black tuxedo. His face was clean shaven and he had cut his shaggy black hair and had it combed back off of his face.

"Eduardo, you look amazing," Rae Ann gasped.

"Well, you know how it is," Eddie said, straightening his tie, "fraternizing with you high society types and all."

Rae Ann laughed and hugged her dearest friend tightly. "I'm so glad you're here."

"You deserve this, Scoop," Eddie said from over her shoulder. "You are a beautiful person. That Spencer guy would have been crazy to let you get away. Now let's go get you married."

~ * ~

The ceremony was fast and quaint. Grant never let his eyes stray from Rae Ann's beautiful face the entire time. Rae Ann could not remember a moment she was so happy, except maybe when she had graduated from college after seven long years of arduously attending night classes while working a full time job during the day. She silently chided herself for comparing the two events. Graduating from college was one of her biggest accomplishments but marrying Grant was not some notch to put on her belt. It was a wonderful, amazing gift that she had been given.

When the last of the guests had kissed the newly married couple and had retired to the ballroom for the reception, Rae Ann took Grant's hand. "Shall we, Mr. Spencer?"

"Um, yeah, Rae Ann, give me a minute, okay?" Rae Ann turned her head in the direction of where Grant was looking and sighed. Elliot Logan stood outside the elevator bank impatiently staring at his watch.

"Oh, Grant, not today," Rae Ann grimaced.

"It will just take a second. You go on without me." Without another word, Grant gave Rae Ann's hand a pat and started off towards his business partner.

"Everything all right?" Eddie asked as he walked up unbuttoning the tuxedo jacket.

"Business as usual, I guess," Rae Ann replied pointing towards the elevator. The doors closed and the two men were out of sight. Eddie changed his facial expression before Rae Ann turned to look at him.

"Come on," he said with a smile, "I've got the urge to dance." Eddie held his elbow out for Rae Ann to take and she smiled at his countenance. Rae Ann allowed Eddie to lead her into the ballroom and onto the dance floor. She was determined to enjoy her wedding reception even if that meant without her new husband.

~ * ~

Settling into life in Rockingham was easy for Rae Ann. Grant gave her free reign over the interior design of the house and hired a housekeeper named Rosie to help her maintain the large property. Rosie was a gentle giant of a woman who came complete with a matching cardigan for every dress she wore. The housekeeper's husband had died suddenly when their son was only eight years old and Rosie had worked all of her life to support the boy. Now her son had his own family in San Diego, California and Rosie's only request was that she received two weeks off during the year to visit them.

Rae Ann had Harold come up and help her with some light landscaping. She was enamored with him almost immediately. The old man took on the qualities that she knew Sally's husband must have had. During those times with Harold, Rae Ann missed Sally so much that a physical ache settled into her chest. Rae Ann knew that marrying Grant had allowed her to shed the protective armor around her heart and now she was bursting with emotions.

At first, Rae Ann suspected but had no real idea how much time Grant would spend at the resort. She knew he was devoted to making the property a success, but still it did not please Rae Ann to eat dinner alone practically every night of the week. Grant, of course, invited her up to the resort for dinner but, unlike their first date, Grant would now stop every diner on their way past to question their approval of the restaurant. During those dinners, Rae Ann and Grant barely spoke ten words to each other.

Once the renovations were complete at the residence, Rae Ann decided to go back to her position at the television station full time. It was just under a two-hour commute into Madison, but Rae Ann missed the excitement of the news. Grant had balked at the idea that she even continue to work at all let alone make such a long drive.

"It's no longer necessary, Rae Ann. You have all that you need here," Grant said. But in truth, the resort held no fascination for her. She had worked so hard to make her grandmother proud of her and she wasn't going to give it up just because she married a wealthy man. In the end, Rae Ann's stubbornness prevailed. Even if the drive had been ten hours one way, Rae Ann was determined not to let anyone take away the independence she had harbored for so long.

"You are so busy with the resort. I'll go to Madison for a couple of days, do some work and be home by the weekend. It will work out, you'll see," Rae Ann said with a smile.

She received no return smile from her husband.

Seven

Wednesday, May 17ᵗʰ

"Did you hear?" Eddie asked, swooping up behind her desk in the station. The mid-May air was heavy with an oppressive heat. It was obvious to Rae Ann that the station had not decided to turn on the air-conditioning yet for the summer. She pulled at the front of her shirt to fan her face.

"Heard what?" Rae Ann asked, her hair flying out to the sides with every flutter of her shirt.

"The going away party is cancelled," Eddie reported.

"What?" Rae Ann's hand dropped from her shirt and looked full on at Eddie, "Again?" Eddie nodded vigorously and picked up a stray paper clip.

"That is the third time Marley has put in her notice and three times she hasn't left," Rae Ann huffed and rummaged through her desk drawer in search of a cigarette. "Damn, I picked a fine time to quit. I just want to know what is going on here?"

"Contract negotiations, I hear. Network wants her, but doesn't want her terms."

"I'm thinking about donating to the cause," Rae Ann mused as she rolled her eyes.

"Well, you could Miss Moneybags," Eddie tossed the paper clip into the air and caught it with one hand.

"It isn't my money. Its Grant's," Rae Ann smiled and glanced at her three-carat solitaire engagement ring and diamond studded wedding band as they sparkled in the overhead lighting. "Anyway, I will be so glad when Marley finally decides to leave."

"Well you'd better hope it is soon before *Mr.* Moneybags gets you barefoot and pregnant," Eddie joked, turning the paperclip over and over in his hands.

"You know, it's funny that you say that. We haven't really discussed children," Rae Ann confided in her closest friend, "I guess I've never really thought about it before."

"Somebody better start thinking about it. You ain't gettin' any younger, sister."

Rae Ann reached over and slapped Eddie's knee. "Such a charmer."

Eight

Monday, May 22nd

Grant Spencer slammed the phone down and cursed out loud. That was the third time this week the housekeeper had called him. He hadn't heard word one from her since the day he sneaked out of his suite leaving her alone in his bed. Then he had gotten married and everything changed. Since then the woman hounded him relentlessly demanding to see him and professing her love for him.

Grant took a fat cigar from the box on his desk and lit it with the sleek silver lighter Rae Ann had given him after she quit smoking. He puffed away as he paced the length of his office contemplating what to do. He should tell Rae Ann about the girl but that would just be foolish. What Rae Ann didn't know wouldn't hurt her, right? Besides, all of this happened way before Grant and Rae Ann.

He wished he could just fire the girl but she was smart enough to inform him that he would be sorry if he did. She said she had a disk full of something that Grant would be very interested to have. The stupid bitch thought she could blackmail him, for Christ's sake. Grant laughed out loud. The thought was preposterous. He pulled in a mouth full of the fragrant smoke and blew it out towards the ceiling. He was sure that no disk even existed and eventually the girl would get over him. Grant had dumped many women in his life without so much as a phone call. They were usually smart enough to figure it out and felt lucky enough to have had him even for a little while. Now he had a real woman. Rae Ann was smart and beautiful and funny but so full of pride and determination. He wished she would quit that silly job at the television station and take more of an interest in the resort.

Oh, the resort, Grant thought to himself. He moved to the silver cart in the corner that held a decanter full of bourbon and poured himself two fingers. Maybe if there really was a disk, he would coerce that disk into his possession. Even if it meant breaking a couple of vows. Until then, Grant needed to think of some way to kick start business at the resort. Now, in the off season, they were losing money fast and if things kept up... Grant let the thought trail off in his head not wanting to contemplate what would happen if he lost the resort. All be damned, if he would lose it to Elliot Logan. Grant drained the dark liquid and poured himself another.

Once an alcoholic, always an alcoholic. Grant drank around his smile. Another thing he had not told Rae Ann.

Nine

Saturday, August 9th

"Grant, please tell me what is wrong," Rae Ann pleaded to her husband as they sat uncomfortably in the kitchen of their home. Grant was drunk. Rae Ann had smelled him the minute he walked in the door.

"Nothing, dear. Nothing's wrong," Grant smiled drunkenly with watery-blood shot eyes and tried to dance Rae Ann around the room. She was visibly disgusted with him as he moved past her to the liquor cabinet.

For months, Rae Ann had noticed that the drinking had become increasingly worse. At first, Rae Ann had been shocked to see Grant drunk for the first time. She had never known him to be a big drinker. But as the months past and the spring fell into summer, Rae Ann watched her husband become more distant and more drunk.

"Elliot Logan called again today. Is that what this is all about, Grant? You have to talk to me. I'm your wife," Rae Ann's voice grew louder and louder as she spoke, hoping her words would penetrate the thick fog that the liquor had left in Grant's brain.

Grant slammed the bottle of whiskey, he had retrieved from cabinet, down onto the table and whirled in Rae Ann's direction. "There is nothing to tell. My business does not concern you. True you are my wife, but you do not act it. You are gone more days than you are here, and when you are here, you are thinking about that damn job."

Rae Ann was taken back by the harsh words that she had not expected from Grant's mouth. At the moment he seemed lucid and logical, but his eyes were still wild and his fists clenched. For the first time in their relationship, Rae Ann was afraid he would strike her.

What he said was true, in the past couple of months, Rae Ann had distanced herself from Grant, Rockingham and the resort. She spent increasingly more time at work to make up for the fact that Grant spent very little time with her when she was home. At first, she had made the nearly four-hour exhaustive round trip drive, every day, to and from the television station. Once Rae Ann realized that Grant never came home at night to see her, she began staying overnight in her Madison apartment. Nowadays, it was rare for Rae Ann to even make it to Rockingham on the weekends.

Never one to back down from a fight, Rae Ann spat, "if I don't want to be here, it is your own fault. You are so wrapped up in the resort that I'm surprised you even remember you are married. I have been more than patient with you, while you try to get this resort going, but I don't know how much more I can take."

With that, Rae Ann turned on her heel and left the kitchen. She paused in the living room unsure of what to do before grabbing her travel bag from the master bedroom and leaving the house. She waved to Harold as she waited for the heavy iron-gate that separated her driveway from the rest of the lodge to slowly open. Harold was mowing the yard around his small cabin in the late afternoon August heat and took a moment to wipe his sweaty brow after lifting his hand to her. He watched her continue on down the mountain and turn onto the main highway before going back to the task at hand.

58

Rae Ann was hurt by Grant's words. All the way back to Madison, she replayed the scene over in her mind. Anyway she looked at the situation, Rae Ann could not think of a way she could have handled it better. She knew there was something Grant wasn't telling her, but what could it be? On the outside, they seemed to have such a happy life, but alone they were merely strangers. Rae Ann didn't want to admit to herself that she had rushed too fast into the marriage and here not six months into the marriage, it was already showing signs of deterioration.

Ten

Thursday, October 23

The next couple of months went much like that day in the kitchen. Rae Ann came home less and less, delving into her work with a more fervent determination to be ready when the anchor job finally opened up.

When she was in Rockingham, Rae Ann barely saw her husband. He lived in his suite at the lodge not even coming home for clothes. Once, Rae Ann caught Rosie in the laundry room folding up some of Grant's things and putting them into a small black suitcase. Rosie's guilty look told Rae Ann that she would be delivering the clothes to Grant at the lodge.

The approaching winter months gave Grant an even bigger reason to spend more time at the resort and Rae Ann was at her wits end. She was determined to make the marriage work. For so long Rae Ann had been on her own, resolving never to depend on another person. She had let Grant Spencer into her heart too quickly, against her better judgment, and it was backfiring in her face. Rae Ann knew better than to trust someone, especially a man, but was she really destined to be alone all her life?

Eleven

Friday, December 15th

"Rosie, hand me that wreath, will you?"

At the beginning of December, Rae Ann decided to take a two week vacation from the station and made a pact to improve her marriage and home life. Her boss, Bob Ashcroft, was shocked at Rae Ann's request for the leave, but knew she had worked very hard for him in her six years at the station. If anyone deserved it, Rae Ann did. She moved full time into the house in Rockingham and helped Rosie bake cookies and decorate a Christmas tree.

Now the two women were putting up the rest of the decorations around the house. It was beginning to look a bit gaudy and the smell of pine from the fresh greenery was starting to make Rae Ann nauseous. But rather than sit around and wait for Grant to make an appearance, Rae Ann kept herself busy with the décor.

On Christmas Eve, Rae Ann was shocked to come home from shopping to discover that her husband was also at the house. "Grant, I'm so glad you are home. If I had known, I would have had Rosie..." Rae Ann exclaimed as she shed her coat and gloves on a chair in the kitchen.

"No," Grant interrupted, "I'm just home for a quick dinner before heading back to the office."

"Oh," Rae Ann was clearly disappointed. She thought of the presents that she had painstakingly picked out for this man that couldn't care less for her, or the Christmas season, and wondered if he would even bother to open them. Grant passed by Rae Ann on his way across the kitchen tile and ventured into the living room. He hesitated at the door to their home and turned back towards Rae Ann, who had followed him.

"Rae Ann," he started.

Rae Ann shook her head and down cast her eyes."It's all right. If you have to go, you have to go."

He approached her slowly and took both of her hands in his own. "I have a lot going right now, but very soon, everything is going to be all right again. I promise you."

"Let me into your life, Grant. Tell me what is going on." Grant shook his head slowly from side to side and gave her hands a squeeze.

"I don't want you to concern yourself with this. It's almost over now." Grant took a small present out of his coat pocket and placed it in her hands. "Merry Christmas." He walked out the door without looking back.

Rae Ann tossed the wrapped token onto the coffee table and sat heavily on the couch. She didn't want what was inside the tiny box. She wanted Grant. For the first time in her life, she wanted someone to be there and Grant couldn't be. Or didn't want to be, Rae Ann wasn't sure which. She watched the headlights of Grant's car meander up the mountain, then turned her back to the wall of windows. He had been drinking again. Of that Rae Ann was sure. If only she could get him to tell her what the problem was, maybe she could help him. Then again, it was possible that Grant didn't want Rae Ann's help. That thought alone was hurtful. Instead, Grant had turned to the bottle. Rae Ann couldn't compete with that. She spent the next couple of days alone in deep thought about what she should do.

In the end, Rae Ann cut her vacation short and went back to work. She didn't see Grant again until their one-year anniversary.

Twelve

Sunday, February 14th

The last thing Rae Ann had planned on doing was going to Rockingham for her anniversary. Then came the message. She received it from the station's office manager late on Valentine's Day.

"Oh, Becky," Rae Ann reached for the slip of pink paper as she caught the young girl's attention, "could you please page Eddie and let him know that we are on for the coverage of the Hearts On Fire Benefit tonight."

"I don't think so, Miss Lewis," the girl replied sheepishly. Rae Ann knitted her brow and the girl gestured toward the message Rae Ann held.

It was a simple invitation requesting Rae Ann's presence at the lodge for a special dinner commemorating her first year of marriage. Rae Ann smiled at the piece of paper. It went on to inform her that a limo would be picking her up in two hours at her apartment where a gown was already waiting.

Rae Ann jumped up from the desk and quickly gathered her purse, "Two hours isn't much time. Could you please tell—"

"Yes," Becky smiled at the reporter, envious of her, "I'll make sure Eddie and Bob both know."

"Thanks," Rae Ann took a moment to survey the desk, careful to make sure she wasn't forgetting something. As she started towards the door, she heard the office manager wish her a happy anniversary. God, Rae Ann hoped it would be happy.

Her arrival at the lodge was swift and comfortable in the long sleek limousine. Rae Ann laid her head against the headrest of the car, careful not to muss her hair, and closed her eyes. This might be the opportunity that Rae Ann had been waiting for, to get her marriage to Grant back on the loving terms where they had started. Already, the night was beginning to feel like their first date. Exciting and new with Grant being his usual generous, passionate self.

Rae Ann touched the sloped neckline of the gown he had sent for her. It was ruby red, cut low to the tops of her breasts and tight fitting to the rest of her body. She had melted into its beaded fabric like a second skin. The deep, rich color complemented her creamy white skin and this time she left her hair loose to swing at her shoulders. Right now she could think of nothing better than an intimate dinner alone with her husband.

In no time the limo was cutting through the slush of a recent snow and stopping in front of the resort's grand entrance. Rae Ann waited patiently while the driver hurried around the car to open her door. The dress's long sleeves were made entirely of chiffon and let the crisp wind in unobtrusively, as Rae Ann walked quickly through the revolving doors.

Inside, the resort was full of life and pulsed with the activity of people. The ski season would be winding to a close soon but, as far as Rae Ann could tell, this year had been a success. She moved towards the elevators to seek out her husband, when a voice behind her brought her to a halt. "Rae Ann."

She turned to him with a beaming smile, her white teeth showing brightly against the red lipstick, "Grant, darling."

They met before the fireplace, their embrace was sweet and, for the moment, Rae Ann thought she could forgive the past few months of Grant's secretiveness and indiscretions.

"Happy anniversary, my love," Grant whispered into her ear.

"Grant, I have missed you so much. Thank you for doing this," Rae Ann breathed into the curve of Grant's neck. Her warm breath caressed his skin and they unknowingly were both remembering how it felt to be close to each other.

"You look beautiful," Grant observed, as he pulled her away and held her at arms length.

"You always know what looks best on me," Rae Ann complimented. She felt giddy again, punch drunk with his attention. When a sudden frown appeared on his face, she couldn't help but be disappointed.

"What? What is it?" Rae Ann glanced down at herself to find the source of his displeasure.

"It's just... well... something is missing."

"Oh, did I forget something? I didn't see anything else in the box." Rae Ann mentally scolded herself for starting the evening off on a sour note.

"No, but I think you need this," Grant said, reaching for a thin square box that was lying on the table between two chairs. He opened it slowly, savoring Rae Ann's look of curiosity and anticipation. When the contents were fully revealed, Rae Ann gasped audibly and looked up at her husband with such a look of love that he thought his very heart would break.

Inside the box, sparkling deliciously under the chandeliers was a slender diamond studded chain that held a simple tear drop shaped ruby as big as Rae Ann's thumb. Matching earrings also made their presence known, with a twinkle.

"They are gorgeous," Rae Ann's tear filled eyes caused her to see the ruby red of the necklace and earrings multiplied a hundred times.

"Now, now, there's no crying," Grant busied himself with the necklace and draped it lightly around Rae Ann's neck, "this is a happy occasion."

Rae Ann dipped her hands into the box and fastened the earrings to each lobe before standing back for his approval. His expression gave her everything she wanted to see and hear and more.

"Rae Ann, I have been a fool, please forgive—" the words rushed from Grant's mouth before Rae Ann put a finger to his lips.

"We are here now. What's done is done. I love you, Grant." He pulled her to him quickly and crushed her against his body. He didn't care that several people had stopped milling about in the lobby to witness the display of affection that was taking place between the owner of this posh resort and his newlywed bride.

"God, I do love you, Rae Ann."

"Come on, let's go have dinner." Rae Ann started for the resort's restaurant until she felt a gentle tug on her hand.

"Oh no, this way," Grant indicated towards the ballroom.

"What? The ballroom? What's going on here, Grant?" Rae Ann's tone was questioning as her husband led her towards the entrance where they first met, and also where their wedding reception had been held. As he flung open the doors, Rae Ann caught sight of the roughly hundred people that filled the interior of the room and her insides lost hold of their solidity. So much for the quite intimacy of a night alone with her husband. Rae Ann tried hard to hold onto the feeling of contentment she had felt moments ago in the lobby, but with each passing step into the ballroom, Rae Ann's heart sunk lower in her chest.

The guests were cordial and congratulatory, but suddenly Rae Ann was in no mood for the festivities. Grant moved through the crowd as if powered by their presence and became the host that Rae Ann knew so well. He had taken *their* anniversary and made it into a resort promoting fiasco. She knew then that he would never change.

Above the noise in the room as the band started up the dinner music, Rae Ann heard herself groan inwardly as she spotted Senator Francis Showalter and his phony wife lounging near the bar. As usual, people were flocked around him, hanging on his every word and laughing at everything he said. Of all people to invite, Rae Ann could not believe that Grant would be so callous to her feelings. This, of course, had no personal bearing on her since she was certain that her husband had not even thought of her as he made up the guest list.

Suddenly the dress, so beautiful only moment's ago, now felt heavy and cumbersome. The jewelry, a bribe, seared against her inflamed skin. Eventually Grant kissed Rae Ann's cheek and was off walking through the crowd, shaking hands. Rae Ann found an open spot at the bar and ordered a drink. She was a drinker by no means and sipped delicately at the mixture of orange juice and vodka. She knew she would never finish it for fear of losing control and screaming out her frustrations right in the middle of the dance floor. Someone elbowed up beside her, but Rae Ann did not bother to move or turn in their direction.

"Congratulations are in order, it would seem," Showy said, assaulting Rae Ann with his words.

She winced involuntarily and spoke into her glass, "it would seem. Thank you, Senator."

"You don't seem very enthused to be here but, then again, you are used to the hustle and bustle of these big crowds. What with your reporting job and all." Rae Ann gave the Senator a sideways glance, not knowing whether that was meant to be a jab or a compliment. His deeply tanned face was smug with self-worship.

"It is my anniversary, Senator, why wouldn't I be happy?" Rae Ann's voice was strained and she hated herself for it. It wasn't often that Rae Ann showed weakness and she'd be damned if she was going to show it in front of this man.

"If you will excuse me..." Rae Ann shifted away from the bar and glanced around for Grant.

"Certainly. I'm sure we'll be seeing more of each other. Millie and I are staying through the week," Showy replied as he caught the eye of his wife and gave her a small wave.

"Great," Rae Ann muttered and tried to lose herself in the sea of people.

First one and then another stopped her along the way to the door, to congratulate her and, before she knew it, two hours had passed. At one point the watered down drink she held had been discarded on an empty table and the heavy ruby earrings were tucked safely into her small clutch purse. Rae Ann managed to dodge the rest of Grant's guests and stumble into the hall of the lobby. She decided just to summon the driver of the limousine and have him take her to the residence.

Just as she reached the check in terminals, Senator Showalter appeared before her like an apparition in a dream. No, a nightmare, Rae Ann corrected. "Leaving so soon?"

"Yes, I have to be up early, but you should enjoy the rest of the evening," Rae Ann replied with forced politeness. She could tell that the Senator had already enjoyed his evening as his eyes were blood shot and watery.

"You know," Showy stepped into her path with surprisingly agile reflexes, "Grant and I are very good friends."

"So I've been told," Rae Ann's sarcasm was lost on the drunken Senator.

"And friends," the Senator slurred as he placed a hand on Rae Ann's red chiffon sleeve, "share."

Rae Ann shook the hand from her arm as if it were a slimy creature, and twisted her face in disgust. "I'm not sure what you are implying here, Senator, but it would be wise if you kept your hands to yourself. I think you have temporarily forgotten that I am a reporter for a widely broadcast television station. And I would say that lately, the last thing you need is more bad press. Now excuse me."

Senator Showalter's face became red with fury, but he let Rae Ann scoot around him. She didn't turn back as she asked the desk clerk to ring the driver and then headed for the parking lot to wait. Perhaps the cool, February air would help ebb some of the fury that she felt towards the whole night. Rae Ann cursed herself as she dug fruitlessly in the tiny purse for a pack of cigarettes. She knew full well that the clutch held none but she looked anyway on the remote chance that a stray cigarette had somehow found its way into her handbag.

Of course, cigarettes were just another thing Rae Ann had given up when she said her vows. She had been planning to quit on her own all along but on her terms. Grant had other ideas. She remembered the note of disapproval in his voice every time she lit up.

"Rae Ann," he began, *"with fame, even local fame, comes a certain responsibility. We can't have our reputation tarnished by something as meaningless as cigarettes."*

What he meant was *his* reputation. And when Rae Ann asked him what the difference was between her cigarettes and his cigars, he just chuckled and walked away. The very thought made her angry and she snapped the small purse shut, furiously.

"Rae Ann, what's going on?" Grant's voice was coming closer along with the tapping sound of his dress shoes as he jogged across the parking lot towards her. "Where are you going?"

"I'm going home, Grant. I've had enough celebrating for the evening," Rae Ann said, not bothering to turn in his direction.

"Well, at least tell me why you seem so upset. I just passed Francis on the way out and he was also visibly troubled. He said you threatened him with some bad press." Rae Ann spun around in disbelief and amazement.

"Threatened him?" she cried.

"Rae Ann, Francis and I are friends. I can't have you treating my friends like that. Not to mention he is a massive contributor to the lodge. You can't just go throwing around your position because you don't like someone."

"I am not a child, Grant, and believe me when I say that I would not risk my position at the television station for a scumbag like Francis Showalter. If that man gets bad press, it is because he has brought it on himself. Don't bother coming home tonight and if you find yourself with no place to stay, then I suggest you try the Senator's room. According to him, friends share." Thankfully, Rae Ann saw the shadow of the limo pulling around the corner and heading towards the curb where she stood with her husband.

"What do you know about the Senator's room, Rae Ann?" Grant's face was menacing in the gloom of the lot.

Rae Ann threw her hands into the air, disgusted. Grant just didn't get it. Didn't get *her*. Without bothering to wait for the driver to open the door, Rae Ann pulled at the handle and scrambled into the back seat. "I asked you a question, Rae Ann." Grant's words were cut off as Rae Ann slammed the limousine door. She pointed in the direction of her house and the driver started off immediately. Rae Ann couldn't speak as tears filled her eyes and choked in her throat. She tried to hold them back as long as possible but it was a failing effort. Rae Ann broke down and let the tears flow soundlessly from her eyes. She had been this miserable before without a husband. Why did she think that a marriage would be the answer to her prayers?

The jaunt from the lodge to Rae Ann's house took less time that it took for the driver to pull the car around to pick her up. She was fidgety while the slow iron gates parted to allow the car entrance and before they even came to a complete stop, Rae Ann was letting herself out of the backseat and stumbling towards the door. Rosie met her halfway into the living room and put a comforting arm around her shoulders as if she knew what had transpired at the resort.

At first, Rae Ann stiffened against the woman's comforting touch, but years of not having a mother's compassion took their toll and Rae Ann leaned in to be embraced by the massive woman. How much more of this was she willing to put up with? If she had had the energy, Rae Ann would have packed her things and moved permanently to her apartment in Madison. Instead, Rosie helped her out of the cumbersome gown and into some soft flannel pajamas. She left Rae Ann with a cool wash cloth for her face and returned momentarily with a tray of hot tea with lemon. Rae Ann had never been more thankful in her life. After a couple of sips of the warming liquid, Rae Ann peered up at the woman. "I'm going to miss you when I leave here, Rosie."

The older woman sighed and straightened her navy blue cardigan over the baby blue dress she wore. She nodded in understanding before taking her leave from the room. Rae Ann replaced the wash cloth over her eyes and was relieved that Rosie had left before a new set of tears spilled over her lashes. Rae Ann had always fancied herself a strong willed person, but now she wasn't sure if she would have the strength enough to leave Grant Spencer. Was it too soon to give up?

Rae Ann left Rockingham the next day without seeing her husband. She felt like a guest that had overstayed her welcome. She wondered if Grant would even miss her at all.

Thirteen

Tuesday, March 2nd

Rae Ann was sleeping soundly, in her comfy Madison apartment, when the shrill sound of the phone brought her to sudden consciousness. The clock on the bedside table read two-thirty seven a.m. and Rae Ann scrambled to grab the phone, praying it wasn't bad news about Grant. In the two weeks since her disastrous anniversary party, Rae Ann had been estranged from her husband. Not even returning home on the weekends to repair the damage he had thrust upon her and their marriage. The bed sheets tangled Rae Ann in their web, but she managed to free herself in time to snatch up the receiver, croaking, "Hello."

"Ms. Lewis?" a strange voice asked.

"Yes."

"My name is Peter Bell. I am a nurse at Grace Memorial Hospital."

"Oh God, is he dead? Is Grant dead? What was he doing in Madison?"

The sudden jolt to her system had left her disorientated and full of uncertainty. She rambled off the questions in rapid fire sequence not allowing for even a breath in between them.

"What? No," the voice faltered a bit, "this isn't about any Grant. There is a young lady here who needs your help."

"I don't quite understand, Mr. Bell, what is it that she wants?" Rae Ann straightened in the bed and rubbed at her sleepy eyes.

"I believe she needs your professional expertise in a matter."

"At two in the morning? Mr. Bell, if you could just have the young lady call my office—"

"She's been raped," the nurse continued.

Rae Ann cradled the phone between her head and shoulder and covered her face with both hands. "I'm afraid you called the wrong person. I can't help this girl. Rape counseling is not in my job description."

"Not even if the rapist was Senator Francis Showalter?" the man's voice took on a disgusted note.

Rae Ann was fully awake now. Had she heard right? Was this nurse telling her that Showy had raped someone? This was the story that every reporter hoped to break and here it was falling right into her lap. "I'll be right there," Rae Ann was already moving the phone back to its place on the night stand before quickly adding, "And Mr. Bell, don't let her talk to anyone until I get there."

Rae Ann fumbled out of bed and flipped on the bedside lamp. The sudden brightness left her momentarily blind, but she continued to move across the room. She staggered into the small bathroom that contained the clothes she had taken off the previous night and dumped on the floor in a pile. Now the shirt and dress slacks looked like better dusting rags than suitable attire for an interview. Especially one of this magnitude. Rae Ann ran back into the bedroom discarding her pajamas en route and quickly grabbed at something in the closet. She was satisfied with a two-piece sweater set and a pair of khaki pants. Rae Ann pulled her bed-flattened hair into a bun and left the house.

In early March, the Wisconsin air was still frigid in the wee hours of the morning. Rae Ann snuggled deep into the fur coat that Grant had given her for her birthday, while her Lexus SUV warmed up. She glanced around the garage and thought about the old Honda she had driven before she married Grant. She had loved the car too much to give it up, even though Grant had purchased the Lexus for her to drive back and forth to Madison. He claimed it was safer and would handle better in the perpetual snow. The Honda now sat unused in the garage at her house in Rockingham. Rae Ann slowly wound through the dark streets of the capital city, trying to remember the fastest way to the hospital.

The nurse had said Grace Memorial, right?

Rae Ann wrestled the cellular phone from her purse and dialed Eddie Torres' number, punching out the illuminated numbers she had memorized long ago. "Lo'," Eddie said sounding like he still had his head stuffed into his pillow.

"Eddie, baby, you are never going to believe this."

"Scoop?" Eddie asked through the static of her phone, "What the hell are you calling me for at three o'clock in the morning?"

"Eddie, shut up and listen," Rae Ann couldn't keep the excitement out of her voice, "I just got this phone call from the hospital."

"What, did your good-for-nothing husband finally drink and drive himself off the ski slopes?" he quipped into the phone.

"Dammit, Eddie, pay attention. This patient is at Grace Memorial, here in Madison, and is claiming that Showy raped her tonight. This could put us on the map, Eddie."

Eddie rattled off something in Spanish and then reverted back to English to say, "I am guessing you are wanting visual on this?"

"You're damn right I want visual on this. Meet me at the hospital in half an hour." Rae Ann ended the call and dropped the phone into the passenger seat. She gripped the wheel tighter in her hands and pressed her foot down on the gas. If this girl was for real, then Rae Ann's field-reporting days were over.

After circling the block, Rae Ann pulled into the well-lit parking lot of the emergency room and spotted the Channel 8 news van. Smoke billowed out of the exhaust pipe in thick clouds which proved that Eddie had not allowed the van to warm up before taking off. Rae Ann pulled her car up to the van and rolled the window down.

"Hey, sunshine," she quipped with a smirk. Eddie appeared to have been sleeping off a heavy night of partying and Rae Ann could tell that he was in no mood to joke. As he rolled out of the driver's door, Rae Ann could see that he had done nothing more than throw on a stocking cap and pull a coat over his plaid pajamas.

"Don't start with me, Rae Ann. I swear if this girl ain't telling the truth..." Eddie trailed off letting Rae Ann use her imagination as to what he might do. She could tell that he was serious, because he rarely called her by her given name. Rae Ann gathered her purse and opened the car door. Her cellular phone started ringing the minute her foot hit the ground. Without checking the caller ID, she stuck it to her ear and said hello.

"Rae? Rae, I need to talk to you," Grant's voice slurred into the phone, "Rae, where are you?"

"Grant, what is it? I am kind of busy."

"No, Rae Ann, listen, you need to come home. You need to come home right now."

"What is it, Grant?" she repeated, both concerned and perturbed at the same time, "Are you all right?"

"I'm fine, but I don't want you working anymore," he said, drunkenly.

"Oh Grant, we have been over this a million times. I am not going to quit working. I am working right now."

"That's what I'm talking about, Rae Ann. Listen, don't go to work."

"Grant, you aren't making any sense. I will call you tomorrow morning, okay? We can talk about this tomorrow." She heard Grant mutter the word *no,* and a couple of other unintelligible sentences, before she ended the call. The phone started ringing again before she could even move a muscle. Rae Ann flipped it over to see the screen and recognized Grant's office number on the caller ID. "I don't need this right now, Grant," Rae Ann said to the still ringing phone as she dropped it into the seat beside her.

Eddie had already retrieved the camera and was waiting for her at the back of the van. Rae Ann glanced at the phone once more before shutting the car door on the annoying ring. The unmatched pair of reporter and cameraman headed for the automatic doors of the emergency entrance, calm and professional, as if this were any other story. But they both knew it wasn't. "What did Eric say about this story, Scoop?" Eddie huffed beside her, referring to the assignment editor at WZZY. When Rae Ann didn't answer, he stopped in the middle of the ambulance bay. "You did call Eric, didn't you Rae Ann?"

Rae Ann stopped a couple steps ahead of him and turned around slowly. Damn, that was twice he had said her name. "I want to see if this girl is for real or not before I bother him," she explained lightly.

Eddie's face contorted considerably, "Don't give me that shit, Scoop. You want this to be a big surprise. A big let's-pat-Rae-Ann-on-the-back-for-a-great-story, don't you? You think that by bypassing Eric and bringing this story straight to Bob, complete with visual, he will have no choice but to give you Marley's job. Plus, you get to drag Senator Showalter's name through the mud as a bonus." Eddie shook the camera at her fiercely.

Again, Rae Ann stood silent. She couldn't bring herself to lie to Eddie, when she knew that what he said was the truth. Since she had received the call, Rae Ann could think of nothing more than the night of her anniversary party, when the Senator had made unwanted advances toward her. She had not liked him before, but now she was out to prove how corrupt he was. "Damn," Eddie muttered as he turned and started walking back to the news van.

"No, Eddie, wait." Rae Ann scampered after her friend. She rounded in front of him and held a hand to his chest.

"Oh, this ought to be good," Eddie said, rolling his eyes.

"Just hear me out, okay?" she asked, breathless in the frigid air. "You're right. I do want to surprise Bob with this incredible story. I do want Marley's job and I do want to knock the Senator off his high horse, but," she rushed on, "I also want to be a good reporter. I love what I do. I deserve this story, Eddie. And so do you."

Eddie jigged his legs in the cold, like a five year old that had to use the bathroom, as he looked around the parking lot. "You're not going to give me that giving-myself-to-the-world-cause-I-promised-my-grandma-speech again, are you?" Eddie smiled in spite of himself as he focused back on Rae Ann.

She smiled too, and dropped her hand from his chest in relief. "Yes. If I must, I will play the grandma card."

Eddie groaned out loud and threw his free arm around Rae Ann's shoulders in a sloppy hug. "Come on, Scoop. Let's go get this story."

~ * ~

"My name is Rae Ann Lewis. I am with Channel 8 news. I am here to see," Rae Ann stammered slightly, "the rape victim."

It suddenly occurred to her that she had not even asked the girl's name. Now she sounded like an ambulance chaser, unprepared. If it sounded that way to Rae Ann, it certainly didn't to the hospital receptionist. The tired brunette rolled her eyes and dropped her Glamour magazine only long enough to point Rae Ann and Eddie in the right direction. Rae Ann thanked the girl politely even as she was already walking toward the door. She paused only briefly outside as she shook out of her coat and then took a deep breath. "This is it. Get the camera ready. I want an initial reaction. Shock value, you know?" Eddie nodded, pushing the stocking cap back off his forehead so he could see more clearly. Rae Ann gave the door a gentle push and entered the room.

In all her days as a reporter, she was not prepared for this. The smell of the hospital's sterilizer hit Rae Ann full force suggesting that the room had recently been cleaned. The back wall was lined with cabinets and drawers painted a sunny yellow with labels such as gowns, sheets and bandages. Scattered gauze and suture kits littered the counter space. Two visitor's chairs sat empty to Rae Ann's left, so she motioned Eddie into the closest one. The bed sat in the middle of the room under a blinding spot light as if on display. The young girl was sitting on the bed with her head down. She lifted it slightly when she heard Rae Ann enter the room. Rae Ann pulled in a quick breath and reined in her emotions at first sight of the girl.

One eye had been blackened and was now in the process of swelling shut. A deep cut arched a second eyebrow over the damaged eye. The girl's bottom lip had been split cleanly down the left side and the puffiness gave the impression of a constant pout. Strands of dark hair clung to the side of her face and she pushed it behind her ear when she wiped her tear stained cheeks.

"My God," Rae Ann exclaimed, bending down in front of the girl.

"I'm so glad you are here," the girl emitted a tiny whisper, "I didn't know who else to call."

The small voice tugged at Rae Ann's heart like a thousand pound weight. Up until now the call had been nothing but a good lead on a great story. Now it was real. "What is your name?"

"Jenna," the girl slurred around her injured lip, "Jenna Ford."

"How old are you?" Rae Ann asked gently. "I'm twenty." Rae Ann backed up from the girl and took the seat next to Eddie.

"Jenna, this is my cameraman, Eddie. He is going to continue to shoot while we talk is that all right?"

"I-I guess," Jenna stuttered as she shifted her eyes to Eddie and then back to Rae Ann. She brought a hand to her face self-consciously touching the bruises and cuts.

"Okay, let's begin. Jenna, why did you call me tonight?"

"I see you on the news all the time. I admire you so much. You are even more beautiful in person." Rae Ann's eyes closed involuntarily against the pain the sight of the girl caused. She could see that Jenna had once been a very beautiful girl before the lowlife, sex-aholic Senator had had his way with her.

"Do you live in Madison?"

"No, I'm not from here. I go to Jamestown College. I have a friend that is a political science major. We went to the lecture last night that Senator Showalter was giving in the auditorium."

"And what happened after the speech was over?" Rae Ann prompted, leaning forward in her seat.

"My friend got a chance to ask the Senator some questions. It was getting really loud in the auditorium so he asked us to step out into the hall with him while he got some air. In the middle of the conversation, my friend had to take a call. I was only alone with him for a couple of minutes before he started coming on to me. I didn't know what to do—he is such a powerful man. I didn't want to ruin this opportunity for my friend, but then he started touching me," the girl cringed against the memory, "So then I did try to leave, but he pulled me into the nearest room and well, you know."

"I'm sorry, Jenna, but I have to hear you say it."

The entire time the girl had been talking she had been looking down at the hospital gown she wore, picking at a tiny hole in the fabric. Now, she looked up straight into the camera and with fierce conviction said, "Senator Showalter raped me." She broke then, putting her hands over her face to muffle the sobs, but the tears leaked through the cracks in her fingers. "I can't believe I was so stupid," she cried, "Why didn't I just leave?"

Rae Ann went to Jenna and enveloped the girl in a hug. Jenna clung to the fabric of Rae Ann's cardigan with clenched fists and sobbed on her shoulder. Eddie lowered the camera and silently left the room to give the two some privacy. Rae Ann reluctantly pulled out of the embrace and grasped Jenna's shoulders. "This is not your fault, Jenna. You are the victim here. You were right to come to the hospital and you were right to call me. I promise you that we will get Senator Showalter for doing this to you. I promise."

"Ms. Lewis?"

Rae Ann turned to the white clad form that appeared in the doorway. "Yes?" she questioned.

"We are going to need to do some more tests before Miss Ford is released," the doctor said, glancing at the girl's chart that he held in his hands.

"Yes, of course," Rae Ann let go of the girl's bony shoulders and straightened her sweater, "I'll be right outside if you need me."

Rae Ann walked to the door and turned back to the girl, "Is there someone you would like me to call? Your parents or your friend that was at the speech with you?"

Jenna shook her head slowly before answering, "My parents were killed a couple of years ago, in a car accident. I have no family. And my friend is the one that brought me to the hospital. But, Ms. Lewis, thank you."

Rae Ann forced a quick smile and ducked around a nurse to exit the room.

As she stepped into the emergency room hallway, she took another lungful of sterilized air. Eddie pushed a steaming cup of coffee into her hand and took a drink of his own. "That's quite a story she's got there."

"Yeah, I know," Rae Ann said, taking a seat on the opposite side of the hallway. The small heels of her shoes beat a path across the freshly polished tiles.

"You know, we just can't take her word for it and make it a story," Eddie said, plopping into the plastic chair beside her.

"I know that too, Eddie. We are just going to have to wait until some of these test results come back." Rae Ann didn't want to look at Eddie, but turned to him anyway. His face showed the lack of conviction that she knew it would.

"Do you believe her, Scoop? Because if you do, this could be very bad for business."

"Or it could be very good for business. Come on, Eddie, I believe this girl. I think that cocky son of a bitch, Showalter, took advantage of that poor girl against her will. Did you even look in her eyes?" Rae Ann threw a hand toward the door of Jenna's room. "She looked lost... alone... and scared."

"But," Eddie protested, "Do you see any family or friends here? We are the only people she called. Vicious, ruthless TV reporters. Don't you find that odd?" Rae Ann let Eddie's comments swirl around in her mouth before she swallowed them.

"She doesn't have any family and, from what I gather, not a whole lot of friends, either. And besides, she's ashamed. She thinks it is her fault." In truth, Rae Ann did not find the situation odd at all. From the look of conviction in her eyes, Rae Ann thought Jenna Ford seemed very in control and wise beyond her years. Just as Rae Ann had had to be when she was growing up. Neither had any family and both were emotionally distant. This is exactly what Rae Ann would have done if she had been in the girl's situation. She would have made it public as soon as possible so the cops or anyone else would have no reason not to believe her.

"You can go back in now," a voice said gruffly, interrupting Rae Ann's thoughts. They watched the heavyset nurse emerge fully from the room with a hand full of vials and tubes, her orthopedic shoes squeaked down the corridor until she was out of sight. Rae Ann pushed back into the room and surrounded Jenna.

"Are you going to put my story on the news?"

Rae Ann exchanged a sideways glance with Eddie. "I'm going to talk to my boss, but we will probably need some proof first."

"Proof?" Jenna huffed, pointing to her swollen face, "how much more proof do you need?"

Rae Ann opened her mouth to respond, but the door swung open suddenly as the doctor and a police officer charged into the room. "Miss Ford, we need to talk about possibly pressing charges," the young policeman said. Rae Ann stepped in front of the girl and switched over to her journalist mode.

"Why, doctor, has a suspect been confirmed?"

"Ms. Lewis, this is private information that should only be heard by the victim."

"No," Jenna interrupted, "I want her to hear this, too."

"Okay," the doctor sighed, holding his hands up in surrender, "we have found traces of semen. If Miss Ford decides to press charges then Officer Frost has been ordered to pick up the Senator."

"He can either volunteer a blood sample to disprove these allegations or hire a lawyer," Officer Frost concluded.

Rae Ann flew around to Jenna. "Yes, honey, press charges. You can get this scum ball."

Jenna pulled in a ragged breath and nodded her head, "Yes, I do want to press charges."

Rae Ann was beaming inside, but her expression never betrayed her. She politely excused herself and Eddie from the room, shutting the door tightly behind her. Finally, a smile broke on Rae Ann's face and Eddie picked her up in an exaggerated hug, spinning her around.

"Can you believe this? I can't believe this," Rae Ann gushed, "Senator Showalter raped an innocent twenty year old student at Jamestown College. I have to go call Bob."

Remembering that she had left her cellular phone in the car, Rae Ann raced out into the cold to claim her story, not even bothering to put her coat back on. She dropped heavily into the driver's seat and slammed the door firmly behind her in attempt to beat the cold from invading the inside of the car. Too late. In moments, her skin was chilled to the bone and her teeth were chattering. With trembling hands, Rae Ann picked up the phone and started to dial the news director's number. She stopped when she saw that the illuminated screen indicated that she had missed nine calls. All of which were Grant's number.

Rae Ann shook her head in sadness wishing that Grant was really worried enough about her to have called this many times, but she knew better. Of course, now, Rae Ann could already see the damage this story was going to do to her marriage. Without another moment's hesitation, Rae Ann erased the display and then eagerly dialed her boss.

After explaining all the sordid details to Bob Ashcroft, Rae Ann waited for a response.

"Why didn't you take this to Eric, Rae Ann? You know he usually screens all of the story ideas."

"Bob, I don't think you heard me correctly. I have a twenty-year old college student claiming that Senator Showalter raped her. If I waited for Eric to act on this story, Channel 8 would be playing sloppy seconds to every other station in town."

"Rae Ann, I know this sounds like a great story, but it also sounds pretty far-fetched. How do you know this girl is for real?" Rae Ann frowned and the air thickened inside the tiny interior of the car. If she couldn't convince Bob, then there would be no story.

"Since when have we waited to know the truth before we tell a story, Bob? Besides, they are picking up Showy for a blood test. That is a story in itself. Even if this turns out to be a hoax, we've got breaking news." She could hear Bob breathing deeply into the phone.

"I really need to run this by the station attorney first, kiddo."

Rae Ann was shaking her head determinedly even before Bob completed his sentence. "I can't sit on this, Bob. This is huge. Let me write the story and get it out there. I promise I won't convict him with my words." Another long sigh and deep breath had all but convinced Rae Ann that Bob wasn't going to let this story fly.

At last, his words were like a blast of warm air in the frigid night. "All right, kid. But listen, if we report this story before the blood test confirms, we could be in real trouble. If it turns out to be someone else's spirit, then there is going to be hell to pay and I have a pretty good feeling that Showy will ask for your head as payment. You two don't exactly share a love for each other."

"Listen, Bob, you didn't see this girl. She's for real. If we sit on this story until the blood work comes back then every station in town is going to have it. I want the go ahead to put this in the works," Rae Ann demanded and then held her breath while Bob made his decision.

"Okay, get the story moving, and Rae Ann, get exclusivity."

Elated, Rae Ann hung up the phone and ran back into the hospital to secure her position as weekend anchor. She was so keyed up that she never even felt the cold.

Fourteen

Wednesday, March 3rd

"Haven't you even been to makeup yet?" Bob's voice thundered across the top of the cubicles in the newsroom like a sonic explosion, causing Rae Ann to jump reflexively in her desk chair.

"What? Make-up? Why?" Rae Ann was clearly flustered with Bob's sudden verbal outburst.

"I read the notes on your story. This rape thing is yours, Lewis. You are anchoring. I suggest you get to make-up and have somebody do something with your hair."

Rae Ann could not believe what she was hearing. Bob was finally giving her a chance behind the desk to prove herself. She quickly lifted from the chair and turned in the direction of the make-up room before addressing Bob. "Hey, what's wrong with my hair?"

Bob Ashcroft's back was to her, but if she could have seen his face it was all smiles. He believed in this one. It wasn't often that someone, with so little training and experience, could ever convince him of what a good reporter they could really be. Rae Ann Lewis had done just that. Bob was willing to bet his life that the ratings for their newscasts would soar, once Rae Ann's face was on the screen. He had been holding her back for as long as he could, to make her truly appreciate the job. But he already knew that she did. Now the only thing he was worried about was the validity of this rape story.

"It's your husband, Miss Lewis," Becky, the office manager was handing Rae Ann a cordless phone as the make-up artist put the finishing touches on her face. The layer of make-up was thick and made Rae Ann claustrophobic from the weight. The look of surprise on Rae Ann's face must have been evident to the young girl, as she shrugged as if to say that she didn't know why Grant Spencer was calling. Rae Ann took the phone and pulled the Kleenex from her collar that protected her dark suit from being dusted with face powder. "Grant?"

"Rae Ann, oh thank God I've caught you. Please hear me out," Grant's voice sounded vulnerable and had a note of urgency. In all the time that she had known him, Rae Ann had never heard him sound like this.

"What is it, Grant? Is everything all right?" The make-up artist finished putting her brushes away and excused herself from the room.

"No, not entirely," Grant was saying. Rae Ann's mind flashed back to their early morning conversation. He had pleaded with her not to go to work, to quit her job. She hoped like hell this wasn't a follow up to that conversation.

Had that really been just twenty-four hours ago?

"I heard about the Senator being accused of rape."

"Yes, well, eventually everything you do catches up with you, Grant." Rae Ann's tone dripped with disgust for the accused Senator, and then wondered where Grant had heard the story. It was a question she wouldn't get to ask.

"Rae Ann, I want you to promise me that you will stay away from this story. Keep your name out of it, please," Grant pleaded.

"Grant, you know I can't do that. This is my story, my chance. Besides, if the Senator is guilty of rape, then the people that elected him need to know what a creep he is. Not to mention a criminal."

"You have no idea what kind of repercussions this story could have." Grant's voice became high pitched to the point of hysteria.

"Repercussions for who, Grant? You?"

"For me. The resort. You."

"First of all, Grant, not everything is about you. The fact that you and the Senator are friends is your problem. Not mine. And as far as I'm concerned, I can take care of myself. I have been doing it for a very long time." Rae Ann was tempted to slam the phone down and leave Grant hanging on the line, but she heard his voice soften.

"Rae Ann, listen, there is a lot of stuff you don't understand. Stuff I haven't told you."

"Then tell me, Grant. Help me to understand," Rae Ann saw a small piece of Grant's mysterious side peel away and she gave it a mighty mental tug. The silence on the phone was endless and just as Rae Ann thought that Grant was ready to divulge his deepest secrets, she heard a tiny whisper. "I can't."

"Then I'm sorry, Grant, but I will be reporting the story. And you should be happy for me, it's almost a given that they are going to offer me the anchor job." A heavy sigh came over the line and Rae Ann closed her eyes from the lava hot tears that scalded her eyelids.

"I'm sorry, too." With that the line was dead and Rae Ann felt another piece of her marriage die with it.

~ * ~

Grant pushed the button on the phone receiver to disconnect the line, then threw the phone full force across the room. It slammed brutally into the wood paneled wall of his office and splintered into two pieces. Everything was falling apart at the seams. If Rae Ann reported the rape story on the Senator, then it would surely sign the death certificate of the resort. Grant had already exhausted every effort with Elliot Logan and had liquidated his assets including a strip mall he owned in Chicago, to keep the place afloat. If he could just get Rae Ann to sit on the rape story for another week, Grant would have everything figured out and would be back in business. But who was he kidding? Grant knew it would be easier to talk the girl out of pressing charges then it would be to get Rae Ann to shelve the story.

"That's it," Grant slapped his hands together and rounded his desk with lightning speed. It was amazing how fast one could move when one hasn't been drinking, he mused to himself. Grant pulled at the bottom drawer to his desk and opened it wide to reveal the small plastic case. The girl hadn't been lying. There was a disk. A very interesting disk at that. Grant picked the disk up gingerly and turned it over and over in his hands. The shiny, metallic side caught a sliver of light from the French doors and cast a rainbow on the wall.

"I can do this, can't I?" Grant asked himself, out loud. Of course, there really was no answer. No easy answer anyway. He had never been the ruthless business type, but now he had to do what it would take to keep his dream alive. If it meant ruining his marriage, destroying business partnerships and bringing down innocent people, so be it.

~ * ~

Rae Ann straightened her suit jacket and took a long, deep breath as someone on the sound stage counted down till she was on air. She caught a glimpse of a couple of the other field reporters standing in the wings to witness her debut. It was like a rite of passage. One of their own had crossed the line to the big time. Rae Ann was glad that Marley Cavanaugh was not among the group. Rae Ann had heard Bob earlier on the phone trying to remain calm while he explained to Marley that she would not be anchoring this once in a lifetime story. Marley had been determined to take over. She, along with everyone else, knew that the network would have to accept her outlandish terms if Marley wrote a blockbuster for the rape scandal.

The lights were momentarily blinding, but when the teleprompter began spewing forth the words Rae Ann had written for the story, she felt right at home. The story had been introduced as a late breaking event and Rae Ann's proverbial fifteen minutes in the spotlight would end when it was over but, for the moment, she didn't care. The dialogue flowed from her mouth, as if she had been born to say it. Rae Ann directed the story to a tape of Senator Showalter being escorted into the police station for his blood test. Showy was ranting and raving to the cameras that he had never heard of his accuser and had gone home straight after the speech at the college. His loyal wife, Millicent, would attest to that. As for the blood test, Showy obliged willingly—which had Rae Ann and the station very nervous. The story wrapped up and faded to a commercial as Rae Ann sat back in the chair, trying to hold onto the moment for as long as possible.

"Way to go, Scoop. That was some good shit," Eddie sauntered up to the carpeted step of the stage and leaned towards her.

"Thanks," she beamed at him, "I just hope Bob feels the same way."

"Oh, I think he does. I heard him talking to the maintenance man about measuring your big head for a publicity shot." Rae Ann playfully socked Eddie in the arm as she passed him, leaving the stage.

"Well, I guess its back to the mundane life of field reporting. Do we have anything on that school fire safety thing?" Eddie fell into step beside Rae Ann, as they entered the newsroom.

"Yeah. My buddy, Dale, is on the fire department. He said we could come over for an interview anytime." Just as Eddie finished his sentence, Bob Ashcroft came at them with a stern expression on his red face.

"Oh God," Rae Ann muttered under her breath. Here it was. Either he loved it or he hated it. There was no in between.

"I want you on this rape thing full time. We are going to have breaking news coverage on it round the clock. Can I count on you for that, Lewis?" Bob's voice was gruff, but Rae Ann could tell that he was pleased with her work.

"Absolutely, Bob. I was just going to head over to the police station to see if I could get some information." Rae Ann tried to remain professional as her inner self was screaming with delight.

"Fine. Take Eduardo with you. Cops make for good tape." Rae Ann slapped Eddie a high five and they scampered out to the van.

~ * ~

"For the third time, Ms. Lewis, I can't tell you."

The police officer was young with a fresh crew cut. Rae Ann could tell he was shy. The entire time they had been talking, the boy had not looked her in the eyes and continually shredded a piece of paper on the counter.

"You're right, Darrin. Can I call you Darrin?" Rae Ann leaned onto the counter and picked up one of the slivers of paper. "I'm not asking you to tell me who shot Kennedy. I just need to know if the Senator has been arrested or not."

The officer was laughing, having found her Kennedy joke far funnier than she had intended it to be. This boy had not even been born when Kennedy was shot and killed. Eddie rolled his eyes toward the ceiling and dropped the camera off of his shoulder. They had been at the station for half and hour and had gotten nowhere. Rae Ann had, however, managed to sneak them in the back door of the station, while the rest of news reporters were just arriving on the front stoop of the police headquarters. They had learned from Rae Ann's news report, along with the rest of the world, that the Senator was being held at the station.

"Is this off the record?" the young officer asked, tentatively. Rae Ann knew this was it. He was going to talk.

"I can't guarantee you it will be off the record, but I can assure you anonymity," Rae Ann let the words roll off her tongue slowly as to not scare the boy away. From the look on his face, she could see he was confused. "What I mean is that I won't use your name in the story," she explained.

"Oh, right. Well in that case, yes," his smile rivaled that of the Cheshire cat.

"Yes, what?" Rae Ann pried. She wanted the police officer to say the words. This way she couldn't be accused of fabricating a story on mere assumptions.

"Yes, the Senator has been arrested." The boy's eyes shifted about to make sure no one in the immediate area was listening. At present, he was the only one at the information desk. Everyone else was busy behind a closed door, pushing at paperwork and their shirt sleeves in frustration.

"But how could they arrest him with no evidence?" Rae Ann was playing stupid to drag the details out of the boy. Eddie loved this part. Rae Ann really was good at what she did. She could woo a source into spilling secrets against their own mother if necessary.

"Preliminary tests have shown the Senator's blood type match the semen collected from the victim." The young cop seemed proud of his grown up dialogue.

Rae Ann wanted to jump for joy but kept her cool. "Wow, that was a great statement, officer. Mind if I quote you?" The boy was putty in Rae Ann's palm. He blushed at her compliment and nodded his head eagerly to agree to the quote.

"Thanks." Rae Ann gave a last fleeting glance in the policeman's direction and winked.

~ * ~

"That must have been some kind of record, Scoop. I think you could have had that one licking your shoes if you had asked," Eddie commented as they skipped down the back stairs and loaded their equipment into the van.

"Well, we didn't get visual, but I think Bob will be more than pleased with what I just heard."

Fifteen

Monday, March 8th

Rae Ann fell into the bed in her Madison apartment, exhausted. She had worked round the clock for nearly a week putting the Senator's rape case on the forefront of every newscast. She had flown to Washington to get an interview from other members of Capital Hill, then back to Madison for a phone conference with Jenna Ford's lawyer. So far, they had been able to keep the girl out of the limelight. Her name and face had not been released and her lawyer was not even letting her talk to Rae Ann.

They conversed through him only, a young man by the name of Alexander Noah. He was a self-proclaimed friend of Jenna's late parents. Rae Ann could tell he was young and inexperienced, but he assured Rae Ann he had nothing but Jenna's best interests in mind. "If I could just speak to her, Mr. Noah, I'm sure it wouldn't take but a minute," Rae Ann was pleading her case for the forth time.

"I'm sorry, Ms. Lewis, Jenna isn't available at the moment."

It was the extent of what she was getting these days. Rae Ann rolled over in the double bed and pushed the answering machine button. She hadn't heard from Grant since their argument about the

Senator and there were no messages now. Rae Ann knew that the marriage wouldn't hold up for much longer. You couldn't live two separate lives in two different towns with contrasting views of life. Soon she would have to be looking for a divorce lawyer. The thought made her physically cringe even now, in the privacy of her apartment. Tomorrow she would think about that, for tonight Rae Ann would bask in the glow of her professional success, even if her personal life was a disaster.

Sixteen

Tuesday, March 9ᵗʰ

The sun rose too soon and Rae Ann dragged herself out of bed. She completed a couple of stretching exercises and pulled on her running shoes. One thing she had always enjoyed was a run in the cool morning air of Wisconsin. She breathed in deep and wound her hair into a makeshift bun before starting down the road in front of her apartment building. The hour was early and for the most part Rae Ann's neighborhood was still asleep. She bounded on the pavement of the sidewalk as her heartbeat escalated to a thunderous roar.

Mentally, she was deciding what to report on today's newscast. Showy's trips out of the country would be attention grabbing, but how could she tie that back to the recent allegations of rape? For a full hour, Rae Ann mulled the words of a story around in her mind as she rounded the city blocks and ended up back on the steps of her apartment. She was winded, but not out of breath and her hair clung to her face in damp ringlets. The run had cleared her mind and she rushed into her building to put the story she had developed in her mind onto paper.

As she approached the door to the place she called home, Rae Ann could hear the muted ringing of her telephone. She fumbled with her keys and managed to get the right one in the lock before the ringing stopped. The cordless receiver was off the hook and to her ear before another ring could begin. "Rae Ann Lewis."

"Scoop, Jesus Christ, where have you been?" Eddie's voice was as shrill as the tone of the phone.

"Running. Why, Eddie, what is wrong?" Rae Ann was instantly concerned.

"The TV, have you watched any TV? Turn on the TV," Eddie's voice escalated to near hysteria as Rae Ann bumbled towards the small television set and flipped it on. Eddie had her unnerved and she had no idea what to expect.

"What channel? What the hell am I looking for? Eddie, what is going on?" Before Eddie could answer any of her questions, a commercial ceased and the morning show news reporter for Channel 14 began her story.

"Just this morning, it has been reported that Senator Francis Showalter's rape victim has dropped all of the charges against him. The victim, whose name has not been released to the press, stated by phone call exclusively to Channel 14 news that her accusations against the Senator were false and that no rape ever took place.

"Furthermore, the accuser went on to explain that she was hired by Channel 8 news reporter, Rae Ann Lewis, to make the false accusation against Senator Showalter to further her own career. As of this newscast, Ms. Lewis was unavailable for comment. Senator Showalter is expected to be released from custody later this morning." The attractive reporter shuffled the paperwork in front of her and moved on to give the morning's weather forecast. Rae Ann sank slowly onto the bed and stared in disbelief. She had forgotten completely that Eddie was on the other end of the phone until she heard him sigh heavily.

"Scoop, I—"

"I don't understand," Rae Ann whispered, "what is she doing?" Rae Ann glanced over at the bedside table and noticed the answering machine was blinking with eleven missed messages. She groped for the remote control and turned the television off.

"Do you want me to come over?" Eddie asked. Rae Ann shook her head at the phone but couldn't speak for fear of her voice breaking.

The distinct beeping of her other phone line sounded in her ear, momentarily blocking out Eddie's voice.

"I have to go."

"Wait, Rae Ann, I'm coming over," Eddie's voice was insistent, but Rae Ann was already recovering from the initial shock of the news report.

"No, I'm going into the station. I've got to talk to Bob and get this mess straightened out." Rae Ann threw the phone on the bed and sprang into action. She was showered, dressed and out the door in a half-hour. Rae Ann stopped at the station's back door with her hand on the knob. She had used the door every day for the last four years, but knew today it would look like she was trying to sneak in. She slung her purse a little higher on her shoulder and made her way around the building to the front door.

Big mistake.

The sidewalk was lined with reporters thrusting their microphones in Rae Ann's face as she made her way through the crowd and into the door. Bob met her halfway and put an arm around her shoulders to shield her from the intrusive mob. "God damn reporters," Bob muttered under his breath, "Are we that relentless?"

"Yes," Rae Ann replied, relieved at Bob's attempt at humor.

"Let's talk in my office." Rae Ann nodded and followed him through the newsroom. Everywhere she glanced, Rae Ann saw people whispering behind their hands and staring in her direction. She had never cared what people thought of her and considered none of them, save Eddie, as friends, but it still hurt to see them try and convict her, before the facts were even out. Bob shut the door to his closet sized office behind her and motioned her into a chair.

Before he could even get comfortable behind his desk, Rae Ann had started in. "Bob, you must know this isn't true."

"I know what they are reporting, Rae Ann, and it isn't good," her boss hung his head low and Rae Ann could tell that the job was weighing on his shoulders heavy.

"Eddie was there. I have a witness. Plus, there is the tape we shot of her telling us the story," Rae Ann paced the room in frustration and fury.

How could Bob not believe her?

"The tape is gone," Bob said, trying to slip the words in unnoticed.

"What?" Rae Ann shrieked, her pacing stopped mid-stride.

"We can't find the tape. There is no proof of the interview at the hospital. The only thing we have is a doctor and a police officer that swear you jumped in front of the girl and told her to 'press charges against the scum ball'."

"And what about Eddie? He will tell the truth." Rae Ann could already see this argument was a lost cause.

"Eddie corroborates your story, but we both know they will say he was in on it. Do you really want to drag Eddie down with you here?" Rae Ann shook her head slowly from side to side. "I didn't think so," Bob agreed, "For the time being, I have reassigned Eddie to another reporter."

The phone on Bob's desk began a series of beeps and flashing lights as all of his lines began ringing. Rae Ann heard him groan and reach for the receiver. Knowing she had been dismissed from the conversation, Rae Ann let herself out of the office. She made her way through the sea of gathering co-workers to the stairs that lead down into the dungeon.

Rae Ann grabbed the arm of a passing tech as he ascended into the light of the newsroom. "Is Eddie Torres down there?" Rae Ann asked, breathlessly trying to keep tears out of her eyes and voice. The guy nodded and glanced down at Rae Ann's grip on his arm. She didn't bother to thank him as she continued down the stairs. As she came to the landing that broke up the L shaped staircase, Rae Ann was tempted to hop through the emergency exit door into the alley and just run away.

As usual the dungeon's lights were darkened and it took a moment for her eyes to adjust as she circled the room. "Eddie, oh thank God," Rae Ann whispered as she found her friend in the stored tape section of the room.

"Scoop, what the hell is going on?" Eddie's whisper was fervent and he nearly dropped a stack of tapes he was holding.

"I don't know. It's a mess," Rae Ann replied, laying her head against the shelf.

"Can you call that girl's lawyer? Get this thing straightened out. I thought Bob was going to have cardiac arrest this morning when he saw the report."

"It just doesn't make sense. I mean, yeah, theoretically I could have paid that girl to report the story but what about the blood type and the semen? There's no way I could have pulled that off," Rae Ann said, folding her arms across her chest. Eddie shrugged and opened his mouth to talk before shutting it again.

"What? What is it?" Rae Ann stood to her full height and tilted her head towards Eddie.

"Maybe this girl is just using you, you know?"

"No, I don't know. What are you getting at Eddie?"

"Well, the Senator is a celebrity of sorts. A wealthy man with lots of power. Just the kind of guy you want to see crash and burn. So you have a little fling with him, scream rape, get paid to keep your mouth shut and if an innocent reporter goes down with the flames, so be it," Eddie concluded by shrugging his shoulders again and went back to shelving the tapes. Rae Ann put a hand on his shoulder and gently pulled him back around to meet his eyes.

"Let me get this straight, you think this girl blackmailed the Senator and is using me as her fall guy?"

"It makes perfect sense to me. Why should she care about you? Plus, the Senator wins as well. He comes out smelling like a rose and that pesky reporter he doesn't like gets canned." Before Eddie finished his sentence, he saw Rae Ann's face pale to a ghostly white. "Rae, wait I didn't mean to say—"

"You think they're going to fire me?" Rae Ann's stomach heaved with nausea. Surely, they would believe her side of the story. She had devoted her life to this station for six years. But really, what choice does Bob have?

"Come on," Eddie soothed, "let me drive you home."

On the verge of tears, Rae Ann simply nodded and let herself be led up the staircase. When they reached the landing, the sound of raised voices and something crashing sent them both running to the main floor. At first glance, Rae Ann knew that this scene only meant trouble. Francis Showalter was barreling through the newsroom at top speed towards Bob's office. In his hasty entrance, Showy ran headlong into an older woman pushing a cart of mail. The wire basket on the cart had slammed into the floor and rang smartly off the tile. Several people ran to the woman's aid and began picking the envelopes and packages off the floor. At the sight, Rae Ann's stomach gave a violent lurch. The door to Bob's office opened and shut, taking in the furious Senator, but not his voice. Everyone in the newsroom could hear the conversation between the two men even though Bob Ashcroft wasn't really getting a word into the discussion.

After several minutes of muted yelling, Bob swung open the door and motioned for Rae Ann. Numb, she entered the office and shut the door behind her. The air in the office was thick and crackled with electricity. It emanated from the Senator and rolled off him in waves.

"Senator, you must know—" Rae Ann began.

"I want her fired," Showalter cut Rae Ann off in mid-sentence and directed his statement toward the station manager. "I plan to sue this woman for defamation of character and malicious persecution and if your television station doesn't want to be named in the suit, I suggest you relieve her of her duties." With that the Senator bounded out of the building and Rae Ann cringed when the door slammed brutally behind him.

"Give me some time, Bob. I will find this girl and figure everything out," Rae Ann pleaded.

A long moment passed where Rae Ann was sure Bob was deciding how to reassign her duties when he finally blurted out, "You have forty-eight hours to get that girl to retract her story."

~ * ~

Rae Ann smashed the phone back into its cradle, picked it up and slammed it again. "Damn," she muttered.

"Find out anything yet?" Eddie slid a chair around to Rae Ann's desk and sat down heavily.

"No, the number I have been calling to reach Jenna's lawyer is now disconnected," Rae Ann replied, eyeing the bag of take out food Eddie set on the desk. It was nearly eleven o'clock at night. The last of the evening news crew had cleared out, leaving Eddie and Rae Ann alone in the newsroom. Rae Ann rubbed her gritty eyes with the heels of her hands and wondered how in this day of other worldly terrorists and crazed sniper shooters that one raven-haired girl could wreak so much havoc. The day had been emotionally exhausting and had taken its toll on her. She wanted only to go home and draw the bed covers over her head. Rae Ann was sure, by now, that Grant had seen the latest story, but she had heard nothing out of him.

"What about that nurse that called you the night we went to the hospital?" Eddie asked as he took a peek in the Chinese food carton he held and then handed it to Rae Ann.

"What about him?"

"The girl must have told him that she was raped by the Senator, before you even got there, since he was the one that told you. They might try to say that you set the whole thing up before hand, but it's worth a shot just to talk to him."

Rae Ann jumped to her feet, abandoning the carton of fried rice. "You're right," Rae Ann pulled the suit jacket off the back of her chair, "if I can find that nurse, he can corroborate that I knew nothing before that phone call. I was clearly confused when I got the call. Eddie you are a genius."

Rae Ann was halfway to the door before she realized Eddie was following her. "What are you doing?"

"I'm going with you. You need all the help you can get."

"Eddie," Rae Ann sighed, "I really appreciate all that you have done for me so far, but I can't let you do this. I am going to end up dragging you down with me and I don't want that."

"No, you listen," Eddie's face was serious, "I am doing this whether you like it or not. You are a good friend, Rae Ann, and you are facing something that isn't your fault. I can't let you go through this alone."

Rae Ann was touched by his words of sentiment. If all friends were like Eduardo Torres, Rae Ann would have a million of them. She threw her arms around Eddie's neck and hugged him tightly. "Thank you," he heard her whisper in his ear.

"Come on," Eddie gave her a brief squeeze back before pulling away, "the night shift should be coming on soon. We might be just in time to catch this nurse." Eddie fished in his coat pocket for the keys to the news van as they entered the brisk night air.

"Hey, Eddie?"

"Yeah, Scoop."

"Can I drive the van?"

"Not on your life."

Rae Ann smiled into the dark.

~ * ~

"I need to see one of your nurses. Last name Bell."

A different receptionist, than the one Rae Ann had encountered on the night of the alleged rape, was working. This one seemed a little more attentive and began rapidly tapping on the keys of her computer. "Nurse Bell is working triage. Right through those doors on the right," the girl smiled pleasantly and tucked her hands under her chin.

Rae Ann thanked the girl and with Eddie in tow entered the triage room. A tall, thin woman clad all in white was bent over the forearm of a man and was dabbing at a severe cut just below his elbow. When Rae Ann entered the room, the nurse raised her head to the intrusion with a questioning look on her face. "Can I help you?"

"Oh, I'm sorry," Rae Ann stammered, "we were told that Nurse Bell was in here."

The nurse stood at full height and began pulling off the latex gloves she wore on her hands, "I'm Marissa Bell."

Rae Ann's features clouded with confusion and she turned to Eddie with an open mouth. "Wrong Nurse Bell, I'm afraid," Eddie chuckled nervously and began backing out of the room, "the Nurse Bell we are looking for is a man. Peter Bell."

The nurse shook her head of short dark hair and frowned, "There's no Peter Bell that I am aware of, that works at this hospital. You might want to check the registration desk on your way out."

Once again in the hallway, Rae Ann wanted to scream out loud. She started to speak, but Eddie held up a hand. "Don't jump to conclusions."

The pair made their way back through the automatic doors of the emergency department and addressed the peppy receptionist once again. "I'm sorry to bother you again, but we were looking for Peter Bell. Not Marissa Bell."

"Oh," the girl said, not losing her smile. She turned again to the keyboard and tapped away for what seemed like an eternity. "I don't see a Peter Bell on the nurse registry. There is a Peter Adkins."

"May I see the screen?" Rae Ann's radar was up and screaming at full volume. The receptionist swung the monitor around towards Rae Ann and pointed to the list. The nurse's names were listed in alphabetical order. First Peter Adkins, then Marissa Bell.

~ * ~

"She set me up," Rae Ann concluded once they were back in the van.

Eddie was silent as he drove through the streets of Madison, ending up back in the WZZY parking lot. He shifted the van into park and leaned forward onto the steering wheel. "You need to think with a clear head. Go home and get some rest."

Rae Ann nodded and slid out of the passenger door. She would indeed go home, but she knew she wouldn't sleep. Her career was hanging precariously at the edge of a cliff. One stiff wind from the Senator would surely send it crashing to its demise. Even if this whole thing blew over and nothing came of the threats against Rae Ann, she could bet that her chances for Marley's job were over. Everyone knew how much Rae Ann wanted the position; they knew how ruthless she was as a reporter. Would it be that much of a stretch to think that Rae Ann could master mind a plan against a man she despised, to further her own career? Even Rae Ann didn't think so.

Her apartment was as she left it. Disheveled and upset from her hasty retreat out the door this morning. Rae Ann absently moved around the small bedroom picking up articles of clothing and a hairbrush. She settled down beside the phone on the nightstand and picked it up. It took everything she had to dial the number to Grant's suite at the resort. "Yeah, Grant Spencer," her groggy husband spoke into the phone.

Rae Ann glanced at the clock forgetting that it was nearly one o'clock in the morning. She instantly felt guilty and almost hung up the receiver. She needed him now more than ever and one wrong word could send her crashing into the deepest depths of despair. Rae Ann's voice was brittle as she sent it out across the miles. "It's Rae Ann."

"Rae Ann, are you all right?"

"No, Grant," Rae Ann could not keep her voice from breaking and hard wracking sobs shook her entire being. Grant waited patiently on the other end until she was able to speak again. "I'm in trouble, Grant, and I need your help."

"What is it, what happened?" The concern in Grant's voice gave Rae Ann just enough strength to spill the events of the day. When she was finished, Rae Ann was exhausted, but at ease. The silence from the other end of the line was so deafening that Rae Ann was sure Grant had hung up on her. When at last he spoke, Rae Ann wished that he had hung up.

"What is it that you want from me?"

"I want you to help me," Rae Ann was exasperated, "I want you to call your *friend* the Senator and tell him to back off. Tell him to give me a chance."

"I told you to drop the story, Rae Ann. You wouldn't listen to me. Why didn't you listen to me? I could have had everything under control." All the concern had left his voice—it was now ragged and sounded tired.

"I was doing my job, Grant." This argument wasn't helping, but Rae Ann couldn't back down from being so defensive. Why was he being so accusatory?

"Are you going to help me or not, Grant?" Rae Ann asked, roughly.

"I can't," his voice was barely a whisper, "I'm sorry, but I can't."

"That's just great, Grant, thank you for being so supportive." Rae Ann was about to slam the phone down when she heard him speak again.

"There are things that you don't know, Rae Ann." It was the breaking point that Rae Ann had been waiting for.

"I'm well aware of that, Grant. You remind me everyday. But unless you are willing to share this information with me, then I guess our conversation is over."

Long after Rae Ann had hung up the phone, Grant sat with the receiver to his ear. He should have helped her, but how could that be possible? It was too late now. If she had dropped the story like he had asked, none of this would be happening. What was done was done. Grant cut off the dial tone by putting a hand on the switch hook. He didn't feel like being alone.

Seventeen

Thursday, March 11ᵗʰ

"The station just cannot take this kind of blow, Rae Ann," Bob Ashcroft was clearly uncomfortable with what he was about to say, "I'm afraid I'm going to have to ask you to clear out your desk."

Rae Ann nodded with reluctant resolve, but remained in the chair across from Bob's desk. She was not angry with Bob or the station or even Senator Showalter for forcing this ultimatum. She was only angry at herself. Rae Ann tried to remember when she had lost her journalistic edge in favor of advancing her career. At one time, Rae Ann could recall that absolutely nothing would have gotten in her way of reporting the truth. She knew she had been preoccupied with the job opening and that was why she couldn't locate the young girl that had accused the Senator of rape.

Of course, Jenna Ford wasn't a student at Jamestown College. No one in the political science department had heard of her or recognized her picture. A fact that Rae Ann never even bothered to check during her reports of the rape story. There were many Ford's listed in the phone book but none of them were listed for Jenna. Rae Ann had gone so far as to call each one but hadn't turned up the girl. Rae Ann had pursued any lead she could to find the girl but every effort had been fruitless.

"We, I mean, uh, the station, is giving you a chance to resign. We don't want to stand in the way of you getting another job," Bob added, fiddling with this tie. He hadn't looked Rae Ann in the eye since she entered the room. Rae Ann nodded and whispered 'thank you' in a voice that was barely audible to the human ear. She stood from the chair on shaky legs and started to let herself out of the room.

"Rae Ann?" She heard the upset in his tone and really wished he wouldn't say anything. She was teetering on the edge and surely any sentiment from Bob would send her catapulting over the brink. But she stopped anyway. She wanted to hear him say that she was a good reporter and she did the right thing. She wanted to hear him say that he had done everything he could to keep her on.

Instead, Bob cleared his throat and said, "You will be missed."

It didn't take long for Rae Ann to have her belongings packed into an empty copy paper box and thrown into the back seat of her Lexus. Except for a wedding photo of her and Grant, Rae Ann had no other personal effects. The reality of it depressed her. She wanted to get out of Madison and was thankful that she still had somewhere to go. What she would face when she got back to the resort, she didn't know. Rae Ann vowed to herself that she would make the marriage work. She had screwed up everything else in her life and her marriage was all she had to hold on to. She would get down on her knees and beg Grant's forgiveness for not dropping the story. Surely, the Senator was not upset with Grant and in time would also forgive Rae Ann. If Grant was willing, then Rae Ann would make every effort to become involved in his life at the resort. She would be the trophy wife he wanted. She would eventually learn to be cordial to Showy, especially if he dropped the lawsuit against her. Rae Ann collected some belongings from her apartment and began the trip to Rockingham. She was ten minutes into the trip when her cell phone rang. "Hello."

"Scoop, I just heard. I'm so sorry."

"Eddie, I'm glad you called. I'm going to be staying up at the resort for a while and I was wondering if you could close up my apartment?"

"Sure, whatever you need."

"Thanks. I'll let you know if there's anything else."

"Scoop?" Eddie let the question hang in the air, "what are you going to do now?" Rae Ann felt like crying but her body was empty of emotion and void of tears.

"I don't know," she replied, honestly, "I'm going to go back to Grant and see where that goes."

"Good luck," Eddie said and Rae Ann could almost hear a smile in his voice, "I know you'll make this work."

~ * ~

Rae Ann by passed the resort and went straight to her home. The ski season was winding down and Rae Ann knew that the resort would be closed soon for the season. This was the perfect time for her and Grant to become reacquainted. She knew it was only a matter of time before the news reporters found out she wasn't staying in Madison. They would track her down here. Grant wouldn't like the bad publicity, but Rae Ann was certain everything would blow over soon. Surely the Senator wouldn't go through with the bogus lawsuit. She just wanted life to be normal again. Whatever that was.

Abandoning her possessions in the car, Rae Ann raced into the house and dialed the number for Grant's office at the resort. She waved to Rosie who came out of the kitchen to see who had entered the house. The older woman dried her hands on a dishtowel and then clapped them together in excitement.

"Grant, it's Rae Ann. I know we haven't exactly been on the best terms these last couple of weeks, but I need to see you. I want you to come home for dinner. I've got some good news." Grant agreed with minimal words to be home around six o'clock before cutting the call short. Rae Ann was too keyed up to notice. She breezed into the kitchen and gave Rosie a brief hug.

"Welcome home, Miss Rae Ann." The older woman held the younger close.

"I wasn't sure if I was welcome here," Rae Ann muttered against the large woman's shoulder.

"This is your home, Miss Rae Ann. Of course you are welcome here. Mr. Grant will be so glad to see you."

"I hope so, Rosie, I really hope so." The two women smiled heartily at one another before Rae Ann pushed up her sleeves. "I would love to help with dinner. What do you have planned?" The housekeeper seemed flustered and looked around the kitchen frantically.

"Mr. Grant hasn't been home in several days. I wasn't planning a meal for this evening."

"Oh well, that's all right. I'm sure there is something we can throw together. Grant and I are going to be making a fresh start tonight and I want everything to be perfect," Rae Ann moved around the kitchen in dreamy splendor. Who knew that being fired would be the best thing to ever happen to her marriage?

Rosie ushered Rae Ann to the door of the kitchen. "You go soak in the tub and get beautiful. Let this old woman worry about the dinner."

Rae Ann surprised them both by hugging Rosie again and planting a kiss on her wrinkled cheek. She took her leisurely time getting ready for the evening. Hoping to recreate the passion of their first date, Rae Ann chose a simple yellow dress that fell just below her knees. To give her small frame some height, she strapped on heeled sandals and then swept her hair off her neck. She felt young and surprisingly happy despite the events that had transpired earlier in the day. She should have taken Grant's advice months ago and quit the station. Already the stress of her work had disseminated and she was determined not to think about Showy tonight.

When Rae Ann heard the front door open and close, she left the bedroom in search of her husband. As usual, Grant was impeccably dressed in a charcoal tailored suit. Although, it was a bit rumpled and creased from his day at the office. He looked tired, the fatigue showing on his face and in the way he held his body.

At the sight of Rae Ann's freshness, he perked up. "Grant," Rae Ann spoke.

"You look beautiful," Grant exclaimed. Rae Ann went to him, practically running across the carpet to fold herself into his arms.

"It feels so good to be home."

He held her awkwardly, but close and breathed in her scent. "Are you? Are you home?"

Rae Ann did not want to start the evening off with an argument so she forced a smile and pulled from the embrace. "Why don't you go take a shower and we will talk about everything over dinner."

While Grant was gone, Rae Ann meandered into the kitchen to help with any last minute details. Delicious smells swirled around her and filled her nose. For the first time that day, Rae Ann actually thought of food and was surprised to find that she was famished. She moved to the small bistro table that had been set for two and lit the taper candles. Rae Ann frowned at the bottle of wine that Rosie had chilling in an ice bucket. Perhaps, tonight they should do this alcohol free. For many months, Rae Ann had become increasingly worried about Grant's drinking. She quickly emptied the bucket and put the wine back on the rack above the refrigerator.

Just as Rosie was placing the last dish on the table, Grant breezed in refreshed and looking more handsome than Rae Ann had ever seen him. His eyes were clear and he seemed to float in a pair of linen, drawstring pants and an orange button down shirt that brought out the deep brown of his eyes. Once seated, Rae Ann felt jittery with anticipation. She picked at her meal even though her stomach continued to growl with hunger. Grant on the other hand, ate with gusto, as if he hadn't had a decent meal in weeks. Rae Ann watched him spear an asparagus tip and slip it into his mouth. The fork took a long sensuous decent from his perfect lips and Rae Ann felt something inside her stir. They hadn't been together intimately in nearly a month now. She missed the feel of his hands on her body. Suddenly she knew the time was right.

"I know we have had a lot of problems but I have a feeling that things are going to be a lot better very soon."

"Oh," Grant's interest was clearly peaked. He put his fork on this plate and focused his deep chocolate eyes on her face, "why do you say that?"

"I have resigned from the station. I am moving back here to Rockingham full time."

"Does that mean that Francis has dropped all of the charges against you?"

"Not entirely. He dropped all of the charges against the station but is still planning to pursue charges against me in civil court."

"Dammit, Rae Ann, we don't need this kind of negative publicity. You need to do whatever you need to do to make this go away," Grant said, angrily.

"Grant I'm doing the best I can with what I have. The only way to get Showy to drop the charges is if I admit guilt, and I am not going to do that. I'm not guilty of anything." This is not how Rae Ann had envisioned the conversation to go. In an effort to smooth things back over, she reached across the table and secured her hand over Grant's. "I don't want to talk about that. What I wanted to talk to you about was the resort."

"What about it?" Grant asked with a heavy sigh.

"I want you to give me a job. Any job. I want to learn about the resort and be involved with that part of your life." Rae Ann felt Grant shrink away from her. Tension in the air became so thick that she held her breath to avoid breathing it in. He gave Rae Ann's face an earnest once over.

Did she know? How could she?

The very thought was absurd, but he certainly couldn't have her rifling around at the lodge. He sat for a long time pondering what he should say.

Rae Ann didn't move the whole time. Her large blue eyes were unblinking and full of hope. At last he could hold out no longer. He pulled his hand away from hers and said, "I don't think there is anything you could do."

"What?" Rae Ann asked incredulously, "what do you mean there's nothing for me to do. I will do anything. Desk clerk, housekeeping—"

"No," Grant shouted, "there's nothing, I'm sorry." He stood from the kitchen chair so fast that Rae Ann was sure it would tip over and crash on the floor. She slumped back in her chair and watched him make a hasty exit into the living room. Moments later the front door slammed shut. *Was this the end?*

Rae Ann took a long time clearing the table and doing the dishes. She shunned Rosie's offer to help, instead needing the time to think. Just before retiring to her own room, Rosie approached Rae Ann at the sink. "I have been contemplating a trip to see my son and his family. Now that you are back, maybe this would be a good time to go."

Rae Ann couldn't bring herself to tell Rosie that things hadn't gone well and decided that it would probably be better if the housekeeper wasn't home to witness the final act of the tragic play of Rae Ann's life. Rae Ann forced a smile and nodded in agreement. The older women, ecstatic, rushed to call her family.

Eighteen

Monday, March 15th

Several days crept by before Rae Ann even realized that they had passed. She never left the house and barely even got dressed, as she wrestled with the decision for her future. During the day, Rae Ann sat propped up in bed watching the latest news release regarding her and the Senator. The pale blue surroundings of the expensive bedding and serenely painted walls were not enough to comfort Rae Ann during the endless hours of the day.

As always, Showy managed to look immaculate and forlorn all at the same time. He chanted endlessly about his devotion to the people of Wisconsin and claimed to have been "deeply hurt" by what Rae Ann had done to him. By the end of the week, he was threatening to file a three-point two million-dollar lawsuit against her. The press hounded Showy relentlessly on how he had come to decide on the number that would restore his character and therefore the faith of the people. He shook his head of snowy white hair and stated, "It's only fair."

Rae Ann clambered over the feather pillows for the remote control and turned the television set off. As usual, she was unavailable for comment, even though the phone rang continually and news reporters were camped out at the gated entrance to her home. Rosie had left several of the messages for her on the bedside table each day and the small pieces of paper were piling up. There were three messages from Eddie and one from Marley Cavanaugh. Rae Ann couldn't believe that the woman would have the audacity to try and interview her, but couldn't really blame her. Rae Ann would have done the same thing if the roles were reversed. An exclusive interview with rogue journalist Rae Ann Lewis would be just what Marley needed as a send off piece before leaving for the network. It would secure Marley's career, just as Rae Ann thought the rape story would do for her.

Of course, during those endless hours and never ending days there was no sign of Grant.

Nineteen

Wednesday, April 5th

It was early afternoon on a Wednesday in early April when Rae Ann stood at the floor to ceiling windows in the living room of her house and stared with hatred at the ski resort. Nearly a month had passed since she was asked to resign from the station and still Rae Ann could not answer the questions that continued to hang over her head as dark and menacing as a storm cloud.

Why didn't Grant want her up there? What was he hiding? Rae Ann had asked herself those questions a million times, but never had an answer.

"Miss Rae Ann?"

Rae Ann turned to Rosie with crossed arms and was surprised to see the woman toting a small suitcase in one hand, her winter white cardigan thrown over the other arm. "Yes, Rosie, are you leaving?"

"Yes, Miss, my trip to see the family," Rosie said, reminding Rae Ann of her plans. For a moment, the older woman was afraid that her boss had changed her mind and wanted Rosie to stay.

Rae Ann waved her hands in front of her face and smiled, "of course, I had completely lost track of the days. You have a wonderful time." The two women embraced and Rae Ann went to the telephone to summon the limo driver to take Rosie to the airport.

"That isn't necessary, Miss Rae Ann."

"Trust me, it is. The driver will let you off right at the terminal so you won't have to walk too far."

"Thank you so much. I will miss you."

"Me too, Rosie."

When the door shut behind the housekeeper, Rae Ann felt a deep silence permeate the entire interior of the house. It felt desolate and unlived in. Rosie took with her all the spirit and joy that a home should possess. Even the freshly cut spring bouquet of flowers on the dining room table seemed less colorful and not as beautiful as it had moments ago. Rae Ann wandered through the house, lost as if she were there for the first time. It didn't feel like home. She spent the day cleaning sporadically around the house and fixing herself a light supper of pasta. She had considered going up to the resort for dinner, but felt like a pariah. She didn't want to show her face, embarrassed that the Senator was still on the television calling for her head; as of yet Rae Ann had not been served with any papers. She was certain the Senator was drawing out the inevitable in order to maximize the sympathy of his constituents.

Around ten o'clock, Rae Ann settled into one of the comfy living room chairs with a magazine and a glass of wine. She had been alone many times before but had never felt as lonely as she did this night. Rae Ann sat reading the same paragraph over and over, preoccupied with hoping that Grant would not come home again tonight, but then again hoping he would. With each passing minute and sip of wine, Rae Ann's eyes grew heavier. She had all but fallen asleep when the living room door burst open and Grant stumbled through.

The commotion brought Rae Ann to full consciousness with a pounding heart and head. Grant was so drunk that Rae Ann found it difficult to believe that he had made it home all by himself. His button down shirt was untucked and wrinkled horribly under an unseasonable long wool coat. His dress pants were creased finishing off Grant's unkempt appearance. He bumbled into the living room where she had been reading and slurred, "We need to talk."

Rae Ann knew that it was the beginning of the end. "I can't talk to you like this, Grant," Rae Ann said, feeling like her head could explode right off her shoulders.

"No, you don't understand. There is something really important I have to tell you." He drew out the word 'really' to try to get his point across, but it only made Rae Ann doubt the actual importance of the conversation. He purposely slowed his words so Rae Ann could make out what he was saying, even though he felt a rush to get the confession off his chest. It was too late for forgiveness, he knew that, but he had to rectify the situation. He knew he was the one to blame for their failed marriage and for Rae Ann's misery. He was trying to put the thoughts together in his head, but the alcohol had practically eaten away his ability to think.

Rae Ann watched him from the chair, unsure of what was to come. Grant sounded so earnest, but still it was hard for her to tell how genuine he was being. While Grant settled himself onto the couch, she smoothed a wrinkle in her linen pants and then glanced up to meet his eyes. They looked at each other for a full minute. In that time Rae Ann thought she caught a glimpse of the man she had married. Through sad eyes, Grant could only see what he was about to lose. There was no other way.

"Rae, please?" Grant reached a hand toward her, but when she flinched he pulled it back quickly.

"I'm listening, Grant." Rae Ann tried to keep the edge out of her voice, but it had found its own way in.

"I don't know where to begin. Everything happened so quickly. I didn't know what to do." Grant, unable to meet her eyes, talked to the floor and gestured wildly with his hands.

"Grant, slow down. You're not making any sense. Let me get us some coffee and then we'll calm down and you can tell me whatever it is. All right?"

Grant nodded in her direction and flopped heavily back against the sofa cushions. Rae Ann unfolded herself from the armchair and crossed the distance that melded the living room into the kitchen. For the first time that day, Rae Ann was glad that Rosie had left on her vacation. She certainly didn't need anyone witnessing this display of impropriety.

While Rae Ann emptied the spent grounds of this morning's pot of coffee and filled the machine with water, she finally decided to tell Grant that she was leaving. The decision had not been an easy one to come to, but in the end it became the only option. For her very sanity, she could not go on like this. She would listen to what he had to say and then inform him of her decision.

Rae Ann poured the steaming coffee into a cup and then cursed as it splashed over the rim, spilling onto the countertop. She retrieved a dishrag and then stood crying silently into the dark liquid until she couldn't shed another tear. Rae Ann wiped up the mess and took the cup with her into the living room.

Grant had slumped back against the cushions of the couch. His chin had fallen onto his chest and from where she stood she was unable to tell if he was breathing. She quickly placed the mug onto the nearest table and rushed to his side. She shook his shoulder vigorously, noticing that he had not even bothered to take off his coat. A small snort escaped him and he repositioned his head to be more comfortable. Not dead after all, just passed out. "Grant?" she gave him another firm shake, "didn't you want to tell me something?"

Rae Ann heard a tiny whisper escape his lips, so she leaned over his body and listened carefully to determine the words. She wasn't expecting what came next, but the three words Grant muttered would forever change her life. "There's a woman..."

Rae Ann straightened off the couch so fast the sudden head rush made her dizzy. What did she think he was going to say? Did she really expect him to say that things were going to change? Had she wanted things to go back to the way they were so badly that she had completely ignored the obvious truth?

Rae Ann took the opportunity to pack the bare necessities into a couple of boxes she found in the garage and randomly pulled clothes from her closet and stuffed them into a suitcase. She carried everything with her into the four car garage and passed up the Lexus Grant had given her, instead choosing to cram everything into the backseat and trunk of the old Honda she had owned before they married.

Rae Ann was about to close the trunk when she remembered the set of pearls her grandmother had given her for Christmas when she was thirteen. Rae Ann dashed back through the living room oblivious of Grant's presence, into the bedroom and back to the open closet. She knelt down and removed a shoe rack from the floor. To the average untrained eye, it would seem like nothing more than quite simply the floor of the closet. But when Rae Ann reached around behind the left bi-fold mirrored door and pressed a code blindly into the key pad, a rather large safe was lifted like an elevator into the closet.

Broken promises and failed marriages, 1st floor, Rae Ann mused sarcastically. The top of the safe was still covered in the carpet that matched the floor of the bedroom, the rest was a cold slate colored metal. Rae Ann quickly twisted the dial into the combination and opened the heavy iron door. Inside there was really nothing of great significance, Rae Ann shuffled through a couple of legal looking documents and an old coin collection to retrieve the blue velvet box that housed the precious strand of pearls. On top of the box, lay a small handgun that Grant kept in the house for safety reasons. She gingerly picked it up and turned it over in her hands. Rae Ann hated Grant at the moment, but not enough to kill him. He would surely suffer enough in the months to come without Rae Ann. At least Rae hoped so. She moved the gun aside. Underneath the pearl's casing lay a manila envelope that Rae Ann had not seen in the safe before. She snatched it up and slipped the paper contents out halfway.

Flipping through the documents, Rae Ann recognized her marriage certificate, copies of Grant's will and blueprints of the resort. Not wanting to waste anymore time she shoved the papers back into the envelope and dashed from the room leaving the safe where it was, the door open. With the pearls held safely against her chest, she paused only once at the door to survey what she had lost in just one short year. Their gorgeous house was now just another broken home. Grant, once the most handsome, sought after bachelor in town was just another drunk, dead-beat husband. Rae Ann turned the overhead light off bringing moonlight in through the bank of windows that made up the north wall of their home. The stars seemed unusually bright and beckoned at Rae Ann to follow them.

She could make out the outline of the ski resort that stood just up the hillside from their property. The corners of Rae Ann's mouth turned down and she lowered her head in surrender. The resort had always been Grant's first love. It was the thing to which he was really married. Rae Ann knew this when they met, but it still hurt to think that she couldn't compete with an overpriced resort for her husband's love.

Then again, she thought, *there was another woman as well.*

Rae Ann wrenched the three-carat solitaire and wedding band off her finger and tossed it into Grant's lap. It was then that Rae Ann realized she was still holding onto the manila envelope of papers. She tucked it in the crook of her elbow along with the pearls and didn't look back. Grant never even stirred when the door slammed shut.

~ * ~

Grant felt the banging inside his head moments before he realized that someone was at the door. "Rosie... Rosie..." Grant slurred into the couch pillow. His mouth and throat felt like they had been covered in cotton, he opened and closed his jaws, feeling his tongue stick roughly to the roof of his mouth. The banging persisted. "Damn," Grant cursed, remembering something about the housekeeper going to California to visit her family.

"Well, she won't be answering the door from there," Grant said laughing drunkenly at his own joke. He groaned audibly and attempted to pull himself into a sitting position. Having forgotten about his uninvited guests, Grant marveled drunkenly at how heavy and awkward his body had become. "Rae Ann, there's someone at the door," Grant yelled into the empty house. The banging sounded harshly again, so Grant picked himself up and weaved a path across the carpet, shrugging off his wool overcoat and discarding it on the floor. As he reached for the handle, there was a loud cracking sound and the door exploded inward towards Grant's outstretched hand.

"What the hell..." Grant muttered, swaying on his feet. He squinted his eyes to focus on the person that had invaded his house and then shut them altogether. Willing his brain to make sense of the situation, Grant opened his eyes and stared intently into the steely eyes of the intruder.

"Where's the disk, Grant?"

Twenty

Friday, April 7th

The beginning of the end, Rae Ann repeated to herself over and over as she clicked on her blinker and crossed two lanes of traffic without even glancing in her rear view mirror. A horn honked alarmingly behind her, but she never even heard it. She was driving recklessly and she knew it, but she didn't care. Rae Ann exhaled slowly and briefly closed her eyes. The night was as black as her mood, crying tears of rain that seemingly had no end. As she meandered across the lanes of the highway, Rae Ann absently wondered how people in previous generations had driven without the aid of those tiny reflective disks that were the only thing keeping Rae Ann out of the ditch.

Long ago, she had turned off the mindless rambling of a radio personality, not really caring whether aliens or homosexuals would be the first to ruin the world. Rae Ann knew that she was would continue searching for the moment when everything had broken and crumbled in her life. It was her specialty. As a reporter, Rae Ann would fine tune every single detail until the story flowed so perfectly and there were no mistakes to be found. *Too bad that doesn't work in everyday life,* Rae Ann mused silently.

She tried not to reflect on the not so distant past, but the lonely stretches of highway had given her plenty of time to think and she could remember in vivid detail the day that had started the changes in her life. The day she had met Grant Spencer. When Rae Ann finally cared enough to glance back to the highway, she could just make out the word "saloon" on a roadside sign about a quarter mile up on the right. Each letter of the quickly nearing sign was a different color casting a distorted rainbow on the rain streaked windshield.

"There's no place like home," Rae Ann whispered, her eyes suddenly welling up with tears. She had no idea how long she had been driving the same endless expanse of highway. What they said was true, it did all begin to look the same after awhile. Rae Ann did know that she was headed west, but that was pretty much it. She had no plan to speak of. She would deal with her divorce and apartment later when she had time to think.

The fluorescent green numbers on the dashboard told her that it had been more than five hours of driving without so much as a bathroom break. Instead of the much desired roadside motel, the saloon would just have to do. Rae Ann pulled off of the highway and entered the fairly full parking lot. As she remembered, the resort had seemingly always been packed. There was never a shortage of people milling about, talking and laughing. Rae Ann had avoided it as much as she could, while her social husband had thrived on the activity and attention. She wondered now, if she had taken more of an interest in it from the beginning, if she would still be with her husband.

With a silent scold, Rae Ann shifted the car into park and paused, the windshield wipers squawked in protest as the rain slowed to a miserable dribble. Knowing that she must look frightful, Rae Ann grabbed her purse in search of a comb and some lipstick. But one long look in the lighted visor mirror was enough to stop the comb dead in its path, halfway into her shoulder length blonde hair. In the dim light of the saloon's parking lot, Rae Ann could just make out the remainders of her once happy home now resting in the cramped back seat of her Honda. She forced a laugh, but tears instantly stung her tired eyes. It was depressing to think of all her dreams and hopes now packed into two boxes and a suitcase headed to an unknown destination. Wordlessly cursing herself, Rae Ann busied her hands, trying to find the discarded pack of cigarettes she kept under the driver's seat.

"God, I wish I hadn't quit," she cursed aloud. She had given up so much for him, her sense of self, her freedom and she had sat back and let him take over. Now Rae Ann was berating herself for not making it work. At that moment she couldn't have hated herself more. This thought made her angry and she hastened her quest for the stale half pack of Marlboros. Instead, her hand came in contact with the leftovers of last nights drive through dinner, a pile of forgotten junk mail and a road map that never got folded back into it's original position.

Giving up her search, Rae Ann settled her head into her hands against the steering wheel, ready to cry the night away, but her car had other plans. The horn honked loudly, as her hands came into contact with that spot you can never find when someone cuts in front of you on the freeway. Rae Ann jumped at the ear-splitting noise then laughed at the absurdity of her situation. Here she was having a breakdown in the parking lot of some no name bar, in some no name town in her pursuit to outrun reality. Rae Ann's laugh had almost reached hysteria when she finally found the door handle and stumbled out of the car into the rain.

Using her purse as a makeshift umbrella, she managed to keep her head semi-dry and dodge the ankle deep puddles. But by the time Rae Ann got inside, her sandal-clad feet were completely soaked. Trying not to imagine her unsightly appearance, Rae Ann melted into the crowd of strangers that lined the inner sanctum of the bar. The atmosphere wrapped around her like a warm blanket and drew her farther inside. She took in the sounds of the music and the smell of the cooking food and felt herself loosening up. Rae Ann smiled at the unfamiliar site and relaxed just long enough to remember that she had to go to the bathroom.

She managed to make her way through the crowded dance floor to the neon sign that announced her arrival at the "indoor outhouse." It was nothing less than expected, instead of stalls the bathroom had old wooden plank dividers and a wooden box had been smartly fashioned around the toilet seat to give the place an authentic look. Rae Ann was just happy to see that unlike their counterpart, these toilets actually flushed. As she washed her hands, she risked a quick glance in the mirror over the sink. Her image stared back as expressionless as she felt. Although a little soggy, she was not the natural disaster once thought. A few quick fixes and she was ready for public viewing again. She dodged around another woman entering the bathroom and broke out into the dimly lit main area. Rae Ann pulled in a deep breath and felt her senses absorb the aroma of barbecue and French fries. Surrendering to her empty stomach, Rae Ann clambered onto a barstool and signaled the waitress.

"I'll take a beer and whatever is easiest to cook," Rae Ann shouted about the crowd.

"Honey, you look like you could use some milk and a good night's sleep," the waitress replied, giving Rae Ann the once over, "You have got a matching set of luggage under those eyes."

Rae Ann looked down self-consciously, but the waitress was no longer paying attention. Her eyes had already wandered onto the dance floor, her hand tapping out the rhythm to the song that blared from the jukebox. When Rae Ann looked back up, the waitress was blowing a huge bubble with her gum. Her fire red hair was twisted into a lopsided bun held only by a pencil. But sometime during the night the pencil had worked its way out far enough to allow the escape of a few loose curls. They coiled their way down the waitress's pale face. The name Terri was stitched in the upper left corner of a T-shirt that was two sizes too small for Terri's well endowed chest making the words Buttercup's Bar stretch around until you could only read "ttercup's B."

Rae Ann chuckled, "you're right. I'll just have the special and iced tea, please." Terri didn't bother to write the down the order, she just nodded her head in time to the music and shuffled off toward the kitchen. Rae Ann took the opportunity to look around the bar. High-backed booths lined the far wall next to a row of electronic dart machines. Small round tables had been pushed back far enough to allow for a makeshift dance floor. Rae Ann scanned the room with her eyes low, taking in first one sight then the next.

The first person that came into focus just happened to be the most beautiful man that Rae Ann had ever seen. He looked as if he had taken time off from his post on the cover of GQ to teach the less fortunate patrons in the bar a good hard lesson in fashion. Rae Ann gaped openly as the Greek God eased his lean frame against the jukebox and ran a hand absently through his thick, mahogany colored hair. He was deep in conversation with two other men. They were cute, but certainly couldn't hold a candle to GQ.

As if she had spoken her last thought aloud, the man tilted his head back and released a husky laugh into the air. His smile produced a dimple deep in his cheek and his pearly white teeth actually did that sparkle thing they show on toothpaste commercials. One of the men standing with Mr. Perfect put a hand on his forearm and then leaned over and kissed him full on the mouth. Rae Ann was so shocked that she had to grab a hold of the bar to keep from falling off her barstool.

She glanced around in confusion, taking in the rest of the bar's customers. A female couple stood to her right with arms draped lightly around each other's waists enjoying a conversation with another lady that had a woman in red cowboy boots perched on her lap. On the dance floor, two men were slow dancing cheek to cheek, their hands resting comfortably on the seats of each other's jeans. Everywhere Rae Ann looked, she saw happy, same sex couples enjoying the music and drinks. She laughed and shook her head.

Geez, Rae Ann, you're looking for a new life but this is pushing it, she thought, humorously.

Her food chose that moment to arrive. Rae Ann rubbed her hands together at the prospect of diving into the mound of pork barbecue that steamed on her plate. "Thanks, Terri, I really needed—" Rae Ann stopped short when her eyes met, not the infamous Terri's, but a new set. This particular pair of eyes shone very green and bright, even in the dim light of the bar. They seemed very at home on an evenly tanned face, set beneath the most business-like eyebrows Rae Ann had ever seen. In his smile she could see both warmth and amusement.

"Sorry to disappoint you, but Terri's shift ended. You're stuck with me." Rae Ann just stared at the man in front of her with eyes narrowed as she sized him up. Slowly a frown replaced the initial shock.

"No, I'm not, if that's what you're thinking."

"What? No. I'm not thinking anything," Rae Ann stammered.

"It's okay. Everyone just assumes, you know? Working here and all, can give you that kind of reputation," the bartender explained as he settled Rae Ann's hot plate of barbecue down on the bar. "And just what is your story?"

Rae Ann's eyes widened at the question and she began to regret coming in the bar.

"I mean, you don't exactly look like the type that normally comes in here either," he waved a hand toward the crowd of gay and lesbian patrons.

"Oh, right," Rae Ann laughed nervously, "I thought I was the only heterosexual in here." As soon as the words were out of her mouth Rae Ann glanced down at her plate. He seemed like a nice enough guy, but Rae Ann knew that the food before her would be ice cold, and possibly days old, by the time she finished telling this stranger the sordid tale of her life that had brought her into the bar.

But then again, Rae Ann had been on the road for a long time with no one to talk to, not even risking a call to Eddie, and if she didn't say something quick the bartender was going to walk away. And as much as Rae Ann hated to admit, she too needed some form of human contact. Besides, this guy was kind of cute. The man stood patiently, a wry smile playing on his lips.

"Well, for starters," Rae Ann sighed, "a broken marriage, a ruined career and a very urgent need to pee brought me right into this fine establishment. Oh, yeah, I also had an appetite the size of..." Rae Ann glanced around and then asked, "What state am I in?"

"Illinois," the bartender said, his eyebrows raising slightly.

"Illinois?" Rae Ann asked incredulously.

Illinois wasn't west of Wisconsin? Hadn't she been heading west? Just how long had she been driving?

Suddenly Rae Ann began to question every single move she had made since leaving Grant. Maybe that wasn't the right thing to do. For Christ's sake, she couldn't even drive in the right direction; what made her think she could start over? Rae Ann shook her head to clear the thoughts of a past life that threatened to snuff out any promise of a new beginning. "I'm going to need a drink. A shot. A shot of anything, quick."

Rae Ann groaned and pushed away the congealed mess that vaguely resembled the barbecue she'd ordered. The bartender was back in a flash offering a small glass of unidentifiable dark brown liquid that smelled like gasoline and felt just as flammable as it hit the bottom of her stomach erupting into liquid flames. Rae Ann was by no means a drinker but this was by no means an average day in her life. She took another quick shot of the alcohol, this time letting it slowly cauterize a path down her throat.

"Hey, are you all right?"

Rae Ann started to lift her head to meet Grant's voice and then realized that it wasn't Grant that had asked the question. It was the non-gay bartender in the gay bar somewhere in the great state of Illinois. Rae Ann burst into tears.

"Whoa, whoa, there's no crying here. Hey, come on now, you're making me feel bad. Listen, I don't even know your name. How am I supposed to be comforting, when I can't even call you by name," the bartender rambled on trying to find the right words to stop this strange woman from melting onto the bar. He looked around for an escape, but found none.

"Rae..." Rae Ann hiccupped.

"Ray? Your name is Ray? Well then you *are* in the right bar," Kyle straightened from his crouched position.

"Ann," Rae Ann continued.

"Ann, its Ann now?" Kyle knitted his brows in confusion. Rae Ann shook her head and tried to calm her breathing.

"My name is Rae Ann," Rae Ann grabbed a bar napkin and blotted at her eyes, "Rae Ann Spencer. No wait, Spencer is Grant's name. I am Rae Ann Lewis. No, Lewis is just my television personality. I guess my name is just Rae Ann. You know, like Cher or Madonna. I am just Rae Ann." The speech had composed her but the realization of not quite belonging to anyone brought on a fresh set of tears.

"Okay, okay, *just* Rae Ann, there is no reason to cry," the bartender soothed pulling a box of Kleenex from under the bar. "My name is Kyle."

Rae Ann stared at the man inquisitively as if she couldn't quite understand what he was saying. The sharp talons of the alcohol were embedded deep in her brain, obviously shadowing her better judgment, because all she could think to do was giggle. She just started giggling and couldn't quit.

"Kyle? Kyle is a child's name," she concluded. The fact that this Kyle had once been a child never crossed her alcohol soaked brain. With tears streaking her face, Rae Ann began laughing loudly covering her mouth to hide her smile. The combination of her laughing and crying bought on the hiccups.

"*You* are drunk," Kyle, the bartender said, matter-of-factly, "Where are you staying? I can't let you drive out of here if you're drunk." Rae Ann's giggles pulled up short. The long, sad face she had gotten used to wearing, sagged another couple of inches toward the floor.

"I don't have anywhere to stay. I am only passing through. I was headed out West. If I'm lucky I will eventually just run out of road and end up at the bottom of the ocean," Rae Ann huffed, a new set of tears balanced precariously on the rims of her eyes.

"Well, what kind of gentleman would I be if I just left you to drown in your own tears?" Kyle smiled, touched by her sadness.

"Don't worry about me. I don't know any gentlemen, so I wouldn't know the difference anyway," Rae Ann squirmed in her chair then rose slightly, "I need to get going. I have a long drive ahead of me."

"Oh no you don't," Kyle said reaching across the bar to push her gently back onto the barstool. Her shoulder trembled slightly beneath his palm and her smallness made his breath catch. "I, uh, I'll be right back."

~ * ~

Kyle moved quickly through the swinging doors that separated the bar from the kitchen. To his right was the employee bathroom and he quickly ducked inside. He had caught sight of her when the door swung open and she rushed in with the wind and rain. The second before she had been swallowed up in the crowd, Kyle heard himself shout her name.

Not her name, not Rae Ann.

Another name.

A name that had left him cold as ice and visibly shaken. His stomach had twisted into a thousand knots and his breathing had ceased all together. She had looked around almost searching for him and then suddenly she was gone. But not like always. This time she had not disappeared, but was only temporarily blocked by the horde of people. She had made her way toward the bathrooms, but in Kyle's mind she had been looking for him. The reflection in the mirror was not of Kyle's face instead he saw a scene of his life playing out like a situation comedy.

She was walking toward him with a stern look on her face. "You know the rules."

Kyle glanced down and realized that he was still wearing his gun and holster on the hips of his policeman's uniform. "Sorry." He quickly unbuckled the holster and placed it on the console table in their apartment. When he turned back she was poised to jump into his arms. They held onto each other until Kyle feared he would crush her with his love, but just before she pulled away she quickly kissed the soft spot behind his ear.

"I love you, Officer Bennett."

Kyle ran the tap cold and then splashed his face. He had to stop thinking like this. That drunk lady at the bar was named Rae Ann Lewis or Spencer or whatever. "That is not your pride and joy out there," Kyle said into the mirror.

At that moment Klein Bennett opened the bathroom door and stared at his little brother, Kyle, with sad eyes.

~ * ~

While Kyle was gone, Rae Ann stared at herself in the mirror behind the bar. Pathetic seemed to be the only word that came to mind. What was she doing here? Wouldn't it have been easier to have just stayed in Wisconsin and worked out her problems? Rae Ann wasn't even sure it was all right for her to even leave the state since the Senator still had charges pending against her. Always on the run did not seem to be the answer, but neither was another night living in limbo. Rae Ann had left so suddenly. It had been two days, but she was almost certain that Grant had not yet noticed her disappearing act. He probably just assumed that she turned tail and went back to her apartment in Madison.

Just how long would it be before he sought her out? Rae Ann wondered. It was hard for her to believe that just two nights ago she had sat in one of the overstuffed armchairs she had picked out for their big comfy living room. A home she would never see again.

"Hey, just Rae Ann? Rae Ann?"

A voice came into Rae Ann's thoughts through the mud that had settled into her brain. She sat up slowly, at one point thinking her head had somehow gotten glued to the bar.

"Rae Ann, this is my brother, Klein. He owns the bar," Kyle said appearing at her side.

"I'm sorry, Mr. Klein, I was just resting. I will leave now. I don't want any trouble." Rae Ann's words slithered out of her mouth like a snake in the sand.

"No, Rae Ann. It's okay. I have to work till three a.m. so you are going to stay at Klein's place tonight," Kyle said placing a hand lightly on her shoulder. Concern showed in his emerald eyes and he wondered how a woman could get so drunk off two shots of Wild Turkey.

"I most certainly am not staying at Klein's place tonight," Rae Ann huffed, suddenly realizing that she was a very vulnerable woman consorting with two strange men. She fought to keep her anger and fear in check as the alcoholic haze lifted slowly from her shoulders.

"Ooh, she's a feisty one," a new voice cracked smartly above the noise, "Calm down, sweetie, I am not some crazy lunatic." Rae Ann turned in the direction of the new voice. An equally adorable man stood to Kyle's right staring at her with the same striking green eyes. Klein. "Plus," Klein continued, "I'm the gay one. I don't want anything you've got under those off the rack Capri pants. If I did, I would get an operation."

Rae Ann smiled in spite of herself and felt the twinge of fear ebbing away. "Well, I can see where that works wonders as a pick up line, but really, guys, I'm fine." Rae Ann stood up to prove her point, perhaps a little too quickly and ended up dropping right back onto the barstool with a thud.

"Yeah, you're fine all right. Now quit arguing and come on," Kyle said, easily slipping an arm around her waist and guiding her towards the door while Klein grabbed her purse. Kyle was very aware of how she felt in his arms and it made his knees feel weak. He closed his eyes briefly to gain his composure. When he finally looked up, Klein was frowning at him and the way he was holding the woman.

Rae Ann did not seem to notice the exchange of glances between the brothers but she was thankful that the rain had ebbed to a slow miserable drizzle. The cool mist on her face was refreshing and she lifted her face heavenward.

Kyle and Klein managed to settle Rae Ann into the front seat of Klein's sleek black Mercedes, without much more trouble. She had suddenly become a rag doll that felt like all her stuffing was about to make a grand entrance. Kyle and Klein had a fleeting conversation and then Rae Ann was on her way. Somewhere.

~ * ~

Kyle watched the car pull onto the highway, then dash out of sight. He let out a slow breath and raised his chin to the night sky. At first, he had thought he was just having another one of his daydreams, but this woman had turned out to be very real. He hadn't been struck by a woman this way since... well for a long time. Kyle smiled now at the thought of her toes barely touching the bottom rung of the bar stool. Water dripping steadily off her shoes and pant legs, leaving a small puddle under the stool. Her arms had been crossed tightly against her chest with her small hands cupping each elbow. She had looked like a scared turtle trying to climb back inside her shell.

Seeing her had sent that pang of pleasure and pain you feel when you need something in the worst way. It was something he never thought he would feel again. Kyle still stared towards the heavens, but when no one answered his silent prayer, he turned and went back into the bar.

~ * ~

A half an hour later, Klein had Rae Ann fixed up in the spare bedroom of his spacious apartment on Clover Street. Two days of non-stop driving and sleeping on second-rate motel mattresses had taken its toll on Rae Ann. She barely took in the surroundings of white wicker furniture and the homemade quilt that blanketed her shoulders before drifting off into the welcome oblivion of sleep.

Klein stepped from the room on light feet, aware that the woman's breathing had already taken on the rhythmic quality of an ocean wave. He couldn't wait to hear his brother's explanation for this. Klein had taken care of Kyle for as long as he could remember. He didn't want to see Kyle hurt again, but he'd be damned if he could tell the boy what to do. Now he had a strange woman snoring softly in his spare bedroom. Klein just shook his head as he shuffled towards the master bedroom. He knew from experience that he could wait all night for Kyle's answer, but with Kyle things were never that simple.

Twenty-one

Saturday, April 8ᵗʰ

A shrill ringing broke into Kyle's restless dream, threatening to steal the pleasant images from his subconscious. He tried to hold on to the images, but they faded in and out of focus before finally disappearing. It had been weeks since the dream. He was sure that his chance encounter with the woman had sparked them back into life. Kyle grumbled and pulled the pillow over his head in an attempt to block out the harsh sound and morning light that spilled through bedroom curtains, which didn't quite meet in the middle. When he realized that the ringing was not going to stop, he slowly unfolded himself from under the protective shroud of blankets and reached for the phone.

"Yep," Kyle croaked into the receiver.

"Kyle! It's seven thirty in the morning," Klein rumbled into Kyle's ear.

"Great, call me at ten o'clock. If it is only seven thirty that means I've only had four hours of sleep. People can't live on four hours of sleep," Kyle explained, moving the phone back to its home on the nightstand.

"What are you going to do about this woman, Kyle?" Klein shouted loudly knowing that his brother was probably about to hang up on him. The question stopped Kyle in mid-motion.

Woman?

"Kyle, I told you I had to meet Ryan at the Buttercup this morning and I am not inclined to leave strange women in my apartment... alone." The last fingers of sleep lost their hold on Kyle and he sat up stretching.

"Okay, okay, I'll be right up. Christ, Klein, she weighs all of a hundred pounds, I think she's pretty harmless. Besides, this isn't the White House."

Kyle smiled at the image his mind had conjured up. He could see Klein standing in the White House Rose garden dictating plans to have a disco ball installed in the Lincoln bedroom. In less than ten minutes, Kyle had pulled on a rumpled pair of jeans and an old T-shirt that proclaimed him 'super stud.' He took the stairs to his brother's upstairs apartment two at a time, his bare feet making light slaps on the hard wood floors. Klein stood at the breakfast bar looking over the order lists for the various types of alcohol that the Buttercup served.

As usual, he was perfectly dressed and groomed. Kyle sometimes wondered if his big brother slept standing up so as to not put a crease in his expensive silk pajamas.

"Coffee," Kyle said, his voice still gruff from sleeping.

"You look as if you could stand to be submerged in it," Klein said, his face showing the blatant disapproval of Kyle's outfit. Kyle shrugged off the comment and took the steaming cup Klein offered. He walked over to the living room windows and looked out over the town.

It wasn't exactly spring yet in southern Illinois. The air still held a crisp bite in the morning, but by afternoon the sun would be blazing. Kyle wished he had the day off, but Klein was counting on him to fill in while he hired a new employee. Rae Ann chose that moment to make her entrance.

"Hi."

Both men looked in the direction of the tiny voice. Rae Ann looked away embarrassed, self-consciously running a hand over her unruly hair, then down over her rumpled clothes. She could feel the heat flushing her cheeks as the brothers stared. She stood all of five feet four, although her driver's license proclaimed her to be five six.

She was thin, almost too thin. Losing your career and your marriage within a couple of weeks can do that to a person.

Rae Ann stood now with her arms at her sides, hands clenched into tiny fists. Her khaki Capri pants and white short sleeved sweater were creased from their use as pajamas. She restlessly shifted her weight from one bare foot to the next, wishing someone would say something to take the focus off of her.

To Klein, Rae Ann looked like a child waking up on Christmas morning. He half expected her to begin rubbing her sapphire eyes with those tiny balled up fists. To Kyle, she looked beautiful. Her freshness seemed to radiate off of her, even in the clothes she had worn the night before. A breath caught in his throat and he had to cough to keep from choking.

"Kyle?" Klein prompted, when his brother simply stood and stared.

"Oh right. Coffee. I mean we have coffee. I mean would you like some coffee?" Kyle stammered, starting for the brewing pot before Rae Ann could even answer.

"That would be great. Thanks." Rae Ann stared at the brothers and wondered how they could ever share the same bloodline. Klein was perched at the end of the marble-topped counter, his posture straight and perfect. His shoes were so shiny, Rae Ann was sure she could see her reflection in them from clear across the room. He wore very smart looking navy blue chinos and a crisp, white shirt that had been ironed and starched so sharply Rae Ann imagined he could use the sleeves as scissors if he moved his arms back and forth in front of him.

Her gaze shifted to Kyle's not so tidy ensemble. He looked as if he had bathed at the local car wash, clothes and all. Regardless of his clothes, the younger of the two brothers was clearly handsome. His sandy blond hair was shaggy and Rae Ann could detect a hint of a curl in the ends. She watched him stretch his arm toward the counter to replace the coffee pot, causing his T-shirt to pull tightly against his body. There was no extra room as the fabric slid across his flat belly. Rae Ann smiled, envious of the carefree attitude Kyle displayed.

Klein pointed a graceful hand towards the counter indicating that she should sit with them. Since Rae Ann had spent the night in this apartment, without meeting an untimely demise, she figured it was her duty to at least be polite. She climbed up on the twisted piece of metal that contemporary art called a chair, feeling as if she had known these two men a lot longer than just one night.

"Your furniture is so interesting," Rae Ann stated, glancing around to the living room. "Yes, well, I travel a lot and pick up different pieces here and there," Klein explained.

"It's so different from the furniture in your spare bedroom," Rae Ann pointed out.

"That was our Mom's stuff," Kyle interjected.

"Oh," Rae Ann didn't know what else to say, so she didn't say anything at all. Klein smiled and winked over his paperwork and she smiled gratefully.

Rae Ann had just finished her first cup of coffee when Klein announced that he had business that needed his attention. "I hope your night was comfortable. It was a pleasure to meet you." Klein kissed her hand and was gone.

"Well, I must have made quite the impression on your brother. I guess it isn't everyday that some strange, drunk woman just happens into your life," Rae Ann muttered nervously, realizing that she was very alone with Kyle. She watched him out of the corner of her eye, but he wasn't looking at her.

"Listen, Rae Ann, don't be embarrassed about last night. Klein and I, we're good people. Most of the people that you are going to meet in this town are friendly," Kyle said, sauntering into the living room area of the apartment and perching on the arm of an orange wingback chair.

"Well, I probably won't be meeting too many more people in this town. Just passing through and all," Rae Ann said, following him, "but since we're talking. Just what town am I in, Mr. Friendly?"

"Harrisburg. Harrisburg, Illinois. Population one thousand two hundred and six," Kyle's voice rose emphatically with every word. Rae Ann's mouth tugged up at the corners and she dipped her head to hide her amusement.

"And you? Where are do hail from?" Kyle asked absently, as if he wasn't really interested.

"Wisconsin. So, do you and Klein live here together?" Rae Ann asked, redirecting the attention off of herself. Kyle didn't press the issue.

"Kind of. I live in an apartment downstairs. Klein owns the building and he lets me live here, if I promise to look out for the place when he is on one of his many vacations. It's not such a bad arrangement," Kyle shrugged.

His honesty struck a chord in Rae Ann. She didn't even know this man, but he seemed to be perfectly willing to tell her his life story. She had never been so candid with anyone about her own life. Not even Grant. And she didn't have any close friends in Wisconsin. Especially if she couldn't count Eddie.

"So, does Klein live here alone?" Rae Ann pried, as she moved toward the purple couch.

"As far as I know," Kyle shrugged again, "we try not to get into each other's business." Rae Ann didn't believe that for a second. Kyle and his brother seemed very close.

"How about you?" Rae Ann absently fingered the tassel on one of the decorative throw pillows "do you live alone?" She hadn't intended to ask. It was really none of her business. Besides, she was a married woman, what did it matter anyway?

"It's just me, oh, and Jasmine," Kyle confessed into his cup of coffee.

"Jasmine?" Rae Ann felt her heart slip a little and silently scolded herself for being so childish. "Is Jasmine your girlfriend?" Rae Ann saw her manner's flying right out the window. She was being rude, but this guy had her so intrigued.

"No," Kyle shook his head and grinned, "Jasmine is my cat."

"Oh," Rae Ann smiled back, "your cat."

"I know, I know..." Kyle groaned, reading her mind, "come on let's get your car from the Buttercup. Plus, you look like you could use a shower." He placed his coffee mug on the glass coffee table and reached out his hands to pull her from the couch.

Still smiling, Rae Ann reached up her arms and allowed herself to be helped up. Only when she was finally standing steadily beside him did she realize how close they were. She stared up into his eyes and felt his piercing stare move deep into her. No one moved or spoke for what seemed like an eternity, until Rae Ann could take the silence no more.

"We should, um, get going," she cleared her throat. This seemed to unlock Kyle from his trance and he stepped back from her.

"Right." Rae Ann grabbed her purse that had managed to find its way into Klein's apartment and followed Kyle to the door. His lanky frame was already bounding down the stairs at top speed. His truck was parked on the east side of the building facing the grocery store and post office. Rae Ann put her hand on the door handle then slowly pulled it back. She glanced around while trying to wrestle her sunglasses from the depths of her purse.

The southern Illinois sun was trying to make an appearance, but was being upstaged by a couple of angry looking clouds that had lingered from last night's storm. People were milling about the streets ducking in and out of the grocery store in search of picnic supplies or just some ingredients for a quick breakfast. Rae Ann had no idea what time it was but her stomach rumbled at the thought of food. Did she eat last night? She didn't think so.

Suddenly, embarrassed by last night's performance, Rae Ann scrambled into the truck and slammed the door. She felt Kyle getting into the truck beside her. Pulling his long body into the seemingly small space that made up the driver's side appeared impossible. Rae Ann was sure that after all the turning and repositioning, he was still not going to fit, but at the last minute he settled into the spot that he had surely sat in a thousand times before.

As Kyle pulled the truck out of the town, everyone they passed raised a hand and waved. Kyle politely waved back. Rae Ann smiled to herself. The town seemed so warm and inviting, the kind of place she would have liked to grow up in. The people reminded her of Harold Spellman, who never had an unfriendly word to say. "You know, Kyle, I don't even know your last name."

"Bennett. Well, that is my stepfather's last name. He adopted us," Kyle said, never taking his eyes off the road. Again, Rae Ann was again amazed at how much information he shared with her. She peered out the passenger window and watched the road whir by her.

The long stretch of highway reminded her of the road that had first brought her into Wisconsin all those years ago.

Kyle gave a casual glance in Rae Ann's direction, but could tell by the pained look on her face that he shouldn't talk. He wondered what she was thinking about that would bring on such an expression of hurt. They continued to ride the rest of the way in silence, but Kyle's mind raced the entire time. He had to think of something and quick. Of course, he had no idea what he could possibly do. The small woman in the passenger seat intrigued him like no one ever had. Here she was, in her obviously pricey clothes, hidden behind expensive sunglasses and looking more out of place than a hula dancer on snow skis.

He glanced over at the petite hands that were casually lying in her lap. There was no tangible wedding ring, but the distinct outline of pale flesh on her left ring finger suggested one had very recently been worn. Last night at the bar she had rambled about a husband and being married. These were all very good reasons to let her off by her sensible Honda and let her drive out of his life. Kyle knew, of course, that he could never do that. Already he was in way over his head.

Rae Ann smelled the Buttercup before it came into clear view. She closed the mental book of her past and perked up in the passenger seat, inhaling the delicious scents.

"Smells so good," Rae Ann whispered to herself.

"Oh," Kyle said, jumping at the opportunity, "are you hungry? This is actually a rare occasion. Klein is having a breakfast meeting with the liquor vendor." He shifted into park beside his brother's massive black car.

"I could eat a horse," Rae Ann exclaimed, hopping out of the truck and starting for the entrance.

"No, wait, around this way," Kyle bounded up behind her and circled her waist with his clumsy hands, "I don't want to interrupt the meeting." He felt her stiffen in his grasp and he pulled his hands back as if he'd been shocked.

Rae Ann felt his hands drop, but she did not relax. It had been a long time since someone had touched her and, from his fumbling mannerisms, Rae Ann guessed it had been even longer for Kyle. They snuck into the back entrance, giggling like junior high kids and skirted around the cooks and delivery men that filled the cramped area of the kitchen. Kyle seated her in a small office off the kitchen, which Rae Ann perceived to be Klein's by the outlandish décor.

Khaki wallpaper was stuck floor to ceiling on every wall and a zebra print border swirled around the room, making Rae Ann's eyes swim if she stared at it for more than a minute. An elephant head was hung on the wall behind the scuffed desk, its trunk curled into an eternal "o" and a six foot wooden giraffe stared at Rae Ann from the far corner behind two bamboo guest's chairs. Several pictures adorned the walls, including one with Klein in full safari gear holding the butt end of a gun.

Rae Ann was still surveying the room when Kyle arrived with a plate full of every kind of breakfast food she could imagine. Fresh fruit and bagels were piled on top of fluffy scrambled eggs, sausage, bacon, and pancakes. Rae Ann dug in as if she had never eaten before, devouring the pancakes and bacon in record time. As she started on the fruit, she realized that Kyle was not eating, he was just staring.

"Aren't you going to eat?" Rae Ann asked through a mouth full of cantaloupe.

"Me? No, I'm fine," Kyle said quietly and sat back, the bamboo chair creaking beneath his weight. He had taken on a solemn quietness and Rae Ann would have given anything to know what he was thinking about. She continued on the fruit, but had lost her zest for eating. The time was drawing near for her to leave and the very thought made the food she had consumed leave a sour taste in her mouth. She managed to polish off the last of the fruit and Kyle had to resist the urge to reach out and wipe away the strawberry juice that dribbled down her chin.

"Thanks, Kyle," Rae Ann said, leaning back in the desk chair. Instead of replying, Kyle jumped up from the chair and busied himself by picking up her plate and fork.

God he wished she would say his name again, he thought.

Uncomfortable with the sudden silence, Rae Ann slipped out of the chair and walked into the kitchen, hands stuffed into the back pockets of her jeans.

"I guess I should be on my way," Rae Ann said, quietly, "I have a lot of ground to cover."

Kyle, who had followed her into the kitchen, slowly placed her empty plate in the sink and leaned over the side. "Yeah, you'd better go." He reached out an absently turned on the water faucet and then turned it back off. He watched the water swirl into the drain and waited for her to say something.

What the hell is wrong with me? Rae Ann thought. Wasn't she on her way to California to get away from her marriage? Was it so difficult for her to remember these details? Besides, she had only met this man last night and now she couldn't find the right words to say good-bye? In fact, she really didn't want to say good-bye. She felt welcome here. Like she belonged. Maybe there was a hotel near by where she could stay for a couple of days. Maybe figure out some things. Rae Ann eyed Kyle and knew he was the reason why she was contemplating this crazy idea.

Kyle thought he could sense Rae Ann's silent struggle and prayed she would give him some time to get to know her. Rae Ann crossed her arms in front of her and sighed heavily. The weight of the world was on her shoulders and it seemed to be teetering a little towards Kyle.

You can't do this, Rae Ann scolded herself under her breath.

"I have to go," Rae Ann said more to herself than to Kyle. She turned on her heel and walked out of the bar's kitchen. The sun was bouncing brightly off the pavement, so Rae Ann shrugged back into her sunglasses, wishing feverishly that they made her invisible. Kyle lumbered slowly into the doorframe, shadowed by the bar's overhang. Rae Ann slid into the driver's side of her Honda, her mood as gray as the interior. She peered through the windshield and squinted in an attempt to see the expression on Kyle's face. It was insane, but she wished he would run to the car and tell her that she wasn't going anywhere, because he wanted her to stay. Make decisions for her like he did last night. She used to be that take charge kind of person, but the events of the last year had changed her. The failed marriage and spoiled career had beaten her down. She wanted someone to take care of her. Grant had been that kind of person until just a few months ago.

Rae Ann had kind of gotten used to having someone do the planning for her. Now, here she was on her own again.

Kyle held his position, one bare foot crossing the other at the ankle. It was probably best this way. Rae Ann certainly didn't need to get involved in anyone else's life right now, considering she couldn't even manage her own. Rae Ann backed out of the parking lot and drove off into the morning light.

When he could no longer distinguish the outline of her car, Kyle stepped into the sunlight and shielded his eyes from the glare. *Well, that was that,* he thought. This was definitely the fastest a woman had come and gone from his life. Kyle shuffled back to his truck, the gravel biting into his bare feet. Heading home, he told himself over and over that he didn't need the likes of Rae Ann Lewis-Spencer. She was trouble, just another complicated female. A married woman for god's sake!

"I don't need her," Kyle said aloud to the empty truck. It sounded even less convincing in the shaky voice that came out of his mouth. He knew it was true, but he couldn't make himself believe it. A silence descended in the cab as Kyle surrendered to his thoughts and let the truck drive them both home. He didn't even take the time to notice his favorite season of the year growing at full force.

Green was beginning to sprout all over the ground and up the sides of the Shawnee National Forest that lay just to the south of town. Kyle had loved growing up in the lush forest surroundings. As kids, he and Klein would run along the trails and clamber over the fallen logs on the forest floor. He would sit endlessly alone among the trees breathing in the earthy scent of the woods. It was one place that Kyle could go and not be judged. He went there when his stepfather had left, again when his mother had gotten sick and then shortly after the accident. Kyle breathed life from the forest and tried to give back what it gave him. He had worked summers there picking up trash and giving tours until his mother's illness had forced him to quit. After that Klein needed him more and more at the Buttercup until he rarely ever had a chance to visit the green surroundings.

Having been nowhere else, Kyle considered life in southern Illinois was unlike any other place in the world. Summers could reach above one hundred degrees and winters could drop well below zero. Sometimes it wouldn't rain for months and then suddenly it would open up and pour for days.

At this moment, Kyle felt like a big, heavy rain cloud, just waiting for the right moment, when his emotions would spill over and drown him with the falling pieces of his soul.

~ * ~

Stepping into the apartment was like entering a mausoleum. It seemed quieter and more depressing than usual. He surveyed the perpetual mess and hung his head in shame. A furry, warm mass curled itself around his legs and purred deeply. Kyle glanced down at the cat and his mood brightened.

"Jasmine, my dear," Kyle bent and scooped up the cat in one swift motion, "you are the only woman I need in my life."

Kyle buried his face into the butterscotch fur and cuddled the cat. The cat's purr rattled in his brain and shook loose an old hurt that he felt every time he looked at the feline. A knocking on the door brought Kyle sharply to the present. He groaned, convinced that it was the last person to which he wanted to explain himself.

Klein.

Kyle knew exactly what Klein was going to say; Kyle had heard the lecture before. But when Kyle finally threw back the door, it wasn't Klein. "Rae Ann," Kyle uttered.

"I was hoping I could take you up on that offer for a shower," Rae Ann's eyes darted past him into the apartment.

"But what, I mean, how did you get here?" Kyle dropped the cat onto the console table and took the suitcase from her hands.

"I went back to the Buttercup and asked Klein for directions."

Kyle smiled behind her as she stepped into the living room, pleased that she had come back. His apartment was identical to Klein's in structure but certainly not in taste. Unfolded laundry littered the mismatched furniture, a pair of cowboy boots had found a comfy home on top of the TV, and from where Rae Ann stood, the dining room table looked like the headquarters for a junk mail distributor.

"Charming," Rae Ann muttered.

"Well, it could use a little tidying up," Kyle agreed.

"It could use a complete professional overhaul," Rae Ann proclaimed with a smile and Kyle smiled with her. "Now about that shower…"

Kyle's grin widened at the lame excuse. "Right, right, let me get you all set up."

Rae Ann followed him into the bathroom and gasped at the sight. In contrast to the hurricane of a living room, the bathroom was impeccably neat and clean. The faucets gleamed under the row of lights above a beautiful beveled mirror. The toilet and tub looked as if Kyle spent hours on his hands and knees scrubbing them with a toothbrush.

"What gives, Bennett?" Rae Ann teased, watching the emerald of his eyes twinkle.

Kyle shrugged, "I can't stand a dirty bathroom. The rest I can tolerate."

He fetched Rae Ann a towel, washcloth, a new bar of soap and mini bottles of shampoo and conditioner, just like the ones the housekeeping staff put out at the lodge. Rae Ann held up the miniature bottles and raised her eyebrows in question.

"Klein," Kyle explained simply.

Rae Ann shook her head in understanding. She already felt as if she had known these brothers all her life. She arranged the towel and shampoo bottles around the shower before starting to pull the bottom of her shirt over her head. It was at that moment she realized that Kyle was still standing in the bathroom with her. She yanked her shirt down hard, rousing Kyle from his trance.

"Oh, right. I'll just be out here if you need anything." He stepped back through the door never taking his eyes from hers. Rae Ann took a step forward and leaned against the frame.

"Kyle," Rae Ann chewed on her bottom lip, unsure of what to say, "I didn't exactly get a chance to thank you for all you've done."

"It was… nothing," Kyle whispered, stepping towards her.

"Well, I wanted to thank you anyway," Rae Ann said quickly shutting the door before Kyle could get any closer. Kyle stood outside the door staring hard at the painted wood. For a moment he couldn't speak or even breathe. Her mannerisms were so similar that for a second he found it possible to believe that it wasn't Rae Ann in the bathroom, but someone else. He shook the thought hard from his head and moved to the living room window. He couldn't help but wonder what her story was. He had felt Rae Ann letting her guard down, just a little. Then suddenly she had slammed the proverbial door shut between them. He sighed in surrender as he heard the water from the shower turn on full force. Of course, he couldn't think he would know this woman in just one conversation. Her life was complex—of that he could be certain.

He did his best to clear the mess of jeans, T-shirts, and socks from the sofa and chair, scooping the boots on top of the mess as he passed the entertainment center. Kyle settled on the chair for a minute before restlessness drove him into the kitchen. He busied himself trying to find the makings coffee and then clearing the week old dishes from the counter top, trying like hell not to think of the beautiful, naked woman in his shower. He was, in fact, so absorbed in scraping the spaghetti sauce off the stove that he didn't hear Rae Ann walk in behind him.

"I hope you're not cleaning on my account."

Kyle startled at the sound of her voice and turned to face her, dishrag still in his hand. She appeared even more beautiful, scrubbed clean and smelling of the spring rain soap he had given her. Rae Ann tipped her head to the left and blotted her sopping hair with the cranberry colored towel. Her blonde hair, darkened by the water, was combed straight back off her forehead. She had changed into a fresh pair of jeans and a short sleeved cornflower blue T-shirt that brought her eyes to a stunning indigo. The neck plunged in a V and Kyle moved his eyes to her feet to keep from staring. He smiled inwardly when he saw that her bare toes sported a pale pink polish with white tipped nails. A French pedicure, if memory served him right.

"Kyle, listen," Rae Ann walked out of the kitchen to break the intense gaze. Kyle chucked the dishrag toward the sink and followed her half-heartedly. The tone of her voice was enough to scatter the cloud he had been walking on since she appeared at his door. "I have absolutely no idea what I am doing here." Rae Ann dropped heavily on the couch, the towel dangling between her knees.

"I thought you came to take a shower?" Kyle teased, trying like hell to lighten the mood.

"Kyle, I'm serious. I drove through this town by accident. I stopped at the Buttercup by accident. And now I am in your apartment, but that was no accident."

Kyle sat lightly on the couch beside her. "You mean you came to see little ol' me?" Again, they smiled in unison. Kyle hooked a finger under her chin and drew her head up to meet his gaze. "Rae Ann, I don't know what you want me to say, but I think I am a pretty good judge of character. You are just confused right now."

"No, Kyle," Rae Ann jumped from the couch, "you don't know me. You don't know anything about me. I just left my husband. I snuck out in the middle of the night and left. I am a coward and I am terrified." Rae Ann paced the living room at top speed. "Besides, I don't even know you. I can't stay here. I don't fit in here. I don't even know why you are being so nice to me." She stopped in front of him and dropped her head into her hands.

Kyle stood up slowly, not wanting to scare her away again. He could see her body begin to shake with dry sobs and he couldn't stop himself from reaching out and placing his hands on her quivering shoulders. Her dripping wet hair had formed a dark blue collar on her shirt and he caught a glimpse of the shadowed valley that formed between her breasts when she turned sideways. She felt like a china doll in his big, clumsy hands.

"When I saw you in that bar, I just wanted to talk to you. I even let Terri off an hour early so I would have an excuse to bring you your food. I have no ulterior motives. You just looked like you could use a friend. You still do."

Rae Ann wiped the tears away as best she could, before she looked up into his eyes. "I do," she whispered.

Kyle slipped his arms all the way around her and pulled her close. He rested his cheek against her cool, wet hair and breathed in her feminine scent. The echo of his words sounded in his head over and over.

No ulterior motives?

Who was he trying to kid? He had not stumbled upon her by accident. The only reason why he had approached her was because of his foolish heart. He felt guilty, but could think of no other reason to get her close to him. Besides, how long had it been since he had held a woman in his embrace?

Too long.

Rae Ann gave in to Kyle's hug and placed her arms around his waist, leaning into his strong body. When had Grant last hugged her? And when had she become so starved for affection? She couldn't remember. A new set of tears pooled in her eyes. Rae Ann found it hard to believe that she was acting this way. Standing in a strange man's apartment, spilling the most intimate details in her life and now being held in his arms. Somewhere along the way she had stopped all rational thinking. Her life had been desolate and void of intimate contact for so long that once she got a taste of how life could be, surrounded by people that cared about you, she didn't want to let go. Kyle Bennett seemed so genuine and caring, even towards Rae Ann, a virtual stranger.

Rae Ann pulled back slightly to look at this new man that had slipped into her life. She was shocked by the unexpected hurt and despair she saw in his eyes. Almost a reflection of her own sorrow. The emerald green iris had dulled to a polished jade. It was just a flash, quickly replaced by the smile and warmth she had become accustomed to seeing.

"I still don't know what to do now. Where do I go from here?" Rae Ann asked.

Kyle only hesitated a moment before exclaiming, "Across the hall."

"What?" Rae Ann dropped her arms from his waist.

"The apartment across the hall is empty. I can talk to Klein about you staying there for a while." Kyle raised his arms in mock surrender, "Until you get back on the road to California, of course."

"Kyle, that would be great, but I can't just take advantage of you and your brother like that."

"No, no, it wouldn't be like that," Kyle rushed on, "I can hire you as my... cleaning lady. You said yourself I needed a professional. Besides, it will take at least a week to shovel this place out. By then you will have had enough time to think of a plan for your future."

Rae Ann instantly dipped her head to hide her guilt. How would this man react if he knew she was married to such a wealthy man? Would he understand that just a couple of days ago she herself had a full time housekeeper and limousine driver? She didn't want to deceive him nor did she want to embarrass him with the truth of her life. Besides, the money was Grant's, not hers. She didn't care to have it anymore than she cared to stay married to a man that couldn't be faithful. Rae Ann opened her mouth to argue, but Kyle put a finger to her lips. "I don't know what you are running from, but I don't think you should pass up this opportunity. The next town you stumble into might not be this nice."

Rae Ann knew what he really meant was that the next *guy* she met might not be as nice. She gave a heavy sigh and nodded her head to accept the offer. *This would give her a chance to plan her next move*, she thought. Of course, her decision had nothing to do with the fact that Kyle would be living right across the hall. That last thought did not sound convincing, even inside her head.

~ * ~

When things had been straightened out with Klein, Kyle helped Rae Ann bring in the two boxes from her car and then directed her where to park around the side of the building. Again the layout of the spacious apartment was the same as Klein's and Kyle's. A small, hardwood foyer led into the living room area with the dining room just off to the left. Beyond that, the galley kitchen's counters gleamed under the overhead florescent light. On the opposite wall of the living room were the two doors leading to the bedrooms. The far room was slightly bigger than the near-closest one. A tiny bathroom, not nearly as clean as Kyle's, was situated directly across from the main exit.

Kyle and Rae Ann took all the covers off the furniture sending up week's worth of dust and grime and moved the pieces to Rae Ann's specification. Rae Ann made the bed with fresh sheets that Kyle had found in the hall closet and then vacuumed the carpet in the bedrooms with Kyle's vacuum. The vacuum cleaner was old and whined loudly, like Bob Dylan singing his greatest hits. The apartment had no TV, so Kyle gave her permission to come over and watch television at his place whenever she wanted.

By the time they were finished setting up Rae Ann's new place, the sun was beginning to dip in the sky. They sat on the couch side by side just staring at the wall. It seemed so peaceful here, not at all like the constant goings on at the ski resort or at the television station.

"Well, I should go. I start my shift in about an hour," Kyle said unfolding himself off the couch and stretching noisily. The task had taken them the better part of the day, but Kyle didn't mind. Even with only four hours of sleep, he was willing to sit with Rae Ann all night if it hadn't been for work.

"Oh, are you sure you have to go?" Rae Ann stuttered, suddenly not wanting to be alone, "we could order pizza or I could—"

"You know I would love to stay, but Klein will have my hide if I miss work."

Rae Ann nodded in understanding and walked Kyle to the door to say good-night. "I truly appreciate all that you've done for me. This place is really great."

"Don't mention it," Kyle replied, sheepishly. He turned his cheek toward her and tapped it with a finger. Rae Ann stood up on her tippy-toes and grabbed his face in her hands. Everything in the moment seemed to have slipped into slow motion. Kyle heard her whisper thanks before planting a kiss on the tender spot below his earlobe. Rae Ann hesitated briefly, taking in his scent and then fell back onto flat feet. Kyle shivered involuntarily and stared down at Rae Ann. If he didn't leave now, he knew he never would.

Without another word he turned and walked through the door. It closed behind him with a dull click. Kyle stood in the hallway and reached a hand up to touch the spot she had kissed. He still felt her lips there and could also feel his pulse racing under the skin, knowing that his face must be flushed and red. Not just with the kiss, but with the memory of a kiss so similar it took his breath away.

"I am so proud of you," she had whispered into his ear after the graduation ceremony. "Now am I supposed to call you Officer

Bennett or am I one of those privileged people that still gets to refer to you as Kyle?"

"Well, lets just see," he had teased, "If you don't respect me as an officer of the law, I will just have to handcuff you."

She threw her arms around his neck giggling and then whispered very softly in his ear, "Promise?" Leaning into him, she kissed the spot that Rae Ann had just managed to find and they held onto each other long after the other people at the ceremony had wandered off toward the refreshment table.

~ * ~

Inside the apartment, Rae Ann absorbed the silence. For tonight she wouldn't think about her predicament, she wouldn't think of Grant sleeping off another alcoholic haze alone in their home. She wouldn't give him the satisfaction. The shock of his cheating had long since worn off and had now settled into a hard realization around her heart. There would be no more worry about whether or not she made the right decision to leave. All the signs had been there. Losing her job, the pending lawsuit by the Senator and a no good husband. It was funny how such a horrible turn of events could have led Rae Ann to a place so wonderful. A place where she instantly felt at home. A place that was home to a man who wanted nothing more than to be her friend just when she needed one the most.

Rae Ann ran into the bedroom and jumped onto the bed, using it as a trampoline. Maybe she hadn't made it as far as California, but this was the beginning of her new life. A new life in Illinois.

Twenty-two

Sunday, April 9th

A lack of curtains in her new apartment brought in the bright sun very early in the morning and a creaking nose above her head suggested that the person that lived upstairs was already in full swing. Rae Ann glanced at the small bedside clock and realized that it wasn't as early as she thought. She threw back the covers and padded into the kitchen, wiping the sleep from her tired eyes. Opening the refrigerator, Rae Ann groaned.

Unfortunately, the furnished apartment did not come with a fully stocked fridge and pantry. She tilted her head to the left and frowned at the old carton of baking soda that sat alone on the top shelf of the refrigerator. Not exactly the breakfast she had in mind.

Rae Ann made her way into the living room, shivering in her thin tank top and pajama pants. She spotted a sweatshirt peeking out of one of the unpacked boxes that housed her life and slipped it on. With no other alternatives, Rae Ann slowly opened the door and peered into the main hallway of the apartment building. She looked both ways twice to make sure that no other tenants were milling the halls and then covered the distance between her door and Kyle's. He had told Rae Ann that he never locked the door and true to form, she let herself inside.

She stood in the small foyer and listened for signs of life. Nothing moved except the camel colored cat, that opened one eye as Rae Ann passed her home on the dining room table. Rae Ann ventured into the kitchen and saw the dishrag from yesterday was still flung over the faucet. There she opened all the cabinets in search of coffee or a tea bag or anything. She found nothing.

Checking Kyle's fridge, Rae Ann decided that three beers and a half empty bottle of ketchup did not exactly sound tasty. She blew a sigh towards the ceiling and leaned heavily against the stove. Through the small window above the sink, Rae Ann watched the sleepy town begin to stir. She watched a mother pull her small child across the parking lot, the woman's mouth was opening and closing like a fish out of water. An elderly couple clad in matching, nylon jump suits walked along the road hand in hand. Rae Ann's smile was bittersweet. It had not been long ago that she believed she would grow old with Grant.

For so long she had held all men at arm's length. Never wanting to get close to them. Rae Ann knew she had let Grant Spencer into her heart too quickly. She furrowed her brow and thought hard for a moment, but still could not pinpoint exactly when the relationship had started to deteriorate.

Of course, from the very beginning there were signs that the union between the two would not work. For God's sake he had vanished into his office with his business partner, Elliot Logan, for most of their wedding night. That alone should have tipped off Rae Ann. But, of course, she had been blind to his errors wanting so much for the spur-of-the-moment romance to work. When had she become so weak? Was it the thought of reaching middle age without ever having loved or been married?

Many nights when Grant did not come home or during the time Rae Ann was in Madison, she would think of ways to get Grant to let her into his life. He had been as guarded as she was, probably more so. At first, Rae Ann understood how it felt to not be able to trust anyone. She had hoped that they would find trust in each other.

Kyle stood staring at Rae Ann a full minute before he spoke. His hands shoved into the front pockets of his jeans, his bare chest pimpled with goose bumps at the sight of her. Rae Ann's pretty blue eyes had glassed over as she stared beyond the present. His heart ached for many reasons. A pain that only certain people ever feel was written in plain English all over her face. The down turned mouth said a lot more than words could express, arms crossed over her small breasts showed her need to hang on to something permanent. Kyle wished she would hang on to him.

Rae Ann reached up and tucked a strand of loose hair behind her ear and an unseen hand squeezed Kyle's heart. Having her in his apartment was like a slap in the face. What right did he have to want her? He had loved and lost, chained to a past that was pulling him under. The similarities were slight, but they were there. More in mannerism than in look.

"Rae Ann?" She turned to face him as if she knew he had been standing there, but wasn't acknowledging him. Her huge eyes blinked twice and she straightened from the counter. "Do you want to talk about it?"

"Talk about what?" She shook herself out of the past and back into Kyle's apartment. "I just came over here for food and you quite simply have none. I am going to change clothes then you and I are going to the grocery store."

With that she walked past him into the living room, a few seconds later he heard the door click shut. Kyle stared off into his own past with eyes closed. Did she have to be so damn stubborn? He knew she needed someone to talk to about whatever haunted her, but when he offered himself, she just shut down. He knew from his own experience that she was letting her pride get in the way of her healing.

Was he still talking about Rae Ann?

Kyle scolded himself for letting the past creep in then went in search of a shirt.

~ * ~

By the time, Rae Ann emerged from her apartment, having deemed herself acceptable to face the public, Kyle had already planted himself on the front stoop.

"Let's go, Bennett. We've got a lot of shopping to do." Rae Ann laid a hand on his shoulder as she walked down the cracked concrete steps.

"Now wait just a minute. I can't shop on an empty stomach. I'll buy everything in the store." Kyle stood taking her hand off his shoulder and placing it in his own. Rae Ann looked at their joined hands then squinted up at him to read his thoughts. A wry smile played on his lips, but she could read nothing into the expression on his face.

Without another word, Kyle led Rae Ann across the street and around the corner. They walked hand in hand as naturally as if they had been together for years, but Kyle's long strides caused Rae Ann to pick up her normal pace in order to keep her arm in the correct socket.

They pulled up short in front of the town's only actual eating establishment. It was nothing less than expected. The exterior of the small diner boasted that it had once been a successful business whose owner had stumbled across a good buy on turquoise paint. There was a yellowing chalkboard balanced on the windowsill between the glass and curtain telling everyone that today's special was a horseshoe and Pepsi, only $2.95. Noting the price of the food, Rae Ann figured that the chalkboard had been there as long as the building. One salmon pink shutter swung back and forth, the rusted hinge that served as its umbilical cord to the window frame moaned louder as the wind picked up.

Above their heads, an old piece of plywood had been painted white and the words "Snappy's Diner" were scrawled in black. Kyle held the door open for Rae Ann and bowed slightly at the waist. Rae Ann gingerly stepped into the diner and back a couple of decades.

A cracked Formica counter ran the length of the diner's only room. Squat, red vinyl covered swiveling stools, which sat empty in front of it. Opposite the counter were a few booths and tables sporting the same red vinyl as the benches. The ancient stove and freezer that loomed behind the counter seemed to be in a deep conversation of hums and buzzes.

In Rae Ann's mind, Ronette, Rae Ann's mother, was behind the counter scooping coffee into the giant machine. She glanced to her left and saw the owner, Randy at his usual post, counting the money in the cash register. Angeline, the Italian girl that worked weekends at the Hot Stop and went to college during the day, was wiping off the booth where Rae Ann would sit and do her homework. Without being prompted, Rae Ann started in that direction.

"Hey?" Kyle's voice startled her out of the daydream. She turned to look at him and then swung her head back toward the open space of the diner. It was now empty. Ronette and Angeline were gone. Randy was no longer counting the money. "You look like you've just seen a ghost," Kyle let the door shut behind them and walked to her side.

"It just reminds me of home," Rae Ann muttered trying to conjure up the image of the Italian girl twisting her long raven colored hair into a bun and securing it with her pencil. Rae Ann still saw her as twenty years old even though she would now be well into her forties.

Kyle and Rae Ann settled into the back booth. She opened her mouth to tell Kyle about the diner in New Jersey when the infamous Snappy slowly lumbered from behind the pie case. His enormous girth caused the dessert plates to rattle against the glass shelves, as if a tiny earthquake had just passed underfoot. He peeled two greasy menus from a wooden box that had been fastened to the end of the counter and headed in their direction. Rae Ann stared, openmouthed, as Snappy flopped the menus down in front of them, then proceeded to wipe his fat, sausage fingers on the dirty apron that covered his mammoth belly.

"I think we're going to need a few minutes," Rae Ann said, never taking her eyes from the man's round face. Snappy shrugged, gave Kyle a pat on the shoulder and slumped back toward the counter area. "If you think I am eating here, you are absolutely crazy," Rae Ann hissed, shoving her menu in Kyle's direction.

"Suit yourself, but this here is the best diner in town," Kyle said, leaning back against the bench seat.

"It's probably the only diner in town, you schmuck." Rae Ann crossed her arms in front of her and scanned the diner from beneath her brows.

"Now I am truly offended. I try to buy you a nice meal and look at the thanks I get. I'm sure this place isn't as fancy as what you've got in Wisconsin, but come on." Rae Ann knew he was teasing and smiled in spite of herself. The thought of Snappy as a waiter in the posh surroundings of Antiquities almost made Rae Ann laugh out loud.

"Sorry, pal, but I think I'll wait till we get to the store."

Kyle shrugged his shoulders and then shouted his order to the owner/cook/waiter that was Snappy.

"And a coffee," Rae Ann pouted.

Without acknowledging his customers, Snappy retreated to the stove to melt a huge dollop of lard on the sizzling surface of the rusted stove.

"So," Kyle leaned forward, lacing his fingers together on top of the table, "what were you really doing in my apartment this morning?"

"I told you. I was looking for something to eat. I know your apartment looks like it could be declared a disaster area, but I still thought you would have enough to put a meal together."

Kyle narrowed his eyes to slits and clenched his hands together making the knuckles go stark white. Actually, he used to love to cook, but those days had come and gone. Cooking for one person depressed the hell out of him, but he wouldn't admit it. He preferred to mooch off Klein or grab a quick bite at the Buttercup or Snappy's. So many things had changed and he no longer enjoyed the task of selecting ingredients and spending hours in the kitchen.

"When are you going to start telling the truth?" Kyle asked, shifting the subject back to Rae Ann, "one of these days you are going to have to let out what you've got trapped inside you. I saw you in that kitchen. You were a million miles away. What is tearing you up inside, Rae Ann?"

The sound of her name made her head jerk to attention. The sound of her name coming from his lips sounded strangely different. Softer, almost breathless, as if he had blended it into one word instead of two.

"I'm not like you, Kyle. I'm not kind to strangers and don't have a lot of friends. I try to be as emotionally detached from everything as possible. I don't even have a cat, for God's sake," Rae Ann said, referring to Kyle's peach colored feline. Kyle cast his eyes away from Rae Ann so she wouldn't see the hurt that flashed through him. If Rae Ann only knew that the cat represented so much more than just a companion, she might not be so kind about Kyle's polite character.

Rae Ann searched over Kyle's face and tried to look deep in his eyes for a trace of mockery or judgment, but there was none. She honestly believed that he wanted to help her sort through the garbage in the landfill that was her life. Why exactly, she didn't know.

Back in Wisconsin, Rae Ann had confided solely in Eddie, but she knew that he was always on her side. Sitting in front of her, this stranger would have a nonbiased ear. He wouldn't know all that she went through in her life. Just what she elected to share. Rae Ann didn't want to be judged for her actions. She just wanted someone to listen.

Slowly Rae Ann let a breath hiss through her teeth and into the diner. "The truth is that my marriage just didn't work out. We, Grant and I, had a whirlwind romance and a fairy tale marriage, but unfortunately three days ago the clock struck twelve on this Cinderella."

Kyle sat still afraid to ruin the moment by speaking. When it was evident that she didn't plan to go on, he reached out for her at hand at the same time she pulled both of her hands down into her lap.

"I'm sorry," he whispered, "where you together a long time?"

"We knew each other only two months before we were married," Rae Ann dropped her eyes and began picking absently at the rotted stuffing that bled from a deep cut in the vinyl seat. "I know how that sounds, but he was so different then. He loved me. I know he did. Then suddenly, after we were married, things just started to slowly fall apart. He started drinking, heavily, and last month I lost my job. In one year my life went from Heaven to Snappy's Diner and from the looks of this place, I wouldn't be surprised if Hell was the next stop on this roller coaster ride."

Kyle slapped a hand to his mouth to hide any visibility of a smile.

"No, it's okay. Go ahead and laugh. My whole life has been a joke," Rae Ann broke the tension with a smile of her own, "maybe I'll tell you all about it sometime."

Kyle's chuckle caught in his throat and his face became serious again. "I hope that you will."

Rae Ann felt as if her heart could burst with emotion. Kyle was so genuine and caring, but hadn't Grant started out that way as well? Rae Ann put her husband out of her mind and focused on the shuffled steps of Snappy approaching their table. Rae Ann and Kyle's smiles returned when Snappy dropped the plate of smiley face pancakes down in front of them.

"You know," Rae Ann managed to say through giggles, "you have really got a great place here. Has it been passed down through your family?" She tilted her head completely back to make eye contact with the giant of a man.

"Actually," Snappy began, smartly, "I bought this place only fifteen years ago. I had to completely redo the inside and out to

155

capture the 1950's ambiance. I think I've finally gotten it. Right down to the vintage ketchup and mustard bottles I bought at an antique flea market three years ago."

Rae Ann stared, unblinking. She had not expected him to say anything, let alone that. Kyle dropped his head to hide the laughter that was bubbling in his throat. When Rae Ann just continued to stare, Snappy shrugged his linebacker shoulders and went back to the kitchen.

"Can you believe that?" Rae Ann shook her head slowly from side to side. Kyle gave her the 'I told you so' look and started into the pancakes. He paused only once with the fork full of dripping syrup and buttery pancakes half way to his mouth when he saw Rae Ann's puppy dog look as she eyed his plate. Kyle leaned away, turning his head and Rae Ann hurriedly gobbled up the bananas, strawberry and blueberries that made up the eyes, nose and mouth of the smiley face.

While Kyle left Snappy a tip, Rae Ann walked up to the counter. "Rae Ann Lewis," Rae Ann held out her hand to be shaken.

"Frank Davis, but you can call me Snappy," the man, said swallowing Rae Ann's tiny hand with his own oversized mitt.

"Listen, Snappy, I didn't mean to come off like such an ass back there. I just—"

"It's okay, Miss Lewis. We all get a little nervous around people we don't know. Although, I feel like I have known you for a long time already."

Rae Ann beamed a smile, "Thanks. I can use all of the friends I can get."

Snappy winked at Kyle as he walked up and then went about wiping off the already spotless counter.

"What was that all about?" Kyle asked as they left the diner.

"Oh, just making friends," Rae Ann replied looking around her. Suddenly the sight before her stopped her firmly on the pavement. "My God," Rae Ann marveled at the sudden slope in the landscape just over the tops of the buildings on the street. She had not seen the looming mountains last night as she drove into town due to the darkness and raining and had apparently not been paying attention as she made her way back into town this morning. Now she marveled at how the thousands of trees melted together on the surface to look like a smooth green cape worn around the neck of the mound. The scene made her unexpectedly feel at peace. Just like the first time she had seen the rolling hillside in Wisconsin.

"Oh, yeah, that's part of the Shawnee National Forest," Kyle explained, "I'll have to take you up there sometime." Rae Ann felt her eyes sting with emotion and she knew at once that stumbling upon this town had been no accident or chance of fate. A new life here was her destiny. She could stop running.

"I thought everything this town had to offer was located on these two streets?" Rae Ann cracked.

"Pretty close. These two streets are the entire town but those hills are their own little part of the world," Kyle said, staring into the distance as if he were seeing the surroundings for the first time as well. "That forest is what roots me to this town. No pun intended," he laughed, reaching over to tickle her in the ribs.

"Hey, I'll race you to the door." He sprinted across the street leaving her in the middle of the road. Rae Ann stopped and stared after his lanky form as it bounded over the pavement. Before this moment she wouldn't have felt like accepting such a challenge but Kyle's energy and exuberance just made her feel like a kid again. Her childhood had been cut short by the selfishness of her mother and inexperience of her father. Rae Ann took another gander at the landscape and stopped analyzing the situation, then just started running to catch up.

~ * ~

Inside the grocery store, Rae Ann and Kyle decided to split up and meet back at the registers in a half an hour. Rae Ann started off in the opposite path of Kyle and then glanced back over her shoulder. He too had glanced back and was looking in her direction. Embarrassed at being caught, Rae Ann quickly turned back to her cart and ducked down the nearest aisle. Kyle couldn't help but smile as he languidly maneuvered the metal basket around a display of paper towels. When she could catch her breath, Rae Ann glanced up and realized she was on the pasta aisle; which gave her a great idea. She had never really had the opportunity to cook for more than two people and suddenly she was giddy with the prospect.

Rae Ann began scanning the aisle to find just the right sauce. She glanced up from eyeing the ingredients of one jar to find the woman next to her staring intently in her direction. Immediately, Rae Ann felt uncomfortable. She slowly put the jar into her cart and then began walking towards the end of the aisle. Still feeling the woman's eyes on her, Rae Ann turned back leisurely and pretended to scour the shelves for something else. As she suspected, the woman still stood in front of her cart staring after Rae Ann. All the while, a small child was standing in the back of the woman's cart pulling things off the shelf while his mother was not paying attention. Rae Ann made eye contact with the woman, but was struck mute. It was something about the way the woman was looking at her. Not at her, but right through her.

Without a word, Rae Ann jerked back to her cart and left the aisle. Did the woman recognize her from the television, or worse yet, the latest news stories involving her and Senator Showalter? *This is how it would be from now on,* Rae Ann thought. Stared at everywhere she went. Guilty in the eyes of the public even if she was innocent. Rae Ann rounded the corner and stopped by the cereal to take a couple of deep breaths. She shook her head and chuckled to herself. What was making her so nervous? No one knew her here. On second thought, she was almost certain that her story had not made national news. Yet. Until then she had nothing to hide.

Rae Ann tried to shake off the creepy feeling and began to shop again hoping she wouldn't see the woman for a second time. She combed the aisles meticulously looking for specific items, but quickly realized that in a town of one thousand people, you get to choose from exactly one brand of everything.

A half an hour later, she pulled her cart up next to Kyle's in the magazine section of the grocery store. "How long are you planning on staying, sugar?" Kyle's eyes grew into huge green lily pads as he eyed the mountain of food in Rae Ann's cart.

"I decided I am going to fix you and Klein dinner tonight. It's the least I can do for all of the help you've given me," Rae Ann explained, sheepishly, "Besides, we certainly can't eat that." Rae Ann pointed to the basket of his cart that held nothing but bread, bologna, and cheese. Kyle smiled at how easily Rae Ann used the word "we" in reference to them.

"You must have been reading this magazine for like twenty-five minutes," Rae Ann laughed oblivious as to what Kyle had on his mind.

"I know how you women are," Kyle replaced the magazine and ducked a slug in the shoulder from Rae Ann. "Besides, now I don't have to buy the magazine." Kyle grabbed his cart and began running down the aisle. At the last minute, he jumped up on the foot bar and rode the rest of the way to the checkout. Rae Ann's laughed escalated as the other people in the aisle stared up from the bottles of juice or soda they held, in disbelief. Rae Ann quickly grabbed a bottle of wine from the shelf of beverages and followed.

Kyle had finished paying for his essential items by the time Rae Ann had emptied her cart onto the conveyor belt. He pulled a crisp five dollar bill out of his wallet and waved it towards Rae Ann.

"I'll be right over there," he said, pointing to the scratch off Lottery ticket machine by the exit, "I'm feeling lucky."

Rae Ann nodded her head and turned to the cashier just in time to see the girl staring googly eyed at Kyle. Rae Ann smiled and dropped her gaze into her purse to search for exact change. Since she had left Rockingham, Rae Ann had used only money that was in her personal bank account. She had no desire to rely on Grant's high limit credit cards. And the one card she had in her name was almost maxed to the limit after paying for her hotel rooms and essentials she had needed in the two days since she'd left home. Rae Ann didn't care about having a lot of money and although she did have a fairly substantial sum in the bank, she would have to watch her spending. Now that she didn't have a job, times would be tight.

"You are so lucky." Rae Ann looked back up at the young cashier.

"Pardon me?"

"I said 'you're lucky'... to be Kyle's girlfriend," the cashier assumed as she began dragging Rae Ann's groceries across the infra-red scanner. Rae Ann blushed to the core of her body. The beeping of the register became the thumping of her heart in her ears.

What had given the cashier the idea that they were a couple? Rae Ann thought to herself. *Did they look like a couple? They had been goofing around in the store, but certainly weren't acting like a couple,* Rae Ann concluded, silently.

"We aren't exactly a couple," Rae Ann began.

"Because," the cashier continued to speak as if Rae Ann had never said a word, "no one ever thought Kyle would recover from the accident." Rae Ann stood still, waiting for the girl to continue.

When it was evident that she was finished, Rae Ann hurriedly asked, "What accident? Are you a friend of Kyle's?" The journalist in Rae Ann took over and she began firing off the questions in rapid succession. The cashier stared out the front windows of the store, perhaps reliving some old memory that included Kyle, but didn't bother to answer Rae Ann's questions. Not specifically anyway.

"I had a crush on him in school. He was a senior when I was a freshman."

Rae Ann pulled her eyebrows into a tight V and frowned.

Kyle was a senior when this girl was a freshman?

That couldn't be right. The girl behind the cash register couldn't be more than twenty years old. Rae Ann guessed her to be working a part-time job to put herself through junior college until she could escape to some out of state university.

"Paper or plastic?"

Both ladies turned to the sudden voice. Kyle stood at the end of the revolving belt, half hidden by a mountain of Rae Ann's groceries. When neither woman said anything, Kyle shrugged and began throwing green peppers and tomatoes into a plastic grocery sack. Rae Ann continued to gape at Kyle even after the cashier turned back to her task.

Just what the hell was going on here?

What accident had the cashier been referring to? Kyle looked perfectly fine to her.

Too fine, in fact.

Rae Ann had never even questioned how old he was. His words and actions seemed to put him right up there with Rae Ann's thirty five years. Now she couldn't be sure. The once masculine face turned babyish right before her eyes.

Rae Ann waited for the last grocery to register in the computer then pushed the money into the clerk's hand. She grabbed what bags she could muster and practically ran out of the door barely waiting for the censor on the automatic door to realize it should open.

Rae Ann and Kyle had managed to carry all the groceries in one trip, but were gasping for breath by the time they dropped everything in the hall between their apartment doors. "Jesus, Rae Ann, did you enter us in a marathon when I wasn't watching?"

Rae Ann wiped a hand across her forehead, unsure of what she should say. "Well, I should get all my perishables inside," she said, jerking a thumb over her shoulder.

"Right," Kyle said, coolly, "me, too."

"Well, I guess I'll see you for dinner. Is five okay?" Rae Ann asked, avoiding eye contact.

"Sounds great."

Rae Ann ducked inside and shut the door firmly behind her. She leaned against the hollow board and closed her eyes. Was it really that big of a deal that he might be younger than she was? It wasn't like she was driving past the local junior high school scouting for prospects. Besides, she wasn't scouting for anyone right now. It was obvious to her that Kyle was an adult. He acted older than many of the people that Grant associated with, including the great Senator. And in any event, they were just friends.

Rae Ann decided that this issue would just have to go on the back burner for now. She would discuss it with Kyle later. Right now, she had a dinner to plan. She heaved the seemingly million plastic grocery bags onto the counter and began sorting through them. She decided on the lower cabinet to the right of the sink for her canned goods and the upper cabinet to the right of the fridge for her boxed items.

Satisfied, Rae Ann stood back to observe her handiwork. She felt as she did when she had rented her first apartment in Madison, shortly after leaving the coffee shop and her father. She had bought a newspaper, called about the first one she spotted and handed over the deposit and first months rent, from the money her grandmother had left her. She had lied on her application, stating she was eighteen instead of her true sixteen. The old woman renting the room hadn't questioned her. Rae Ann could tell she was more interested in the money.

To save what little money she had, the apartment had been a one room furnished apartment. But still it had been more of a home than Rae Ann had ever known. By now Rae Ann could barely remember the trailer where she and her mom had lived in New Jersey, and her father's small house in Pennsylvania had been merely a stopping point.

In Madison, Rae Ann had stocked the shelves with her favorite foods and bought three books to place on the single bookshelf below the television. Once Rae Ann began her classes at the University, she quit work at the restaurant and got work at the local newspaper, answering phones. It wasn't elegant and didn't pay well, but the steady schedule worked fine around her classes.

Plus, Rae Ann loved the hustle and excitement of the news. She relished the rush of the reporters working on a last minute story before press time. It only took her six months of working there to realize that reporting was what she wanted to do, but not behind the scenes. Rae Ann wanted to report the news on camera, sitting behind the small news desk with a picture of downtown Madison behind her. She could imagine herself smiling at her co-host and laughing at some witty impromptu comment he had said regarding the story. She voiced the aspiration to her boss at the newspaper and his confidence in her was all she needed. He was a stout older man with the bushiest white eyebrows Rae Ann had ever seen. Having no children of his own, Rae Ann's boss considered her the daughter he never had. The elderly man was more than happy to help her and made a couple of calls on her behalf. He introduced her to his old golfing buddy, Robert Ashcroft, the news director at WZZY.

It was the first time Rae Ann felt like she was taking control of her destiny and living her life as she wanted and not how two dead-beat parents saw fit. She promised herself that she would never let anyone dictate her actions ever again. And when she had first met Grant, Rae Ann had never suspected that he would soon be telling her how to act or what stories to report. Of course, maybe her stubbornness had gotten the best of her with the latter. Maybe if she had listened to him she wouldn't have reported the Senator's rape scandal and would have never lost her job. But it was over now, her opportunity for greatness was gone. She would begin from here, take control of her destiny again and this time she wouldn't fall. Not for a glamorous job or a handsome man.

A handsome man like Kyle.

Rae Ann walked out of the small kitchen and turned back to look at the open cabinet doors. She hadn't realized it before, but now noticed that the cupboards contained no pots or pans. Rae Ann groaned and jammed her hands at the waist of her jeans. How was she going to make this fabulous dinner with no cookware? Rae Ann looked apprehensively at the door to the apartment. She couldn't explain it but at this moment; she did not want to see Kyle. Rae Ann walked to the door and stopped.

"If this is what you call taking control, well then you need a dictionary," Rae Ann spoke to herself out loud. Throwing her hands up in surrender, Rae Ann crossed the hall to Kyle's apartment. He had left he door open a crack.

"Kyle?" Rae Ann said, peeking her head through the narrow space. "Kyle?" she asked again into the silence. Rae Ann didn't hear anything or anyone inside the apartment, but was almost certain that he hadn't left after their return from the grocery store. She crossed the floor of the living room on light feet and peeked into the kitchen.

Nothing.

As she started back towards the door, she spotted him. He was sitting in the bedroom just off the living room. He was perched on the bed with what looked like a million pieces of paper spread out in front of him.

"Kyle?" Rae Ann whispered, approaching the door cautiously. Suddenly sensing a presence, Kyle jerked his head towards the open doorway. "I called your name, but you didn't hear..."

"Rae Ann, what is it?" Kyle jumped from the bed as if it were made of hot coals and rushed through the door, closing it firmly behind him. "What is it?" he repeated more urgently.

"Nothing," Rae Ann stammered, flustered by his insistent tone, "I just wanted to use your pots."

"What?" Kyle asked, his face twisting in confusion.

"Your pots and pans," Rae Ann explained, "I don't have any. Kyle, are you all right? You kind of freaked me out there." Kyle ran a hand through his sandy hair turning back into the Kyle she had met just yesterday.

"I was just..." he began, glancing over his shoulder at the bedroom door, "You just caught me off guard is all. I'm not used to beautiful women just waltzing around in my apartment." Kyle's suddenly casual tone made Rae Ann's reporter intuition perk up.

"Anyway, about those dishes. Yeah, sure, help yourself," Kyle shrugged, "Actually, why don't you just use my kitchen instead of hauling it all over to your place?" An unexpected creak above their heads sent both faces looking toward the ceiling and then back to each other.

"Klein must be home," Kyle stated.

"Oh. Well, I guess I should go invite him to dinner," Rae Ann glanced at her watch, the face already showing quarter past twelve. "I am going to change clothes, then I'll be back at three to begin cooking, if that's okay."

Kyle nodded his head in agreement and escorted her to the door. Rae Ann stepped into the hallway and then turned to question him, but Kyle shut the door abruptly, cutting her off in mid-inhale. Rae Ann blew a sigh up into her bangs. One minute it seemed as though he was trying to get her to open up and then the next minute it was him that was being mysterious. She decided that this probably wasn't the best time to become Rae Ann the reporter, so she turned and bounded up the stairs to the second floor.

Rae Ann tapped lightly on Klein's door and it swung open almost immediately. As usual, Klein was dressed to kill. He was immaculate from the tiny plaid button down shirt to the shiny wingtip shoes that had clicked their way across the hardwood floor.

"Rae Ann," Klein exclaimed, "how lovely to see you again."

"I hope I'm not interrupting anything."

"Don't be silly. Do come in." Klein led the way across the apartment to a stack of mail he had been sifting through on the dining room table. "What can I do for you?" he asked, picking up an envelope and tearing into it.

"Well, I wanted to cook dinner for you and Kyle. To show my appreciation. Will you come? It's at five." Rae Ann stopped herself from rambling by pulling her lower lip between her teeth.

"Let's see," Klein said, holding his hand out, "That is very thoughtful. You don't have to do that. I'd love to come and five sounds great." He ticked off each statement with the fingers of his left hand. "But I can't stay long. I have a date."

Rae Ann smiled at Klein's last statement. It was so nice to see someone in love. Rae Ann gave him the rest of the details, then headed for the door. She turned the knob and then stopped. "Klein, can I ask you a question?"

"What is it, love?" Klein asked, never looking up from the letter in his hand.

"Is there something Kyle isn't telling me?"

Klein's head snapped back as if he'd been slapped. "What do you mean?"

"Never mind," Rae Ann said, "I think you just told me what I needed to know." With that Rae Ann closed the door between them.

Klein tapped his wingtip hastily on the floor and considered going after her. At last, he turned back to his mail and decided not to get involved in matters of the heart where his brother was concerned. Kyle would tell her in his own time.

Maybe.

Twenty-three

Back in her apartment, Rae Ann went through both of the boxes and her suitcase for something suitable to wear. She had been hoping that the task would keep her mind off Kyle for even a little while. Hosting a dinner party had obviously not been on her mind when she packed her clothes. She rooted through jeans, leggings and sweatshirts until she found a long flowered dress that she had worn last on her honeymoon.

Rae Ann slumped on the bed, pressing the soft material to her face. If she breathed really deep, she was sure she could smell some of Grant's cologne that had rubbed off into the fabric. Tears welled up in Rae Ann's eyes and she didn't fight them. She could recall everything that had happened from the moment she'd met Grant right up to this point.

Rae Ann tried hard to think of a good reason to just pack her bags and go back to Wisconsin where she belonged, but at long last nothing came to mind. The truth was, there was absolutely no reason to go back. Grant had become just a shell of the man he used to be, her career in television was over and to her the resort was just the wedge that had finally driven them apart. She was thankful that she would never have to deal with it again. During their short marriage, Grant and Rae Ann had never discussed nor finalized any type of will or prenuptial agreement. The two had continued to lead separate lives and would leave the marriage with only what they had brought into it. As if it never even happened.

Rae Ann lay down on the bed, the cool fabric of the dress still pressed to her wet cheeks. Her marriage had simply dried up like the Sahara Desert and she vowed to never again shed a tear for what could have been. But what had been lost would linger in her mind forever. Rae Ann didn't move on the bed for fear of breaking the new vow she had just made to herself. Eventually, she fell into a fitful sleep, dreaming of a past that promised no future.

~ * ~

Kyle paced his apartment restlessly. Things were getting out of his control. He wasn't supposed to be feeling like this, was he? About a married woman? Every time he looked at Rae Ann he could just melt. He was acting like a damned teenager. Kyle recalled the first time he saw her in the Buttercup and then again this morning in his kitchen. She seemed to fit in so perfectly, as if she had been searching for this place all her life, and finally found it. Who was he to turn her away? He knew he wanted her so bad he could taste it, but then the guilt would take over and leave a bitter aftertaste.

Kyle scooped the cat off the dining room table and began clearing the junk. "What should I do, Jazz?" Kyle asked as the cat sauntered into the living room ignoring him. He couldn't decide whether or not he should just cut his losses and get out or forget the past and move on with his life. He threw the pile of mail that he had been picking up back onto the table and plopped into the nearest chair. He should have known it was about time for his four year upset.

Four years ago, the accident had turned his life upside down. Four years before that his mother had died from her battle with breast cancer and four years before that his step-father had taken a business trip with a female co-worker and had never come back. Kyle had never been one to keep secrets, so he decided to tell Rae Ann the entire truth after dinner.

Dinner!

Kyle had been so wrapped up in his thoughts that he'd completely forgot about the dinner Rae Ann was cooking. He glanced at the wall clock and then dashed into his bedroom to rummage through the clothes in his closet for something decent to put on. Most of the garments hadn't been touched in four years or better. He pushed aside

some of his less casual shirts and ran headlong into a plastic bag. His
patrolman's uniform still hung the way he had left it. It was secured
tightly in a plastic dry cleaner's bag from Sander's Dry Cleaning over
in Prairie Sun. He had picked it up the Tuesday before the accident.

The department had expected his leave from the force to be short,
but it was now bordering on three and a half years. He had tried to
return the uniform to the Sergeant, but he wouldn't hear of it. He had
told Kyle that someday he would be back and, until then, let the
uniform remind him of where he belonged. Kyle now shoved it to the
back and quickly picked out a shirt and jeans. It had been a long time
since he'd worn them and all he could hope was that they still fit.

~ * ~

Rae Ann came out of the hot shower feeling newly refreshed. She
used a tiny balled up fist to wipe a circle of steam off the vanity
mirror. Observing her reflection, she decided that getting dressed up
could really do wonders for a girl's self esteem. She eyed the way the
long dress clung to all the right places and hid all the not so flattering
points. Not that Rae Ann had many of those.

The dress itself was sleeveless and scoop neck, showing off a lot
of skin above the waist. The princess seams pulled the dress in tight
around her tiny waist then cascaded down over her curvy hips almost
to the floor. Unfortunately, she had only packed a pair of running
shoes so the sandals she had worn the night she left would just have to
do.

Rae Ann had never been one to weigh herself down with heavy
makeup so she just dabbed on the bare essentials. She remembered
running home from the nightly broadcast and scrubbing off the
pounds of makeup the job required her to wear. A weary sadness crept
slowly over Rae Ann's head, but she shrugged it off, determined to
have a great evening.

Her blond tresses were just long enough to put up, so she dug a
clip out of her bag and slipped in into a French twist, letting the ends
hang free. Rae Ann surveyed the final product and frowned. With her
hair up and the scoop neckline of the dress, the void area of skin
between felt naked and exposed. Rae Ann thought of the blue velvet
box she had packed when she left.

Locating the bigger of the two cardboard boxes she had brought, Rae Ann dug to the bottom. The pearl necklace her grandmother had given her lay in its special box. She picked up the box and ran her hand along the crushed velvet exterior. She opened the tiny clasp and puckered her brow. The pearls were slithering back and forth along the display bottom like a snake on the desert sands. The two slits in the casing were supposed to hold part of the necklace in place on top and then house the rest of it comfortably under the false bottom. She did not remember ever leaving it loose but, then again, she had worn them last on her wedding day. She had been so energized with emotion that it was possible she hadn't been so careful in putting them back. Rae Ann clamped her eyes tight against the vision of her wedding day, but it only became more vivid. She had been standing in the bathroom of the dramatic lavender guest suite as she slipped the string of precious beads around her graceful throat and fastened the clasp. Oh how she wished her grandmother could have been there.

You should wear them on your wedding day and I pray that you will be as happy as your grandpa and I were. The reflection of her grandmother's words made tears sting the back of her eyes.

"I'm sorry, Grandma," Rae Ann muttered now as she struggled to secure the clasp. She could see it as if it had happened yesterday. Of course, it had only been a year ago. Not exactly the forty-two years that her grandparents had spent together. Perhaps if she hadn't rushed into the love affair so quickly things would have turned out differently. She should have taken it as a sign when Grant ushered his business partner, Elliot Logan, up to his private office right during their lavish reception at Pine Trails and remained behind closed doors for almost two hours. It had broken Rae Ann's heart, but she knew going in, that his business was extremely important to him and demanded a lot of his time.

Rae Ann really wasn't in the position to argue since she had refused to give up her job with Channel 8 news and move completely to Rockingham. Grant had balked at the idea of Rae Ann keeping her job and simply couldn't comprehend why she was adamant about working. That she was determined to make it behind that news desk, and was close enough to seize the dream. He just assumed that any woman would be more than willing to stay home and enjoy only having the job of being Grant's wife. That realization alone had Rae Ann wondering if Grant had ever really known her at all.

Finally satisfied with herself, Rae Ann went into the kitchen of the tiny Illinois apartment and began carrying over the ingredients for the lasagna she had planned for the main course. There were also the makings of a salad, a loaf of garlic bread and the chilled bottle of wine. All in all Rae Ann made three trips across the hall to Kyle's apartment bringing the reinforcements for a fabulous dinner.

Juggling the last of the vegetables, Rae Ann shut the door to Kyle's apartment with her foot and headed back toward the kitchen. She heard the water running in the shower so she took it upon herself to clean off the dining room table and set it. Surprisingly, Kyle had a lovely pattern of dishes with all the matching accessories. Rae Ann also found two sandalwood scented candles which she set up on the table and lit.

With the lasagna in the oven and the tossed salad in the fridge, Rae Ann poured herself a glass of wine and wandered into the living room. The place screamed bachelor pad, but Rae Ann could hear the whisper of a home in the background. The furniture was mismatched, but arranged in a cozy conversational circle. Pictures in frames littered every surface and there was one particular frame on the console table behind the couch that drew her attention.

Cradling the glass of wine to her chest, Rae Ann picked up the picture. Two boys about seven and ten years old were standing on a snowy mountain, their skis planted upright in the powder covered earth. All that showed beneath the heavy mass of clothes were cherry red noses and cheeks, four sparkling eyes and the biggest, brightest smiles the boys could muster. Between the boys, a stunning woman was down on her knees with arms draped around the boy's slender shoulders. Most of her face was hidden by oversized ski goggles, but you could tell that her smile matched those on the faces of the boys. Rae Ann smiled back at the picture involuntarily.

"Hey."

Rae Ann had been so engrossed in the photograph that she had not heard Kyle emerge from the bathroom. She turned to him, but any words that she had planned on saying lodged one by one in her throat. His still damp hair was combed back off his face giving his jaw line an even sharper angle. Emerald eyes shone like a cat's in the moonlight against the sea foam color of his short sleeved polo shirt. He wore dark denim jeans that fit tight to his lean hips, so much so that she had a hard time pulling her eyes away from his sculpted physique. All the way down to the boots she had seen on top of the TV yesterday, Kyle no longer looked like the boy she saw in the super market this afternoon, but a man. Rae Ann willed herself to move, but knew that once her feet started moving she was going to run into his arms. It was crazy, but at that moment it felt right.

"You look beautiful," Kyle said softly, reading her thoughts. He thought she looked as fresh as a peach and just as tasty. The flash of heat in her eyes had been unmistakable and instantly his stomach had knotted with desire. He would have given anything to kiss that little dip where her neck swooped into her shoulder. Kyle wished so much that they had met under different circumstances. He silently went over the speech he had rehearsed to say to her after dinner and, as if a bucket of ice water had been doused over his head, Kyle snapped back to reality and saw what was really before him.

A married woman.

Rae Ann watched the torment in his eyes a second before he broke the spell. Kyle sauntered across the floor towards the kitchen, the heel of his boots tapping on the wooden floor. Rae Ann quickly replaced the picture and followed him, still caught up in the moment.

"Smells delicious," Kyle started and then stopped just as suddenly almost sending Rae Ann crashing into the back of him. He stared open mouthed at the burning candles on the dining room table. No other light illuminated the three sets of dishes that had been placed upon it.

"Is something wrong?" Rae Ann kicked herself for not asking permission to use the plates, "I can put them back. I think there might be some paper plates—"

"No," Kyle cut in, "that's what dishes are for, to be eaten off of, right?"

Rae Ann knew he was trying to ease her mind, but she could still see tension in his raised shoulders. "How about some wine?" Rae Ann cut in front of him to the fridge and poured them both some of the blood red liquid. Her nerves had been so jangled at the sight of him that she could barely keep the bottle pointed into the glass while she poured. Kyle accepted the glass with his right hand and reached out his left to grab her wrist before she had a chance to pull it back.

"Rae Ann, listen I—"

"Knock, knock." A voice cut in from the hall stopping Kyle in mid-sentence.

Kyle dropped her hand and said, "We're in the kitchen, Klein."

Klein strolled in looking just as Rae Ann had last seen him. "Everything looks fabulous, Rae Ann. Doesn't it Kyle?"

Rae Ann smiled at the flattery, but was sure that the glow on Klein's face was for his upcoming date and not her dinner. She waited for Kyle to politely respond, but when he didn't she ushered them into the dining room. "I am actually ahead of schedule so why don't we get started."

Klein insisted on helping, but Rae Ann turned him down hoping that Kyle would take the hint and assist her in the kitchen. She dawdled an extra minute behind the refrigerator door before realizing he wasn't coming. Rae Ann didn't understand how things could go from the heated look they had shared in the living room to the aloofness he was showing her now. She didn't understand the sudden harshness when she was certain that he had been trying to win her over since she'd arrived. Rae Ann placed the food on the table in front of Kyle and sat to his left in the seat across from Klein. Almost instantly, Klein picked up on the tension that hung between Kyle and Rae Ann. It was almost another physical presence in the room. The trio ate their meal in thick silence.

"So, Rae Ann, have you decided on how long you'll be staying with us?" Klein asked trying to lighten the mood. "Of course, you are welcome to stay as long as you like."

Rae Ann looked to Kyle for a sign or clue that said he might even in the slightest bit want her to stay. From what she could see there was no such sign. "I imagine it won't be much longer. I, of course, will stay until Kyle's apartment is clean. That was the deal."

For the first time since their moment in the living room, Kyle stared in her direction. "Don't be stupid, Rae Ann," he spat at her, "You don't really have to clean my apartment. I only said that so I could get past your pride and convince you to stay."

Rae Ann pulled back as if Kyle had physically slapped her. Heat flushed her face bright red. Never could she have imagined Kyle being so cruel towards her and she had no idea what had brought on the verbal attack.

True to her nature, Rae Ann stuck her chin a little higher in the air and retorted, "well, Kyle, it's a good thing you don't have any pride in your home or you wouldn't have had any excuse for me to stay."

Klein watched Rae Ann take a deep breath and smile to try and lighten the situation, but he could see that Kyle's comment had struck a chord in her. He turned to Kyle who had lowered his head and was staring at his plate. Of course, Klein knew this side of Kyle and had seen it many times when it came to women. It was Kyle's way of saying that he was getting too close and was trying to emotionally detach himself. Up until now it had worked, but Rae Ann was a different woman, from a different place and Klein was certain that Kyle wasn't going to scare her away as easily.

Klein worked up a smile and pointed it in Rae Ann's direction. She smiled back pleasantly. Too him, Rae Ann seemed someone that could take care of herself and had been doing it for quite a long time. She was a tough fighter packaged in a beautifully frail container.

Having finished with his dinner, Klein excused himself from the table. "I hate to eat and run, but my date is probably waiting."

"Don't be silly," Rae Ann said also rising from the table, "You have a great time."

She picked up her wineglass and drained the last of the liquid. Walking Klein to the door, she linked her arm through his.

"Thank you for the lovely dinner, darling, and please don't let my rude brother run you out," Klein said, patting her upper arm. Rae Ann promised that she wouldn't and then shut the door lightly behind him. It took her temper only a minute to reach the breaking point.

Turning on her heel, she stomped back into the dining room and planted her hands at her hips. Kyle sat in the same place she had left him as if he had been rooted to the spot.

"How dare you embarrass me in front of Klein? If you have something to say to me, I suggest you do it in private. I have been nothing but nice to you and this is how you treat me? I'm sorry I ever stopped at your stupid bar in the first place. I thought you actually wanted to be my friend, but if this is the way you treat your friends, then forget it." Rae Ann could think of nothing more to shout about so she busied herself cleaning up the dishes.

Unfortunately, getting Klein's plate meant she had to reach across Kyle. Just as she was pulling back, Kyle reached out and placed both hands lightly on her hips, crushing the thin fabric of the dress. With hands full of dishes, Rae Ann was helpless. He stared up at her in the dim light from the candles. The wine and anger had flushed her cheeks a deep crimson and Kyle thought she had never looked more stunning. Being seated, he had an eye level view with where he knew her belly button would be under the thin sheath of material. He pulled her to him, resting his cheek against her flat stomach.

Rae Ann had no idea what she should do. She could feel the heat from his hands and face pass through her clothing, searing the skin underneath them. She wanted just as badly to wrap her arms around him and squeeze him into her, but her pride kept her at an emotional distance.

"I'm sorry, Rae. I don't mean the things I say it's just..." Kyle trailed off, leaving Rae Ann in suspense.

"It's just what, Kyle?" Rae Ann pulled back slightly, but Kyle still held her firm in his grasp.

"I don't know. I need some time."

"Well, time is a luxury I don't have. Certainly not the kind of time you are looking for."

With that Rae Ann slipped from his embrace and carried the dishes into the kitchen. She was filling the sink with soapy water when she felt his breath tickle her neck. A shudder ran the length of her body, as if she had been jolted with electricity.

"The farther and farther I try to distance myself from you the more and more I want you," Kyle whispered. Rae Ann tried to move, but someone had seemingly replaced her sandals with concrete shoes.

"Kyle, I am a married woman."

"But you left," Kyle said quickly, setting her on fire with his hot breath. He pulled her around to meet his gaze. The two unblinking orbs had become as cool as the ocean waters.

"You hurt my feelings," she uttered almost breathlessly.

"I know. I'm sorry. I'll never hurt you again. No one will ever hurt you again." Kyle cut off his own words by pulling her mouth to his. His kiss was soft but firm. Rae Ann felt as if she was being swallowed whole and the feeling was wonderful. His tongue danced over hers, drawing her deeper and deeper. Kyle pressed his whole body into the kiss, the edge of the counter bit into Rae Ann's back. Her arms and legs had suddenly become liquid but her hands managed to tangle themselves in to the back of his hair. Rae Ann pulled out of the kiss gasping for air, her breasts heaving up and down with each intake. Kyle was rubbing the curve of her hip and staring straight into her eyes. The deep blue irises could barely be seen around her dilated pupils. Rae Ann pulled him back towards her, eager for another kiss when suddenly she cried out as water tumbled down her back side, soaking her to the bone.

In their heated moment, Rae Ann had left the water running in the sink and now it was overflowing onto the floor. Rae Ann quickly shut off the faucet and pulled the drain plug while Kyle scrambled through the drawers in search of a towel. They both crouched down on the floor and began mopping up the soapy mess. When their eyes met, they both began laughing uncontrollably and added joyful tears to the puddle of water on the floor. Rae Ann continued to sop at the water, but Kyle could do nothing but watch her. When the last drip had been soaked up, they stood awkwardly not knowing what to do.

"Well, I guess I should go put on something dry," Rae Ann said, looking down at the pretty dress that now hung limply off her shoulders.

"No, don't go. I'm sure I have something you can throw on. Besides, we still have half a bottle of wine to go."

Rae Ann let herself be dragged into the spare bedroom. "Wait here. I'll get you something." Kyle said, disappearing. A moment later he returned with a sweatshirt and some old basketball shorts from Abraham Lincoln High School. She quickly shed the clammy, wet dress and melted into the warm fabric of Kyle's clothes.

Feeling that her pearls didn't exactly compliment the outfit, she slipped them off and placed them next to the soggy dress. Rae Ann joined Kyle in the living room, after he too had changed out of his dinner clothes. The bottle of wine and two glasses sat on the coffee table in front of him. A place beside him on the couch had been cleared off, the miscellaneous items now rested on the floor at his feet.

"What should we do now?" Rae Ann asked tentatively.

Wickedness flashed in Kyle's eyes, but Rae Ann just laughed at his expression. "Sorry, Romeo, that impromptu bath really killed my mood."

She settled into the seat beside him and he pulled her close. It just felt good to be here. Kyle reached for the remote and began flipping through the channels aimlessly. He stopped on the nightly news to listen to the weather report. A flat-chested, redhead was giving out the highs and lows of tomorrow and then directed the attention back to news desk. When Rae Ann heard the name of the anchorwoman, she grabbed the remote and flipped off the TV.

"Do you have it in for the weather?" Kyle asked, confused.

"Not the weather, just the anchorwoman," Rae Ann explained.

"I don't get it. Do you know her?"

"Yes. Her name is Marley Cavanaugh. We used to work together."

"You were a reporter?" Kyle asked, incredulously. Rae Ann nodded and then held the remote up under her chin as a microphone. "Reporting live from Madison this is Rae Ann Lewis for Channel 8 news."

"Very nice," Kyle commented, "I am guessing that this is the job that you got fired from last month."

"I didn't get fired," Rae Ann shot out defensively, "I was asked to resign. There is a big difference."

"I'm sorry. I shouldn't have said it like that," Kyle said turning towards her on the couch. "You know," he continued, "if you ever wanted to tell me your problems, I would be here to listen."

Rae Ann gave him a sideways glance and sighed. She wanted so badly to tell him the squalid tale of the Senator's rape scandal. At that moment she needed desperately to get it off her chest. To hear from another person that she did the right thing and it wasn't her fault. People paid good money for this kind of therapy and here Kyle was offering up his ear for free. Maybe it was the wine that made her tongue loose or maybe the kiss, but Rae Ann just opened her mouth and out came the details.

"It happened about a month ago," Rae Ann started, completely losing herself in the memory, "It was the biggest story of the century. I couldn't pass it up. I was up for weekend anchor. Marley Cavanaugh's job. She was getting ready to leave for the network job." Rae Ann gestured toward the blank television screen. "I had worked for the station for almost six years, the competition was fierce. This story would have made me a shoo-in for that seat and would have set me up for life."

Rae Ann closed her eyes and the memory played like a movie behind her eyelids. She recited every point in graphic detail. No fact or figure about the situation was omitted. As she finished telling Kyle the story, the last sentence rushed out of Rae Ann on a breath of relief. It felt wonderful to have the story out in the open, but now Rae Ann braced herself for Kyle's judgment. But the judgment never came.

Instead, she heard him take a slow, deep breath in and utter, "That sounds like a fascinating story. How could it ever have gotten you fired? I mean 'asked to resign'." Rae Ann looked from her glass to Kyle. An innocent aura swirled around his head in bright colors. The cheap wine had driven nails into her brain and a pounding headache was building behind her eyes.

When had she started drinking so much?

"She was a fraud," Rae Ann said as she sat the wineglass on the coffee table in front of her and dropped her hands between her knees. "We aired the story the following morning as the Senator was at the police station consorting with his lawyer. I did no other research than to send the tape down to be edited. My boss even let me anchor the story. It was better than I had ever dreamed."

Tears formed in Rae Ann's eyes as she remembered the exhilaration she had felt behind the news desk. It was a strain to will them away before she continued. "The Senator went ballistic, which was to be expected. Of course, his lawyer instructed him not to submit the blood sample even though he proclaimed his innocence, on a rival station, the very next chance he got. Against advice, the Senator willing gave blood and I just knew everything was falling into place." Rae Ann paused only briefly, afraid that if she waited long enough the rest of the story would not get told, but would just rot away inside her.

"We continued the coverage several times that day and when I had a break I tried to call Jenna's lawyer on the phone. As it turned out, the number was suddenly disconnected. The hospital had no real record of her existence, since she had given false information when she checked into the emergency room. She was, of course, not a student at Jamestown College and therefore no phantom friend in the political science department was ever found. I had been so absorbed in getting this story out on the scene that I hadn't done any of the background work. I failed.

"A week later she showed up on Channel 14 stating that I had coerced her into making the false accusations. Can you believe that? She actually named me as the person responsible for setting the whole thing up. She said that I doctored the tape and incriminated the Senator to further my own career. Then to make things worse, the tape pulled a disappearing act and was never found."

"I'm sorry," Kyle said, leaning forward and placing a hand on the small of her back. Rae Ann shook her head.

"Don't be sorry. I wanted that job so bad that I let it cloud my better judgment. Everyone warned me about this girl, about this story, but I didn't listen. Even my own husband tried to get me to drop the story. At the time, I thought he was just worried about his own status with the Senator."

"And now?" Kyle's hand began moving in small circles over the sweatshirt.

"And now, I still think that Grant was worried about only himself." Rae Ann smoothed a piece of hair behind her ear and focused on the feel of Kyle's hand on her back.

"So the Senator didn't rape the girl?"

"Oh, well, that's where it gets complicated. Eddie's cousin, Denise, works at the hospital and risked her job to get us the lab results. As it turned out, the policeman was right, the semen sample matched perfectly with the Senator's blood type. Of course, it would have taken weeks to get a positive DNA match, but for all intents and purposes, Denise was certain that the specimens matched."

"Then he was having an affair with her?" Kyle asked, confused.

"It would appear that way," Rae Ann glanced up at him, with an equally perplexed expression, "I still can't figure it out, but my best guess is that this girl just made up the phony rape as a way to get money out of him. The alternative is just too incredible."

"And," Kyle said, still rubbing her back gently, "what is the alternative?"

"She was trying to ruin me," she said, fighting back the tears again, "I don't know why she named me as the instigator unless I was either convenient or she was trying to destroy my reputation. The Senator and I were constantly at odds. If he was having an affair with this girl it is possible that *he* set this whole thing up to get me fired. I just can't believe he would risk his entire political career to see me go down in flames. If that's true then I am even more in the dark than I thought."

"But you didn't know the girl, right?"

"No," a tear trickled a slow path down Rae Ann's cheek, "I didn't know her. After that, I didn't know anything anymore." Rae Ann stood up to pace the room, dropping Kyle's hand from her back.

"Of course, the Senator threatened to sue me and the station for wrongfully slandering his name. My boss was furious, but he convinced the station to let me dutifully resign instead of having to publicly fire me. What really killed me was that the people didn't even care that their precious Senator had been accused of rape or that he may have had an affair, but they wanted to see me drawn and quartered. I was a public pariah.

"My relationship with Grant had been teetering on the edge before, but this sent it plunging over the cliff. I just couldn't live like that anymore. The night I decided to leave, Grant told me that there was another woman. I thought if I ran away and went somewhere, where no one knew me, I could start over again. I have been running all my life and it has seemed to work so far."

Rae Ann stopped pacing the room and placed a hand on top of the entertainment center to steady herself. Kyle stared from the couch.

"I never imagined," his voice trailed off. She looked so fragile when she turned to him with tear filled eyes, that it broke his heart.

"Me neither."

He went to her quickly, before he changed his mind, and gathered her into his arms. He was amazed at how perfectly she fit against him. Every angle and curve slid neatly into the angles and curves of his own body. The feeling made him shudder to the very core of his being. He felt tears dampen the front of his shirt, but Rae Ann stood as still as a statue against his frame. She was not sobbing or whining. She had clearly accepted her life and the events that brought her to this point. And she may not have felt sorry for herself, but Kyle felt sorry enough for both of them. It was obvious to him that Rae Ann did not deserve all of the dreadful things that had happened in her life but, then again, neither did he.

Kyle reluctantly pulled back from their hug and placed his hands on her tiny upper arms. Every effort was made to avoid his stare so she glanced around the room, her gaze settling on the picture of the ski clad kids and the beautiful woman.

"Is this your mother?" Rae Ann ducked out of his grasp and went to the console table that held the frame.

"Yes," Kyle replied, his voice barely above a whisper.

"She's beautiful," Rae Ann said, tracing the frame's intricate design with her finger.

"Yes, she was. She was diagnosed with breast cancer shortly after my step-father left. She died when I was sixteen."

"I'm so sorry." Rae Ann set the picture frame down and picked up the one beside it. She had not noticed this one earlier. This picture contained only Kyle as an adult. He was leaning against his truck, smiling brightly. The picture would not have caught Rae Ann's attention except for the fact that Kyle was wearing a policeman's uniform. Rae Ann opened her mouth but closed it almost immediately. She turned the picture to Kyle in question. "You're a police officer?"

"Used to be," Kyle rubbed his neck absently, "for just a short time."

"Why? What happened?" Rae Ann narrowed her eyes and tried to scrutinize Kyle's expression. Gone was the sentiment from a moment ago. Now he held just a blank face, void of emotion. This was clearly not a favorite subject of his.

At last he sighed, "I was one of those guys that was going to change the world, you know? But when the world let me down, I just sort of forgot why I did it in the first place."

Rae Ann nodded and decided it was best not to push the issue any further. She tucked the reporter inside of her away. Soon she would have to learn how to suppress that part of her character all together.

"Rae Ann, there is something I need to tell you." She looked at him, patiently waiting, the photograph forgotten in her hand. Kyle stepped toward her within arm's length. "I was with someone. I mean a girl. I mean a girlfriend."

Rae Ann stepped back, and a puzzled expression shifted her face. "You have a girlfriend?"

"No, no, I *had* a girlfriend. I haven't talked about it in a long time, but you have been so honest with me. I feel like I should be honest with you."

Rae Ann placed a hand on his mouth to silence the tormented words. A sudden pang of guilt pierced through Rae Ann. Had she been completely honest? That answer was no. She had not told Kyle about her husband's wealth or the true nature of his friendship with the Senator. Rae Ann did not deserve Kyle's honesty and she couldn't stand to let him bare his soul in front of her knowing that she had kept the entire truth from him.

Quickly looking for a scapegoat, Rae Ann remembered the cashier from the grocery store and asked, "Is this about the accident?"

Kyle nodded his head slowly never pulling his eyes from hers. "Its okay, Kyle. We don't have to talk about this tonight. I can tell this is hard for you, but we have plenty of time."

At the moment, Rae Ann did not like herself.

"Does that mean you're staying?"

Rae Ann nodded with a fleeting smile and ran her hand down his cheek. Kyle released a breath that he had been holding since this amazing woman walked into his life and he deflated with a sigh.

"Goodnight."

Rae Ann turned to the door and paused. She didn't know what she was waiting for, but she waited anyway. When nothing happened, no sign from God, she placed the picture back in its place and let herself out of the apartment.

Once outside, she stood in the hallway and counted slowly to ten. Still, Kyle did not emerge from the apartment. If he had, Rae Ann would have given herself to him. Telling the past to this more than willing stranger who had become a friend was more cathartic than she ever thought possible. Rae Ann didn't want to scare him away by overwhelming him with her once extravagant lifestyle. She certainly didn't want him to think her superficial and shallow.

Rae Ann had wanted to hear his story, but the pain in Kyle's face and eyes told her that it was too much for him. It was the perfect excuse to omit the fine points. Rae Ann walked into her desolate apartment and shut the door with a click. As she started to walk across the wooden planks of the floor, a small piece of paper on the floor caught her eye. She picked up the scrap gingerly, certain that she hadn't left it there before.

Collapsing on the couch, she opened the single flap. On the inside, crudely written were the words, "I want my disk back." Rae Ann squinted her eyes and re-read the message.

Tilting her head, Rae Ann thought hard, but could not place the message on the note. It meant nothing to her. She came to the conclusion that someone had slipped it under her apartment door by mistake. Someone else in the building must have borrowed someone's disk and hadn't given it back. She made a mental note to herself to bring it to Kyle's attention tomorrow. For now she would try to get him off her mind.

Rae Ann knew it wasn't wise for her to fall for Kyle, but a part of her was aching to run back into his arms and spend the rest of the night helping him forget the terrible accident that had claimed his love and his life. But how could she help someone else pick up the pieces of their life when she was barely strong enough to hold her own together? She was no good for Kyle. They both needed someone who could provide support and understanding without adding their own baggage to the mix.

Of course, you can't choose who you fall in love with. She had learned that lesson once with Grant and never dreamed that after having just been hurt so badly she was willing to rush back into a romance that most likely had no future. This thought lingered in Rae Ann's mind as she drifted off to sleep still holding the cotton fabric of Kyle's shorts.

Twenty-four

Monday, April 10th

Rae Ann startled to full consciousness and quickly took in her surroundings. A heavy sigh escaped her as the familiarity of the apartment sank in. It had been the dream again. The dream that Rae Ann just couldn't put her hands on the moment she awoke. While asleep, she silently struggled with the demons, but once awake could not put her finger on what had been so upsetting about the dream. It had plagued her for a very long time.

Rae Ann stretched and groaned, as her muscles and joints protested. She had awakened very early it would seem. The couch had not been a comfortable choice and had left her with a sore back, which Rae Ann also attributed to age, and a splitting headache, compliments of last night's wine.

Having nothing else to do, Rae Ann decided that she should get back into the habit of her early morning exercises. She had always made it a point to run at least three times a week to help keep herself in shape. Although, this morning, she was hoping the exercises would also help clear her head. Another quick survey through her clothes told Rae Ann that she would have to go shopping soon if she planned on staying as long as she let Kyle believe last night. She emptied the boxes and suitcase into the dresser drawers, but the paltry contents didn't even fill up two drawers full.

Rae Ann changed from Kyle's shorts into leggings but kept on the sweatshirt he had loaned her and then grabbed her tennis shoes. She was anxious to get outside for a while, but still was hoping to avoid the town's curious eye.

Unfortunately, the town had other plans.

When Rae Ann stepped on to the dilapidated front stoop to stretch, there were already numerous people walking on the sidewalks and driving down the road. Meeting new people had never been her strong suit. Her journalistic background made her come off as too curious and forward. Rae Ann froze completely, still hoping that it would somehow make her invisible. It didn't.

"Hi there."

Rae Ann looked down from the steps to the voice in front of her. A woman that looked to be somewhere in her fifties looked back at Rae Ann, with a sudden stricken expression on her face. One hand shielded the woman's eyes from the glare of the sun and the other was resting comfortably on the railing. Her left foot was cocked up on the first step as if she were about to enter the building.

The older woman was dressed in a brightly colored warm-up suit, with small heeled dress shoes. She wore plenty of jewelry, her arms lined with bracelets and her neck held at least three necklaces that Rae Ann could see. The makeup she wore would have been better suited for a night on the town and her well preserved hairstyle wasn't moving despite the slight breeze. Her eccentric appearance made Rae Ann smile at the lady.

"Nora Presley," the woman stuck her gnarled hand out for Rae Ann to shake, "no relation to the king."

"Rae Ann Lewis," Rae Ann chuckled, "it's a pleasure to meet you."

"My goodness, you remind me of someone I used to know." When the woman pulled her hand back to once again shield her eyes, the fabric of her multi-colored warm-up suit swished noisily.

"Oh?" Rae Ann asked, all at once uncomfortable with the woman's intense stare.

"Anyway," Nora continued replacing her curious countenance with a crooked pink smile, "Do you live here in the building?"

"I'm staying in number three for a while," Rae Ann answered.

"Three you say?" Nora took a moment to pat her stiff hair.

Swish, swish, swish.

"I live in six. So all that creaking in the ceiling you've been hearing is me."

Rae Ann ducked her head and smiled. It was true that she could tell exactly what room the woman was in just by hearing her walk across the apartment.

"Well, welcome. It's nice to see someone closer to the boys' age around here."

"The boys?" Rae Ann inquired.

"Klein and Kyle," Nora explained, never losing her smile, "I have tried to look out for those boys, after their mother passed, and I always said that it was going to take just the right woman to give those boys a change of heart." Nora exaggerated a wink in Rae Ann's direction. Rae Ann was certain that she was referring to Klein's lifestyle, but was still too polite to come right out and say it.

"You seem to be the perfect one to do it, you know. You're just right for Kyle," the woman babbled on talking more to herself than to Rae Ann. "I didn't think that boy was ever going to snap to but now look." Nora held her arms out wide to take in Rae Ann. "Well, I shouldn't keep you. I've said enough. Enough talking for the day. Too many things to prepare for." Nora Presley rushed past Rae Ann and entered the apartment building. The swishing noise was so prominent that Rae Ann couldn't hear the rest of what the lady was saying.

Rae Ann shook her head at the encounter and bounded down the steps. If everyone in this town was as harmless as the Bennett brothers and Nora Presley, then she was going to get along just fine.

Finally off the porch, Rae Ann did a few stretches and began running. She chose the path that had taken her and Kyle to Snappy's Diner yesterday. Snappy was changing the daily special in the window as she passed. He raised his meaty hand in a wave.

Once past the diner, the buildings got fewer and fewer and soon there was no civilization at all. The lush green of the Shawnee National Forest rose around her and sort of encapsulated her in its green embrace. The sight of the hilly terrain was so comforting and peaceful.

Rae Ann jogged faster and faster in an attempt to catch up with the feeling of content. She pumped her arms and legs until her lungs felt like they were on fire. When Rae Ann felt like she couldn't take anymore, she slowed to a stop in the middle of the road and doubled over to her knees.

What was she trying to outrun? Herself? Grant? Kyle?

Rae Ann crumbled to the ground in a heap of boneless flesh. If she had just stuck to the plan, she wouldn't be sitting here thinking about Kyle. But, then again, where would she be? Alone somewhere in California or in Mexico looking for a quickie divorce lawyer.

Rae Ann looked to the sky for answers but there were none. *How could she have left her husband, met someone and then managed to fall in love with that person in just four days time?* That must be some kind of record—or maybe she was just a glutton for punishment.

Rae Ann was so deep in thought that she didn't hear the car coming towards her in the distance. She slowly picked herself up off the ground and dusted off her leggings. Raising an arm to wipe the sweat from her brow, Rae Ann caught a glimpse of a dark blur racing towards her. A horn blared as Rae Ann jumped out of the roadway and scrambled into the ditch. The car never slowed as it zoomed past her out of town, the tires throwing up a handful of rocks.

With her heart racing, Rae Ann once again stood from the ground and surveyed herself. Nothing damaged or broken. Her elbow hurt as it had bounced smartly off the hard earth. Rae Ann retraced her steps back to where she had been standing when the car came up behind her. Clearly she had been off the pavement of the two lane road, on the shoulder, and had been facing the traffic. But the car had been coming right at her. It had skimmed by within inches of where she stood, which meant the driver had purposely swerved at her. The thought made Rae Ann's blood run cold.

Why would anyone want to scare her like that? Rae Ann shook her head. *It had to have been some local kids trying to get a rise out of the unfamiliar face in town,* she thought. A quick survey convinced her that no one else had witnessed the incident. She could also not see the dark car anywhere in sight.

Slowly, Rae Ann turned towards the reassurance of the small town and headed back. She hadn't realized how far she had run until she finally reached the edge of the town limits. She was physically and mentally exhausted, as well as thirsty. By now the morning sun was blazing down full force. Rae Ann could see Snappy's Diner like a mirage dancing in the distance and decided to stop in for some water. And possibly some advice. She pulled open the door and peered in. There were no signs of life inside and Rae Ann was thankful the place was empty. This time her mother and the other ghosts from her past stayed tucked away. Rae Ann's tennis shoes squeaked across the freshly waxed floor as she made her way to one of the swiveling stools. She flopped down heavily and placed her head and arms on the counter.

"Miss Lewis. How nice to see you again." Despite his mammoth size, Snappy had snuck up on her.

"Hi," Rae Ann croaked around the lump in her throat, unexpectedly she felt on the verge of tears.

Without another word, Snappy pulled up his own chair and took a seat in front of her. "Do you want to talk about it?" Concern was clear in his voice.

"I don't want to burden you with my problems, but you are really the only person that I know in this town besides Kyle, and well, that's just the problem. Kyle, I mean."

Snappy glanced around at the empty diner, then back at Rae Ann, with a ghost of a smile on his face. "Since I don't have any other pressing engagements, why don't you tell me what's going on. I have a feeling that I have just as much to say to you as you do to me."

Rae Ann gaped in confusion, but Snappy did not continue. He did, however, get up from his chair and fix them both a cup of coffee. As hot as Rae Ann was, the coffee felt good as it heated up her mouth and throat. When Snappy was seated again, he motioned for her to start talking with a wave of his hand.

"Well, for starters, I'm married," Rae Ann stopped for a reaction, but got none from the gentle giant. When she was certain that he wasn't judging her, she continued. As she told the story, she felt a great weight lifting from her shoulders. She left nothing out, including even the details she had not told Kyle. She told him about her childhood, her job, the Jenna Ford ordeal, Grant, the resort and now Kyle.

As an afterthought, Rae Ann decided not to mention the episode with the car moments ago. It now seemed foolish. The roads were narrow and unlined. The driver had surely been trying to warn her to be careful of the traffic while she was running. After all, her mind had not been on the issue of the road.

When Rae Ann had finished, she took a sip of the now cold coffee and stared up through her eyelashes at Snappy. He sat in the same position, arms crossed in front, eyebrows pulled into a deep V. "Seems to me like you've got a lot on your plate, young lady." Rae Ann smiled. She couldn't remember the last time someone had called her young lady.

"Thank you for listening," Rae Ann said as she rose from the stool. "You're better than a shrink and certainly cheaper." Snappy reached out to place his giant hand over hers before she could move any further.

"Kyle has been through a lot too, you know?" he said, gently.

"No, Snappy, I don't know. Kyle doesn't volunteer much information and when he tries to, I run in the opposite direction. I don't know what I am so afraid of. He has truly been a friend and there is no one I would rather be with, but we just aren't good for each other. If we had met at a different time, maybe things wouldn't be so complicated."

Snappy patted her hand and released it from its imprisonment beneath his. "I helped look after those boys."

"Seems like the whole town is looking out for the Bennett boys," Rae Ann drawled sarcastically. Snappy came around the counter to walk Rae Ann to the door.

"No, I mean it. I offered Kyle a job shortly after his mother died, but he was too stubborn or too proud or both. He said that Klein and he could make it and they didn't want anyone's help." Snappy shook his head sadly. "I still can't believe it has been eight years since the good Lord took that woman."

Rae Ann stopped halfway to the door and turned to face Snappy. "What woman?"

"Alicia Bennett. Kyle and Klein's mother."

"But, you said she died only eight years ago," Rae Ann's breath caught in her throat.

"Yes, that's right. She battled the cancer for so long, but in the end," Snappy's voice trailed off, but Rae Ann wasn't listening anyway.

"But, he said he was sixteen when his mother died," she muttered to herself, "that would only make him twenty-four years old. Oh my God, Snappy, I have to go." Rae Ann bolted for the door, not allowing Snappy to say another word, but then quickly brought herself up short. "One more thing. Do I remind you of anyone?"

Snappy gave her a toothy grin and crossed his meaty arms in front of his body. "As a matter-of-fact, you do."

Rae Ann didn't want to hear the answer but she asked anyway, "who?"

"You look like Kyle's pride and joy."

Snappy gave a little chuckle and turned back towards the counter. Rae Ann didn't know what to say, so for once she didn't say anything. She had come here for answers, but she certainly didn't like what she heard. Although, the conversation did give Rae Ann a way out. The only question was would she be brave enough to take it? And, even after all of this, did she really want to go?

And what the hell was this 'pride and joy' business? Rae Ann thought to herself.

Once outside the tiny diner, Rae Ann's thoughts didn't get any clearer. The hot air was pushing into her head, taking up the rest of the space that wasn't occupied by her thoughts of Kyle and his age.

His young age.

Rae Ann walked until she could see the apartment building. Her first thought was to just pack up her car and get out before she had to answer anymore questions. Something she probably should have done a few days ago. But just as she crossed the street, Kyle pulled up next to her in his truck.

"Rae? What are you doing?" Kyle rolled down the driver's side window, releasing a blast of cold air from the vehicle's interior. Rae Ann stood rooted to her spot unable to utter a word. She had questioned his age yesterday at the supermarket, but now she knew. He was eleven years younger than her. Eleven very significant years. As far as Rae Ann was concerned he hadn't even lived yet, he was still a baby.

"I was," Rae Ann managed to squeak out, as she looked around for a possible explanation, "I was going to the supermarket to buy some cleaning supplies. I hope to have your apartment clean by tomorrow. See ya later." Rae Ann turned back in the direction of the sidewalk, relieved at her quick thinking and began marching towards the store.

"Rae Ann, there's no hurry. Don't worry about it. Rae Ann, come back here." Rae Ann could hear Kyle's voice continue to rise as he tried to get her attention, but Rae Ann kept her eyes forward and walked onward. She avoided the curious stares from the townspeople and was grateful when the automatic doors of the grocery store welcomed her inside.

Kyle watched her go. He wanted to follow her into the store and ask her why she wouldn't meet his eyes. A beeping horn sounded behind him and didn't allow for any more thought on the subject. Kyle put his finger on the power button that raised the window and took his foot off the brake. He let the truck creep past the store front, but the windows had turned opaque from the glaring sun.

A slow smile spread across his face, when he recalled their kiss from last night. He figured that she too was maybe a little embarrassed at all that they had shared the previous evening. And damn but didn't she look good wearing his sweatshirt. With that thought, Kyle put his foot heavy on the gas pedal and sped out of town toward the Buttercup.

~ * ~

Rae Ann pushed open the door of Kyle's apartment with her foot and dropped the bags of various cleaners next to the console table. Jasmine was resting comfortably on the sofa and didn't even give Rae Ann a second glance. A quick look around the apartment told her that most of the cleaning would just require some picking up and putting away. The bathroom was still gleaming, so the only real dirty work would be the kitchen. The dishes from last night's dinner were still on the kitchen counter and on the dining room table. Rae Ann decided to start there. She cleared off the table and wiped it down.

Putting away the candles, Rae Ann took a moment to sniff the mild sandalwood scent one last time. She was trying desperately not to remember the kiss they shared last night, but the memories flooded back into her mind. Rae Ann stood in front of the empty chair that Kyle had occupied last night. Her eyes drifted shut of their own accord. She could feel his strong arms wrapping around her waist, his flushed cheek pressing against her belly.

"You've got to stop this, Rae Ann," she said aloud into the empty apartment. Her voice seemed to echo back at her from the stark walls.

To cause distraction, Rae Ann sauntered into the living room and flipped on the television. It was on the same station that she had turned off last night. She absently picked up clothes from a pile on the floor and folded them properly as she heard the distinct tone of Marley Cavanaugh's voice. Rae Ann smirked, as her only consolation was that the network must have Marley operating twenty-four hours a day.

After folding the pile of clothes, Rae Ann rolled up the sleeves of Kyle's sweatshirt and tackled the mess of Kyle's kitchen. She scrubbed all the dishes and pots till they were gleaming and placed them back into the cabinets where she found them. She wiped off all of the counters and stove top before filling a bucket she had found in the pantry with mop water. Rae Ann looked everywhere but could not find a mop so she dropped to her hands and knees and began scouring the linoleum surface with a dish cloth.

The task was arduous but gave Rae Ann something on which to focus her attention. The kitchen was nothing more than a galley space and Rae Ann mopped and backed slowly towards the door that led into the dining room. Once she reached there, something inside her seemed to snap and she couldn't make herself put the rag down. She quickly grabbed a broom and swept the hardwood surface of the dining room floor and then set out again on her hands and knees to wipe down the entire floor.

When at last she reached the entrance to the living room, Rae Ann stood and admired her work. A huge smile danced on her lips as she felt proud of her accomplishment. And for at least two hours, the thought of Kyle, or anything for that matter, had not crossed Rae Ann's mind. In the living room the numbers on the clock proclaimed the time to be quarter till two in the afternoon. Rae Ann had never dreamed that she'd worked so long and hard on cleaning just two rooms. As if to convince her of the time, Rae Ann's stomach growled with hunger. She decided to go back to her apartment and fix a quick lunch, then she would tackle the living room and be done with Kyle's cleaning.

Once in her own pristinely clean space, Rae Ann felt grimy from the day's task and decided that a quick shower before eating would not interfere with finishing her job. Of course, she had all day. From what she knew, Kyle was working an early shift at the bar today. He wouldn't be home until around seven or seven thirty. Surely everything would be finished by then. Rae Ann would be packed and gone before Kyle ever knew what happened.

The hot water bounced deliciously off Rae Ann's skin and stung the scrape on her elbow where it had earlier kissed the ground. She was scrubbed clean and dressed within a half an hour and had snuggled into a kelly green top and another pair of jeans she had brought with her. Rae Ann fixed herself a small salad and heated up a can of soup in a saucepan she had smuggled from Kyle's kitchen.

Truly, Rae Ann knew that she would miss this place. If she had not chosen to complicate the situation by falling for Kyle, she could have seen herself making a home here. The fact of the matter made Rae Ann sad. She finished her late lunch in the silence of her apartment and washed up the meager dishes. Thinking now would be a good time to finish cleaning Kyle's apartment, Rae Ann headed for the door. Just as she was about to pull the doorknob towards her a soft knock echoed on the other side. Rae Ann was startled to see Kyle before her.

"Come with me," he reached out his hand to her. "I have a surprise."

With the sight of him, every plan that Rae Ann had made to leave simply vanished into the air. "I'm not finished cleaning," Rae Ann uttered even as she reached her hand out to his.

"It can wait." A wry smile played on his lips and the excitement in his voice made Rae Ann forget everything. Kyle loaded her into his truck and took the same road out of town that Rae Ann had run on just this morning. She gazed out over the grassy lands that steadily rose upwards.

After several twists and turns in the road Kyle pulled into a visitor's parking area of the Shawnee National Forest. As Rae Ann slid out of the passenger side of the truck, Kyle rounded the front and held out his hand once more, for her to take. Rae Ann slid her tiny hand into the welcomeness of Kyle's palm and allowed this young boy to lead her.

Without another word, they started along the flagstone trail and pushed into the wilderness. Kyle moved nimbly in front of her, blocking most of what she could see. Rae Ann breathed in the smells of the dirt and leaves. The budding spring was evident in the blooming wildflowers. They walked past a small bubbling stream and Rae Ann stopped to place her hand in the cool water.

When she looked up at Kyle from where she crouched, he seemed like the vision of a God. Sunlight had found its way through the thickening leaves of the forest trees with the strength of a magnetic force and bounced lightly off the blond waves of his hair. A second ray had reflected off the water in the tiny stream and pierced deep into the green of his eyes. The pair sparkled and shined as they watched Rae Ann, unblinking.

Satisfied with the stream, they once again continued on the path, until Rae Ann's legs were shaky from walking. Suddenly Kyle stopped in front of her sending her almost crashing into the back of him. Rae Ann placed a hand on the waist of his jeans to steady herself and the contact made them both aware of how alone they were. Kyle slowly pulled her around in front of him and Rae Ann peered over the most beautiful sight she had ever seen.

In Wisconsin, she had fallen in love with the hills instantly, but their snow covered tops seemed stark and cold compared to the full, lush landscape that lay before her. The view was outstanding and so breathtaking that Rae Ann momentarily lost herself.

Softly behind her, Kyle whispered, "it is called the Garden of the Gods."

Rae Ann beamed and breathlessly replied, "How appropriate."

After several minutes of silence, Rae Ann spoke again, "Kyle, this place is amazing. I can see now why you would never want to leave here."

Kyle shoved his hands deep into his pockets and moved up to stand beside her. She turned to him, but his eyes were lost on the forest. The vision of times gone by, no doubt reliving themselves inside his mind.

"I used to come here a lot. To think. This spot seemed to be the only one where I could really get an answer or come up with a solution. After Klein and I lost our mom, we didn't know how we would make it. I came up here and I just knew that somehow everything would just work out." Rae Ann knew without anyone telling her that Kyle had come here again after the accident. She absently wondered if he would come back later after she was gone in hopes of forgetting her as well.

Rae Ann turned her attention back to the lay of the land, while Kyle continued to speak. "Can you imagine in this world of advancement and technology that here in this little corner of Illinois are three thousand acres of virtually undisturbed land. Land that has survived flooding and rain and snow and sandstorms. I guess I kind of feel like the land, you know. I've been through a lot but if the land can survive, then I can, too."

At that moment, Rae Ann loved Kyle. For better or worse, she loved him to the very core of her being. Nothing in the world could have meant more to her at that moment then being here in the Garden of the Gods with Kyle Bennett. Not his age or her age seemed even to have any significance. Rae Ann reached her arms out to encircle his waist and laid her head against Kyle's chest. He too moved his long arms around her small body and leaned in close. The steady beating of

Kyle's heart spoke to Rae Ann and she could have stayed in that instance forever.

"Let's go," Kyle broke into her silent conversation, "there's more." Rae Ann could not imagine anything more amazing that what she had just witnessed, but followed along as Kyle escorted her farther up the trail. He showed her Camel Rock and then kissed her sweetly as they admired the Devil's Smokestack. More wildflowers were sprinkled along the path as they completed the trail.

By the time, they finally made their way back to Kyle's truck, the sun had dipped low in the sky and Rae Ann was weary from the experience. Much to Kyle's delight, Rae Ann slid over from the passenger side and settled into the middle of the bench seat next to Kyle. He slung his arm behind her and draped it across the back of the seat.

Rae Ann felt small against him but not smothered. Any further thoughts of her leaving tonight were all but erased from her mind. Rae Ann was still buzzing with excitement from the day's events, but Kyle seemed calm. He drove only a short distance, back the way they had come, but this time turning sharply onto a road that Rae Ann would have missed. A small sign noted Karbers Ridge Road and they bounced along coming to rest in a clearing not five hundred feet from the main highway, but it seemed like a whole other world.

Kyle slipped the truck into park, but didn't cut the engine. The headlights shone out over the bare piece of land as the light slowly faded from the sky. From the bed of his truck, Kyle produced a cooler, a picnic basket and a faded chambray blanket. Rae Ann helped him spread the soft material over the bumpy earth and took plates and silverware from the basket.

"Where did you get all of this?" Rae Ann asked incredulously as Kyle began pulling cheese and crackers, chicken salad and croissants from the cooler.

"I hate to admit this, but Klein helped. If it had been me, we would have been dining on the bologna I bought yesterday at the store."

Rae Ann laughed softly and replied, "I doubt that." The musical rhythm of her voice carried over the wind and caressed Kyle like an embrace. He watched her delicately bite into the food and for a full minute forgot that he was in the process of opening a bottle of wine.

After the food had been consumed and cleared from the blanket, Rae Ann placed her wineglass aside and laid her head in Kyle's lap. By then, he had shut the truck's headlights off and the stars were shining in full force.

"In Madison, you can't see the stars. There are too many streetlights," Rae Ann pointed out with a note of sadness in her voice.

"That is too bad," Kyle said, stroking her blond hair away from her face. "I can't imagine not being able to see the stars. People think that small towns aren't good for anything."

"Yeah," Rae Ann agreed, "I used to be one of those people. When I moved to Madison, I thought I had died and gone to heaven. I wanted out of the small, backward town that my father lived in so bad I could taste it."

Kyle stared down at Rae Ann in the dark. "That is the first I have heard about your family."

Rae Ann sat up and moved her mouth close to Kyle's. "Someday maybe I will tell you the whole story and then you can tell me your story."

"Why don't you tell me now?"

"Because it is a long story. One that I have tried really hard to forget. I no longer speak to my parents. I haven't spoken to them in a long time," Rae Ann's voice was forlorn and for a moment she was sorry that she had been so callus toward the people that had given her life.

"Now might be a good time to start over, Rae Ann," Kyle said, softly as he ran a hand along her smooth cheek.

"Hmm," Rae Ann sighed, "say my name again."

"Rae Ann," Kyle uttered breathlessly, "your name is so beautiful. At the very least you should thank your parents for that."

Rae Ann tossed her head of blond hair to the sky and laughed. "Actually, just my mother and I'm not so sure I have her to thank." Kyle's look of confusion spurned Rae Ann on. "My mother told me once that she actually named me Rain. I don't really know whether it was a mispronunciation or some nurse just felt sorry for a little baby being cursed with such a name, but it somehow became Rae Ann.

"Anyway, the birth certificate was filed before my mother realized the mistake and by then it was too late. She decided it was fate. Her name was Ronette, so we became Ron and Rae. Stupid, huh?"

"No," Kyle shook his head, "it's not stupid at all. I can tell that you really care, Rae Ann. I think you have tried to suppress that side of you, but I think you should call her sometime. You know, in reality we aren't all that different."

"Maybe you're just rubbing off on me, Bennett."

Before Kyle could reply, Rae Ann crushed her mouth on to Kyle's and kissed him deeply. He leaned slowly back on the blanket bringing her with him. Their bodies melted together on the ground as Kyle's hands began exploring Rae Ann's body. Her breathing became rapid and Kyle felt her shiver on top of him. He ran his hands up her bare arms and felt the goose bumps. Stupidly, he had thought his passionate kisses had caused her shivering, but now knew that she was getting cold in the rapidly dropping temperature of the night.

"Let's go somewhere warm," Kyle stated and Rae Ann agreed with a laugh and a nod of her head. They quickly picked up the remnants of their picnic and raced to the truck, eager to be close to each other again. They were giggling like junior high school kids on a first date as they entered the apartment building. Rae Ann started towards Kyle's apartment, but he stopped her. "Can we go to your place?"

"Sure. I just assumed that—" Rae Ann started.

"I think we would be more comfortable," Kyle interrupted and then hurriedly added, "your place is cleaner."

"Not for long, mister," Rae Ann retorted as she let herself into her apartment, "that place is going to be spotless by tomorrow." Kyle stopped her halfway into the living room, grabbing her arm at the elbow. Rae Ann winced slightly as his hand came in contact with the scrape from earlier.

"You don't really have to clean my apartment," he said tenderly.

"I know. But it actually been really cathartic for me," Rae Ann explained, "plus it looks a hell of a lot better now."

Kyle laughed with her and pulled her into the apartment and up against him. Moments before his lips made contact with hers a knock at the door sent both of them away from each other like boxers retreating to their opposite corners of the ring.

"Come in," Rae Ann called out once she was at a safe distance from Kyle. Klein entered the apartment and looked between the two. He could easily tell that he had interrupted something.

"Rae Ann, I'm sorry to intrude, but I thought you should know that someone was in the bar asking about you this evening." Rae Ann's body chilled to the bone.

"Oh God, its Grant. He's found me." Rae Ann stepped up to the small kitchen table and grabbed a hold of it to steady herself. "I knew he would find me. He has every resource at his disposal," Rae Ann rambled on, unaware that she was alluding to Grant's wealth and power with her words.

"Who's Grant?" Klein asked, clearly confused by the topic.

"Did you see him? Was he angry?" Rae Ann continued, ignoring Klein's question.

Kyle quietly explained a brief version of Rae Ann's situation to his older brother while Rae Ann stood lost in her thoughts. She remembered the night in the kitchen when she had confronted Grant. Over the months of their marriage, Grant had become increasingly volatile as he drank more and more. At first, she assumed that Grant would be indifferent to her disappearing act, but now she was concerned with wondering if Grant had been furious when he realized she had left him. There was no telling what he was capable of doing.

From where Kyle stood, he could tell that Rae Ann was visibly shaken. He crossed the room in record time and placed his hands on Rae Ann's shoulders.

"No, I didn't see him," Klein continued, his eyes softened by the predicament of his new friend, "Terri told me about the man. She said he was handsome, well put together. He had a drink at the bar and was there a full ten minutes before even mentioning you."

"Well, that certainly sounds like Grant. Especially the drinking part."

"Of course, she told him that you had stopped there on your way through town, but she didn't know where you were now. Anyway, I just wanted you to know," Klein turned towards the door then stopped. "I think it would be best if Kyle stayed here with you tonight. Just to make sure you're all right."

"Yes," Kyle agreed, relieved that he had been given the approval by his big brother, "I think that's a good idea." Rae Ann nodded and thanked Klein. When the elder Bennett had left, Kyle turned Rae Ann towards her.

"Whatever has happened between you, Rae Ann, I will not allow Grant to hurt you." Rae Ann clung to Kyle and his words, hoping that both were as solid as they seemed. Again, all of the passion between the pair had been doused, only this time not with water from the sink but with the remnants of Rae Ann's past.

"Will you just hold me, Kyle?" They retreated to the bedroom of Rae Ann's apartment and settled onto the bed. Rae Ann lay facing the wall and felt Kyle's body move up tightly behind her. He draped his arm over her waist and she laced the fingers of her left hand with his right. Rae Ann felt the soft whisper of his breath on the top of her head and fought hard to keep her eyes open. In the end, the rhythm of their heartbeats lulled Rae Ann into a dreamless sleep.

Twenty-five

Tuesday, April 11th

It was nearly noon before the walls started closing in on Rae Ann. She had been in the apartment all morning, alone. For once, she had been allowed the luxury of sleeping late. Perhaps the warmth of another person in the bed beside her had prolonged her slumber, or maybe the emotional stress had finally taken its toll, but in any event Rae Ann awoke rested in the safety of Kyle's arms. He was already awake, staying beside her to let her sleep. But now he was gone. Kyle still had a life to lead, an existence that did not include Rae Ann.

As she sauntered from room to room she wondered about getting a job in this town. If she planned on staying that was really the next logical step. Of course, now that Grant had shown up looking for her, it wasn't clear whether or not staying would be a good idea. Kyle had told her to stay put, but Rae Ann couldn't spend one more minute alone.

She crossed the hall to Kyle's apartment, determined to expend some of her restless energy on cleaning up the rest of Kyle's apartment. Rae Ann settled in front of the television once more to finish folding the clothes in the pile on the floor.

Just like yesterday, Rae Ann reached for the remote and flipped on the television for some company. Before she knew it the pile had been sorted and arranged neatly. Now all she had to do was find a home for the junk. She picked up the assorted clothing and turned to the closed door of Kyle's bedroom.

Rae Ann put her hand on the knob before she realized what she was doing. This was not her apartment and she was not in the habit of entering a person's private space. Even if Rae Ann and Kyle had shared some intimate moments, that did not give her the right. She simply placed the load of treasures in front of the door and went back in search of the vacuum.

The rest of the cleaning went fairly smoothly, especially since she really hadn't done much of the cleaning in Wisconsin. Rae Ann didn't spend all that much time at her small apartment in Madison, therefore, it never really got that dirty and she had Rosie up in Rockingham to take care of the house full time.

Suddenly a voice from the living room caused her to stop her task and retreat to a spot in front of the entertainment center. Coming from the television were the familiar introductory sounds of a late breaking special report, but what had caught her attention were three words.

Pine Trails Resort.

They had drawn her into the living room like a snake charmer's flute draws a snake from a wicker basket. The story was just beginning, but Rae Ann would never see the end. The camera was now directed at a beautiful young reporter sitting perfectly poised in front of the camera. Her tasteful powder blue suit and neatly bobbed hair reminded Rae Ann so much of herself that she reflexively reached up and smoothed her tousled tresses. A look of mock sympathy and concern that had been perfected years ago graced the woman's elegant features. But it was the words that were tumbling from the woman's mouth that had Rae Ann entranced.

"It seems as though the raging spring snow storm in Wisconsin is not the only natural disaster this week. This just in, our station has been informed that Grant Spencer, owner and operator of the Pine Trails Resort, was found dead in his home early this morning. Let's go now to the home of Mr. Spencer where Shelly Burke is on the scene. Shelly?" The screen flashed from the warm, lively anchor woman to a frozen, humorless field reporter. Rae Ann sympathized with her immediately. It was obviously cold in Wisconsin and snow was falling in a steady pattern around the woman's shoulders. Rae Ann glanced out the window at the shining sun and for an instant could believe that the story was fake. The woman's words convinced her that it was all too real.

"Thanks Lynn," Shelly said, her words came out in a plume of white breath, "this spring snow storm was certainly unexpected to the citizens of Rockingham, but the true shocker is the story of Grant Spencer. The prominent business man was found apparently murdered in his home early this morning. A missing person's report was filed with the Rockingham police department just yesterday by a member of Spencer's staff when he failed to show up for work. When Mr. Spencer's housekeeper arrived back from vacation this morning, she discovered the body in the ransacked living room.

"Although results of a complete autopsy are still pending, authorities speculate that Mr. Spencer has been dead for several days. The wife of Grant Spencer, Rae Ann Lewis, resigned from her field reporting position at WZZY Channel 8 news out of Madison early last month following an alleged incident regarding Senator Francis Showalter. Ms. Lewis is currently unavailable, but is wanted in questioning for the death of her husband..."

That is precisely the point where Rae Ann stopped listening. A million thoughts began swirling in her mind. What were these people trying to say? Was Grant really dead? Had her husband just been reduced to 'a body in a ransacked living room'? Rae Ann felt sick. She gazed at her surroundings in shame and disbelief. What was she doing here? If she had been at home where she belonged then her husband might not be dead. But no, she was in someone else's apartment. Someone that she was likely in love with.

Rae Ann replayed the story in her mind and cringed when the reporter had mentioned her resignation from the station and the scandal with Showy. What were they trying to imply? Could the reporter have been alluding to the fact that Rae Ann killed her husband? She should have been prepared for how the reporter would twist and distort the truth. She herself had done it many times. It gave the story depth and piqued the interest of the viewer. It had certainly piqued Rae Ann's interest.

Without a moment's hesitation, Rae Ann became furious when she realized that they had only reported on Grant's murder because he was *her* husband. A woman shrouded in suspicion due to her involvement in the defamation of Senator Showalter. Rae Ann dashed from the apartment into the hallway. She slammed the door shut behind her, not even thinking about the vacuum left out in the middle of the floor. The air seemed much easier to breathe in the hallway so she paused to catch a ragged breath. Her lungs were on fire and a jackhammer had somehow found its way into her brain. Oddly though, there were no tears.

I'm just in shock, Rae Ann told herself, unconvincingly. Why wasn't she crying? Her husband had just been found dead for Christ's sake. She had to get out of here and back to Wisconsin. She had to find out what had happened. The woman on the news said that she was wanted for questioning.

How could they think that she was capable of killing her own husband? Of course, who really knew her? Only her faithful camera man really, but that part of her life was over. Rae Ann had had no real association with the people that frequented the resort or even those that were employed there. Only Howard, but what could he say besides she had waved to him every time she passed his cottage or saw him on the grounds. In truth, the facts didn't make her look good. Rae Ann was a public figure gone bad. It wouldn't be too hard to assume that she went crazy with jealousy after losing her job and killed Grant in some lover's quarrel. Then, of course, she fled the scene. She had never wanted to go back to Wisconsin, didn't want to have to face her shortcomings as a wife, but now she was left with no choice. Rae Ann was going to have to clear her good name and make sure the real person, that killed Grant, was brought to justice.

Rae Ann suddenly felt a sense of purpose and this thought motivated her into action. She was just two feet from her apartment door when the entry way door swung open dramatically. Klein entered with the bright Illinois sun flooding in behind him. He put on a smile, but quickly changed his countenance when he saw her state of distress. Rae Ann's pale complexion grew even whiter as he stepped up to her side. "My dear, what's going on?" His concern was genuine, but Rae Ann did not have time for a heart to heart. She had hoped to be gone from the apartment building before Klein or Kyle returned. Something she should have done days ago. This way she wouldn't have to explain anything.

Rae Ann searched Klein's face. She couldn't tell him that Grant was dead. Without knowing what else to do, Rae Ann put on her best smile. The effort was tremendous. "Klein, hi. Nothing's wrong. Why do you ask?" Her phony display was so transparent that even she cringed. Klein sighed and slipped his hands inside his pants pockets.

"You're leaving aren't you? Did something happen with Kyle?"

Rae Ann's smile faded in spite of her attempt to appear normal. "Klein, listen, I am leaving, but this has nothing to do with Kyle. I can't tell you. I wish I could, but I can't. I have to go. I'm sorry."

In an afterthought she added, "Please don't tell Kyle."

Rae Ann shut the door on Klein's hurt stare and felt terrible. She stood with her back against the door and her eyes shut, but it seemed that no amount of deep breaths was going to fill the void that had settled itself into the middle of her chest. Rae Ann wished she could just slide down on the floor and disappear through the cracks in the wooden planks. Here she was running again.

She pulled the boxes and her suitcase from the hall closet and threw them on the bed. That's when she remembered the necklace. The pearl necklace that her grandmother had given her was, as far as she knew, still sitting on the bed in Kyle's spare bedroom along with the dress she had worn to dinner. Rae Ann knew she couldn't leave it. It was her only link to her childhood.

Tiptoeing to the door, Rae Ann listened intently. From the lack of noise, there didn't appear to be anyone in the hallway, but she cautiously peaked out just in case. There was no one. Apparently, Klein had retreated to his upstairs apartment, most likely to ponder the strange way Rae Ann had dismissed him. A quick glance at her watch told her that Kyle would still be occupied at work for the next four hours. This would giver her plenty of time since she didn't have much to pack.

Kyle's apartment was just as she had left it moments ago. The TV still blared endlessly and Rae Ann stepped over the vacuum cord to get to it. She pushed the power button violently as if to punish the television for delivering her the devastating news of Grant's death.

Marching towards the spare bedroom, Rae Ann ignored the cat that had found a new resting spot on top of the clothes she had placed in front of Kyle's bedroom door.

The necklace was gone, so was her dress.

She had not encountered either item in any of the rooms she had cleaned earlier and was certain that Kyle had not returned them to her place. *Where could they be?* Rae Ann stood in the middle of the room with her hands planted firmly on her hips. She did not need this wild goose chase, but knew she wouldn't be leaving Illinois until her necklace was safe back in its blue velvet box. The only other room in the apartment that hadn't been checked was Kyle's bedroom. Rae Ann's hand hesitated on the doorknob for only a second. She pushed the door open wide and stepped over the small obstacle in front of it.

Cat and all.

Her eyes swept the room for the pearls, but settled on something else entirely. She moved farther into the room, head cocked slightly to the right. Her eyes narrowed reflexively as she focused on the object that was perched on top of Kyle's chest of drawers. A simple 8 x 10 wooden frame housed a picture that made Rae Ann completely forget why she had entered the room in the first place.

At first Rae Ann wondered how Kyle had gotten a picture of her. But when she got closer she realized that it was not her in the picture but a different girl. Their hair color and cut were virtually identical and both had the same piercing blue eyes. But this girl's face was softer, more innocent. She had a smaller, pointed chin and the tiniest nose Rae Ann had ever seen. She was like a pixie, tiny like Rae Ann but also much younger. It wouldn't be a far stretch to assume that Rae Ann could have been this girl's older sister or perhaps an aunt. Such ferocious sweetness was harbored in the girl's smile that Rae Ann choked up. She couldn't even remember when she had smiled so genuinely.

Next to the large frame there was a smaller picture of the same girl, in fact, the whole top of the dresser was covered with pictures of her. Some with her hair in a short ponytail lying in the sun. There was one where the girl was hanging upside down from a set of parallel bars in what looked like a gymnasium. Rae Ann tore her gaze away from the dresser and surveyed the rest of the room. Every available table top was covered with photos. Most were duplicates of the same picture that Rae Ann had first picked up. The whole room was some kind of makeshift shrine to this beautiful girl. This beautiful girl that just happened to remind Rae Ann of herself.

She spotted her pearl necklace on the nightstand beside Kyle's bed. Her knees felt weak and Rae Ann sat heavily on the bed. The necklace lay silently beside yet another picture of the girl, only this time the frame was different. It was fancy, intricately carved gold colored border with a smooth silver colored inner border. At the bottom, Rae Ann could just make out the lovingly inscribed words: *To my one and only. Love, Your Pride and Joy.*

Rae Ann's heart dropped completely down to her toes and then bounced back up into her throat. She recalled her conversation with Snappy just this morning.

Do I remind you of anyone?
As a matter of fact you do.
Who?
You look like Kyle's pride and joy.

"Oh my God," Rae Ann muttered now. She remembered the stares she had gotten at the grocery store and the way Nora Presley had done a double take on the stairs yesterday morning. They had undoubtedly known this young lady and were wondering why this phantom new woman bore such a striking resemblance to her. Except Rae Ann had never passed this girl on the street. Where was she? Anger flashed like lightning across the sky of Rae Ann's mind. The girl was obviously not here, but Rae Ann was. And she seemed to be the next best thing. That night after dinner, Kyle had tried to tell her about an old girlfriend, but she had cut him off. Was he going to tell her about this particular girlfriend? Was he going to casually mention that they were extremely similar in appearance? Or was he going to tell Rae Ann that he was only falling for her because she looked like a girl he obviously cared for a great deal?

Rae Ann surmised that Kyle must have been looking at this girl's pictures that day she had startled him before dinner and it was no wonder why he steered her away from his apartment last night when they came home from the forest. These thoughts only inflamed the anger and frustration that Rae Ann felt. How could she have let things get so far out of control? When Rae Ann worked as a reporter, she was always the one in charge. She called the shots and certainly didn't let anyone get the best of her. Well, not until last month anyway. It pained Rae Ann to think that the mindset of a career, she had trained and worked at for so long, was already slipping from her mind. She could let no more of these thoughts get in the way of her leaving.

Rae Ann picked up the necklace and left Kyle's apartment, the picture still firmly clutched in her grasp. Once safely back in her own apartment, Rae Ann pulled open the chest of drawers fiercely and closed her eyes to the contents. She had been a fool to think that she could have made a home here.

She removed the meager amount of clothes and shoved them hastily into the nearest box. A sheen of molten lava tears blinded her, but she never slowed from her task until the boxes and suitcase were full. Rae Ann bent to pick up a forgotten sweatshirt when her eyes settled back on the picture frame that she had thrown on the bed. It lay undisturbed right where she had dropped it. Rae Ann could have surrendered to her grief right then, but the sight of the picture only turned up the burner under the pot of fury that was boiling inside of her. She was motivated back into action.

Rae Ann roughly grabbed her makeup bag from the larger of the two boxes and headed into the bathroom to gather up the few toiletries she had placed in the medicine cabinet. She was more than halfway finished when she heard the front door open and close.

"Rae Ann?!"

Damn.

She had almost made it. She finished putting her assorted lipsticks and eye shadows into the bag hoping Kyle would just go away. He didn't. When Rae Ann turned to the bathroom's only exit, Kyle's frame filled the space, blocking her way out. "What's going on? Where are you going?"

Rae Ann didn't answer, she simply studied the yellowing, plastic light switch cover with great interest. He knew she was ignoring him—or at least trying to do so. "Rae Ann?" Kyle reached out to touch her but she shoved his hand away roughly.

"Don't touch me."

Kyle reeled back in shock, which gave Rae Ann just the opportunity to slide past him through the doorway.

"Whoa, hang on here. What did I do?" Kyle asked, following her into the bedroom.

"You know, Kyle. Not everything is about you." The fury inside her was starting to boil over the sides and she was unable to contain it. Rae Ann picked up the smaller box and then set it firmly back down. She carefully placed both hands on top of the cardboard, wishing the corrugated surface could absorb some of the anger that was coming off of her in waves.

Turning her head slowly, Rae Ann faced Kyle for the first time since he arrived. A stricken expression was frozen on his face. He had no idea what was about to hit him and for one sick moment Rae Ann relished the attack she was about to launch. There was so much to say that she had no idea where to start. "You know, maybe I'm wrong Kyle. Maybe this *is* about you. Maybe this is all about you." Rae Ann didn't even stop for a breath before posing the next question. "How old are you, Kyle?"

Rae Ann's arms locked on top of the box, fingernails digging into the sides leaving half moon indentions. There was no more grief for her lost husband, not at the moment. Only anger, pure white-hot anger pulsing through her veins. Anger at Kyle, at Grant, at whoever was responsible for Grant's death, but mostly at herself. Rae Ann had left Grant by himself in a vulnerable condition and now he was dead. This thought alone was enough to put a lid on the pot of inner turmoil and for the time being, calming her. Rae Ann looked back to Kyle for an answer. He hesitated only a second.

"I'm twenty-four," he blurted, "but I don't see—"

"Twenty-four years old," Rae Ann said more to herself than to Kyle.

Finally, the truth.

"Do you even know how old I am?" Rae Ann asked.

"No and I don't care about—" he said taking a step towards her.

"I'm thirty-five, Kyle," Rae Ann interrupted harshly, "that makes me eleven years older than you. Eleven years, Kyle." She released her death grip on the box and sat down heavily on the bed. Kyle made another move toward her, but she held up her hand to stop him. "You're just a baby, Kyle. I know it may seem like a very short time to you, but the eleven years that separate twenty-four and thirty-five are very extensive. You have so much left to do with your life. Things to do, to go through, to see.

"You shouldn't be expected to settle down, not yet, and it's obvious that isn't what you want. You continue to live under your brother's protective cocoon because it is safe and unthreatening. You haven't lived yet. You don't even know what life is."

Even as the words were pouring out of her mouth Rae Ann wanted to take them back. She didn't even have to look at Kyle to notice the change that had transformed him. He stood rigid in the center of the room. His muscular arms were glued stiff, straight to his sides ending in fists held so tightly, Rae Ann could see the whites of his knuckles.

"Kyle," she started.

"I don't know what life is?" Each word delivered through clenched teeth was clearly enunciated so that she wouldn't misunderstand. "I'm not the one who drove up in my car, wearing expensive clothes, wanting everyone to feel sorry for me because things weren't going my way. Because things were out of your control. Now, I don't know where you came from, but I do know what my life has been like. I've had people taken from me right and left and still I push through. I make the best of things. I stick with it, but you, you just run away. You didn't stay and face your problems. You just pick up and leave them behind hoping that the next life that you start will be the one that makes you happy. So don't sit there and say that I'm the one who doesn't know what life is, because as far as I'm concerned you're the one with the seriously distorted perception of reality."

The room was so silent in the wake of Kyle's booming voice that Rae Ann uttered a small sound to make sure she still had hearing. Kyle fixed a hard, green stare on her until she had to look away or risk being blinded as well.

211

"I don't know what to say," Rae Ann muttered, delicately. Her eyes were downcast like a child that has been sent to the corner for punishment. She absently ran her hands over the knit fabric of her pants.

"Just forget it. We both said some things we didn't mean." When she didn't reply, Kyle turned and headed for the door.

"I'm going back," Rae Ann blurted out as if that was going to make things better. Kyle glanced back at her over his shoulder, but didn't come back into the room like she had hoped.

As if he already knew the current situation in Wisconsin Kyle said, "There's nothing left for you there."

Rae Ann could tell that the anger was gone from his voice. Now she could only hear defeat and hurt in his tone. Kyle looked at her full force. He was ten feet away from her, but the look he gave, reached out and ripped Rae Ann's heart from her chest. She knew she loved him, but she could never say it. A full minute passed before Kyle broke the barrier between them with his words.

"Don't go. We were just getting close."

"Kyle, stop, please. I'm eleven years older than you. It can't work."

"Jesus, Rae Ann, would you stop with that damn age difference excuse? It doesn't matter if I'm twenty-four or forty-four. The truth is... I love you. You can continue to lie to yourself or whatever helps you sleep at night, but I am in love with you and nothing is going to change that." Rae Ann groaned inwardly and leaned forward, clasping her hands between her legs.

It was true she had been less concerned about age differences when she had learned that Grant was nearly ten years her senior. Being with Kyle had made her feel young but now knowing his youthful age it just made her feel old.

"You have known me less than a week, Kyle. That isn't love," she argued.

"You're right, Rae Ann," Kyle smirked, his voice dripping with sarcasm, "a week is too soon, but a month or two goes by and hell, its true love, right?"

"That wasn't fair," Rae Ann retorted, jumping to her feet.

"No, Rae Ann, life isn't fair. I love you and I know you feel it, too. Even if you don't say it, but I can say it now or a year from now and it will still mean the same thing. Age difference or not. You can't choose who you love," he finished dramatically.

The rage inside her was again instantaneous. It raced a mean course through her body and she snapped her head up to meet his cat-like stare. "Really, Kyle? Because I think that is exactly what you've done. When I first came here, I was overwhelmed with how honest you were with me, about your life, about everything. Now I know you're just like everyone else."

"What are you talking about?" Kyle's voice trembled slightly. Rae Ann turned back to the bed and picked up the picture frame half hidden by the disheveled bedspread. The bottom of Kyle's stomach dropped out and his inner workings became liquid. He knew what Rae Ann held even before she showed him.

His pride and Joy.

"Did you love her?" Rae Ann croaked, her throat felt coated in cotton. Kyle stood dumbfounded, his tongue glued to the roof of his mouth.

"What were you doing in my room?"

Rae Ann closed her eyes and shook the picture fiercely. "Did you love her?"

"Yes," Kyle said fumbling over himself, his words barely audible.

"Did you *choose* to love me because I remind you of her?" Rae Ann didn't really want to hear the answer, but she waited for the response anyway with eyes still tightly shut.

"Maybe at first, Rae Ann, but not now. When I first saw you sitting in the bar, you reminded me so much of her. I couldn't even take my eyes off of you. But then I got to know you, Rae. It's you I love, not her. She's long gone." Rae Ann had tried her best to tune out the hurtful words, but they had penetrated her inner defenses like knives through raw silk. There was no fight left in her body.

Rae Ann held the picture out for Kyle to take and then opened her eyes. He reached out timidly as if she would attack him and then picked the picture from between her fingers. In her eyes, Kyle saw nothing but hurt and pain. Something he had promised he would never do to her.

"Good-bye, Kyle," she whispered.

"Don't do this, Rae Ann. We have something real. I am not a wealthy man and I have nothing to offer you, but I will never hurt you or lie to you again. I won't treat you like he did. He doesn't deserve you. When will you let go and move on with your life?"

"Like you've moved on from her?" Rae Ann asked, pointing to the picture.

"Joy is a different story," Kyle tried to find the right way to explain.

Rae Ann clucked her tongue and mumbled, "Your pride and Joy. That's cute, but Kyle I don't see how it's any different."

Kyle stared at the picture so intently, that Rae Ann wasn't sure if he had heard her last sentence. His next words made it painfully clear that he had, "It's different because I killed her."

~ * ~

To Rae Ann, time completely ceased inside the tiny bedroom. Overhead, Nora Presley went about her business in a series of creaks and protests from the ceiling, virtually unaware of the sudden stall in the conversation below her.

"What do you mean you killed her?" Rae Ann tried to keep the tremble out of her voice, but the efforts were fruitless. She had already begun backing away from Kyle, desperately trying to figure a way out of this predicament. Kyle still stood rooted to the same spot, but he had placed his hands over his face to hide the shame and guilt. The picture of the girl was still caught in Kyle's hand. Rae Ann thought it looked silly just hanging there in the air.

Nothing in the room moved or changed for what seemed like hours, but was in reality only a few seconds. Kyle could have turned to stone for all Rae Ann knew or cared. She was about to attempt a drastic escape through the room's only window, when she heard his muffled voice through the open cracks between fingers. "I took her up there. I made her go."

Moments ago she had wanted him to tell her the whole story, but now that he was actually speaking, she suddenly didn't want to know. Rae Ann held up her hands to ward off his words.

"You know, maybe this isn't such a good idea. I've seen enough movies to know that when the killer confesses to the innocent victim then they have to be killed, too."

Kyle shook his head in haste, his eyebrows pulling together tightly. "No, it wasn't like that."

"It wasn't like what?" Rae Ann questioned breathlessly, "Because the last time I checked when someone says 'I killed her,' it generally means that they killed her." Kyle walked to the bed and sat down amongst the packed boxes. He was only feet from Rae Ann, but she held her ground.

"I want to tell you what happened. I wanted to tell you after dinner the other night, but you stopped me." Kyle looked up at her expectantly and patted the space of empty bed beside him. "I just did what she wanted, but I still feel as guilty as if I had taken a pillow and smothered the life out of her."

Rae Ann blinked her blue eyes and rested her hand at her collar bone. As if having a mind of their own, her feet began moving one in front of the other toward the bed. Toward Kyle. Rae Ann sat beside him, their knees brushing as Kyle turned to face her.

"If we are going to be honest with each other from here on out, then I think you should hear this story. I want you to know every little detail about my life up until this point," he stared unblinking, "or I'm afraid you're never going to love me."

Rae Ann opened her mouth, but closed it with only a click of her teeth. He was ready to continue the story and Rae Ann was finally ready to listen. Kyle's eyes stared right into her, but they were slightly unfocused. Not staring at her, but beyond her seeing something that she did not.

"Joy had just graduated from high school. And she had actually agreed to marry me that following December. Hell, I had proposed to her right there at the graduation ceremony. She was so beautiful."

Rae Ann dropped her head down to look at her hands. The last thing she wanted was Kyle comparing the likeness of her features to those of his long lost love. "I called her my pride and Joy. It started as a joke, but it used to make her smile every time I said it, so I said it all of the time. I would have said anything to see her smile." Kyle smiled now at the small picture.

"About a month before our wedding, we got invited up to Shepard's Mountain for the weekend. That is in Wisconsin," Kyle added as an afterthought for Rae Ann's benefit. Rae Ann nodded silently, having never been to that ski resort herself.

Kyle continued, "Joy said we shouldn't go because we were knee-deep in wedding plans, not to mention helping Klein with the grand opening of the Buttercup. But I pushed her to go. I have loved to ski since I was a kid, but Joy had little use for the sport. I thought that if we were going to share our lives with each other we should also share a little of what we enjoyed. After all, I had helped her pick out ribbon and dresses and jewelry for the wedding. I didn't enjoy doing it, but I did it for her. I guess I thought the least she could do was go skiing with me."

A pained expression took control of Kyle's features and twisted them harshly into a grimace. "I admit it was pretty selfish of me and I guess I made her feel guilty, because she finally agreed to go." Kyle stopped again. Rae Ann could see that his shoulders had slumped lower and his head hung farther down on his chest. It seemed as though the retelling of the story was draining the very life from him.

What surprised Rae Ann was that her hand had somehow found its way onto Kyle's knee without her knowledge. She tried subtly to slip it back onto her own lap, but it ended up dangling awkwardly in the air so Rae Ann promptly returned it to the warm spot she had created on the leg of Kyle's jeans. Kyle looked from Rae Ann's hand to her eyes, perhaps seeing her for the first time since he began talking. He wanted to say something to her, something loving, but when he opened his mouth the rest of the story just came pouring out of him in torrents.

"The first two days were great. We bought Joy all the new ski clothes at the resort shop and she was actually excited. She picked out the brightest purple ski jacket I had ever seen," Kyle said smiling involuntarily at the image, "The weather was perfect, so we started spending more time on the slopes. Towards the end of the weekend, I thought she might even want to come back sometime. Maybe even for our honeymoon. Sunday came too quickly. We were getting ready to check out, but I suggested that we hit the slopes one more time before we had to go. Joy told me to go on ahead while she finished packing because she was worried that we wouldn't make it back on time.

"I wouldn't take no for an answer and she finally, reluctantly gave in. It had begun to snow a little by the time we were on our way up, and it was making her nervous. I wouldn't back down. I thought she had done well enough the last few days to go all the way up, but she just kept saying no, that she didn't want to do so. We started arguing. Joy kept telling me to keep my voice down because the people behind us would hear. Of course, that just made me want to shout louder and by the time we go to the top we were practically screaming at each other.

"I was so agitated that when the chair lift reached our drop off, I just jumped off and raced down the mountain leaving Joy behind me. I thought a minute alone would help me cool down. I was right. By the time I reached the bottom, the only person I was mad at was myself for leaving Joy alone. By now the sky had darkened and the snow had really started to come down. I decided to wait at the bottom so I could beg for her forgiveness the moment she arrived."

A sob choked off Kyle's voice, not allowing him to continue, but Rae Ann was certain she knew what was coming next.

"She never came down did she?" Rae Ann voice wisped out like a tendril of smoke. Kyle shook his head in agony, huge tears spilled out from beneath his closed lids.

"I waited and waited, but she never came down. In the meantime, it got darker and the snow fell harder, but still I waited. I don't even know how long I stayed there just peering up at the mountain waiting for that silly purple ski jacket to come bounding down in front of me.

"Finally, I went back to the chair lift. I don't know why. I guess I thought that she had rode the chair lift back down or had gotten off at the top but was just waiting for me to come back. She wasn't there. Not at the chair lift and not at the top of the mountain so I started skiing down again. I got scared, really scared at this point. For the first time I realized she could be hurt, lying somewhere in pain. I was positively frantic.

"It was so dark and the snow was so heavy. It covered over the ski tracks almost as soon as they were cut into the snow. I couldn't believe how bad the weather had gotten in such a short time. Then over the first jump, I saw some more tracks leading off to the right into some trees. I was a little relieved because I figured that Joy had somehow gotten off track and that's what had taken her so long to get to the bottom. Surely by now she had made it to the bottom. But then I heard voices shouting from the direction of the trees. I figured it was much too dark for anyone to be starting a run, so I followed the voices."

Kyle knew he was sitting on the bed in Rae Ann's apartment, but he felt the cold mountain air penetrate his skin and heard snow crunching underfoot. The blanket of trees along the slopes had caught most of the snow so Kyle could see a little better here. He shook the vivid images out from in front of his eyes and focused again on Rae Ann. "About a hundred yards away I could make out the shapes of several people. Two were part of the search and rescue team, huddled close to the ground wearing red jackets with big white crosses on the back. Two other people were standing off to the side. I skied over as fast as I could but the snow felt like it had turned to quick sand. I started praying then. Praying for something small like a broken arm or leg."

He flashed back on to the scene again. This time all of his senses were sharp and alert. There was almost like an electric current, sparking in the air and before he even saw her lying in the snow, the metallic scent of blood hit him square in the face. Even now he physically jerked back from the hateful stench. A grotesque, red halo was steadily forming around Joy's head, melting away the snow where her head had hit the tree. The silence was deafening.

"The rescue workers went about their business never even looking in my direction but I could feel the stares from the bystanders. I didn't know what to do, so I just stood there trying to understand what was going on. I wondered why she didn't just get up and say 'It's just a scratch. I'll be okay.' And then I would turn to the rescue crew and say 'see this girl fellas? You'd better take good care of her because she is my pride and Joy.' And of course that would make her smile."

Rae Ann felt her own tears scald her cheeks before she even realized she was crying. She had turned her shoulder to Kyle, but he kept his head down and his eyes shut. "I kept saying her name over and over again. I wasn't even sure if I was talking out loud, but I kept saying it. I just knew she could hear me on some level." Kyle was choked by the tears and memories. "I kept holding on to the smallest shred of hope that she was okay, because in the middle of this mess was that silly purple ski jacket and my whole life."

Kyle reached out blindly to grasp the hand that Rae Ann had placed on his knee. He gripped it tightly as a drowning man would clutch a life preserver. As if trying to inhale Rae Ann's energy into his own spent body, Kyle took two deep breaths and exhaled only reluctantly. Finally he opened his eyes. Rae Ann could see the emerald green iris twinkling in a sea of torment and unshed tears.

Kyle searched her face for the unmistakable sign of disappointment he was sure would show in her eyes. Rae Ann didn't smile or frown nor could he see the contempt and disgust that Kyle felt towards himself. Instead, as if the story had just soaked in, Rae Ann's blue eyes softened and understanding crept on to her face. She realized then that she had never really known love as it is supposed to be. Rae Ann had not shed a tear even after just having learned that her husband was dead, but Kyle was still torn up over his lost high school sweetheart nearly four years later. Rae Ann could see Kyle's devotion to the dead girl, but only through his love for Rae Ann. She nodded in understanding. It was this look that enabled Kyle to go on.

"Then I realized they were shouting something. Their voices were distorted and slow, like I was underwater, but I guess I broke through the surface because suddenly I could hear them loud and clear. One of them was shouting, 'I've got a pulse, I've got a pulse.'"

Rae Ann felt her muscles relax in relief as if the day was saved, but then remembered that the girl was obviously dead, no matter what happened during the course of the story.

Rae Ann's muscles were no longer relaxed.

Kyle was sitting so still on the bed that Rae Ann couldn't be sure he was still breathing. He had turned away from her and placed his hands between his knees. Rae Ann wanted to touch him, but didn't for fear that he would shatter and fall to the floor in a million jagged pieces. Before she could say or do anything, he continued, "They got her off the mountain as quick as they could, but the snow and darkness made for slow moving. When we finally got to the hospital, no one would let me see her. Everyone was rushing around shouting out things that I didn't understand. I just assumed that everything would be all right. I mean, after all, she was alive.

"I sat in the waiting room with her family until the doctors allowed me to see her. I had no idea that nine hours had passed. In a million life times, I would have never been prepared for what I was about to see. It was a surrealistic nightmare. For a second, I thought I was in the wrong room because the person in that hospital bed did not look like my Joy. Her face was all bruised and swollen and they had shaved her beautiful blond hair during the surgery to repair her damaged head. She was hooked up to so many machines, with tubes running in and out of her, I couldn't stand it. I felt responsible for the whole mess. I mean, I did it. I made her go. I picked the fight. I pushed too hard, I always do. God, I loved her so much."

Kyle's voice broke and more tears rushed forth, both Kyle's and Rae Ann's. It hurt her to see that Kyle had endured so much pain. Life was truly unfair, but Rae Ann knew that all of the trouble she had endured in her childhood, nothing compared to Kyle's loss. His pause was brief, "they told me that she was brain dead. A machine would go on pumping her heart and filling her lungs with air, but for all intents and purposes, she was dead. I just couldn't make myself believe it, you know? I thought nothing like this could ever happen to us. We just loved each other too much.

"I was in complete denial. I convinced myself that she was just in a coma. I had seen TV shows where people have been in comas for long periods of time, sometimes years, and one day they just wake up. I was positive that was going to happen with Joy. I vowed never to leave her side in case she did wake up. I wanted to be there, no matter how brief it was. I wanted her to see me so I could tell her how sorry I was, and how much I loved her. I needed to hold on to that, so I took a leave of absence from the police force and stayed at Joy's side night and day. I showered there, ate there, lived there, period.

"Her family came up whenever they could, but it was not easy traveling in the winter weather. This went on for about three weeks and then one afternoon her doctor pulled me into the hallway and showed me a piece of paper. It was a Do Not Resuscitate Order. Do you know what that is?" Rae Ann nodded her head, but Kyle explained anyway. "It was this piece of paper that Joy filled out saying that she did not want to be helped on life support if anything were to happen to her. The doctor explained to me that no heroic measures should have ever taken place. Had the rescue team on the mountain been informed of this DNR, Joy would have been left to die in the cold.

"In fact, she would not have been kept on at the hospital except the paper had been misplaced until just recently. Of course, he had other reasons for telling me all of this. It just so happened that an old man in Oklahoma needed a heart transplant and Joy was a perfect match. They wanted to shut off Joy's machines so that they could give her heart to someone else," Kyle said still in disbelief of their request. "I could not believe what they were saying. They kept saying that this is something she would have wanted and I knew that, but nobody ever asked me what *I* wanted." Kyle's voice suddenly took on a wistful quality, as he recalled perhaps the most difficult time in his life.

"In the end, it didn't matter anyway. We weren't married yet so her family had all the rights. They made the decision to turn off the machines even as I held on to that little bit of hope that she was going to wake up. I held her in my arms and for two minutes she managed to hold on, but then she just took in really deep breath and sort of sighed.

"Of course, they saved the man in Oklahoma. In fact, she also saved three other people that day with her liver and kidneys. And on our wedding day, instead of marrying her, I put her in the ground." He stopped talking and wiped away the remaining tears, but he did not look in Rae Ann's direction.

"You didn't kill her, Kyle. You were just helping to fulfill her wishes." Rae Ann's throat was dry from her sobs.

"I know, but it still hurt just the same. I have never skied again after that. I just can't bring myself to relive that horrible day. I tried once, about two years ago, but by the time I got to the top of the mountain, I was physically sick." Rae Ann reached out and touched his smooth cheek with her hand. He responded by leaning into her touch and closed his eyes.

She wanted him desperately.

Rae Ann pulled him close and kissed the smooth spot behind his ear. He shuddered and reached out to encircle her waist with his powerful arms.

"I love you, Rae Ann," he muttered softly. She knew it was true, felt it in the room like another physical presence. There was no way she could deny it any longer.

"I—" Rae Ann started.

Unexpectedly a loud banging on the apartment door interrupted her speech and sent both Rae Ann and Kyle to their feet. They both glanced around awkwardly like kissing teenagers caught by their parents.

"Rae Ann? Are you still in there?" a voice called out from the hallway.

"It's Klein," Kyle said matter-of-factly starting for the door.

"Oh you're here, too. Is everything all right?" Klein's words were breathless.

"Fine," Kyle said, wiping the last of his tears.

Klein nodded with a look that said we'll-talk-about-it-later and continued into the apartment. "Rae Ann, dear, have you seen the news?"

"Yes, I know I owe you an explanation. I was just about to tell Kyle."

"Tell Kyle what?" Kyle asked.

"I have to go back to Wisconsin."

"Rae Ann, I thought we just—" Rae Ann held up her hand to silence his words.

"Kyle, Grant is dead—and they think I killed him."

Kyle stood stunned gawking back and forth between Klein and Rae Ann.

"I know you don't understand. I don't understand either," Rae Ann whispered sympathetically. Klein ushered her into a chair at the kitchen table and then joined her.

"Honey, what would give them the impression that you had anything to do with this?" Klein inquired.

"Well, even I can admit that it looks suspicious. Everyone knew that my marriage was on the rocks and I vanished from town virtually overnight."

"This doesn't make any sense," Kyle said, finally speaking up, "What happened? Where did they find him?"

"I don't know what happened," Rae Ann shook her head, "but he was found in our house. The news report said it had been ransacked. A robbery or something. So you see, I have to go back. I have to find out what's going on and tell them I didn't do it." Kyle began pacing back in forth in front of the kitchen table.

"Rae Ann, you're safe here," Klein said, softly, "and it's too late to do anything about this today. We'll all get a good night's rest and figure this out in the morning." Rae Ann glanced towards the front window of the apartment and was shocked to realize that it was dark outside. She had been so involved with Kyle and his heart-wrenching story that she had not noticed the hours ticking away. She nodded her head in agreement and reached across the table for Klein's hand.

"Thank you."

"Although," Klein continued, "I don't think you should be alone. Kyle has some things left to do at the bar so I suggest you bunk at my place."

The look of relief on Rae Ann's face was evident to all in the room. "Let me just go get some things." As Rae Ann got up from the table she looked up at Kyle expectantly.

As if reading her thoughts, his features softened and he said, "of course. I'll come up after I get back from the Buttercup and stay with you." Rae Ann smiled then and left the two men in the kitchen. Kyle could feel Klein's eyes on him and for once he turned to meet the gaze of his older brother.

"I told her. Everything."

"Well, that's a start," Klein mused, "she seems pretty special."

Kyle turned to face the bedroom door and crossed his arms over his heavy heart, "you have no idea."

~ * ~

Rae Ann could hear the mumbled talk of the brother's, but only concerned herself with gathering a couple of items to get her through the night at Klein's place. She stacked some toiletries on top of a pair of jeans and a white T-shirt on the bed and then looked around the room expectantly. She found the pearl necklace still on the bed.

Rae Ann couldn't bear to leave it behind so she searched through the roughly packed boxes until she found the blue velvet case that housed the precious jewels. Amongst the half folded clothes, Rae Ann's hand brushed the crushed velvet exterior and she snatched it up in haste.

Somehow her clumsy fingers slipped off the box and it tumbled through the air landing severely on the floor. The tiny clasp that held the lid closed popped open and the false bottom of the display jumped free. Rae Ann rushed over hoping that she had not permanently damaged the box that was so valuable to her.

As Rae Ann approached it, something glinted in the bottom, catching the illumination from the overhead light. Bending over the box, she peered inside. Fitting very snugly in the bottom of the box was a thin plastic case. Rae Ann picked up the small package and tipped it over onto her hand. The casing hesitated only a moment before falling squarely onto her palm. It was what she had thought, a CD case. But how it had gotten into her jewelry box, she didn't know.

Rae Ann dropped the velvet box onto the bed and worked open the lid of the case. Inside was a shiny, metallic disk. She turned it over and over in her hands, but it had no distinguishing marks or music group logo. Rae Ann walked it into the kitchen and held it up for Klein and Kyle to see. They had been in deep conversation, but halted at Rae Ann's expression.

"What's that?" Kyle asked.

"I don't know. I found it in the bottom of my jewelry box," Rae Ann shrugged. "Does anyone have a computer?"

The brothers exchanged glances.

"There's one at the Buttercup," Klein answered.

Kyle was already walking towards the door, "let's go."

~ * ~

No one spoke inside Klein's Mercedes as they raced into the night towards the bar. Rae Ann sat in the back seat holding the disk in her hands as if it would disappear. Kyle twisted around in the passenger seat twice to look at her but never uttered a sound. His unspoken words had Rae Ann tense and visibly shaking by the time they pulled into the parking lot, leaving a trail of dust from the highway.

"Are you ready?" Klein asked, catching Rae Ann's eye in the rear view mirror.

"Yeah, let's do this," Rae Ann replied, even though she was not ready to jump out of an airplane with no parachute. They were a somber crowd walking towards the back entrance of the building. Kyle fell in step beside her and captured her hand in his.

"It's probably nothing," he said, giving her hand a reassuring squeeze. Rae Ann nodded but was unconvinced. There was something sinister about the way it had been hidden in her jewelry box, locked in the safe. They weaved through the sparse cars in the lot. Being a weekday night, the bar wasn't full. For this Rae Ann was thankful.

Klein went on ahead to unlock his office and Kyle stepped ahead of her to hold open the kitchen door. Rae Ann slowed to almost a stand still and stared at the back of Kyle's head. A pang of guilt filled her insides as she remembered what they had just shared in her apartment. Kyle had poured out his heart to her and she had barely said three words about it before the situation had focused on her again. She made a mental note to make it up to him after all of this was over.

Rae Ann cast a fleeting look over her shoulder at the highway and wondered why fate had ever pulled her car into this parking lot. When she turned back to the bar, both men were peering in her direction. No doubt trying to understand what kind of person they had brought into their lives. Rae Ann dropped her head, ashamed, and stepped inside the building.

The trio entered through the kitchen just as Kyle and Rae Ann had on Saturday morning. It seemed like ages ago. The cooks and waitresses smiled and shouted out hellos to the Bennett's and then

225

lowered their voices to whispers to discuss who the mysterious blond was. Klein pushed open the door of his private office and flipped on the overhead light. The harsh fluorescence hurt Rae Ann's eyes and she squinted to cease the burning sensation. Her eyes felt gritty from crying earlier and a pounding headache was beginning deep in her brain. At the moment, the comfy office seemed more like an interrogation room. The wooden giraffe now stared accusingly at her and the elephant seemed frozen in perpetual scowl. Klein lowered the bamboo shade that covered the room's only window and then moved behind the desk to boot up the computer. It seemed to take forever groaning and buzzing in protest all the while.

"Here let me have it," Klein said, removing the disk from Rae Ann's hand and placing it in the CD Rom drive. "There's only one file," Klein stated to no one in particular.

"What is it? Kyle asked moving around the desk to get a better view of the monitor, "audio or video?"

"Video," Klein said, simultaneously double clicking the icon to run the file. Before she changed her mind, Rae Ann stepped around behind Klein, too, and focused on the screen of the computer. Kyle placed his hand lovingly on her back and although Rae Ann wasn't comforted, she looked up at him with a grateful smile. None of them were prepared for what was on the disk.

The black screen took on a fuzzy green hue and a picture began flashing on and off the screen. Rae Ann could make nothing of the distorted images or the hissing sound track, but suddenly felt sick to her stomach. She wanted to rip the disk from the machine and toss it out. She wished she had never found it desecrating her jewelry box with its awful secrets. With her right hand, Rae Ann reached out to Klein who was trying to fiddle with the screen's adjuster knobs.

"It won't get any clearer," she explained absently, never taking her eyes off the screen. Klein pushed back from the desk and landed heavily against the back of his office chair just as the screen stopped blinking. Rae Ann gasped. Through the twisted picture, Rae Ann could make out two people. They seemed to be engaged in some sort of masochistic foreplay that was more vile than Rae Ann had ever imagined.

The star of the video was a woman on all fours on a bed in front of a beastly man. She was wearing some sort of black plastic corset that left her heavy breasts to swing freely in front of her. Around her neck was a spiked dog collar with a leash attached to it.

The man positioned on his knees behind her was holding the leash in one hand and a small whip in the other. A black mask covered the entirety of the man's head with only small holes for his eyes and mouth and he wore black leather underwear that had a hole in front to allow his jutting manhood through it. The whole scene was grotesque and frightening, but Rae Ann couldn't tear her eyes away.

A thick silence had settled on the room, but Rae Ann could see out the corner of her eye that Kyle's mouth hung open in disbelief. The couple on the screen were now occupied in brutal intercourse. The three watched as the man cracked the whip viciously and pulled roughly on the dog leash around the woman's neck. Each time he jerked at the leash, the woman's head would snap back violently and was held at an impossible angle for longer and longer periods of time. It looked painful and degrading, but each time the man let his grip loosen on the leash, the woman would chant "yes, more, harder."

It was almost too much to bear. Rae Ann felt sick to her stomach and even bent slightly at the waist to keep the dizziness at bay. The man yanked on the leash again and held it high above his head shouting out an ear splitting war whoop, but this time the woman did not scream out her sadistic mantra. Her head had snapped back a little too sharply and she fell limp onto the bed not even stretching out her arms to catch herself. The man dropped the leash and whip onto the bed and tore off the mask, grinning broadly. Rae Ann squinted through the hazy reception to make out the face of the now unmasked man.

"How was that baby?" the man's toothy grin shown as a fuzzy white blob on his face. It was evident that he was oblivious as to what had just happened to the woman.

"Turn it off," Rae Ann demanded, breathing heavily through her mouth. When no one moved, she raced to the machine and pulled the disk roughly from the drive even before it had a chance to close. Rae

Ann slammed it on the desk and then leaned over it to keep from vomiting.

"Rae Ann," Kyle rushed to her side and put both hands on her tiny waist. He felt her sway slightly to the side and tightened his grip to keep her upright. She could see Klein out of the corner of her eye as he remained sitting in the office chair. He had templed his hands up under his chin and was staring at the floor. Rae Ann pulled in a couple a breaths through her nose and blew out through her mouth. She sensed Kyle behind her but her body had become numb to the effects of touch.

An unseen hand squeezed Kyle's heart at the sight of her, but he couldn't keep from asking, "Was it Grant?"

Rae Ann tensed under his hands and looked up at him through a sheen of unshed tears. "I don't know," she shook her head miserably, "the image was too fuzzy." The realization that her husband could have been caught up in this malevolent and immoral situation hit her full force.

"Right before I left him," Rae Ann said, straightening from the desk, "he told me there was a woman. Maybe he was trying to tell me about this."

Klein, who had been silent so far, interjected, "I think its time to consider that your husband wasn't killed in some random robbery." Rae Ann nodded and dropped her face into her hands. She was so ashamed. Ashamed of Grant, for keeping such a vile secret from her, and ashamed at herself for being so naïve. Rae Ann had kept her heart guarded for so long until she'd met Grant. She had rushed headlong into her relationship with Grant and now it was falling apart around her.

Rushed in just as she was rushing into a relationship with Kyle.

Rae Ann was being forced to realize another side of her husband that she never would have considered possible just one short day ago.

"Maybe Grant didn't know about the disk. Maybe someone put it in your jewelry box to find," Kyle thought out loud, grasping at straws. Rae Ann was shaking her head even before he finished speaking.

"The box was locked in our personal safe. No one had access to it but me and Grant."

Klein got up from his chair and covered the small distance between him and Rae Ann. "Whoever it is, do you think he actually killed that girl?"

"I don't know. I mean, yeah, it did look like that," Rae Ann stumbled over her words.

"Let's get you home. This has been a very traumatic day." Rae Ann leaned over and hugged the older Bennett tightly. When she pulled back Klein could see in her face what she was going to say.

"Thank you for everything, but I'm going to get on the road. It's a long drive, but I need to get this disk to the police. It might answer some questions that they have and it could clear me. I'm so sorry that I involved either of you in this mess."

Kyle took only a second to formulate what he was going to say. He didn't want to scare her off, so he decided on a more diplomatic approach. "Rae Ann, you have to consider the possibility that the police might see this disk as your motive for murdering Grant. Like Klein said, you're safe here. Take a few days to figure out what you are going to do. Nothing will get accomplished by you leaving tonight and, besides, what kind of friends would we be if we sent you out there alone?"

Rae Ann wanted to run and hide. She couldn't let herself get caught up in a new relationship right now, but Kyle was determined not to let her slip away.

"Klein, could you please excuse us for a moment," she asked patiently. As Klein stepped quietly from the room, Kyle took the opportunity to get comfortable in one of the guest chairs. He knew he wasn't going to like what Rae Ann was about to say. When the door had shut out the noise from the kitchen, Rae Ann went to Kyle and knelt in front of him.

"Kyle, please understand. This whole thing is turning into a nightmare and I don't understand any of what's going on. I'm just so confused right now. It wouldn't be fair to you or to Klein." Kyle leaned forward in the chair and captured her face in his hands.

"Don't worry about us right now. We'll get this misunderstanding straightened out. Just promise me you won't go back." Rae Ann had prepared an argument, but in the end she couldn't deny him.

"I'll stay for a couple of days until we can figure out a way to get proof of who did this to Grant." He pulled her into his arms and kissed her sweetly on the mouth.

Klein and Rae Ann bid Kyle farewell in the parking lot of the Buttercup. As hard as it was for Kyle to let her out of his sight, he knew she would be safe with Klein, until he finished up his business at the bar. For Rae Ann, the car ride back to their apartment building was no more relaxed than the car ride into the bar. The initial shock of the disk's contents had worn off and they continued to make sense of it.

"If it is Grant on the disk, then it is possible that someone was blackmailing him," Klein posed.

"That is the most logical explanation," Rae Ann offered, "he was a very wealthy man." A little bit more of Rae Ann's life bobbed to the surface.

"But if they were blackmailing him, why would they kill him? Unless he wasn't paying," Klein said, answering his own question.

"I'm still not convinced it was Grant," Rae Ann said to her reflection in the passenger door window. "The image was just so fuzzy. If I could have seen the man's face..." Rae Ann trailed off.

When they finally reached their destination, Rae Ann was physically drained and thankful that Kyle had talked her into staying. They bypassed Kyle and Rae Ann's apartments on the first floor and went directly to Klein's upstairs residence. Rae Ann laid the disk and its loathsome contents on Klein's dining room table and went straight to the spare bedroom that she used the first night she arrived in Illinois. Klein was close behind her.

He stopped at the door and inquired softly, "will you be all right?"

"Yes," Rae Ann replied, crawling into the comfy linens of the bed, "just don't go too far."

"I'll be right outside," Klein came to her then and kissed her forehead. Rae Ann couldn't remember feeling surrounded by such warmth. It made her smile.

Sometime in the night, Rae Ann heard the door open slowly and a thin shaft of light made the figure a dark shadow. She raised her head from the pillow and rubbed at her tired eyes.

"Don't be scared. It's just me," Kyle's voice was deep and gruff with the late hour. He came to the bed and reached for her in the darkness. "I just wanted to make sure you were all right."

"As well as can be expected," Rae Ann whispered, hoping that their conversation would not disturb Klein.

"I will be just outside on the couch if you need me. I would love to stay with you, but Klein would have a hemorrhage. He's so old fashioned."

Rae Ann suppressed a giggle as she asked, "But he's gay, how can he be old fashioned?"

Kyle laughed at her question and then stopped them both with his words. "I am glad that you decided to stay."

"Me, too," Rae Ann replied.

"I love you, Rae." A moment of silence between them seemed to drag on for miles.

"Don't be upset that I can't say it back," Rae Ann finally broke the silence, "It's not that I don't feel it, it's just that—" Kyle put a finger to her lips to quiet her and then replaced it with his warm mouth.

"Good night."

Twenty-six

Wednesday, April 12th

Rae Ann woke slowly, but no more refreshed. The memories of last night flooded back into her conscience and she wondered how she was going to solve this puzzling conundrum. Someone had killed her husband and it may or may not be related to that awful disk she had found in her jewelry box. Rae Ann stumbled from the bed and entered the hallway. The whisper of voices made her strain to hear the conversation before she realized that the voices were coming from the television set in Klein's living room.

The Bennetts were already up and watching the set intently. When her foot came across a small creak in the wooden floor, both men spun in Rae Ann's direction. The scene seemed to play out a lot like the first night she had met these men, except now the looks on their faces made it evident that something was terribly wrong.

"What is it?" Rae Ann asked, apprehensively approaching the couch where Kyle sat.

"Rae Ann, I think you should sit down," Klein motioned her to the empty space next to Kyle. Behind them the news reporter droned on about a vandalized construction site.

"Why? Just tell me what's going on," Rae Ann became nervous and something in her stomach hardened. Before either man could say another word, the reporter turned to his on screen partner, none other than Marley Cavanaugh, who began a new story.

"Late developments in the Grant Spencer murder case. Forensic tests concluded that a gun left at the scene was used in the slaying of the Pine Trails Resort owner. Police are now treating Spencer's wife, Rae Ann Lewis, as the prime suspect in her husband's murder, since confirming her fingerprints on the murder weapon. Any information regarding the whereabouts of Rae Ann Lewis should be directed to the Rockingham Police Department."

A publicity shot of Rae Ann from her days at Channel 8 news flashed up on the screen and Rae Ann gasped audibly. The story concluded and went to commercial before Rae Ann could even speak.

"You were married to *the* Grant Spencer? The multi-millionaire?" Rae Ann heard the accusation in Kyle's tone.

"You know who Grant is?" Rae Ann was dumbfounded. How could this small town in Illinois know anything about her husband?

"He owns a string of strip malls in the Chicago area. We have seen him on the news more than once," Klein explained.

"I wanted to tell you," Rae Ann started, "but there never seemed to be the right time."

"Never the right time? To tell me that you were rich? It was better just to let me make a fool of myself by offering up my humble lifestyle."

"No, Kyle, there is no reason why you should be embarrassed. I have never felt more at home than when I have been here. Grant never provided a home for me. I never cared about the money and I hated the resort."

"Well, I guess you should learn to love it, 'cause it is now all yours." The comment stunned Rae Ann into silence and sudden tears were brought to her eyes. She knew this would happen. Damn her for not being honest up front.

Instead of pursuing the unpleasant topic with Kyle, Rae Ann turned to Klein. "When did you first see this story?"

"We saw it earlier this morning," Klein said, gesturing to include Kyle, "We wanted to tell you before you saw it."

"My God, what am I going to do?" Rae Ann croaked, her voice still heavy with sleep, "The police actually think I killed Grant."

"Well, maybe you could explain how your fingerprints got on the gun that killed him."

"Klein!" Kyle admonished. Rae Ann could tell he was upset with her, but still wouldn't allow even his brother to be accusatory.

"I'm sorry, Rae Ann, I don't mean to be insensitive, but everything seems to be working against you here," Klein explained from his place on the wing back chair. Rae Ann shook her head trying to remember when she had ever handled the .45 that Grant kept in the house for protection.

"I've never held that gun," Rae Ann said incredulously, "I don't know how my fingerprints could have gotten on it. Grant always kept it locked in the safe." Realization hit her just as the words came tumbling from her mouth.

Her face contorted into a pain filled grimace, "I picked it up. I picked it up when I got my jewelry box out of the safe the night I left. The gun was sitting on top of the case and I had to move it. I only held it for a second." Rae Ann suddenly felt a deep stab of guilt, as she recalled her hatred for her husband that night. Kyle got up from the couch and began pacing.

"We need to find out who it is on that disk. We need to make sure that it is Grant so we can take it to the police and get you out of this mess," he continued his short walk across the apartment before turning back towards Rae Ann and Klein. "If only the image was clearer."

"Eddie," Rae Ann shouted, jumping from the couch. Both brothers sat silently waiting for her to shed more light on what she had just said. "My camera man, Eddie," Rae Ann explained, "if we can get him the disk, he could use the equipment at the television station to clear up the feed." She waited for nothing. but began walking intently towards the door.

"Where are you going?" Klein asked standing.

"To get my things. I've got to get to Eddie."

"Are you nuts, Rae Ann?" Kyle said, following behind her out of the door and to the flight of stairs, "I know you've never been a murder suspect before, but if you go back to Wisconsin the police are going to track you down and throw you in jail. I'm sure they would love nothing more than to solve the case of their golden son, and that doesn't include listening to your half-cocked theories about who killed Grant." Kyle's voice echoed in the empty hallway as he took the steps three at a time.

Rae Ann stopped in mid-step, but wasn't sure she could face him. "You have to make up your mind, Kyle. You say you love me, but that means you have to take me as I am. Impetuous, stubborn and determined. Yes, I should have told you I was married to Grant Spencer, but I didn't. You know now, so accept it or let me go." Rae Ann had already reached the bottom and was approaching the door to her apartment.

"I do love you, Rae Ann," Kyle explained from behind her, "I'm just worried about you."

"Well, I have to do something and if you're so worried about me, then come with me," Rae Ann shouted out and flung open the door to her makeshift home.

"You're being impulsive. We need to talk about this. I don't want you going anywhere," Kyle roared back coming up short behind her. Rae Ann had stopped at the threshold and was peering in but made no attempt to go any further into the room. As he got closer and finally reached her side, Kyle stole a look inside the apartment and was taken aback.

The entire living room and kitchen area had been tossed. Couch cushions and canned goods had been flung from one side of the room to the other. The room's only chair had been turned upside down and was leaning over the coffee table. The curtains had been torn off the window letting the bright sun permeate every corner of the desecrated room. Kyle pushed past Rae Ann and entered the bedroom, which was in worse shape.

All of Rae Ann's clothes had been dumped on the bed or floor along with her makeup case. Someone had poured an entire bottle of shampoo over the bundle and then smeared it on the mirror above the sink in the bathroom. Klein, who had followed the duo down the stairs, stood in the bedroom doorway, but Rae Ann was nowhere to be seen.

"What the hell?" Klein asked, surveying the room with amazement. Both stopped moving when they saw the words written above the bed. In a pale shade of pink, almost invisible on the eggshell walls, the words 'give back the disk' were scrawled cruelly. Kyle moved quickly back through the bedroom to the front door where Rae Ann stood stoic.

"Did anyone see you leave that night?" he asked roughly, grabbing her by the shoulders. Rae Ann did a double take as Kyle shook her from the momentary trance.

"Why?"

"Just answer the question. Did someone see you leave that night or did you talk to someone before you left?" Kyle's brusqueness unnerved her and she began to tremble slightly.

"Just Harold," her voice quivered, "he's the groundskeeper. He opened the gate when I left and I waved to him." Kyle released her arms and placed his hands on the hips of his jeans.

"I always wave to Harold," Rae Ann said absently.

"If the news story is right, and Grant has been dead for several days, then he certainly wasn't the one asking about you the other night at the Buttercup." With the recent events of the last couple of days, Rae Ann had completely forgotten about the mystery man at the bar.

"If it wasn't Grant, then who?" she whispered, rhetorically.

"Go look in the bedroom," Kyle said pointing behind him. Rae Ann didn't hesitate, she pulled up next to Klein in the bedroom and stared at the wall above the bed she had slept in just recently.

"They found me. *They found me?*" Rae Ann never even considered that someone had seen her leave or knew where she had ended up. After all, she had only been leaving her husband, not the scene of a crime. She thought back to when she had fled into the night. It had been late, almost ten, but Harold was still hard at work on the shrubbery around the iron gate that led up the driveway to Grant and Rae Ann's house. Rae Ann had been grateful that she only had to face Harold and not the scrutinizing eye of the resort staff. Rae Ann had been a wreck. Upset at the revelation that Grant was cheating on her. Harold had stepped from behind a large hedge and come over to the car.

"Mrs. Spencer?" He asked through squinted eyes. Harold was the only one that she knew who called her that.

"Yes, Harold, it's me. I'm going out for a while. Could you please open the gate? My electronic opener is in the Lexus." Harold nodded but continued to approach the car.

"Taking your Honda, are you? I heard it might snow later. Some spring snow storm coming in. You be careful now, okay?" Rae Ann smiled genuinely at the little old man and fought the tears. She wouldn't be coming back and knew she would never see Harold again. He retreated back to the concrete embankment that held the iron gates in place and pushed the small button that opened the gates. The heavy iron creaked and gave a lurch before splitting smoothly down the middle and separating. Rae Ann had crept through the opening, barely allowing them time to part wide enough for her car to fit through.

After hitting the open road, she had never glanced in the rear view mirror. But now, as she stood staring at the debased wall, she couldn't help but feel phantom eyes prying into her personal space.

"Wait a minute," Rae Ann moved back into the living room and began pulling the tipped chair off of the coffee table. It flung brusquely to the floor and landed on its side. Rae Ann dropped to her hands and knees and began searching around the wooden base of the table.

"What are you looking for?" Kyle probed.

"This," Rae Ann told him, holding up a small piece of paper, "I found this on the floor that night after dinner." She handed the scrap to him and turned to Klein. "I thought someone had slipped it under the wrong door. At the time, I didn't know anything about a disk."

"My God, Rae Ann," Klein said peering over Kyle's shoulder to read the contents of the note, "these people have been following you since you left."

"And that day before we went to the forest, I went running. Someone in a car almost hit me. Do you think it was the same person?" Rae Ann was flustered and near hysteria.

"Come on," Kyle said, crumpling the note in his palm and ignoring her question. He grabbed her hand and started towards the door.

"What? Where are we going?"

"Wisconsin."

"But you said—" Rae Ann started, as they crossed the hall and entered Kyle's apartment.

"Yeah, I know what I said," Kyle interrupted, "but we've got to find out what kind of people we're dealing with. You could be in some serious danger here. The only way we're going to find out any answers is to face what's back in Rockingham. If they know you're here, maybe they won't think you'd ever go back."

"Well, you can't just go out there with guns blazing," Klein stated, trailing the couple and taking a seat at the freshly cleaned dining room table. All of this upheaval, in his otherwise normal existence, was showing in his face.

"We'll call Rae Ann's friend, Eddie—if he's willing to help us, then we'll start there," Kyle said matter-of-factly.

"We need to get into the resort, too," Rae Ann said, trying to be helpful, "That's where Grant kept all of his legal papers. Maybe that will give us some idea of what he had gotten himself into." Rae Ann made her way over to the table and stood next to Klein's chair.

"I don't know how that will be possible, Rae Ann. We can't just drive up the hillside, through the entrance and waltz in the front door of this resort," Kyle pointed out.

"No, you couldn't," Klein agreed, "but the police could."

Without another word, Klein pushed up from the table and went through the house to Kyle's bedroom. Rae Ann looked up at Kyle with an inquisitive look, but he pretended not to see. Klein was back in a moment holding a plastic drying cleaning bag with the Sander's Dry Cleaning logo on the front.

"Klein, no," Kyle said firmly.

"What? What is it?" Rae Ann asked.

"It's Kyle's police uniform. He could wear it. Pretend he was gathering evidence from the resort or something and if anyone saw him they wouldn't suspect a thing."

"Yeah," Rae Ann agreed, "you could even question some of the staff."

"You both are forgetting that I was just a beat cop, not a detective."

"Well, due to the circumstances," Klein declared, "you've just been promoted."

"It's going to take more than a uniform to protect us against these people," Kyle argued.

"You're right," Klein said, "You can take my gun."

Kyle raised his eyebrows at his brother who sighed and said, "Yes, I have a gun. It's for protection. Besides, this isn't about me. Are you going to help Rae Ann or not?" Kyle stood in front of them as if on trial. He tried to think of any good excuse to tell them no, but when he looked at Rae Ann's expectant face, he couldn't think of one.

Finally he sighed, "let's go call Eddie."

~ * ~

Kyle thought it best not to use her cell phone, so they had driven over to Snappy's Diner to use the pay phone. The ringing on the other end of the line just kept on until she was convinced that Eddie was not carrying his phone. Then at the last minute she heard a tiny click and the gruff voice of Eduardo Torres spring from the ear piece. It was one of the sweetest sounds she had ever heard.

"Eddie?" she whispered.

"Scoop? God, Scoop is that you?" Eddie asked in disbelief.

"Yeah, Eddie it's me."

"Where are you? Have you seen the news and what's going on up here? It's some crazy shit," Eddie rambled on, "they sent me up to your house to cover the story. Can you believe that? The place was totally trashed."

"Eddie, stop," Rae Ann didn't want to hear anymore details, "I need to ask you a favor."

"Yeah, shoot."

"I found a disk in my jewelry box. It has a video file on it. I don't know where it came from, but it is essential that we find out who is on it."

"You didn't watch it?" Eddie inquired.

"No, we watched it, but it is distorted, fuzzy. I need to you to take it to the station and enhance it," Rae Ann rushed the last sentence out. When Eddie didn't respond right away, Rae Ann went on, "I know this is asking a lot of you. I'm probably involving you in some sort of crime, but I don't know who else to call, Eddie."

At last Rae Ann heard him say, "They think you killed Grant."

"I know," Rae Ann became resigned to the fact that Eddie wasn't going to help.

"This is going to be tricky. You'll have to come during the day when the techies go to their meeting." Rae Ann stood, momentarily stunned, while Eddie continued. "Stay at the North's Pride Motel just outside of Madison. Call me from the pay phone across the street at Mae's Luncheon, it's no Mama Torres' but it's got good—"

"Eddie, focus," Rae Ann said.

"Oh right, anyway, call me about eleven o'clock—that should give you enough time to drive over, if the coast is clear. I haven't seen the disk so I don't know how long it will take to enhance, but we'll give it a shot."

By the time he quit speaking, Rae Ann had tears in her eyes, "Eddie, thank you."

"Never mind all that. You'd better get off the phone before the police have a chance to trace the call."

"You've been watching too much *Law & Order*, Eddie," Rae Ann mused with a smile. They ended the call and Rae Ann joined the Bennett brothers in the same booth she had sat in with Kyle that first morning. Rae Ann gave them a briefing on the call with Eddie and then they decided to order a late breakfast before starting their journey. Snappy was his usual jovial self, saying not ten words, but smiling brightly at the sight of them. This time Rae Ann ate slowly, picking at her plate.

When the last bit of eggs, pancakes, sausage links, and oatmeal had been consumed, they lingered over coffee, unsure of what to do next. Rae Ann swirled the dark liquid in her cup, a look of concern covered her face.

"What is it? I thought we were doing exactly what you wanted," Kyle stated, wiping at a ring of coffee on the table left by his cup.

"We are... it's just, I don't know. I feel like we're going into this blind, unprepared," Rae Ann explained.

"I don't see what else we can do until we get to Wisconsin."

"I just wish we could figure out what kind of trouble Grant had gotten himself into. How these people got a hold of the disk. If people were blackmailing him, then they had to have been powerful people. Grant was no pushover."

"But you said yourself, Grant kept all of his business and legal papers at the lodge," Klein volunteered. Rae Ann chewed on her bottom lip, her eyes full of thought.

"Not all his papers," she said, leaning forward in the booth. "When I got my pearls from the safe that night, there was a manila envelope full of documents underneath the box. I was in such a hurry to get out of there that I didn't realize I had taken them until I got in the car," Rae Ann rushed on.

"Where is the envelope now?" Kyle asked, eagerly.

"I threw it in the trunk of my car. I suppose it is still there." Rae Ann hadn't finished the sentence before she was out of the booth and heading out of the diner, the boys close behind her.

~ * ~

Rae Ann turned the envelope upside down and dropped everything out onto Kyle's dining room table before tossing it aside.

"Just look for anything suspicious," she told them. Each grabbed a third of the sheaf of papers and began sifting through the contents. Rae Ann came across an old deed to some property in Massachusetts that she wasn't even aware Grant owned. In fact, the more in depth Rae Ann got into the papers, the less she felt like she even knew the man that had shared her bed on and off for the past year.

After several moments, Kyle pulled one of the papers from his stack and held it out for all of them to see. "Who is Elliot Logan?"

"Elliot?" Rae Ann asked, pulling the paper closer to her, "he's Grant's business partner. They bought the property for the lodge as a joint venture and then Grant bought him out."

"Not according to this," Kyle said. Rae Ann gave him a perplexed look and took the paper from him altogether.

"According to this," Kyle said, "Grant still owed Mr. Logan quite a bit of money."

"How much?" Klein probed.

"Two point seven million dollars."

"What?" Rae Ann shouted incredulously, "that's impossible. I witnessed the buy out with my own eyes. We even went out to dinner with the Logan's to celebrate." Rae Ann scanned the document with swift eyes, but found no evidence of a pay off in the ink.

"This paperwork is dated January," Kyle pulled the paper back for another once over.

"Was that before the buy out?" Klein asked. Rae Ann shook her head slowly.

"Wait a second," Kyle said, examining the document further, "this looks like a second draft. Maybe Grant needed the money back and took out an extension on the payback."

"What are you saying... it was all a show?" Rae Ann said aloud, "Maybe Grant wasn't the wealthy resort owner he had everyone believing? Maybe the resort was actually losing money? Why wouldn't he just tell me? I would have helped him." Neither Klein nor Kyle could provide her with any answers. Rae Ann sighed heavily and got up from the table.

"Two point seven million dollars sounds like a motive to me," Klein said, into the silence of the room.

"You know, we could be looking at this all wrong," Kyle interjected, "if Grant owed Elliot Logan the money, maybe he set Logan up. Grant caught him on tape with that woman and was using the disk to get out of paying him the money."

Klein shrugged and nodded in agreement, "yeah, and Logan killed Grant to get out of the blackmail and to cover up his own problems with the girl."

"But if Elliot killed Grant, then he wouldn't get the money that Grant owed him. Besides, Elliot isn't a killer," Rae Ann pointed out.

"Maybe the money wasn't as important to Elliot as his freedom was. Whoever it is on that disk is a murderer whether it was intentional or not," Klein said slowly.

Rae Ann knew immediately what he meant. Her mind flashed back to a conversation she had witnessed. Without a word, Rae Ann jumped from the table and retraced her path back to her car. She rummaged in the trunk through magazines and around a tire iron before finding the voice activated tape recorder.

As Rae Ann ran back into the apartment building, taking the front stoop stairs two at a time, she pushed the rewind button in hopes of still having captured the conversation on tape. She reentered Kyle's apartment through the already open door to face the questioning stares of the two brothers. Rae Ann hit the play button and held the small tape recorder out for all to hear.

The tape picked up in the middle of the conversation "...*should hope so, Grant. I really do. A deal is a deal and I don't want to think about what could happen if—*"

"*Elliot, we shouldn't make a big deal out of this. I told you I would take care of it. I said that, didn't I?*"

"*Yeah, you said it. But I haven't seen anything happen yet, Grant,*" Elliot Logan said, "*You'd better make good on this deal. I would hate to have to send my boys.*"

"I accidentally recorded that on my first date with Grant," Rae Ann explained. Kyle and Klein exchanged matching expressions. "But that doesn't mean that Elliot killed him. Oh God," Rae Ann cupped a hand over her mouth, "it actually makes Grant sound very guilty."

"But why the disk?" Klein asked.

"It was a threat," Kyle explained, "Grant wasn't paying so Elliot set *him* up. Elliot wanted to catch Grant in the act, you know, a little extra incentive for him to pay up. Especially if he knew Grant was cheating on Rae Ann. Logan would have no way of knowing that Grant was going to kill that girl."

"Why wouldn't Logan just take the disk to the police?" Klein asked, intrigued.

"He would never get his money if he did that," Rae Ann clarified.

"Right," Kyle agreed, "the worst he could do was threaten to show Rae Ann, but he never could, of course, because Rae Ann might take it to the police."

"If Grant knew all that, then he might have blown off the disk."
The situation was suddenly becoming clearer to Rae Ann. "It
wouldn't have forced him to pay and when he didn't—"

"They killed him," Kyle finished.

"If these are the kind of people that we're dealing with, we've got
to get you guys packed up," Klein stated.

~ * ~

Rae Ann dug through the pile of shampoo covered clothes and
couldn't find anything salvageable to pack. She borrowed a shirt from
Kyle, but would be stuck in the same pants she had slept in. Everyone
split up to take showers and gather what they would need for their
trip. An hour later the trio met in front of Klein's car that was housed
in the single car garage behind the apartment building. Kyle loaded
the rest of their things, along with Klein's gun, into the trunk and
slammed the lid.

Rae Ann hung Kyle's uniform from the hook in the back seat.
Klein had stepped to the back of the car and was telling his brother
good-bye. She watched the scene playing out through the rear window
and was overcome with emotion for the brothers she had met only
days ago.

"Be careful, okay?" Klein embraced his brother.

"Don't worry so much. I'll be fine." Kyle hugged his brother back
and then pulled away to look him square in the eye.

"But I do worry about you. I've been worrying about you since the
day they brought you home and it only got worse when Mom died,"
Klein explained.

"I know. But this is something I have to do on my own," Kyle's
mouth was set in a serious line.

"You love her, don't you?"

"Yes, I do," Kyle admitted.

"Then go," Klein gave him a slight shove, "take care of business
and bring her back safe."

"Thanks, bro," Kyle said embracing his brother again. Rae Ann
ambled to the back of the vehicle and stood awkwardly while the
brothers shared their moment.

Klein straightened at her presence. "Take care of yourself and my little brother."

"No problem," Rae Ann's tone came out a little less confident than she had intended. Klein reached in quickly and pulled Rae Ann close. Before she could react, he had straightened away and started back towards the apartment building.

Rae Ann settled into the back seat and lay down. If anyone was watching her or following her, Rae Ann.wanted them to think she had entered the apartment building and was, for all they knew, still there. Kyle started the ignition and pulled out slowly from the garage. He could see no visible cars in his rear view mirror, but kept a watchful eye on their surroundings.

Once they crossed the city limits, Rae Ann wriggled over the seat and plopped down in the passenger seat next to Kyle.

After a moment of fidgeting with her hands she finally said, "I just want to thank you for doing this."

"It's nothing," Kyle replied, keeping his eyes on the road ahead.

"No, really," Rae Ann emphasized by turning her whole body in his direction, "you are really putting yourself on the line for me and no one has ever done that."

Kyle took his right hand off the wheel and cupped her face. "This is what you do when you love someone, Rae."

To both their amazement, Rae Ann rested her head against the warmth of his palm and gave a deep sigh. Kyle smiled inwardly and outwardly and, for just a moment, could forget that they were headed into a world of danger. They settled into a comfortable routine. Rae Ann found a mellow radio station that played the oldies and Kyle grinned to himself when she starting humming along.

They stopped only twice along the way. Once to grab a quick dinner, although neither were very hungry, and a second time to shop for clothes. Rae Ann quickly grabbed a couple new pairs of jeans, some shirts and both invested in heavy parkas, gloves, hats and snow boots. The further north they drove the more the news was geared towards the escalating snowstorm in Northern Illinois and Wisconsin and they wanted to be prepared for the abnormal spring weather.

Until now, Rae Ann could pretend that this road trip was fun but, with no more stops between now and what lay ahead, her mood became somber. She rested her head against the cool glass of the passenger door's window and watched the passing landscape. For all her life, she would never understand how someone could take another person's life. How a man as wealthy as Elliot Logan could kill over mere money. She prayed deeply then, prayed that it wasn't Grant on the disk. It was hard enough to imagine her husband involved in such a kinky sexual environment where he violently killed a woman. Even with all of his faults and shortcomings, Rae Ann could not believe that was in Grant's nature. She hoped he hadn't suffered.

At some point, Kyle turned on the windshield wipers as they drove into the ever-thickening snow. Soon the rhythmic motion lulled Rae Ann into a dreamless sleep.

"Rae." She felt the gentle touch on her shoulder but fought against its attempt to rouse her from the peaceful slumber. "Rae Ann," Kyle leaned close to her ear and took in the deep clean scent she emitted. He hated to wake her, but couldn't very well let her sleep in the car. It was shortly past eleven and the temperature had dropped to nearly twenty-two degrees. Finally Rae Ann stirred under his hand, "Where are we?"

"We're at the motel, just outside of Madison."

"My God," Rae Ann's eyes widened as she came fully awake, "how long have I been asleep?"

"Just a couple of hours," Kyle said, glancing at his watch, "why?"

She stepped from the car, "It's just that the same trip took me two and a half days." Kyle dropped his chin to his chest to hide his smile, but Rae Ann detected his amusement.

She gave his arm a light punch. "Hey, no jokes about woman drivers."

"Ssshh," Kyle whispered into the dark, "we'd better be quiet. I only registered one person at the desk in case the police are looking for you." Rae Ann's bright smile disappeared instantaneously at the remembrance that she was a wanted fugitive. Kyle grabbed the suitcases and headed for their room. Rae Ann pulled her sweater tight around her shoulders and cast furtive glances into the shadows.

"Relax," Kyle said, "no one even knows you're here." Rae Ann shook her head, but was not convinced. The people after her seemed omnipotent. They had found her in Illinois and they would find her here, of that she was certain. The motel's rooms all sported outside entrances, so there was no front desk clerk to sneak past. It would make coming and going easier.

Once safely inside the well-lit room, Rae Ann was able to relax enough to unclench her fists. She released the breath she had been holding since she set foot out of the car. Rae Ann took a quick look around small space. It was glamorous by no means.

An old sagging bed, covered in an obnoxious orange bedspread, took up most of the room's free space. Next to it was a round bedside table with a dim-watted lamp and a radio clock that perpetually flashed twelve o'clock. Another table and two chairs were pushed into the corner of the room under the large picture window.

On top of the table a Bible was tattered and had a cigarette burn clean through the brown synthetic cover. Behind the entrance door, an open closet held extra blankets and one empty hanger and next to that an open door showed the outlines of bathroom fixtures. All of this surrounded by four sad, brown-paneled walls and finished off with dilapidated brown carpet that had been nearly crushed to death by years and years of unkind foot traffic.

The only thing good about the space, that Rae Ann could see, was that the room contained no television set. The last thing she wanted to do was see her face on every channel, including the one for which she used to work.

"Charming," Rae Ann muttered.

"We'd better get some sleep," Kyle said behind her, "sorry about having only the one bed. I thought it would look funny if I asked for two."

Rae Ann nodded in understanding and perched on the edge of the bed. "If you want I can just get a pillow and camp out on the floor," Kyle said, nervously moving towards the bed. Rae Ann had spent the night in his arms before, but somehow tonight felt different. Something about being away from the safety of Klein's apartment building had pulled Kyle back into himself.

There was a crackle of nervous energy around him as he circled around Rae Ann and removed the pillow. Rae Ann rubbed the material of her sweater between her fingers and watched him as he went to the closet to get a blanket. With his back to her, she finally found the courage to speak.

"Kyle."

Something deep in her voice spoke the depth of her loneliness and he turned to her with the same aching need.

"I don't want you to sleep on the floor," she whispered, tiny tears sparkling in her sapphire eyes. At once, he knew that Rae Ann meant more than just wanting Kyle to hold her. In the swift moment it took her to inhale, Kyle was across the room pressing his mouth to hers. It was the same fervent desire she had felt when they had kissed in her apartment, and again in the clearing by the forest. Every part of him that was touching her felt wonderful and perfect and at that moment Rae Ann gave herself to him.

Kyle lowered her tiny body onto the mattress and stopped to marvel at how beautiful she looked despite the eight-hour road trip and seedy motel surroundings. He reached over and turned off the bedside lamp, plunging the room into total darkness.

From somewhere beneath him, he heard her say, "I love you, Kyle."

Twenty-seven

Thursday, April 13th

Rae Ann awoke in his arms amidst the tangled sheets and smiled sweetly, even before opening her eyes. The heavy motel curtains were lined with a faint ring of sunshine. She knew they should get up and get moving, but knew the day would hold no joy for them. She wished they could just lie together in the bed forever. Rae Ann did not want to face the people that had killed her husband and could not even make herself consider that she or Kyle would not come out of this unscathed.

As if knowing her thoughts, Kyle stirred in his sleep and subconsciously pulled her closer to the warmth of his body. Rae Ann had never felt such love. Kyle had ignited in her passion that she had thought long dead. Even with Grant, Rae Ann wasn't able to fully let herself go. Their physical relationship had been good, but wasn't emotionally fulfilling. Now, after having been loved by Kyle, Rae Ann wondered how she could have ever settled for less.

"Hey you," he spoke without moving, for fear that he would frighten her away. When she turned to him, Kyle could see in her eyes that everything would be all right. Rae Ann snuggled deep against him and sighed in contentment. From here on out she wanted to share her everything with this man beside her.

They showered and dressed, taking their time. "So what's the plan?"

Kyle hopped back onto the bed beside her, scrubbed clean and smelling delicious. Rae Ann felt as giddy as a school girl, despite the seriousness of the subject.

"You get dressed in your police uniform and go to Logan's office to ask him questions. You shouldn't have any problem getting past his secretary with your handsome face and charisma."

"That's your plan?" Kyle asked, incredulously.

"Well, I'm sure it won't be that easy, but you get the idea. Just get dressed." Rae Ann pushed him back off the bed and he faked a stumble into the middle of the floor. Rae Ann laughed and it felt good. She was still chuckling to herself when he took the police uniform into the bathroom to change. When he emerged, Rae Ann frowned involuntarily.

"What? Too tight?" he asked looking down at himself.

"No," Rae Ann said, tapping her upper lip with her index finger, "it's just not believable. What kind of police department sends a uniformed officer to question a suspect? On TV shows it is always a plain-clothes detective. Plus, if anyone looks close enough they're going to see that your patch says Prairie Sun Police Department."

"You're right, this is an insane idea," he said, grabbing her around the waist and pulling her close, "let's just go back to Harrisburg and live happily ever after."

"You mean as happily ever after as an alleged wanted criminal and her young lover could?" Rae Ann placed her arms around his neck and hopped up on her toes to kiss the soft spot behind his ear.

"You know," she said, seriously, "after this is all over, we still have a lot to talk about."

So there it was.

In his mind, a mental needle moved closer to his balloon of happiness, threatening to burst it. "I was afraid you were going to say that. But right now, I'm going to change back into some normal clothes and we're going to grab something to eat."

~ * ~

It was only ten minutes till ten when Rae Ann and Kyle settled into the booth at Mae's Luncheon. They had over an hour to wait before she could call Eddie. Rae Ann thought Kyle looked more the part of the detective dressed in crisp blue jeans, a button down shirt and a tweed blazer. His only pair of cowboy boots had also made the trip. He could have been a young Chuck Norris in *Walker, Texas Ranger*. The thought made Rae Ann smile.

She had dressed in jeans and a sweater. She pulled her hair under a stocking cap and kept her dark sunglasses on until the waitress was out of view. As she flipped through the sticky laminated pages of the menu, Rae Ann thought her life was doomed to play out in a greasy diner. But strangely, she thought only of Snappy's and the owner that had become a friend. She didn't reflect on the long ago life at the Hot Stop or her mother.

"Well, this is no Snappy's," Kyle declared, speaking Rae Ann's thoughts. He sipped at his coffee and grimaced. Rae Ann forced down the soupy eggs and soggy toast. She felt ill but was certain it didn't have anything to do with the meal. She glanced at her Rolex repeatedly, no less than twelve times in the last fifteen minutes and stared out the window at the frozen landscape. The snow was steadily falling and beginning to stick against the dirty curbs.

When she finally couldn't take it anymore, Rae Ann pushed out of the seat, "I should call Eddie." Kyle stared up at her for a full minute in silence. Rae Ann gave a fleeting look around and saw only the waitress leaned back against the counter watching a TV set mounted high in the corner opposite Kyle and Rae Ann. The only other customers had left minutes ago and Rae Ann was thankful. They would have thought she was crazy just standing in the aisle like she was.

Rae Ann directed her attention back to Kyle but he was staring intently at the television set. Another news report was giving more details about Grant's murder. Until now, she didn't realize that they were watching Channel 8 news. Rae Ann could barely make out the words but saw her picture again flash onto the screen. She recognized the reporter from the weekly staff meetings but only knew her name was Laura.

The nail biter that took the Sheridan murder right before I got assigned to the resort, Rae Ann thought, bitterly. She strained to hear the report but didn't want to call attention to herself by asking the

251

waitress to turn it up. So far she hadn't been recognized. Most of the information was the same as what they had already seen but the last sentence made Rae Ann struggle to take in the muted voice.

"Last seen in Illinois."

She cranked her neck back around to stare at Kyle. "I guess we can't go back now," Rae Ann said.

"Yeah," Kyle concluded, "let's do this."

They walked to the back of the diner and, using the pay phone, dialed the number that Eddie had given her. The phone rang only once when she heard the voice of Eduardo Torres say, "It's empty. Use the emergency exit." Rae Ann waited to hear the click before hanging up the phone.

They had agreed that she shouldn't speak in case someone was keeping an eye on Eddie. In truth, Rae Ann actually preferred the police to the faceless people that were hovering over her shoulder. She nodded the okay to Kyle and they headed back to their room to collect Klein's gun.

~ * ~

Arriving, Kyle parked in the alley behind the WZZY station house and waited in Klein's car until Eddie opened the door and motioned them inside. In typical Eddie fashion, he was sporting a bright yellow tee shirt with the words 'Poke Me' underneath a picture of the Pillsbury Dough Boy. The tee shirt looked thread bare and Eddie started shivering in the few seconds he was holding open the door.

"Thank you, Eddie," Rae Ann whispered as she hugged him tightly.

"Hey, I'm just glad to see you're okay. I've been worried since the moment I heard you were missing and that... Grant was dead. By the way, I'm sorry about that."

"Thanks," Rae Ann pulled back, but didn't let go of Eddie until she noticed him staring over her shoulder. "Oh, right, Eddie this is Kyle Bennett. He's, uh, a friend of mine."

Eddie gave a closed mouth smile and shook Kyle's hand vigorously. Rae Ann looked up at the flight of stairs that would take them to the main floor of the television station. How many hours had she spent up there writing stories and preparing for on camera appearances? *Too many,* she thought. So many, in fact, that she had neglected her personal life, and ended up a fugitive from the law, accused of her own husband's murder. The thought was devastating.

The group moved off the landing that led to the emergency exit and descended the stairs into the basement, with caution. Eddie had said it was deserted, but he gave the room another once over. The first shift of techies got off at eleven and the next shift didn't start until one. During this shift change they held a geek meeting of the minds which gave the reporters and newscasters a chance to use the equipment.

Rae Ann retrieved the disk from her purse as Eddie settled in behind the high tech computer. She couldn't bear to watch the gruesome scene play out again, so she took the opportunity to meander through the seemingly endless shelves of tape. If she looked close enough she would see tapes of news stories that she had done not so long ago. She smiled at the memories of her and Eddie freezing outside in sleet and snow just to report on the number of birds that hadn't yet flown south. In this moment Rae Ann really missed her job and the atmosphere of a breaking news event, but now wasn't the time to start feeling sorry for herself.

"Jesus Christ." Rae Ann heard Eddie mutter. She came up behind them,but kept her distance until Eddie turned off the monitor. Kyle, who had been leaning over Eddie's shoulder, straightened and crossed his arms.

"Well, he killed her. That's for sure. As for who it is... can't quite tell, but it should be easy to clean up the feed. Do you think it's Grant?" Eddie swiveled in the chair to face Rae Ann.

"I don't know. I can't tell either. But we found some papers that gave us the impression that Logan may have been using the disk to blackmail Grant. If Logan was involved in the blackmailing, it may not be too difficult to assume he was involved in Grant's murder as well. Or it might be Elliot on the disk. We just don't know."

"Elliot Logan? Really? What sort of papers?"

"I'd rather not get into it,until Kyle gets back from Logan's office."

"Yeah," Kyle leaned over and kissed Rae Ann quickly on the cheek, "you stay here with Eddie until I get back. You'll be safe here."

"Hey, whoa, wait a second cowboy," Eddie said, jumping from the chair, "You're going over to chat with a murderer all by yourself?"

"First of all," Kyle explained, "we don't know that Logan was the one that killed Grant or the girl on the disk. But just in case, I am taking my friend." Kyle pulled out the gun and displayed it for Eddie.

"I don't know man." Eddie shook his head and eyed the gun. "These rich dudes have people that have people. I mean one phone call and boom, your car explodes." Kyle could see the anxiety creeping into Rae Ann's face.

"Eddie's right, Kyle. Maybe we're in way over our heads here. We know that Grant owed Elliot Logan a lot of money and if that's all it takes to kill a person..." she trailed off and began wringing her hands as she looked back and forth between the guys.

"Listen," Kyle grabbed both her arms above the elbow and drew her to him, "we know that getting proof of who killed Grant is the only way to get you cleared. Now come on." He guided her to the chair that Eddie had just vacated. "The faster I get out of here, the faster I'll be back."

Rae Ann nodded numbly. She had known this was the plan all along. but couldn't help feeling disturbed, now that the time had finally come. Kyle shook hands with Eddie and was gone before she could utter another word.

"Well he's quite the guy, Scoop," Eddie said, leaning on the desktop, "and he's obviously in love with you. Where did you find this guy anyway?"

Rae Ann stared at the door that Kyle had just exited from.

"Where else... the Garden of the Gods."

~ * ~

Kyle sat in the car outside of Elliot Logan's office for almost ten minutes before the nervousness in his stomach settled enough for him to confidently get out of the car. He mentally reviewed what he was going to say to the prominent business man and hoped that his meager police training would be enough to fool the guy.

As he waited for the secretary to announce his presence, Kyle glanced around the posh downtown office building. It was stark and sterile in decoration. The art was modern and colorful, thrust into corners and hung on the crisp, white walls. Klein would have loved it. Kyle made a mental note to call his big brother to make sure that everything was still all right with him and to let him know that they had made it to Wisconsin.

"Detective?" Kyle realized from the tone of the secretary's voice that she had said it more than once before he turned towards her. "Mr. Logan will see you now."

Kyle nodded and headed towards the direction that the woman pointed. He took a deep breath and entered the room.

"Ah, detective... come right in." The gentleman behind the massive oak desk gestured Kyle farther into the room with a pleasant enough smile. His office, in contrast to the waiting area, was much warmer in appearance. It was full of wood and burgundy leather, a real man's sanctuary. The man himself wore a cream suit with a slate colored button up shirt underneath it. Kyle figured this was a casual day as Logan wore no tie at his throat. His hair was nearly black with just a hint of white at the temples. Kyle guessed to have just a couple of inches on the guy.

"I must say, I was surprised when my secretary said there was a cop waiting to see me. You must know that detectives have already questioned me about Grant Spencer's murder.

"Yes, well, Mr. Logan, as you must know, the investigation has crossed state lines and we are not in the notion of getting into a jurisdiction war with the great state of Wisconsin." Kyle settled into a chair, just as Logan stood from behind the desk, putting him at the advantage. Kyle silently scolded himself for falling into the trap.

"And just what state did you say you were from, Detective...?" Spencer questioned as he shrugged out of the tailor made suit jacket.

"Klein," Kyle croaked out his brother's name. "Detective Klein with the Illinois State police department." Kyle did not want to allude to the fact that he was *actually* from Illinois but after seeing the news report this morning, felt he had no choice but to fess up. It was better if he followed the facts of the story rather than to trap himself in a lie.

Logan kept talking without skipping a beat. "So Rae Ann was seen in Illinois?" He walked leisurely around the desk and perched on the front corner not three feet from Kyle. Kyle cleared his throat and sat up straight in the chair.

"She was, uh, allegedly seen there yes. But that's not what I want to talk to you about, Mr. Logan."

"Of course it isn't, Detective," Elliot Logan said smugly and leaned toward Kyle with narrowed eyes. Kyle was almost certain that this man could see through straight through his façade, with those cool grey eyes, and he realized that if Logan attacked him, there was no way he would get to his gun in time.

~ * ~

Rae Ann tapped her foot annoyingly against the floor until Eddie put a hand on her knee. "Stop it."

"I'm sorry it's just that its twelve-thirty and we haven't heard anything from Kyle. The new shift is going to start in half and hour and we haven't made any headway on the disk."

"I'm sure Kyle is fine and as for the techs, you may just have to chill out in the van until I figure something out here." He gestured to the still screen. He had been able to enhance the picture of the man's face and was in the process of clearing up the blur so they could see who it was.

"I feel like I should be doing something," Rae Ann pressed.

"You should," Eddie said, "sitting still." He turned his attention back to the screen while Rae Ann paced behind him.

"Over the last couple of days, I feel like I don't even know who Grant was. Like I never really knew him at all," Rae Ann said thinking out loud. Eddie stopped his business at the computer and turned to face her. She knew what he was thinking and shook her head. "Don't feel sorry for me. After all, I had left him."

"This is still a difficult thing to go through, Scoop. You guys didn't have anything official saying you weren't together. Now you not only have this murder investigation but the resort to deal with."

"Oh, God," Rae Ann groaned, "I haven't even thought about the resort. I wouldn't and don't want to know anything about running a resort. That's exactly the kind of stuff I'm talking about. I feel like his business partners and friends were the only people in his life." Rae Ann began rubbing her temples to push away the threatening headache.

"What friends?" Eddie cracked and then pushed the chair into a crazy spin. Rae Ann suddenly stopped rubbing her head and quickly looked up. She reached out and grabbed Eddie's shoulders in mid spin and bent to his eye level.

"His friend," Rae Ann began, "the Senator."

"What? You're nuts."

"That's it. I need to talk to Showy. If anyone knows anything about Grant's dealings it would be Showy. Grant and the Senator go way back."

"Senator Showalter is not going to talk to you. Don't you remember an incident, not so long ago, where you dragged his name through the mud and then stomped on it. He would love nothing more than to see your pretty wrists in handcuffs and hauled off to jail. As I recall, he's threatened to send you there before."

"Yeah, but this is different. If the Senator and Grant were as good a friends as Grant let on, then he should be glad to help me. Showy knew that Grant tried like hell to get me to drop that rape story."

"No," Eddie said flatly, "no way." He took her hands off his shoulders and stood up. "Let's get you settled in the van." Eddie walked to the desk opposite the computer and picked up his coat.

"This is Rae Ann Lewis, could I please speak to the Senator?" Eddie crossed the room in record time but Rae Ann shielded him from pushing the plunger on the phone to disconnect the call.

"Have you lost your mind completely?" Eddie hissed through clenched teeth. Rae Ann motioned for him to remain quiet and he threw his hands up in defeat.

"Yes, Senator, this is Rae Ann Lewis." Rae Ann pointed at the phone and mouthed the word 'Showy.'

"No shit?" Eddie asked sarcastically.

"Senator, there is some business of Grant's that I would like to discuss with you," Rae Ann said, pointedly, "and I hope you agree that there should be no reason to involve the police."

Rae Ann held her breath until she heard the Senator exhale sharply through his nose and say, "be here in half an hour."

Rae Ann hung up the phone and beamed at Eddie. "Sounds promising."

"Sounds like a bad idea. Showy is probably going to have the SWAT team waiting for you when you get there."

"Come on, Eddie. I'm a reporter. I live for stuff like this."

"Correction, Rae Ann, you *were* a reporter and even if you still were, this time it's different. This time *you* are the story." Rae Ann recoiled from his harsh words.

"Ouch," she muttered.

"Besides," Eddie continued in a softer tone, "If I let you leave here, your boyfriend is likely to kick my ass."

"Eddie, at this point you could go to jail for harboring a fugitive and tampering with evidence and you're worried about Kyle?"

"No, Scoop, I'm worried about you," Eddie sighed and reached in his pocket to fish out the keys to the van. "You're just so damn stubborn," he said holding them out for her.

"Eddie, you are the best." Rae Ann snatched the keys before he could change his mind. She hurried over to the desk that held her purse and coat before heading towards the door. She was at the bottom of the stairs before she realized that Eddie was following her.

"What now?" Rae Ann asked, preparing herself for another round of their argument.

"I'm going with you," Eddie said simply, zipping up his coat.

"What? No, Eddie you have to stay here and work on that disk. That disk is the key to unlocking this whole messed up deal. We have got to be able to see that man's face before any of this will make sense. It is my only chance to being cleared."

"God, I hate it when you're right," Eddie replied, pulling back down on the zipper. "I'll stay, but only on one condition. You turn on your cell phone and you leave it on. I know you're afraid that the police will try to trace it, but I have to got to know you're just a phone call away."

Rae Ann dug deep into her handbag and pulled out the pocket sized silver rectangle of her phone. She pressed down the power button until she heard it come to life. "Deal."

She hopped up a couple of stairs to make her taller than Eddie and then patted the top of his head gently. "You're a good friend, Eduardo," she said genuinely.

Eddie blushed through his dark complexion. "Yeah, well, don't make me drag a camera out to a crime scene at Showy's in this freezing snow."

Rae Ann ascended the rest of the stairs, but Eddie shouted after her, "You know they've got me paired with a dude now." Rae Ann shut the door on Eddie's words, but couldn't help smiling. She felt alive at the prospect of being the investigative reporter again. If only in her mind.

Rae Ann backed out of the station lot and glanced at her Rolex. If she broke every speed law and ran all the red lights, she might just make it to Showy's before the half-hour deadline.

~ * ~

If Elliot Logan knew about Kyle's fake identity, he gave no indication. Grant's former business partner remained poised on the edge of his desk, body positioned slightly forward. His perfectly tailored cream suit pants creased in all the right places and he made no other move than to twist the mighty ring on his pinky. "Well, Detective, ask away. I am quite busy."

"Oh, of course, sir." Kyle took out a small notebook and a pen that he had bought on the way over to Logan's office. Kyle really didn't know if real cops did this or just the ones he saw on television. In any event, he did not want to forget what this partner of Grant's was about to say. "It has come to our attention that Mr. Spencer owed you a great deal of money. Legal documents found at his house indicated that Mr. Spencer was supposed to buy you out as a silent partner."

"That was the initial deal, yes." Logan slid off the desk and meandered to the window.

"The initial deal?" Kyle raised his eyebrows.

"Yes. Initially, Grant was to pay back to me the sum of three million dollars within six months of the grand opening." He peered out over the city like a king over his kingdom. "About three months ago, Grant paid the last installment of the money. But then came to me not three weeks later and asked for the entire sum back. He said he needed an extension on the loan. Now this isn't typically the normal practice, but I knew Grant. I knew he was having trouble with his wife. I knew the resort was paying out more than it was making. I gave him a break. We compromised on another six months at double the interest."

Kyle jotted the facts down in his little spiral notebook, his mind racing. *Grant had had the money to pay Logan but suddenly needed it back?* This didn't make any sense to Kyle.

Surely, Elliot Logan wasn't going to loan Grant the money to pay his own blackmail ransom. Kyle looked hard at Logan, trying to get a feel for the man seemingly void of emotion. Of course, Logan could be lying to Kyle to cover his own tracks, but then why wouldn't he just say that Grant had paid him and kept his name out of the situation altogether?

"I'm sure a man with your savvy business ethics would have a record of such a deal. I can't imagine anyone loaning even a good friend three million dollars on just a handshake and a smile. Can I see the extension papers, Mr. Logan?"

"I would happily show you the papers, Detective, but they are now a moot point." Elliot Logan was again seated behind the behemoth desk. He took out his own pen and paper.

"Mute because Grant is dead," Kyle concluded.

"No," Logan corrected, "mute because just last week Grant paid me in full. The papers were never filed with my lawyer due to his busy schedule. I had them rescinded immediately." Logan's tone took on a note of boredom with the entire conversation.

"Grant didn't owe you any money?" Kyle said more to himself than to Logan.

"No, he didn't," Logan reiterated never lifting his eyes from the writing pad.

So there it was, Kyle thought, *Logan was covering it up. Grant must have blackmailed Elliot Logan with the disk so he wouldn't have to shell out the money that Grant knew he could never repay. So*

Logan killed him or had him killed in an attempt to get the disk back,
but it was nowhere to be found in the ransacked house. Rae Ann had
already left by then and now Logan wanted it back.

"Thanks for your time, sir," Kyle stood up from the chair and
immediately headed for the door before remembering to keep up the
pretense of his cop cover. Kyle turned back into the room as he
reached for the door knob. Logan had abandoned his writing pen and
unbuttoned the cuff of his sleeve. He carefully rolled it up, smoothing
out the creases before beginning another roll.

In the instant before he spoke, Kyle caught the inside of Spencer's
right forearm. On it was a small marking. "You have a tattoo?"

"What? Oh yes," Logan turned his arm back out for Kyle to see
the outline of the dove. "It was something I got in the Navy. I try to
keep it covered up now, but all be damned if it didn't seem like a
good idea at the time," he said with a smile.

"Thanks again, Mr. Logan," Kyle said absently as he crossed the
threshold.

"Oh and Detective Klein or whoever you are?" Spencer's words
stopped Kyle in his tracks. "Tell Rae Ann that I'm on her side. If it
means anything, I don't believe that she killed Grant."

"Yeah, well, if you didn't kill him and Rae Ann didn't kill him,
then who did?" Elliot Logan shrugged his shoulders if the question
didn't mean anything to him. "If you don't mind me asking, how did
you know I wasn't a detective?" Kyle couldn't help but need to know.

"Your car," Spencer said pushing back from the desk and crossing
his arms over his chest, "I don't think they give detectives a Mercedes
to drive around."

Kyle left the office at almost a dead run. He jumped into the car
and headed down the street in search of the nearest pay phone. He
spotted one across the intersection and nearly ran the red light to get
to it. His fingers were shaking as he dug Eddie's cell phone number
out of his pocket and punched it into the phone. It was answered on
the first ring.

"Rae Ann?"

"No, Eddie, it's Kyle. Listen closely, look at the disk and tell me if
the guy has any sort of tattoo on the inside of his right forearm."

Eddie was silent for several agonizing moments before he came back on the phone.

"No, nothing like that, why?"

"Logan. Logan has a tattoo. It isn't him on the tape and Grant didn't owe him any... wait a second, why did you ask for Rae Ann when you picked up the phone?" Eddie knew he was had. He blew out a long breath and ran his hand over his shaggy black hair.

"She left."

"What?" Kyle shouted into the phone, "Where the hell·did she go?"

Twenty-eight

The ornate door of the Senator's mammoth home opened before Rae Ann even had a chance to knock. A stiff British butler motioned Rae Ann into the foyer with his white gloved hand. "Please come in. The Senator will see you in his office."

She followed the butler just down the hall of the grand house. The office door opened with a small creak and again the butler motioned Rae Ann inside. She prepared herself for the worst. What she hadn't expected was the Senator's casual appearance. She had never seen him outside of a suit until today. His tan was as dark and rich as ever, set against a flaming orange shirt and khaki pants.

"Sampson," Francis Showalter addressed the butler, "please put my luggage in the master suite, I will unpack it after my meeting."

"I could unpack it for you, sir."

"No," the Senator said hurriedly, "I will unpack it, thank you." The butler nodded quietly and closed the door.

"Traveling, Senator?" Rae Ann asked.

"I've been out of the country, yes. But you probably already knew that, right? You always did have a knack for being in my business," the Senator quipped, "In any event, I don't really think you are here to talk about my recent vacation are you? You mentioned business on the phone."

"Yes, of course," Rae Ann agreed.

"I guess I didn't realize that you had a hand in Grant's dealings."

"Well, I don't, anyway I didn't until—" Rae Ann started to say.

"Don't you think you've caused enough damage?" the Senator interrupted. Rae Ann held up her hand and lowered her head.

"I know that I'm the last person you want to talk with right now, but you have to understand that I want an explanation."

"Ms. Lewis, my business with Grant doesn't concern you. I don't appreciate you coming out here to strong arm me for ammunition. Now I agree that there is no reason to get the law involved, there are lives at stake, but in any event I am still planning on pressing charges against you. Our conversation is over."

Eddie was right.

The Senator did not want to discuss anything with her, even if it meant squandering the opportunity to see her pay for what she had done to him. Rae Ann started through the exit when the Senator's words stopped her cold. "And you can tell Grant that as far as I'm concerned we are square."

Rae Ann turned her head slowly, her feet feeling as heavy as cinder blocks. A small warning bell began clanging somewhere deep in Rae Ann's mind and as hard as she tried, she could not ignore its incessant ring. "How long did you say you were out of the country?"

"Ten days. Why?" The Senator had already turned his attention away from her, seemingly bored with the entire conversation until Rae Ann spoke.

"Grant was murdered almost a week ago." Even though the Senator was not looking at Rae Ann she could tell that his face took on a stricken expression.

"Grant is dead?"

"If you didn't know that Grant was dead, then why didn't you want to involve—" Suddenly the phone rang shrilly in the small office and the Senator fumbled over himself to snatch it up immediately. He uttered a couple of yes's and okay's before covering the receiver to address Rae Ann. "I really need to take this, but if you could just wait in the salon, I really think we need to finish this discussion. Maybe there is some sort of solution to this silly lawsuit thing."

"Of course," Rae Ann stammered and pulled the door shut behind her. "What the hell is going on around here?" she muttered into the empty hallway.

The Senator had been genuinely shocked when she'd told him that Grant was dead, but it was obvious that he was hiding something. Rae Ann wandered across the foyer into the salon and debated whether or not it was wise to stick around here. She may not have gotten the information she came for, but the possibility of the Senator dropping the lawsuit may have made the trip worthwhile.

Just when Rae Ann had made up her mind that it was in her best interest to leave, the front door opened and the Senator's driver tumbled in loaded down with bags.

"Hey, Sammy," the driver said as the butler appeared at the top of the stairwell, "that's the last of them."

"Thank you, David. Just leave them and I'll bring them up when I'm finished building the fire."

"Suit yourself, old buddy," the driver said and left the same way he had come in. The butler wiped a gloved hand along the stair rail and also went back to his duties on the second floor. Neither had noticed Rae Ann standing just out of view behind a tall marble column. She peered out at the luggage curiously.

Maybe, she thought, *something inside the luggage would reveal where the Senator had been and what he had been doing.* The only kind of business that she knew of that was conducted outside of the country involved smuggling drugs. If Grant had been involved in drugs too, Rae Ann thought her sanity would break. She didn't know how much more of this she could take.

Rae Ann deduced from her own traveling that the most important stuff was always packed in the carry on, so she bypassed the two larger bags and knelt down beside the small one. "Damn," Rae Ann said, pulling at the lock on the zipper. She sat back on her haunches and blew a sigh up towards the ceiling.

As an afterthought, she clawed into the front unlocked part of the bag and smiled coyly as she pulled out the key. People were usually so worried about losing their luggage keys that they never even take them out of the bag. "Amateur," Rae Ann whispered. She twisted the key around in her hand and moved it toward the lock.

Without warning the quiet interior of the hallway was interrupted by the unnerving jangle her cell phone. Rae Ann was so alarmed that she dropped the tiny key onto the tile floor and dug the phone out of her bag before it alerted everyone in the house. She knew Eddie wouldn't call unless it was important.

"Scoop, its Eddie. Are you all right? What's going on with Showy?"

"Eddie I don't have time to gossip right now. If there's something you need to tell me then out with it."

"Ok, listen, Kyle called here and besides the fact that he is pissed, he said that Logan had nothing to do with Grant's death."

"How does he know that?" Rae Ann began searching for the dropped key.

"Well, he didn't really say. Just muttered something about a tattoo and that he would explain later."

"Well no offense to Kyle, but he is a really trusting person. I'm not sure we should dismiss Elliot Logan so easy." Rae Ann pinched the phone between her ear and shoulder so she could lift the bag. Seeing that the key had not bounced under it, she put it back on the floor and resumed her hunt.

"Anyway, that's not the only reason why I called," Eddie said drawing out his words. Rae Ann lowered the phone away from her ear and made sure she could still hear the Senator on the phone in his office.

"Spit it out, Eddie. I'm on borrowed time here." Rae Ann crawled on her hands and knees in circles trying desperately to find the small gold colored key. Finally her hand connected with the cool steel and she snatched in up.

"I was working on the disk, right and I wasn't having much luck with the face so I decided to pan out and take in the room." Rae Ann had the key in the lock but Eddie's words kept her from turning it. "I focused in on a book on the bedside table. It turned out to be a room service menu." Rae Ann held her breath. "Rae Ann, it was a room service menu for Spencer's Grill."

"Are you sure, Eddie?"

"I'm positive. It had the Pine Trails Resort logo embossed right on the leather." Rae Ann tried frantically to make sense of what Eddie was saying. She shook her head to clear the confusion and focused on turning the key. Finally unlocking the suitcase, Rae Ann flipped open the top.

After what seemed like an eternity, Eddie asked, "Scoop, are you still there?"

"Yeah," Rae Ann said, sifting through the pile of toiletries and set of spare clothes, "there's nothing here. I'm heading back over to the station."

As she started to close the lid, Rae Ann noticed something shiny sticking out from under the false floor of the suitcase. At first glance, she thought it was a coin but as Rae Ann reached down her hand came in contact with a zipper. Rae Ann gave it a tug and the whole bottom of the bag lifted up.

"Scoop, I know this is tough but hear me out. This disk would be the sort of thing that could be very bad for Grant and his business. Who else would be using a room at the resort? I think it's time you start to accept that it is Grant on the disk. That Grant murdered that girl and someone was using it to black mail him."

"Oh Jesus," Rae Ann gasped when she realized what she was holding. "No, Eddie it wasn't Grant," she said with conviction.

She heard Eddie sigh, "Rae Ann—"

"Eddie, stop. Have Kyle take you to our motel. I will meet you there and don't forget the disk." Rae Ann shoved the leather mask into her purse and attempted to heave the scattered clothes back into the case.

"Rae Ann, what aren't you telling me? What the hell is going on over there?"

"I'll explain later, just get out of there." It had been less than ten minutes since Rae Ann left Showy's office, but she now felt like every second was working against her. She walked as quickly and as quietly as she could to the front door.

"Ms. Lewis?" the Senator called out behind her, "I would like to finish our discussion now."

"I'm sorry, Senator. I'll have to take a rain check."

"Wait a minute. What the hell?" the Senator questioned. "Rae Ann, come back here!"

Rae Ann slammed the door hard and raced for the van. As she backed out of the narrow lane, she glanced anxiously at the front door. She expected a couple of the Senator's goons to bust through with guns blazing and cut her down before she even got off the property. It was only a matter of time now before the Senator realized *she* had the disk. She weaved around the tree lined driveway and bumped recklessly onto the main road. She tried to control her breathing and found it nearly impossible. Her heart beat wildly and after a couple of miles, Rae Ann realized she was crying. In the midst of all the confusion and disgust Rae Ann felt, she never even saw the car that pulled onto the highway behind her.

~ * ~

By the time Rae Ann reached the hotel room, she was hysterical. The snow had begun falling again and had made the trip more treacherous. The wind stung her eyes and froze the tears instantly to her cheeks. Kyle rushed out to meet her in the parking lot and helped her inside. Eddie had been sprawled on the bed reading the newspaper but sat up when he saw the state that Rae Ann was in. "Jesus, Rae Ann, what happened? You scared the shit out of me on the phone."

Kyle waved for Eddie to be quiet and then helped Rae Ann into one of the chairs at the small table. He gave her a quick once over and then quietly asked, "Are you okay? Did anyone hurt you?"

Rae Ann shook her head and with a couple of deep breaths was able to talk. "What did Logan tell you?"

"We don't have to talk about this now."

"What did he tell you, Kyle?" Rae Ann asked a little more forcefully. Kyle could tell that she would not be dissuaded. She stared intently into his eyes and something inside him stirred. Kyle suddenly had the urge to kiss her. Every part of her. He had been so mad when he found out she had left the station to see the Senator, but it made him proud that she was so determined to get to the bottom of this mystery.

Kyle ran a hand beneath her hair and rested it on the back of her neck. He started to pull her towards him before remembering that Eddie was in the room.

"Grant paid him off just last week," Kyle said, answering her question, "With interest I would say around three point two million."

Rae Ann groaned, doubling at the waist. "It's true, it's all true." She felt sick.

"What? What's true?" Eddie bent next to Kyle in front of her. Rae Ann could see sweat gleaming on his forehead.

"It's Showy on the disk. Showy killed that girl." Rae Ann broke into harsh sobs. "Somehow Grant knew about the Senator's extracurricular activities and set him up in a room in the resort. Grant used that disk to blackmail Showy and then used the money to pay off Elliot Logan."

Rae Ann was crazed with the sudden knowledge of the months past events and couldn't stop talking even if she wanted to do so. "The night I called Grant and asked him to call the Senator off, he wouldn't do it. He said there were things that I didn't know about. He was talking about the disk. Grant was already blackmailing the Senator and wanted me to drop the story because he knew that if the Senator went to jail, Grant would never get his money. He wouldn't be able to pay Elliot Logan and would be forced to sell the resort. It was enough to see my career ruined so Grant could save face and his precious possessions.

"After all that, Showy wanted his money back so it was only fitting that he threaten to file the three point two million dollar lawsuit against me, the exact amount that Grant had taken from him. It was sweet revenge."

"That's why the Senator was so cooperative today and said he would see you," Eddie added and Rae Ann agreed with a nod of her head.

"He thought I knew about the disk all along. I told him we shouldn't involve the police and he agreed because he thought I was talking about him, not me. He didn't even know Grant was dead."

Kyle pushed off of his haunches and moved around the room. "But if the Senator didn't know that Grant was dead, then we still don't know who killed him." Tension was as thick as fog in the room, but Rae Ann could especially see it in the way Eddie held himself. She watched him stretch to his full five foot seven inch height and cross the room in measured steps. When he finally turned back to Rae Ann, Eddie's eyebrows were draw tight and he was chewing roughly on his bottom lip.

"What is it, Eddie?" Rae Ann sat forward in the chair and dropped her hands between her knees.

Eddie threw his hands into the air and let them slap on his thighs. "I'm on your side here, Scoop, you know I am, but we've accused this guy before and it backfired. I just don't know…"

Rae Ann remembered her purse and scanned the room for where she had dropped it. She spotted it just inside the door. Rummaging to the bottom, Rae Ann found what she was searching for and pulled out the leather mask for the guys to see. "I found this in the bottom of Showy's suitcase."

"Holy shit," Eddie mumbled.

"Does that mean that you believe me?" Rae Ann mused.

"My God, Rae Ann, he could have caught you," Kyle said from the corner of the room.

"Well, he didn't," Rae Ann lashed out.

Sensing an explosion between the two, Eddie stepped between them to defuse the situation. "So that's it, right? We've got the proof. We go to the police."

"I wish," Rae Ann retorted, flinging the mask into the center of the bed and then wiping her hands on her jeans. "The disk isn't clear enough for a positive ID and I don't think the police will just take our word for the fact that the mask came from Showy's. They don't look too kindly on people removing evidence. What we need is something a little more solid."

"Like what?" Kyle inquired to the room.

"Like the room at the resort," Rae Ann offered, "Eddie said that the room service menu had the Pine Trails Resort logo on it. There must be records of the Senator staying there."

"I doubt it would be that easy," Eddie said, "If Grant was trying to frame the Senator, he probably would have offered to fudge a couple of records. It's unlikely that the Senator wanted everyone to know about his extracurricular activities or the fact that he was using the resort at all."

"Besides," Kyle picked up where Eddie left off, "if the disk was ever found it wouldn't be good for Grant either, because the murder took place at the lodge." The three of them were spent of ideas. The cold crept in under the door and brought silence along with it. Both permeated every inch of the room. They paced in their own personal area and then every so often switched for a change of scenery.

After twenty minutes of no one speaking, Rae Ann settled onto the bed and leaned her head against the headboard. She shut her tired eyes so she wouldn't have to stare at the hateful leather mask that sat in front of her. Eddie had taken one of the flimsy chairs from the table and tipped it back on its hind legs. He was tossing a wadded up piece of paper into the air and catching it. Rae Ann sensed Kyle to her right, standing in the bathroom doorway. His arms stretched high above his head, holding onto the door jam. He stared at his feet and took a slow deep breath. He had been trying to think of someway to avoid the inevitable, but knew they were running out of time. If the Senator knew that Rae Ann had found the mask, Kyle knew it was only a matter of time before the Senator tracked them down and would come after her.

"I'm sure that isn't the only disk that Grant made. And, even if it is, he had to have some way to make it in the first place," Kyle said aloud.

Rae Ann opened her eyes at the sound of his voice. "We have to get inside that room at Pine Trails."

"But how will you know which room it is? That place has got like a billion rooms," Eddie exaggerated.

Rae Ann sat up off the bed, "He said 'The Senator's room. What do you know about the Senator's room?'"

"What?" Kyle and Eddie asked in unison.

"The night of our anniversary party, the Senator came on to me. When I told Grant that he could just stay in the Senator's room, he freaked. He started asking me what I knew about the 'Senator's room.' I thought he was just drunk."

"That still doesn't narrow down—" Eddie began.

"Storage," Rae Ann sat up straighter. "The other room," she stuttered, "on the third floor. Grant told me it was storage. I never had any reason to look inside. If what I'm thinking is true then the Senator frequented the room more often than we thought. That's how Grant knew to set him up there. You're right, we have got to get into that room."

"I don't see any other way around it," Kyle agreed. He walked to the bed and edged her over so he could sit down.

"I've been trying to avoid going to the resort all day," she sighed.

"Me, too," he whispered and lightly placed a hand on the knee of her jeans.

Eddie, who had stopped tossing his makeshift ball said, "You can't just stroll in the front door in broad daylight, a dozen people will see you. And just how do you expect to get up to the suite level? I'm sure there is some sort of security system that won't allow just anyone onto that floor." Eddie let the chair fall forward and it landed roughly on all four legs.

"Oh, Eddie," Rae Ann scoffed as she scrambled off the bed and once again retrieved her purse. "You're forgetting that the ski resort is closed for the season. Only the restaurants and lodge portion are still open. There is minimal staff on duty. Plus, I was married to the owner." Rae Ann jangled a ring of keys in front of her mischievous grin.

"This one," she explained, pointing to the thick brass key, "can be inserted into the elevator lock. Once turned you are allowed access to the suite level. This one," she plucked another key from the group, "is a master key. It will open every room in the lodge, including Grant's office."

"And we will just wait till dark," Kyle added, "I will wear my policeman's uniform and tell the staff I was assigned to patrol the grounds for safety purposes."

"Sounds good to me," Eddie said, resuming his toss and catch game, "as long as I don't have to wander around that haunted mansion in this freezing weather." Kyle looked to Rae Ann, but she still had a perplexed look on her face.

"What now?" he asked.

"It's nothing. I just wish that we could get back into the station so Eddie could do some more work on the disk."

"Ah, I've got that one covered, my queen," Eddie reached over to the table and patted a black soft leather briefcase. "I knew the tech geeks would be swarming the dungeon so I loaned myself the lap top. I will need to download some files and the software is not quite as sophisticated but should be enough to help us."

"Well, then we're covered," Rae Ann announced, "I guess we just wait for dark."

Eddie stood from the chair, stretched and rubbed his generous belly. "I, for one, just can't sit here. Besides, we have got to eat. I'm gonna jet over to Mama Torres' and pick us up some grub. You guys sit tight." Rae Ann's stomach growled at the thought of some authentic Mexican food prepared by Eddie's mother. Eddie grabbed his coat and then hesitated. "Hey, Kyle, can you give us a moment."

"Yeah, sure," Kyle patted Rae Ann's leg and then stepped out the door into the bitter cold.

"Scoop—"

"Eddie, forget about it," Rae Ann said reading his mind.

"No, I want to apologize. I shouldn't have doubted you."

"You had every right. I don't exactly have the best track record when it comes to the Senator."

Eddie dropped his chin to his chest and chuckled under his breath. "So we're okay?"

Rae Ann smiled at her dearest friend, "we're better than okay." He pulled open the door and let in the frozen wind and a shivering Kyle.

"You'd better get some rest," Kyle said over the sound of the door shutting behind him, "it might be a long night." Rae Ann went to him and held his face in her hands.

"You are such an amazing person," she told him, "Thank you for helping me find out who killed Grant. I'm not just interested in clearing my name. I may not have loved Grant anymore, but I can't let his murderer go unpunished."

"I know," he took her hands in his and kissed each palm. "It's just another reason why it is so easy to fall in love with you." She circled his waist and hugged him tightly. When Kyle hugged her back, Rae Ann had never felt safer. He pulled her with him onto the bed and they settled in beside each other. Rae Ann thought she would be too keyed up to sleep,but soon found herself drifting off. She could hear and feel the even rhythm of Kyle's breathing behind her. It made her sad to think that their entire relationship could change in a couple of hours. Of course, there was no guarantee that things would work between them, no matter what lay ahead in the dark of the evening. But one thing she was sure of was that she had been changed by his love and hoped that he could say the same.

~ * ~

"I found her. They are staying at North's Pride Motel just outside of Madison," the man said triumphantly.

"What took so long?" a commanding voice demanded from across the shadowy room.

"She brought that man with her, they used cash and registered under a false name. It wasn't that easy, you know."

"You're right. You did good. Now get the car. It's time we pay this bitch a little visit."

~ * ~

It had been two hours since Rae Ann fell asleep beside Kyle, even though it felt like she had closed her eyes only minutes ago. She swam in the murky waters of twilight sleep, until an unfamiliar noise startled her to the surface of full consciousness. Kyle was already staring at the door. Rae Ann looked alarmingly at Kyle who motioned for her to be still. He moved off the bed as silently as possible and slid the cumbersome curtain only a quarter inch away from the window. The pane was foggy but Kyle could make out a dark form in the gray of the afternoon. A quick rattle of the doorknob made Kyle jump and he dropped the curtain back into place.

"Who is it?" Rae Ann whispered. Kyle didn't answer, but scampered across the floor and pulled the gun from his coat pocket.

"Get in the bathroom," he mouthed to Rae Ann and she quickly heeded his advice. Kyle could feel the heat building under his shirt and beads of sweat breaking out on his forehead. He inched towards the door holding the gun at arm's length in front of him. The doorknob continued to jiggle, the noise grating on Kyle's nerve endings. He took a couple of deep breaths, twisted the doorknob and flung the door open wildly.

"Don't move." There in front of him a startled Eddie held two large paper bags of food with a third bag clenched tightly between his teeth.

"Jesus, Eddie," Kyle dropped the gun and breathed a deep sigh of relief, "you scared the shit out of us."

"I in't ean oo," Eddie muttered around the paper bag. Kyle grabbed the bag from between Eddie's jaws and motioned for him to come in. "I thought you guys knew I was coming back?" Eddie said, sitting the food in the middle of the table.

"We did. I guess you just startled us," Kyle walked to the bathroom door and opened it for Rae Ann. She was sitting on the edge of the tub, her hands holding her elbows.

"Just Eddie," he explained.

"Food," Rae Ann replied and scurried past him. Eddie unloaded the bags and set out plates and silverware. They stuffed themselves on tamales, burritos, refried beans, quesadillas, tacos and Spanish rice. Rae Ann was in heaven. In those moments, Rae Ann reveled in the delicious food and wonderful company.

Without warning, the lap-top beeped, stating that the necessary files had been downloaded. She glanced casually at her watch but it was enough for the talk and laughter to cease immediately.

Kyle leaned back in his chair and parted the curtains. The unseasonable snowstorm was in full swing. The massive flakes were falling thick and steady. "Maybe we should hold off. This snow storm looks intense."

"I know it looks bad but it might actually work to our advantage. Less people will be out. Hopefully we can get to the resort and back without being spotted."

"Hopefully?" Kyle asked with raised eyebrows.

"You know what I mean," Rae Ann said, absently picking up the garbage and leftover food on the table. She headed for the garbage, but Eddie blocked her path. He rescued the tamales from her grasp.

"Some of us are staying here," he explained. Rae Ann smiled and obligingly handed over the food. Eddie returned to the table, tamales in tow and began working on the computer. Kyle changed into his uniform while Rae Ann wrestled into her coat and boots as they prepared to venture out into the storm.

The razor sharp air pierced the back of Rae Ann's throat and took her breath away. She bent her head against the wind and allowed Kyle to lead her to the passenger side of the car. She was relieved when it slammed shut cutting off the wind. Kyle settled in beside her and made a move to start the engine before hesitating. He turned to her and marveled at how innocent and fragile she looked, all but lost inside the heavy parka.

She could read the concern plainly written on his face and as if reading his mind said, "I have to."

"I know," he whispered, reaching out to touch her cheek. The cold had turned it as red as a rose, but it still felt as soft as the petals. "I just have a bad feeling about this."

Rae Ann rested her cheek against his palm and closed her eyes. She recalled the night they had shared and hoped it wouldn't be their last. Without another word spoken, they pulled out of the lot and headed for Pine Trails Resort.

Somewhere behind them another car pulled into the parking spot they had vacated. The driver cut the lights, but kept the engine running, plumes of white smoke billowed from the exhaust pipe. From deep in the shadows an angry voice hissed, "it's time to get my disk back."

Twenty-nine

The journey to the small town of Rockingham was uneventful but making it up the slick hillside was treacherous. Klein's car was not exactly equipped for heavy snow travel. The back end slipped precariously around a turn before straightening back onto the road. Rae Ann held the door handle and her breath while Kyle sat hunched forward in his seat. His knuckles were white on the steering wheel and the windshield wipers thumped violently in an attempt to keep their field of vision clear.

Rae Ann hoped they could find evidence quickly and be back at the motel before the snow shut down travel on the roads altogether. She had seen it happen only twice before since her relocation to Wisconsin, and never in April. But after what she had been through the last couple of days, anything seemed possible.

From the driver's seat, Kyle was praying silently under his breath. The amount of snow was making him very nervous and suddenly the heat inside the car was making it hard to breathe. He scolded himself at being even the slightest bit apprehensive. *It's not like it doesn't snow in Illinois,* Kyle thought. He glanced sideways at Rae Ann and knew that the weather had nothing to do with his current state of near panic. Rae Ann was the source of all his concern. Kyle was so afraid that he was going to lose her, after all these years of searching to find her.

They came to the turn-off to the mountain and Kyle looked to Rae Ann one last time. "Last chance to turn around."

"We've come this far. Let's get it over with," Rae Ann said. She wished that Harold had been out on the grounds. If she could have only seen the sweet little man that waved to her every day, she might have been able to attach some semblance of normalcy to the night.

As they continued to inch their way up, Rae Ann's fear mounted until she thought her sanity would reach the breaking point. Kyle pulled into the parking lot and positioned themselves between a Chevy Suburban and the resort.

"I'll go in first," Kyle said, slamming the car into park, "when I have the desk clerk's attention, you walk in and go straight to the elevators as if you are a guest. I'll be right behind you." Rae Ann nodded, but made no attempt to get out of the car.

"Can you do this?" he asked her.

"Yes, just promise me you'll be okay." Kyle pulled her towards him and kissed her deeply on the mouth. His lips warmed her in the dropping temperature of the car. Kyle got out of the car and began walking in the ankle deep snow, his head bent against the wind. Rae Ann took a deep breath and opened the door. Kyle had turned off the automatic dome light switch that kept her shrouded in darkness.

The cold was bitter and hateful. It seeped in around the collar and found its way up the sleeves of her coat. Within seconds Rae Ann's teeth were chattering and her face felt numb. She scurried towards the resort to outrun the arctic conditions. Taking the steps two at a time, she came up short just to the side of the revolving doors. Rae Ann peeked around the corner and could see Kyle lounging languidly against the front desk counter. He was smiling sheepishly and already had the young female employee blushing furiously. A twinge of jealousy sparked in Rae Ann and, at the moment, she actually laughed out loud before remembering why they were here.

"Get it together, Rae Ann," she mumbled to herself. Her mouth felt anesthetized making her voice sound funny. She pulled her collar up tight against her throat and covered her mouth with a scarf. Now most of her face was hidden from view. Rae Ann stepped into the glass enclosure of the revolving door and gave it a push.

Before Rae Ann could change her mind, she was rushed into the lobby of the lodge in one fell swoop. The warmth was absolute and revitalizing. For one fleeting second it made her feel like they might actually pull off this charade. That was before she became aware of the fact that the reservation desk clerk had directed her attention away from Kyle and onto Rae Ann.

"How are you doing this evening ma'am?" the young girl asked her with a smile. Rae Ann could see that she was trying to impress Kyle and decided the best course of action would be to just play along.

"Very cold," Rae Ann's voice came out muffled through the scarf. She wiped her boots on the expensive rug and started towards the elevator. "Good night then," she added although her efforts were lost as she saw the girl staring back at Kyle. Rae Ann kept having to tell her feet to slow down as she crossed through the room past the fireplace and up the short hallway to the elevators.

Behind her, she heard Kyle say, "yeah, I'd better be getting to making my rounds. Good talking to you, Julie."

Rae Ann couldn't hear the girl's response over the rustling sound her coat made as she dug in the pocket for the elevator key. She held the button to keep the doors open until she saw Kyle fast approaching. He nodded silently and she simultaneously let go of the button and inserted the key. Kyle stepped into the elevator just as the doors swiftly shut. He let out a rush of breath and grabbed a hold of her as they began their ascent.

"Are you okay?" Kyle asked.

"Yeah, you did great," Rae Ann assured him. "Let's just get a quick look around and get—"

Suddenly the elevator gave an abrupt lurch sending Rae Ann crashing into Kyle and the couple was plunged into darkness. Rae Ann gave a sharp gasp and gripped Kyle tightly. As quickly as it had gone off, the power was back on and the elevator again heaved upward. "Oh God, did they find us?"

"No, I don't think so. The power must have gone out for a second," Kyle surmised.

"Right, sorry, my nerves are so jumpy," Rae Ann's voice reached out across the elevator.

"On top of everything, we do *not* need the power to go out," he sneered.

"Well let's just hope that doesn't happen again," Rae Ann muttered, realizing she was still holding fast to Kyle's coat. The ride to the third floor took an eternity and Rae Ann cringed when the indicator dinged loudly proclaiming they had arrived.

"We should be safe up here. No one should be up on this floor," Rae Ann whispered, peering out into the hallway.

"Then why are you whispering?" Kyle asked following behind her as she moved across the carpet.

She stopped and looked at him, "Just nervous, I guess."

Rae Ann glanced across the hallway at the beautiful lavender suite that she had used on her first date with Grant. She shook her head to dismiss the thought and concentrated on using the master key to unlock the secrets of what lay behind the mystery door. Grant had told her it was used for storage, but when the door swung open and Kyle flipped on the lights it was evident that he had lied.

The suite was just as luxurious as the one across the hall but was definitely more accurately decorated for a man. The fixtures and wallpaper were the color of antique gold. Rae Ann recognized the deep magenta bedspread from the scene on the disk. A large cherry cabinet held a television set and state-of-the-art sound system. Small speakers had been distributed throughout the room for a surround-sound effect.

Two large paintings in gilded frames stared at each other from opposite walls. Ornate cherry tables flanked either side of the bed, but nothing lay on top of them. In fact, the entire room was spotlessly clean and unwrinkled in every way. There was no evidence that a horrific crime had taken place here. Rae Ann started into the room but Kyle stopped her.

"Keep your gloves on," he said, "we don't want to leave any fingerprints."

"Right," she agreed and set about searching for any indication that Showy had been in the room.

Rae Ann and Kyle scoured the bathroom, under the bed, in the drawers, behind the wooden cabinet and found nothing except the room service menu from Spencer's grill in the drawer of the bedside table.

In defeat, Rae Ann leaned against the wall. "There's nothing here. This place looks like it has been sterilized."

Kyle placed his gloved hands on his hips and gave one last look around him. Indeed the place looked like a reconstructed simulation of an actual room. Something about it seemed not quite real. "It's clean," he said.

"Yeah, it looks like it has never been used," Rae Ann decided, gesturing towards the bed. She crossed her arms and glowered at her reflection in the blank television set.

"How do you suppose it got so clean?" Kyle inquired. His expression was blank, but Rae Ann could tell he was on to something.

"The housekeeper must have scoured it," Rae Ann stated before realizing what she had just said. "The housekeeper's closet," she shouted and sprinted for the door. She stopped only briefly to retrieve the skeleton key out of the suite's door.

They busted into the small interior of the closet and were met with a housekeeper's cart. Both had to retrace their steps back out of the room and Kyle dragged the cart with them. Rae Ann could barely wait until the back wheel crossed the threshold before she squeezed into the small space. They were looking over every inch of the interior when Rae Ann came across the tiny hole in the wall.

"And look at this," Kyle said, directing her attention to a small locker in the corner. Inside was a lap top and connecting cables for a web cam.

"You stay here," she told Kyle and dashed around the corner back into the suite. "Now talk to me," he heard her shout.

"Okay," he drew out trying to think of something to say," okay I've got it. When all of this is over and we get back to Harrisburg, I am going to buy the property I showed you, off Karbers Ridge Road. We could build a little house there, you know? I could finally move out of Klein's place and you could forget about all of the problems you had up here. Maybe we could even think about—"

"I found you," Rae Ann interrupted in a small voice. Kyle left the small closet and wound around into the suite. Rae Ann was perched high on her toes pointing to the wall, "there's a hole in the painting. They must have set the camera up there."

"Did you hear what I was saying in there?" Kyle asked, leaning against the door jam.

Rae Ann fell back onto flat feet and smiled. "It all sounds wonderful." She began walking back towards the door when again the room they were in was suddenly plunged into total darkness.

"Stay where you are," Kyle said. Her breathing became rapid and she held her arms out toward his voice. She waited while he made his way toward her and at last her fingertips came into contact with the slick material of his coat and she crushed herself against him. The seconds ticked by slowly and Rae Ann became convinced that this time it wasn't the storm that had extinguished the power. She waited in Kyle's arms and listened intently for any indication that they weren't alone on the floor. The lights flickered once and then surged back to life.

"Let's get moving," Kyle instructed her, "we've got the computer. Maybe that and the disk will be enough to show the police that Grant was killed by the Senator because Grant was blackmailing him."

Kyle closed up the suite and housekeeper's closet doors while Rae Ann followed behind and locked them. They made it to the elevator before Rae Ann took a hold of Kyle's coat sleeve. "Wait a minute." She turned towards Grant's office and froze. "The housekeeper would have gotten paid," she said, aloud.

"Yeah, so what?" Kyle pushed the elevator button impatiently trying to make it arrive faster.

"There would be employee records. Grant kept all of the employee records in his office. Maybe that housekeeper would have more information about Showy. Maybe she overheard Grant and Showy arguing or anything that would help me."

Kyle took his eyes off the elevator doors and looked down at the woman he loved. "Damn, you were a good reporter, weren't you?"

Rae Ann tugged him along with her and used her key to open the lock. She wasn't expecting the wave of emotion that threatened to pull her under at the sight of Grant's office. Her breath caught firmly in her throat and she swept her eyes around the familiar surroundings. A single lamp on the desk provided the only light. The world beyond the French doors was so dark that Rae Ann could not tell where the glass ended and the wooden wall began except for the occasional flicker of a snowflake that showed it was still snowing. A small drift had pushed itself against the door as if begging to come in from the cold.

Rae Ann moved into the room and ran her hand along the silver cigar box. She pulled open the lid and shut her eyes against what she knew would be there. The lighter once given to her by the station manager of WZZY was perched atop the expensive tobacco. She had passed it on to Grant as her prize for having quit smoking. He had never smoked the cigars that she had seen, but doled them out to guests, lighting the end with his gift from Rae Ann. She gingerly picked it up, opening the lid and then ran her thumb along the wheel that sparked the flame to life. It burned blue orange in the dim light of the office.

"Rae Ann?"

She flipped the lid shut. Now was not the time. Rae Ann slipped the smooth silver rectangle into the back pocket of her jeans and moved to the filing cabinets. They were in no particular order. Rae Ann pulled a bundle from the top drawer and dropped them onto Grant's desk.

"Here. Look through these for anything pertaining to the third floor," she said, continuing to flip through the seemingly endless paperwork. Kyle settled into the oversized desk chair and delved in. After fifteen minutes of looking, neither had found so much as a mention of the third floor.

"Something isn't right here," Rae Ann concluded. Her arms ached from reaching over the tall drawer of the file cabinet, "there isn't anything about the suite level in these files."

Kyle looked up from his pile, his eyes weary and tired. Dark shadows appeared under the dull jade orbs, making him look like a football player ready for the field. "If Grant was trying to hide something, then he probably wouldn't have left the records out for everyone to see." Kyle looked around the immediate area where he was sitting and began pulling at the drawers in the desk. They were locked.

"Use this." Rae Ann pulled a letter opener from the pencil cup on Grant's desk and Kyle jammed it forcefully into the lock. He twisted and turned it, yanking on the handle of the drawer. It seemed like a fruitless effort but just when he was about to give up, the lock suddenly gave and the drawer flew open. Rae Ann looked at him in disbelief.

In the bottom of the drawer was another manila envelope like the one Rae Ann had taken from the safe in her home. Kyle took no time in jerking it from beneath a glass paperweight and dumping the contents on the expensive glass blotter. Above the rushing sound of the blood in her ears, Rae Ann heard the elevator door ding as it slid open. Kyle and Rae Ann simultaneously froze.

"Someone's on the floor," Rae Ann whispered.

"We've got to get out of here," Kyle said.

"No, no one knows we're here. We'll be fine if we just stay quiet. Keep looking through the file." Rae Ann moved to the door and pressed her ear to the solid wood. Of course, she heard nothing. She took a deep breath and slid the lock on the door into place. The click was barely audible, but Rae Ann felt as if it had been blared over a loud speaker.

"Wait, here's something," Kyle muttered from behind the desk. He held the file up under the small lamp to get a better look. "The only housekeeper that was ever assigned to the suite level was Jennafer Stanford."

"Great, write it down and let's get the hell out of here."

Kyle picked up a pen and scribbled it onto a small piece of paper. "I've never seen it spelled that way," Kyle muttered more to himself.

"What spelled what way?" Rae Ann asked, her ear once again pressed to the door. She could have sworn she heard another door opening down the hall.

"Jennafer. It is spelled with an 'a' instead of an 'i.'"

"What?" Rae Ann jerked her head away from the door and rounded the desk to stand behind Kyle. As she stared at the piece of paper, she almost couldn't believe what she was seeing. Confusion clouded her expression and she reached out to the paper. Kyle held it firmly and watched her cover the 'fer Stan' of the name.

"Jenna Ford," Rae Ann said out loud. It took Kyle a moment to realize that Rae Ann had actually uttered words. Her tone was so breathless that, if not for the still of the room, it would have sounded like nothing more than a sharp intake of breath. The doorknob suddenly gave a violent twist and then rattled impatiently. Rae Ann and Kyle both looked expectantly towards the room's entrance. A brutal pounding disturbed the door and it jangled on its hinges.

"Oh God, they found us. We've got to get out of here," Rae Ann looked up at Kyle with fear in her eyes.

"Where are we going to go? That door is the only way out."

"Just give back the disk, Rae Ann, and there won't be any problem," a voice hollered out.

"No, we can go out the French doors," Rae Ann turned away from him and headed for the doors."

"We're on the side of a gigantic hill, Rae Ann. I don't know how far we will get on foot."

Rae Ann wished the pounding would quit so she could think clearly. "We'll ski. In the closet, Grant has ski equipment. Mine and his. There is a private run out those doors. It winds around by kitchen. If we can just get there, we can call the police." Rae Ann moved to the cabinet and rifled through the gear. She pulled out Grant's skis and held them behind her. It took a minute to realize that Kyle had not followed her. He stood rooted to the spot across where she had left him. Kyle's face was ghostly white.

"I can't," he uttered.

"Rae Ann, open the door. Let's talk," the voice from the hallway lashed out again.

"Kyle you have to do this. Whoever is on the other side of that door is going to kill me if they get in." Suddenly the wood around the doorjamb crackled as it was hit with tremendous force. Rae Ann jumped, flinched against the noise and scurried again to get the rest of the gear. She threw Kyle goggles and then shoved the skis, ski poles and boots into his arms.

Just then their world was again plunged into darkness as the power gave out under the weight of the storm. Rae Ann yanked open the glass door and was taken back by the force of the wind. It was nearly impossible to see in the darkness of the night. The snow swirled ferociously around her face and the cold turned her fingers stiff. She struggled into the boots as the door once again splintered behind them. Rae Ann watched Kyle reluctantly slip on the boots and move onto the deck beside her. The skiing would not be an easy task. She could read the fear in Kyle's eyes even as they hopped down the last of the steps onto the powdery earth.

"Kyle, look at me," Rae Ann shouted above the wind, "everything is going to be fine. Just go and don't look back. I'll meet you at the bottom."

"I can't do this, Rae. I'm sorry, but I can't," Kyle shook his head and grabbed her arms tightly.

"Yes you can," Rae Ann squeezed him back, "You believed in me when no one else did, just like I'm believing in you now. I love you, Kyle."

Those four small words seemed to do the trick. They were not just a ploy to get him on to the ski trail. Rae Ann had meant them. Kyle dug his ski poles into the ground and slipped into the skis. Before Rae Ann could say another word, Kyle plunged ahead of her, the murky surroundings swallowing him up. She quickly slipped on the rest of her gear and risked a glance behind her. A final break told her the door had finally given way and she took it as her sign to go.

The snow choked her nose and mouth and the darkness threatened to send her off course but she pushed on, twisting and sliding in one direction and then the next. For a moment she imagined that everything was all right and that she and Kyle would make it, just before she saw him.

At first, Rae Ann thought her imagination was in overdrive. She blinked several times to clear her vision, but the image remained. Kyle was ahead of her about a hundred feet down the trail, lying on the ground and not moving. Rae Ann was suddenly immobilized. A sob caught in her throat and tears blurred what little vision she had. She directed her skis toward the motionless form and dug her feet in towards each other to stop beside him.

"Kyle," she cried above the raging wind, "oh God, Kyle, I'm so sorry." She ripped off her gloves and felt around his body for any indication of his injury. "Kyle talk to me," she grumbled low in her throat. The wet snow was melting through her thin jeans and she could feel her core begin to freeze. She had told him it would be okay and it wasn't. None of it was. She should never have brought him back here and involved him in her problems.

Rae Ann wanted to lay her head down beside him and just cry, but what good would she be to either of them if she gave in to her tears. She struggled back to her feet, when behind her a snapping twig rung out in the night. Something hard came down on her shoulders and an envelope of darkness slowly sealed around her.

~ * ~

Rae Ann woke slowly coming up through a thick layer of haze that never fully left her vision. She blinked continuously until she realized it made her head throb so she stopped. Something was making it hard for her to breathe but when she reached her arms around to touch her chest she discovered her hands were tied and yanking on them tightened the rope that encircled her upper body. Something was also holding her ankles fast to the legs of the chair but amazingly her mouth had not been taped shut.

It took a moment for Rae Ann to realize she was no longer outside but in a warm dark place lit only by a dozen or so candles. She absently wondered if the power was still off, or if her captors were just trying to set the mood for terror. Next to Rae Ann was a table and beyond that she noticed a bed. On it lay a small person with their back to Rae Ann. The person's snow-white hair was disheveled and half of it was darkened with a red substance. A small puddle of the red liquid had also formed on the pillow beneath the person's head. Rae Ann knew at once she was in the groundskeeper's cabin near the bottom of the hill.

"Harold?" Rae Ann croaked. She cleared her sore throat and mustered everything she had to say the name again. The effort was wasted as the frail little man did not respond. Rae Ann's shoulders ached with the weight of her head and the sound of her own voice made spots form in her eyes. "Harold?"

"He can't hear you, bitch," the same voice from the hallway outside of Grant's office lashed out of the shadows. Rae Ann squinted into the black of the room, fighting to keep her eyes in focus. She could make out only a shape.

"What do you want?" Rae Ann whispered and then more assertively added, "Where's Kyle?"

"Oh, how quickly the Widow Spencer has bounced back from the tragic death of her husband. That won't look good in court, Rae Ann." The dark form moved farther into the room and stopped just behind a table that held a small blue votive candle. The stranger picked up the flickering candle and brought it up to his chin. The light caused hard angles on the surprisingly handsome face. He smiled wide revealing straight white teeth.

"Boo," he said, the smile never leaving his face, "scared you didn't I?"

Rae Ann was reassured by the fact that she wasn't already dead. If she wasn't dead, then that meant that this psycho wanted something from her and that gave Rae Ann the upper hand.

"Listen, you can tell the Senator—" Rae Ann started.

"The Senator?" the man interrupted, "The Senator is an imbecile." He spoke through clenched teeth and then slammed the votive back onto the table. The liquid wax sloshed high over the sides, extinguishing the flame and spilling onto the man's fingers. If it burned him, he made no indication of his pain. Rae Ann took this to be a bad sign. He stepped towards her around the small table and then perched on the edge. His black jean clad legs stretched out in front of him, casually crossed at the ankles. Beads of melted snow clung to the knitted fabric of his black sweater, causing a million tiny twinkles of light from the candles.

Rae Ann twisted and pulled at the ropes on her wrists but gained nothing but the burning sting of the ropes on raw skin. Her feet also bound fast to each leg of the chair couldn't be moved. Rae Ann stared at the man long and hard. She did not immediately recognize him or even have an inkling in the back of her mind that maybe she had seen him somewhere before. Absently she noticed that he was not at all unattractive and obviously in good shape.

Good looking, physically fit and an obvious psychopath. Well, two out of three ain't bad.

The man met Rae Ann's gaze and stared back, daring her to look away. His icy expression made Rae Ann squirm as far back in her chair as she could. She felt the tiny wooden spindles bite into the bones of her shoulders.

"What do you want? The disk? You can have it, but you have to untie me first," she challenged.

The man dropped his chin to his chest and chuckled out loud. "No, Rae Ann, we already have the disk."

Rae Ann cringed and thought of Eddie alone at the motel. She no longer had the upper hand. Now her mind was filled with the endless possibilities of torture and she wondered what this man had in store for her.

"What we want is to kill you."

It took Rae Ann almost a full minute to realize that the stranger in front of had not spoken those words. She turned her head in the direction of the new voice, a smaller voice that came from behind her. Rae Ann craned her neck around to the new presence and stared in disbelief as a young woman stepped into her view. She blinked again to make sure that her eyes weren't deceiving her, but even in the dimness of the cabin she was certain of who was before her. The face sprang from her memory and Rae Ann gasped audibly.

Jenna Ford stopped a few feet from Rae Ann's chair and tilted her head to the left. "Remember me?" Rae Ann tore her eyes away from the girl and glanced back to her male companion. "That's Chad. Oh wait, you probably know him as Nurse Peter Bell. No, wait, he's my lawyer, Alexander Noah."

The two captors shared a hearty, sadistic laugh and then Chad busied himself trying to re-light the candle he had snuffed out earlier. Rae Ann was certain she couldn't speak even if she had wanted to do so. A thousand questions flurried through her mind. She fought to restrain her emotions and summoned her voice.

"Why did you tell me the Senator had raped you?" Rae Ann asked.

"That's what you want to know? Out of everything that has happened to you, you want to know about the Senator?" Jenna asked incredulously. The firelight caused Chad's smile to dance across his face.

"Yes," Rae Ann said pointedly.

"Okay then. I wanted to expose the slime ball for what he really is. It's really as simple as that." Jenna moved farther into the room and swung her long dark hair over her shoulder.

"Then why didn't you follow through with it?" Rae Ann kept glancing between the two of them.

"Because, as it turned out, I had the opportunity to ruin you and I wanted that even more. And I must say, it worked perfectly."

"You had sex with the Senator to ruin me?" Rae Ann was flabbergasted.

"Ew, no," Jenna stopped pacing and twisted her face in disgust.

"But the semen... it was the Senator's," Rae Ann said in utter confusion.

"Framing the Senator was easy. He's a buffoon," the girl's attitude was so nonchalant, "I worked at the resort as the housekeeper. I knew what went on in that room. I just got a used condom out of the trash and used that to... well, you know. Then I got Chad here to knock me around a little." Jenna casually flung a hand in Chad's direction and he air boxed for effect.

"*Voilà*! Instant rape victim." Jenna didn't give Rae Ann a chance to comment, before she continued, "if you hadn't been so greedy you would still have a job, but I knew you couldn't resist this story. Even Grant tried to get you to drop it."

Rae Ann's head snapped back and she was certain she would have fallen off the chair if she wasn't tied to it. "What did you say?"

"Grant. He told you to drop the story, didn't he? He told you like a million times... didn't he?"

"Yes," Rae Ann's voice was barely above a whisper. She felt tears stinging her eyes.

How could this girl know such details about her life?

"Yes, he did ask you to drop it. But you wouldn't, and that's where we're different. When Grant asked me to drop the rape charges and said I'd made it all up, I did. I did it because Grant asked me to. Of course, he didn't tell me to blame it on you. That was my idea,"

Jenna was gesturing wildly into the air, her voice booming off the interior walls.

"Grant asked you to drop the charges against the Senator?" Rae Ann knitted her brows in confusion.

"You're just full of questions aren't you?" the young girl began to pace again in the space between Rae Ann and Chad. "Yes, Grant explained to me what good friends he was with the Senator, and so I reneged on what I said to the press and told them that you just coerced me into making up the story." Jenna made it sound so matter-of-fact, as if they were talking about a recipe or how to play bridge.

"But you said that you did it all to ruin me."

"Well," Jenna stopped her forward movement and let the thought swirl in her head before saying, "that turned out to be a bonus. The fact is," Jenna's pacing was beginning to make Rae Ann nauseous, "I loved Grant and you didn't. In fact, I hated you since the first moment that I saw you kissing Grant that night after dinner. And even though Grant betrayed me, I still felt the connection between us."

Rae Ann closed her eyes, but the image did not go away. Grant sat before her on the cozy couch in their living room, his lips weren't moving but she heard the words playing over and over like a broken record. *There's a woman... There's a woman... There's a woman...*

"That was you," Rae Ann suddenly felt sick to her stomach, "that day in the lobby. I saw someone staring at Grant and me, that was you. And then later on the third floor, you brought the housekeeping cart up and ignored me when I called out to you. You were checking up on Grant."

Jenna nodded at Rae Ann's observance with a small smile on her lips, "All true. Very good, Rae Ann."

"Then how?" Rae Ann's voice was scratchy. She didn't want to ask these questions, but needed to know the answers. If she could just keep the girl talking it might give her a chance to free her hands from the amateurly tied ropes.

"How what?"

"How did Grant betray you?"

"'Cause he didn't love her," Chad, who had been quiet since Jenna entered, piped up from across the room.

"He did, too. He did love me," Jenna growled vehemently at Chad, although she never moved her eyes from Rae Ann. "I thought that if I gave him the disk, he would see how much I loved him and how much I wanted to protect him. Then he would leave you. But he didn't see it that way. He was mad and took the disk saying he would destroy it. But he didn't do that either. He betrayed me."

Rae Ann's body went limp under the exertion of maneuvering and manipulating her bound hands. "What do you mean *you* gave him the disk?"

Jenna threw her hands into the air and turned to Chad with exasperation on her face. "She just doesn't get it does she?" Chad's wide grin moved side to side in the firelight. "It was my disk to begin with. I made it."

"We made it," Chad clarified. He began swirling his hand above the flame on the candle moving it closer and closer until Rae Ann was certain the heat was burning him, although he remained stoic and unflinching.

"Right, we made it. Please pay attention from now on," Jenna sighed. Rae Ann's head had cleared a bit, but her shoulders still ached mercilessly from the initial blow.

"You planted the computer and the web camera in the housekeeper's closet to catch the Senator in his kinky sex act. You didn't know that you would catch him killing someone," Rae Ann stated.

"That's right," Jenna smirked at her own ingenuity, "Chad here is a computer whiz. He hacked into your credit cards and that's how we found you in that little piss ant town in Illinois."

Rae Ann reflexively thought of her scraped elbow and felt the whole situation becoming clearer. "But you didn't take the disk to the police. Instead you showed it to Grant, but he was furious because he knew that it would be bad for the resort and for his friend."

"Well, that's what Grant said at first, but then I guess he decided it could be of good use to him."

"He used it to blackmail the Senator so he could pay off his debt to Logan," Rae Ann concluded.

"Yeah, hey, you are smart, aren't you?" Jenna commented, "If he had just said *thank you* for giving him the disk, this whole thing would be a non-issue. Chad," Jenna turned her attention to the handsome young man, "be a dear and bring in our other guest."

Rae Ann exhaled slowly and relaxed slightly. If she could just see that Kyle was all right she would be more at ease with the realization that she was about to die. Chad hesitated only briefly before slipping from the cabin. A blast of frigid air whistled in for a split second through the open door.

Rae Ann's mouth opened and she spoke before she even considered what she was saying, "you must have been pretty upset to learn that the Senator had Grant killed over the disk."

What was she doing? Sympathizing with this psycho?

"No," the look on Jenna's face was pure confusion, "you killed Grant."

"No, I didn't. Why would I kill my own husband?" Rae Ann's eyes were wide and unblinking.

"Because you didn't *love* him, but you didn't want anyone else to have him. When you found out about us, you killed him and then skipped town."

"No, no, no," Rae Ann shook her head fiercely. "I was upset when I found out about your affair with my husband, but when I left him that night, he was still very much alive."

"What affair?" The words hit Rae Ann just as the cold air did. The door to the cabin slammed shut and Chad stood in the doorway struggling with his hostage. Rae Ann strained to see the squirming figure, but couldn't be sure of whether or not it was Kyle. The person looked shorter than Chad, but if they would just stop moving, Rae Ann could get a better grasp on the situation. Whoever it was, their mouth was taped shut—Rae Ann could hear the strain of a muffled scream from behind the shiny gray tape. She wanted to shout out to whoever it was, but she held her tongue.

"Shut up, Chad," Jenna warned.

"Tell her, Jen, tell her the truth," Chad urged, taking out a gun and putting it to the hostage's head. The struggling form became instantly still. Rae Ann saw a flash of bright yellow T-shirt between the open flaps of a coat and felt sick.

"I don't need this right now," Jenna shouted, holding her head between her open palms.

"They never had an affair," Chad continued, undaunted by Jenna's threats.

"Chad, I'm serious. Shut up."

Rae Ann followed the exchange between her captors hoping they wouldn't realize that the rope on her left wrist had loosened slightly.

"Admit it, Jennafer," Chad drug out the pronunciation of her name in disgust. "He never had any real interest in you. He used you, because he knew you worshiped him. And besides, you set him up. He was so drunk that night you sneaked into his suite, that he couldn't even remember how you got there in the morning. He only thought you had slept together because you undressed him while he was passed out."

Suddenly all of the fight in Chad's voice left and he asked, "Why can't you see that I'm the only one that cares about you?"

"What the hell are you talking about, Chad? You aren't making any sense," Jenna sneered at her companion.

"Oh God," Rae Ann uttered aloud without even thinking.

"Now what?" Jenna screeched, "What the hell is going on here?"

The last piece of the sordid puzzle snapped into place in Rae Ann's mind. She could suddenly see the entire scene playing out before her eyes as if she had been a witness to the entire murder.

Again, she heard Grant murmur drunkenly, *"There's a woman."*

"He wasn't trying to confess an affair. He was trying to warn me. And that night at the hospital, he called me and told me not to go to work. It's because he knew what you were going to do," Rae Ann's voice broke in the tiny groundskeeper's cottage and she no longer cared what her captors had in store for her. She deserved whatever torture they had in mind. "My God, if he had only told me the truth about what was happening I would have dropped the story. I would have saved us all the trouble that *you* caused." Rae Ann's tortured words were directed towards the dark-headed girl. ·Rae Ann stared hard at Jenna, tears balancing precariously on her lower lids. "He loved me and he was trying to protect me,but I just left him. I left him alone and..." Rae Ann slid her unblinking eyes to Chad, "you killed him."

Chad still held fast to Eddie, but now he looked more as if he leaned on Eddie for support.

"What? No. Like I'm really going to believe that," Jenna huffed. She flung her head back and forth violently causing her silky dark hair to fan out around her face.

"Chad," Rae Ann said, cautiously, "I understand." Her voice was calm and soothing, "I know why you had to do it." Chad began moving his head slowly up and down with the rhythm of her voice. He pushed Eddie back against the wall. Since his hands and feet were bound, Eddie lost his balance and had no choice but to sit down heavily on the floor. "You couldn't possibly have just stood by while he continued to hurt the woman you loved."

Rae Ann felt the ropes on her left wrist fall away and knew she had to keep talking. She could just make out Jenna standing motionless inside her peripheral vision and hoped she could be quick enough to react if Jenna decided to strike. "You helped her make the disk and stage the rape and pretended to be her lawyer, because you thought she would see that you would do anything for her. Anything she wanted." Chad brought both heels of his hands to his eyes the gun still clutched in his right hand. "But Grant didn't appreciate what Jenna had done for him. You both gave him the answer to his financial troubles without so much as a thank you. Grant had ignored her before, but this was the last straw. You knew you had to make him pay for upsetting her so you went to my house that night."

"Chad?" Jenna questioned, breaking her silence.

Rae Ann continued as if the girl had never spoken. "You just wanted to scare him. To get him to see how wonderful Jenna was."

"Yes," Chad said with tears in his voice, "I just wanted to scare him."

"Chad?" Jenna's voice raised a notch and she took a step toward him, "You told me that Grant was dead when you got there. He had been shot with his own gun, for Christ's sake. Shot by her." Jenna's arm thrust out in Rae Ann's direction and for a moment Rae Ann was sure she was about to attack.

When Jenna finally turned back to Chad, Rae Ann took advantage of the dim lighting and continued trying to wrestle her hands free. She prayed the power would stay out long enough for her to formulate a plan. "I did. I did just went to get the disk back. I went to his office and couldn't find it anywhere. The more I looked, the madder I got. Furious over how he treated you, and how I never had the guts to tell you how I feel. I never found the disk, but I could see out the glass doors that there were lights on in the house."

Rae Ann closed her eyes and wished she could shut the sound off in her head but instead would hear the last moments of her husband's life played out between two crazy people. "When I got to the house, Grant was a slobbering drunk mess. He kept babbling about the damn maid being on vacation and needing a drink. I completely ransacked the place while he sat on the living room floor drooling onto his expensive, monogrammed shirt." Chad spit the words out as if they tasted bad in his mouth.

Rae Ann felt the rope on her right wrist finally give way and she sprang her eyes open to see if anyone had noticed. She kept a watchful eye on the couple, but they seemed to have completely forgotten about her or Eddie. Even though Rae Ann was free from the poorly knotted ropes, she kept her hands behind her back while she thought of a way to get her, Eddie and Harold out of the cottage alive.

"Then you left, right Chad? You couldn't find the disk so you left," Jenna's last words came out as more of a statement than a question.

Chad sobbed into his hands and continued to plead his case. "The safe was open. There was a gun in it. He called you a stupid kid. He said you didn't know the first thing about real life. I told him to shut up. That he didn't know what he was talking about, but he just started laughing and he wouldn't shut up. He just kept laughing and laughing and I couldn't stand it," Chad spoke with wild eyes and clenched teeth. "Before I knew it the gun was in my hand and... I shot him."

"No," Jenna whispered.

"I'm sorry, Jen, but I did it because I love you." He said it with conviction and Rae Ann was sure that the murder was justified in his own twisted mind. Chad held his arms open to Jenna and motioned for her to come close. She took a small lunge towards him and then covered the rest of the distance in record speed. Jenna wrapped herself in his embrace and hugged him tightly.

Rae Ann was amazed at the events unfolding before her eyes, but continued to focus primarily on finding a weapon or something that she could use to defend herself. She slid her hands around the spindles of the chair and briefly wondered how easily the chair would break. She quickly dismissed the notion since her ankles were still bound to the legs of the chair. She maneuvered her hands silently under the seat of the chair and then over the back pockets of her jeans. She slipped her hand into the pockets and touched the smooth square exterior of the lighter she had given Grant. Rae Ann thought of Kyle and decided that she did want to live. She had to get to him and save him as he had saved her. She owed it to him. She loved him.

Across the room, Jenna stepped back from Chad. He reached his right hand out to touch her face and then realized he was still holding the gun.

"Give me that, silly," Jenna said taking the weapon out of his hands with a smile. Chad happily turned it over to her and wiped his eyes and nose with the sleeve of his sweater. "Let's go finish this." Jenna nodded her head in Rae Ann's direction.

Jenna moved only three steps across the room before turning and shooting Chad twice in the stomach. The blasts reverberated off the walls and stunned Rae Ann into complete lack of movement. Eddie clamored away from the falling body and just got out of the way before Chad slammed forcefully onto the floor. Too shocked to feel the pain, Chad busied his hands against the open wounds trying to make sense of the blood. Tears streamed relentlessly from his terrified eyes and a small gurgle from his throat spilled blood over his beautiful white teeth.

"Let me just get this straight," Jenna said matter-of-factly, as if the last few moments had not even taken place. "You shot him because he was laughing?"

Chad slumped to one side and began gasping for breath. He held up a bloody hand to Jenna, but she made no attempt to help him. Instead, she pointed the gun at him and hissed. "How could you have ever thought that would make me love you. You are a pathetic, sniveling idiot that has to be told every single move to make. I used you like a puppet and now you are no longer needed. I hate you for what you did and I hope you burn in hell."

Rae Ann wasn't sure if it was the actual bullets that killed Chad or Jenna's hateful words, but in any event his chest stopped heaving and his fixed gaze looked even sadder in death.

"All right," Jenna said turning her full attention back to Rae Ann, "this whole thing is starting to bore me."

"You're insane," Rae Ann spat at her.

"I'm rubber and you're glue…" Jenna mocked and chuckled to herself. She had retreated to the far corner of the house and was busy with something on the floor. Rae Ann watched her walk back across the room, struggling under the weight of whatever she held in her hand. "Damn," Jenna cursed as the heavy liquid sloshed over the top of the container and saturated the sleeve of her sweater. The girl pulled up short of Rae Ann and set down the container. It spilled out again onto Jenna's shoes. Rae Ann caught the first whiff of the gasoline and she coughed to get the pungent smell out of her nostrils. It mixed with the metallic scent of Chad's blood and sent her head racing.

How will I get my feet untied from the chair before Jenna douses me in the gas and sets me on fire? The thought was disturbing, and she didn't allow herself time to contemplate this scenario. Rae Ann glanced at Eddie. He sat still in the corner, watching Jenna with frightened eyes. He had scooted as far away from Chad's body as he could. Rae Ann knew she was the only hope for him. She watched Jenna walk to the small table with the blue glass votive on it. She picked it up in her left hand and moved within feet of Rae Ann. The container of gasoline was now between them.

"Your pretty face will be so charred, they are going to need dental records to identify your body."

"They'll know that I didn't kill Grant and they will come looking for you," Rae Ann said in a surprisingly even tone.

"Even you thought the Senator had killed Grant. It won't be a far stretch since he killed the girl on the disk. I will simply leak the disk to the press and let them run with that theory. Who would ever suspect a little old housekeeper like me?"

Rae Ann's eyes fluttered about to take in a mental image of the cabin's interior. If things happened quickly, she didn't want to get disoriented in the shuffle. "Why don't you just shoot me?" Rae Ann nodded her head to the small table where Jenna had left the gun in place of the candle she now held.

"It is more fun this way. More exciting." Jenna glanced over at the gun, which is exactly what Rae Ann wanted. She took the opportunity to reach her recently freed arm out and shove the container of gasoline over towards Jenna. The metallic ping of the container on the floor sent Jenna's head whirling back to Rae Ann. Rae Ann watched comprehension spread across the girl's face as she watched the gasoline puddle around her feet.

"You stupid bitch," Jenna spat as she quickly extinguished the candle she was holding.

"That's okay," Rae Ann stood, the ropes on her chest falling away from her body and reached both of her aching arms around in front of her. She flipped open the lid to the lighter, "I brought my own." Rae Ann flicked the dial and sparked the flame. Realization was evident as Jenna tried to back pedal towards the gun.

Rae Ann gave the lighter a gentle toss and prayed the flame wouldn't go out as it sailed through the air. It landed with a dull thud beside Jenna's left foot. She clambered away from the yellow orange light and gave one last lunge for the gun. For a sick moment, Rae Ann was sure that she would make it and then she saw Eddie. He was lying on his back next to the table with his bound legs splayed in the air. He kicked the table forcefully just as the lighter hit the gas fumes.

A mighty roar and blast of heat pushed Rae Ann back against the chair. Jenna let out a war cry of anger and pain as the flames licked at her pant legs and continued to travel up her clothes until she was engulfed in the fire. Eddie rolled out of the way as Jenna tumbled to the ground and began twitching from side to side. Rae Ann pulled her upper body free of the ropes and began untying her ankles.

The mass of flames that was once Jenna rolled into a recliner and set it on fire as well. The whole place was going to go up. Rae Ann knew she had to get herself unbound and fast. She yanked at her foot in attempt to free it from the ropes but it was tightly secured. The awful screaming seemed to penetrate every fiber of her being and for a second she couldn't distinguish between her own and Jenna's.

Giving up, Rae Ann dragged the chair, still attached to her leg across the room to Eddie. Beads of sweat were standing prominently on his forehead and the firelight flickered wickedly in his moist eyes. She gripped the tape across his mouth and yanked it off.

"Scoop," his breathing was rapid and painful. She noticed that his eye was swollen and beginning to blacken. "Get out. This place is going to fry."

"I'm not leaving you here," Rae Ann stated as she began to pull at the duct tape that encircled his wrists.

"We're never going to make it. You've got to save yourself," he stammered.

"Listen," Rae Ann stopped her task and looked at him full on, "Harold has been hurt. He's on the bed over there and I can't carry him out. You *have* to help me, so stop talking nonsense and start helping me." Eddie nodded and pulled harder at his wrists. Rae Ann knew that the tape must be cutting in deep but she clawed at it anyway.

Finally able to tear through it, Eddie took a moment to rub his wrists before grabbing the rope around Rae Ann's ankle to release her from the chair. She moved to his feet and began the daunting task of pulling off the tape, but the smoke and heat were making her vision blur. She coughed a sickening noise deep in her chest and blinked the spontaneous tears from her eyes. The rumble and crackle of the fire was deafening.

"We're not gonna make it." She heard Eddie shout. The fire crept ever closer and was surrounding the bed where Harold lay motionless. Rae Ann wiped her eyes with the back of her hands and turned to look at Eddie. She wanted to say so many things to him. To thank him for being a friend. But when she faced his direction she felt a blast of the most exquisite cold air ever to touch her skin. A bright light was blinding her vision and she squinted against its harshness. A tall figure lumbered in the door and ran to her side.

"Are you all right, ma'am?"

Rae Ann was stunned speechless to see a fireman looming above her. She nodded her eyes wide with shock. "My friend," she managed to get out and pointed to Eddie. The fireman hollered back over his shoulder, but to Rae Ann his voice was lost in the growl of the flames. Two more firemen bounded into the room with hoses and began spraying down the great fire.

Rae Ann vaguely remembered being carried outside and placed gingerly on a waiting stretcher. Eddie was next to her with an oxygen mask over his face. She pulled at the fireman's coat before he had a chance to get away. "There's another man in there. On the bed. I don't know if he is still alive and another man that has been shot." Her voice was raw with tears and smoke, "and a burned woman."

The fireman nodded and headed back into the cabin. Rae Ann could see him through the window. It was decorated with curtains of fire. An EMT was busy trying to put an IV in Rae Ann's arm but she stopped him. "Ma'am, I need to—"

"Wait, you can do it in a minute. First I need you to get the police or the ski patrol. Do you know how to get a hold of the ski patrol? There's someone on the slope behind the lodge. You have to help him. He's hurt," Rae Ann hurriedly said.

A nearby policemen stepped to her side by the EMT. "Did you say there is someone hurt on the ski slope?"

Rae Ann nodded, tears streaming from her eyes. "Please help him. I love him."

"You mean the guy in the policeman's uniform. Kyle something?" the policeman asked, consulting a small notebook he had pulled from his breast pocket, "Kyle Bennett."

"Yes," Rae Ann croaked, clinging to the front of his shirt.

"That's how we got here, ma'am. He's the one that called us. He must be safe at the hospital by now. I'll put a call into dispatch and check on him for you, if you want." The words sent relief flooding through Rae Ann's body and she slumped back against the stretcher. She was physically exhausted and emotionally drained from all that had happened. Blindly she reached a hand across the space between her and Eddie and squeezed his hand. The night air was cold but she breathed it in gratefully. It was clean and tasted wonderful.

At one point, she realized that it had stopped snowing. The acrid residue of smoke still lingered in her hair and clothes but she was oblivious to its scent. She was safe. Eddie was safe. And most of all, Kyle was safe. The cabin was unsalvageable. It burned to the ground and took Jenna's body with it.

Thirty

It was three days before Rae Ann summoned the courage to go see Kyle in the hospital. The same hospital where she had first met Jenna Ford. Rae Ann felt devastatingly guilty and could do nothing but stand in the hallway outside of Kyle's room for several minutes while she garnered the nerve to face him. Thankfully Klein was not around.

Rae Ann had escaped with mere bruises and a broken bone in her wrist. She touched the small cast and took a deep breath. Her psyche had taken the brunt of the scars, but even those would fade with time. The white clad nurses bustled around her carrying medicines and food trays. Twice a nurse stopped and asked Rae Ann if she could be of help to her. She simply shook her head with tears in her eyes and continued to hold vigil just outside the door.

Finally she couldn't take it anymore. She knew she either had to leave or face him. The door opened smoothly without protest. Kyle was sleeping. His leg was propped up on pillows. A cast covered the length of his leg from hip to toe. The nurse had told her it was broken in several places, exacerbated by the fact that he had dragged himself up to the resort to call for help. There had already been two surgeries to correct the damage and it would take months for him to be healed, a long painful process that might still result in a permanent disability.

Rae Ann crept to the bedside and hovered over him. She wished she could see the bright green of his eyes, to kiss his petal soft lips.

"I'm sorry," she whispered, "but thank you for saving me."

Rae Ann left.

In a few weeks he would be well enough to go back to Illinois. Back to a life that didn't involve Rae Ann. He would no doubt be constantly reminded of her every time he winced from the pain in his leg, and she wouldn't be surprised if he was sorry he had ever helped her that night at Buttercup. The best thing she could do for him was to leave him alone. Let him settle back into his normal existence and forget about her. Rae Ann's thoughts seemed logical but they still made her heart ache as she pulled her car from the hospital lot. She cried all the way to her tiny apartment in Madison and well into the night.

Epilogue

Four months later...

The summer was almost over, but the August heat of southern Illinois was still forceful and oppressive. Eddie pulled his Ford Explorer off Clover Street in a cloud of dust and stopped next to Rae Ann's Honda. She sat in the passenger seat gazing up at the apartment building with expectant yet fearful eyes. They had come to collect her belongings, but now that they were here, Rae Ann wanted to just keep on driving.

About a month after the events at the lodge took place, Rae Ann received a call at her apartment in Madison. There had been nothing on the other end of the receiver except a tiny muffled clicking as the line was disconnected. She was sure it had been Kyle. Never once had she tried to get in touch with him.

Eddie reached over and patted her bare knee. The bruises and cuts that the duct tape had left around his wrists had vanished with time. Only one thin scar remained where the tape had cut deeply. Eddie loved it and told her the women found it sexy. "Let's get this over with, Rae Ann."

Some time over the past four months, Rae Ann noticed that Eddie had stopped calling her Scoop. On occasion she missed it, but mostly she was thankful that he didn't try to remind her of a previous life that was no more. She dug the Honda's keys out of her purse and got out into the sunshine. It instantly warmed away the chill from the Explorer's air conditioner.

Eddie moved around beside her and squeezed her shoulder. "I'll get your things from inside."

"No," she said stopping him, "I'll do it."

Eddie shrugged his shoulders and stepped back so she could pass. Rae Ann moved slowly up the steps to the entrance of the apartment building. She had not called ahead to let anyone know she was coming. Part of her desperately wanted to see Kyle and the other part told her that things were better left the way they were. She loved him. She would always love him, but couldn't stand to watch herself destroy what was left of his already broken spirit.

The hallway between Kyle's door and the apartment where she stayed was deserted. Without knowing whether someone had rented the apartment or not, Rae Ann knocked softly. When no one answered she twisted the knob and was surprised that it was unlocked. She moved quickly into the apartment and shut the door quietly behind her. The stillness of the surroundings was disturbing.

Someone had cleaned up the mess that had been left when Chad and Jenna ransacked the apartment looking for the disk. The furniture was upright again and covered by the dust clothes that she had stored in the closet. Her clothes had been washed of the shampoo mess and folded neatly, packed away in the boxes and suitcase she had brought with her all those months ago. The sight made her feel sad and unwelcome. Rae Ann picked up the suitcase and exited the way she came. She would send Eddie back in for the boxes.

Stopping in the hallway, Rae Ann stared at the door to Kyle's apartment. Somehow the suitcase found its way to the floor and suddenly she was rapping softly on the wood. Nothing stirred inside. Rae Ann reached out and rattled the door knob. It was locked. Kyle's door had never been locked before. She turned to go when she heard the door locks being manipulated and it swung inward.

"Oh dear," Nora Presley said a hand fluttering to her heart.

"Nora?" Rae Ann asked as surprised as she was confused.

"Rae Ann, how are you? Please come in."

"No, uh, thank you. I was actually looking for Kyle."

"Well, he doesn't live here anymore. Moved out about a month ago. Something about needing to grow up. Klein let me take this

306

apartment, being on the ground floor and all. My old bones just can't take the stairs anymore," Nora rattled on, but Rae Ann had stopped listening.

"Where?" Rae Ann said breaking into the conversation.

"Where what, dear?" Nora asked.

"Where did he go?" Rae Ann's voice took on a note of desperation and she suddenly felt the need to see Kyle. To see that he was all right.

"He built a place out past the edge of town."

Rae Ann turned to the noise in the hallway and saw Klein standing at the bottom of the staircase. "Klein." Rae Ann ran into his arms and pulled him close. He returned the embrace and then pulled back to look at her.

"You know where it is, right?" She nodded fiercely. "Then go to him." Rae Ann didn't argue or even take time to think. She sprinted down the hallway past Nora Presley and her abandoned suitcase, out the door. Eddie, who had been leaning back against the Honda, straightened up as she clambered down the steps towards him.

"I'll be right back," she said getting into the driver's seat of her car and slamming the door.

"Wait, I'll come with you."

She pushed the button to roll the window down and said, "No, this won't take long. Just load up my things. Klein will show you where to get them."

"Rae Ann, wait," Eddie knelt beside the open window and looked inside. "Don't let him get away this time."

Rae Ann stared at her friend and smiled, "You're the best, Eddie." He straightened away from the car as she backed out and sped off down the road.

The drive wasn't a long one, but each mile stretched in front of her in a never-ending scheme to keep her away from Kyle. Rae Ann left the window down and turned her face into the warm wind. Snappy's Diner whirred by on the right. Rae Ann hoped it wasn't too late to tell Kyle how she felt.

She almost missed the small dirt path that turned off the main road. It was dusty and overgrown. At first Rae Ann thought she had steered onto the wrong lane when suddenly a break in the trees revealed a tidy little house centered in the middle of the clearing where she and Kyle had had their picnic. It was a beautiful cedar sided cabin with a bright green roof. Dormer windows blinked up from the second floor and a wrap around porch supported by thick wooden beams smiled a toothy grin. Rae Ann didn't see Kyle anywhere, but she knew if she didn't get out and do this now, she never would. She crunched her way over the gravel driveway and stepped onto the porch. "Hey, Jasmine," Rae Ann bent and scratched the butter yellow cat behind the ears.

Rae Ann heard Kyle before she saw him. A rhythmic *thump, thump* of Kyle's cane mocked the pounding of Rae Ann's heart. He came around from the back of the house wearing a white T-shirt and a well worn pair of jeans. His blond curls were tousled from being outside and Rae Ann reached up to smooth her own windswept hair. She could see the green of his eyes even from where she stood across the porch. His face looked wiser, small lines creased around his eyes as he squinted into the sun.

"You have a beautiful place here," Rae Ann said, breaking the silence. Kyle looked around as if seeing the surroundings for the first time.

"Yeah," he finally agreed, "it's peaceful. Why are you here, Rae Ann?" Something inside her chest gave a mighty squeeze on her heart.

"I... I wanted to see you."

"It's been a long time. Why now?" Kyle moved across the floor slowly, his leg looking stiff and uncomfortable. He settled into the porch swing and laid his cane beside him on the floor.

"I don't know why now. I just came to get the things I left here," Rae Ann said, defensively. It wasn't what she had wanted to say, but his nonchalance towards her made the confrontation difficult. Kyle nodded and seemed satisfied with the answer. He pushed back with his good leg and let the swing fall forward of its own momentum. The chains above him creaked with each swing. Rae Ann wanted to say something about how he looked or how well he was doing, but she couldn't find the right words in her brain.

"I had a lot of things to work out back in Wisconsin. I couldn't get here until now."

He nodded again, "yeah, it must take a lot of one's time to run a ski resort."

The response was cold and Rae Ann could tell this was her cue to leave. She walked down the steps and then turned back to him. "Senator Showalter was arrested for embezzlement of campaign funds and has been indicted for the murder of the girl on the disk. You will probably be called to testify at the trial. It turns out that all of his trips out of the country were to some hedonistic resort in South America. I suppose his tan will be fading behind bars. Oh, and in case you cared, they closed Grant's case. All the charges against me were dropped."

Rae Ann started towards her car when she heard the squeaking of the swing's chains stop.

"Rae Ann?" Rae Ann laid a hand on the hood of her car to gather herself but she did not turn around to face him. "I'm sorry… about that night. I'm sorry I wasn't there for you."

"Is that what this is all about? This cold shoulder routine?" Rae Ann turned to look at him, but his eyes were scanning the ground at her feet. He stood at the railing as if trying to steady himself.

"I couldn't save you," Kyle's voice quivered.

"Oh, Kyle, but you did save me," Rae Ann moved quickly towards him and folded herself into his arms, "you saved me in more ways than one."

He pulled her close and breathed in her scent deeply. She didn't want to let him go but had to look him in the face and explain the truth. "You *did* save me that night, Kyle. You saved me and Eddie. We couldn't get free and the smoke was overwhelming. If the police and fire department hadn't shown up when they did… I don't even want to think about what could have happened."

"I tried to get to you, but the snow was everywhere. I got turned around and confused. I'm not even sure how I ended up at the resort. The power was still out, but thank God the phones worked," Kyle rushed, eager to tell her everything.

"Shh, it's okay, really. We're all okay now," Rae Ann quieted him with a touch of her fingers to his lips. She felt his weight shift slightly onto his bad leg and he winced from the pain. She led him back over to the porch swing and then sat down beside him.

"Harold didn't make it," she explained to him, "The blow to his head was... fatal."

"Oh, Rae, I'm so sorry. I know how well you like him." Rae Ann nodded as tears fell silently from her eyes. "Who did this? I've heard sketchy details on the television, but I don't really know what happened."

Rae Ann looked into Kyle's expressive green eyes and took a deep breath. To the best of her ability she spun the tale of her husband's corrupt business practices and habit of consorting with the worst people. She told him about Jenna's obsession with her husband and determination to make her life miserable. Rae Ann did not know many details about the girl's life but explained what she could.

After she was finished talking, Kyle was momentarily speechless. He shook his head slowly from side to side. "My God. You mean that this whole ordeal was brought on by one girl's hatred and jealousy? How could that twenty year old girl and her friend have exposed a Senator, ruined a career and a marriage and killed a man?"

To that Rae Ann had no answers.

"I was just so worried that I was never going to see you again," she said into her lap. Kyle hooked a finger under her chin and drew her eyes up to meet his.

"Here I am."

Rae Ann smiled and wiped at her streaming eyes.

"I've been doing a lot of thinking over these past few months," Kyle told her, "I never stopped thinking about you for one second. I wanted to wait for you, to build this house together like we talked about, but in the end I decided that I needed to do it for me. You were right. I had a lot of growing up to do. I had to get out from under the safety of Klein and be an adult. I hope you will give us a chance. I don't know how it will work, you being in Wisconsin and all, but I think we both deserve to try."

Rae Ann took his face softly in her hands and drew his lips into a powerful kiss that left them both breathless. "I had a lot of things to figure out for myself, too," she replied, "I had to face everything that has happened to me before I was able to start a new life. I am sick of running away from everything and everyone that I love." Rae Ann paused a moment before continuing to let her words sink in. "Grant left everything to me. It could take years to figure out. I'm in the process of selling Elliot Logan the resort and I don't think I would be very good at a long distance relationship."

Kyle appeared dejected. His shoulders slumped, but he nodded his head in understanding. His look of pure disappointment spurred Rae Ann into action. She left the porch and headed again for her car. Rae Ann opened the driver's door and started to get in. Kyle remained on the swing on the porch, but leaned forward with his hands clasped together between his knees.

"Where are you going?" he shouted out across the yard.

"Back to town. I need to make a few phone calls. I believe the last time I was on this piece of property you told me I needed to call my mother," Rae Ann explained.

"That's where you're going... to call your mother?" Kyle was clearly exasperated.

"Yeah, that and there's this great apartment I want to rent on Clover Street." Rae Ann got into her car and backed around so the driver's side window was facing Kyle. "I told you I wasn't good at long distance relationships."

Rae Ann watched Kyle casually lean back into the shadows of the porch's overhang, a grin still evident on his handsome face.

Courtney E. Michel

Courtney lives in Central Illinois with her husband and two sons. Although she has written for many years this is her first published novel. After completing her Master's Degree in Gerontology, Courtney hopes to soon explore the psyche of the elderly mind in a future work.